# DEAD DUCK

*also in this series by* PATRICK MACNEE

DEADLINE

PATRICK MACNEE

---

# DEAD DUCK

*A John Steed adventure*

An original novel, based on
the theme of the A.B.C. Television
series, THE AVENGERS

HODDER AND STOUGHTON

Copyright © 1966 by Patrick Macnee and Peter Leslie

FIRST PUBLISHED 1966


Printed and bound in Great Britain for
Hodder and Stoughton Ltd.,
St. Paul's House, Warwick Lane,
London, E.C.4
by Hazell Watson & Viney Ltd.,
Aylesbury, Bucks

Patrick Macnee gratefully acknowledges the
help given to him by Peter Leslie in writing
this book

# CONTENTS

| Chapter | | Page |
|---|---|---|
| 1 | The Death of Three | 7 |
| 2 | An Interrupted Meal | 12 |
| 3 | Steed Smells a Rat ... | 18 |
| 4 | Hearts Come Up Trumps! | 23 |
| 5 | "It looks like one of ours." | 31 |
| 6 | The Corpse In The Cardboard Coffin | 36 |
| 7 | Enter a Girl With a Shotgun! | 44 |
| 8 | Conversation With a Poacher | 49 |
| 9 | Bella Goes To Work | 58 |
| 10 | The House On The Marsh | 67 |
| 11 | A Ghost In a Battered Bowler ... | 80 |
| 12 | Matters of Migration | 88 |
| 13 | Below Stairs For Emma ... ... And Steed In a Cupboard! | 98 |
| 14 | Exit a Journalist! | 114 |
| 15 | Operation Worthington | 126 |
| 16 | A Touch of the Sun | 138 |
| 17 | Mrs Peel Passes Out | 147 |
| 18 | You Can Always Duck ... | 159 |

# 1

## THE DEATH OF THREE

THROUGHOUT the morning, the tramp sat in the shelter of a black-thorn bush, facing the high storm-beach cutting off the view of the sea on the far side of the road. Behind him, tall reeds clattered and bent in a wind gusting inshore from the East.

The road appeared to one side of a clump of trees crowning a slight rise to the North, vanished briefly in a shallow dip and then arrowed southwards across the flat countryside for nearly two miles before it twisted out of sight round the grassed bank of a dyke. No other human being, no building broke the monotony of the featureless landscape, though birds shifted from branch to branch in the foliage behind the barrier of reeds and an occasional seagull soared momentarily into sight above the shingle ridge. Beyond the incessant, invisible surge of waves, no sound broke the moaning of the wind and the macadam stretched away empty and desolate on either side of the seated man. At his feet, a ring of stones from the beach preserved the ashes of a fire on the wide verge, on top of which a battered billycan held the remains of a meal. Beside a shabby bundle nearby, an enamel plate glinted in the pale sunlight.

Then, in the early afternoon, when the sun had risen far into the pale, clear sky and the shadow of the storm-beach had withdrawn from the road, a moving dot manifested itself on the horizon. Rapidly it approached down the incline, disappeared into the dip, rose into view again much nearer, resolved itself into a small tradesman's van and passed the tramp in a swirl of dust. Soon it was dwindling once more to a speck, to be cut off abruptly by the wall of the dyke.

The dust subsided; the roadside grasses resumed their leaning stance away from the inflexible wind. The tramp remained motionless, facing the blank mound of stones across the road.

Later a Jaguar hissed past on its way North, and before it was out of sight, a clergyman in an ancient Austin passed slowly in the opposite direction.

The sun crawled across the high sky. Slowly, inexorably, the shadows swept the grass, charting the passage of the day. Flights of wild geese in formation flew out to sea, calling hoarsely, as a bank of cloud blew up behind the shingle mass.

When the sun had crossed the road and was sinking behind the distant dyke, seven army lorries in close convoy thundered past towards the North, hugging the side of the road. The wind of their passage threshed the branches of the blackthorn and tossed the reeds behind the seated man. As the birds startled from their perches by the din settled protestingly down again, he leaned slowly forwards and pitched to the ground, his sightless eyes buried in the cold ashes of the fire.

\* \* \*

A half hour later, as the olive-drab convoy roared through the village of Bratby in the gathering dusk, the driver of the leading vehicle swore, flashed his headlamps, stamped on the heavy brake pedal, and then swerved desperately in an attempt to miss the small saloon which persisted in edging out from the side road across his path.

The big lorry slewed sideways in the narrow street, clipped the high curb on the offside, bounced back into the middle of the road and turned completely round, the covered tail smashing into the *Keep Left* bollard of an island refuge and snapping off the pole of a street lamp behind it. There was a vivid blue flash, and the whole length of Bratby High Street was plunged into gloom. Before the scream of brakes from the following members of the convoy had died away, the driver of the leading vehicle and his mate had wrenched open their doors, dropped to the ground, and were sprinting across the broken glass towards the car which had caused the accident.

"Crazy bastard!" the driver panted as he ran. "Crawling out of a ruddy side street with no lights on like that! I'll show the bleedin'—"

"Hasn't even stopped, for Chrissake," gasped his mate. "*Look!*"

The two men halted, staring, in the middle of the road.

The saloon had crossed the main road behind the crashing lorry, missing the gyrating tail by inches, and penetrated a narrow No Entry street opposite. Now, as they watched, it was moving away from them at a slow walking pace towards the lights of a small square at the far end of the one-way thoroughfare. Deliberately, almost caressingly, it scraped along the side of a parked Mercedes before veering to the other side of the road, mounting the pavement, and rasping itself along a brick wall. Through the rear window they could see the silhouette of the driver hunched over the wheel.

"Come on, mate," the driver said suddenly. "Something wrong here. Let's go . . ."

Together, the two men raced after the car. But before they caught up, it had entered the square. The driver appeared to lurch to one side, the exhaust note rose abruptly, and the little saloon leaped forward to crash with shattering force into a stone horse trough on the far side of the open space.

In the sudden silence after the appalling impact, the noise of the soldiers' boots pounding on the road sounded unnaturally loud. A piece of broken glass dislodged itself from somewhere and tinkled to the ground. Petrol from the saloon's ruptured tank splashed to the ground and spiced the chilly evening air with its aromatic tang.

Then windows were being thrust up in the timbered houses, voices called, people trooped into the street to join the other members of the convoy who had followed the driver and his mate. Before the soldiers reached the wrecked car, the square was echoing to the noise of many feet.

The driver yanked open the offside door. "Blimey," he cried, "I reckon this bloke's had it, and all . . ."

The middle aged man who had been the saloon's only occupant had been forced half through the fragmented windscreen by the crash. On the crumpled bonnet, his face lay pierced by wicked shards of glass. The thin steering column with its distorted wheel had torn the overcoat away from his right shoulder, so that this arm now splayed grotesquely behind him, a limp hand dangling from the lanced sleeve.

"Jesus," the driver's mate said. "Let's get him out of there. Hold the door open wider, Charlie. Wider . . . Come on, now, folks : give us a bit of room, will you? . . . There—thanks, mate : get a hold of that leg, would you? —easy does it. *Easy* . . . Look, for Chrissake let's have a bit of *room* . . ."

"All right, you people," the crisp voice of the sergeant in charge of the convoy spoke behind them. "Stand back there and give the bloke a chance. Lay him on the floor there, Foster. Gently now. You, Reed, strip off your jacket and put it under his head. That's it. Now . . ."—he swept the peering villagers with a glance—". . . anyone here tell me where the local doctor lives?"

"He *is* the local doctor," someone volunteered.

"But he don't *live*," Foster, white-faced, spoke from the ground by the victim. "He's copped it, Sarn't. He's dead."

"Dead before the smash, too, I shouldn't wonder," the sergeant replied. "Hardly any blood, see? Though how the hell that car came all that way on its own . . ." His voice trailed away.

"Oh, it could, Sarn't," one of the other drivers said. "It's a Fiat 600, see. The wife's brother has one. They're so light, the engine'll drive 'em along in bottom without you touching the accelerator. If they're in gear, I mean."

"That must of been it," Foster said. "Then, when the car hit the wall, the body moved and his foot pressed the pedal and sent it roaring into this." He gestured at the stone trough.

"Heart attack, probably." The sergeant's voice became assured and authoritative again; all phenomena accounted for. "Still and all, we ought to get a doctor. Police, too. Anyone here got a phone?"

"Jamie's gone for the police," a woman said. "You can use my phone across the road there. The only other doctor around here's Maltby at Great Hornham. The number's two-one-seven."

As she led the sergeant across the road to the lighted doorway of a cottage, the villagers stood uncertainly around the crashed Fiat, embarrassed in the presence of death. Off to one side, the soldiers muttered among themselves in a separate group. The driver, Reed, stepped forward and knelt by the flat-tyred, buckled front wheel to spread a handkerchief over the dead man's lacerated face.

But Dr Maltby was out on a case, the sergeant found out when he telephoned. "He's over seeing that young woman, the painter, who lives in the Martello tower at Star Point," a woman told him in her soft East Coast accent. "If it's an emergency, you could get him there." She gave him a number.

The sergeant dialled again.

\*     \*     \*

The phone rang as Dr Maltby was packing up his bag in the big, bare room in the converted tower. Canvases were stacked around the walls, propped against the cheap table, resting on easels. Most of them were landscapes—flat, low-key marsh scenes with water birds in the foreground. Wind stammered the small-paned windows in their frames and boomed in the stone stairway. The girl lay in a huge bed under the single oil lamp, her long gold hair spread fanwise on the pillow. A faded pair of blue jeans, inside out, had been dropped across a chair. Below, a paint-splotched sweater and a torn brassière were crumpled on the flagged floor.

The doctor's hands were trembling as he sought for the telephone among the books, jars of brushes, sheets of paper and twisted paint tubes in the shadowed reaches of the room.

"Yes?" he said absently, mopping his brow with a paint rag. "Yes, this is Maltby speaking . . . An accident, you say? In Bratby? . . . Doctor—why, that must be Atherley! Good God! How dreadful . . . Yes. Yes, of course I'll come . . . I'll be there as quickly as I can . . ."

He continued talking, half to himself, as he replaced the receiver.

"Most extraordinary thing I ever saw," he mumbled. "Fantastic. Nothing worse than a simple streptococcus infection of the pharynx . . . and then to collapse like that! It's not natural. Girl's heart was as sound as a bell . . . Checked on it myself less than an hour ago. And now another . . ."

He shook his head, picked up his bag and moved towards the door, hesitated, then sighed and crossed the room to the telephone again.

Behind him among the pillows, the girl's contorted face pointed rigidly at the high ceiling.

# 2

## AN INTERRUPTED MEAL

"THE whole point about a good *sauce vinaigrette*," John Steed said, "is that it's a completely *personal* thing : you can't make it to a formula. It's your particular, private blend of oil, vinegar, salt, pepper and mustard that counts. That's what makes or mars it; any fool can hurl in the chopped capers or gherkins or parsley or whatever."

Across the table, Emma Peel smiled indulgently at him over the rim of her Suze. "Brillat-Savarin might disagree with your principle," she said, "and De Nobrega would certainly quarrel with the mustard—"

"There you *are*, you see !" Steed interrupted triumphantly. "That's just what I mean ! Anyway—let's go and sample Mark's, shall we ?"

Taking her solicitously by one elbow, he piloted the girl through the press of people thronging the aperitif bar towards the dining room.

The "Ely Cathedral" boasts a clientele considerably more recondite than its position or appearance would suggest. The inn lies at the foot of a steep hill between Little Hornham and Boston— an L-shaped 17th-century building of no particular architectural merit : lath-and-plaster, exposed beams and East Anglian thatch disposed agreeably enough in a curve of the river which winds towards the Wash. Its fishing is passable, its shooting negligible, the accommodation comfortable, if limited. Yet the small car park across the footbridge on the far side of the water is always jammed with machinery of the most expensive and récherché kind. Besides Steed's blown 4½-litre Bentley, there were on this particular evening a Ferrari, an Iso Rivolta, a brace of 2600 Alfas, a Matra-Bonnet Djet and a covey of Marcos GT's among the more pedestrian Rolls, Aston Martins and E-Types standing there—and the registration marks testified to journeys from as far afield as London, Chester, Shrewsbury and even Edinburgh ...

The reason for this was simple : Mark Lurchman, the owner,

had learned to cook at the "Pyramide" in Vienne, that Rhône valley gastronomic shrine whose table earns it the coveted three rosettes in the *Guide Michelin*—one of only a dozen in the whole of France. And although the proprietor himself now rarely officiated in the kitchens, his influence was still strong enough to make the "Ely Cathedral" (in the words of the famous guide) well worth a detour.

The head waiter seated Steed and Emma at a corner table from which they could comfortably survey the rest of the panelled dining room. It wasn't large—a central dispense buffet with a superb cold table arranged on it, a ring of well spaced tables, and an alcove at each end—but everything in it was well chosen, well displayed and in perfect condition. There was a subdued hum of conversation, a discreet tinkling of silverware and fine china below the illumination welling softly outwards from concealed ports in the blackened ships' timbers which served as beams for the white ceiling. Behind Steed, the glass of a framed Morland engraving reflected the sudden flare of light from a trolley on the far side of the room where a pineapple *flambé* was being prepared.

Steed glanced at the picture as he shook his napkin free of its starched convolutions and dropped it across his knees. "Oh," he said, "I see Mark's managed to get the wildfowling one at last. Makes a good pair with the fishing scene on the other side of the alcove, don't you think? . . . I always wondered, though, why the coloured retainer was so much better dressed than the shooting party itself—and why on earth he's sitting on a kitchen chair in the middle of a skiff !"

"He probably brought it along because he knew very well he'd have to wait an age before he ate," Emma Peel murmured mischievously.

"My dear Mrs Peel ! Do forgive me . . . One does run on, doesn't one? Now—to what Lucullan dish may I tempt you in expiation?"

The girl smiled at him once more across the table. In the diffuse top-lighting, her tawny hair glowed softly against the turquoise *lamé* of an evening trouser suit. Above the high cheekbones, her enormous brown eyes held Steed's ironic grey ones for a moment before she turned her attention to the menu. Daughter of a shipping magnate, widow of a supersonic test pilot, rich enough to be her own mistress and nobody else's,

Emma Peel was still zestful enough, at 27, to relish a dinner date with a civilised and charming companion.

"I see they have leeks *vinaigrettes*," she said. "After your dissertation, no self-respecting woman could avoid choosing them. As for the rest, though—since you brought me all the way out here just because the food was so good, I think it's only fair that you should be allowed to select whatever dishes you feel can justify the journey!"

"A challenge!" Steed said. "Right. There's a bottle of Alsatian Tokay—fruity but very dry—cooling for us. A bottle of Grands Echézeaux should have been opened in here half an hour ago . . . yes, there it is over there on the sideboard, look. I suggest that we have a simple *truite aux amandes* with the former, and Mark's speciality for tonight with the Burgundy."

"What is the speciality?"

"Duck *à la Rouennaise*," Steed said impressively. "You don't often get it in England, and it should be pretty good here."

"I'm terribly sorry, Steed," Emma said contritely, "but I don't know what it is."

"Splendid! That'll give me the chance to tell you. It's a—"

"Mr Steed! How very nice! Welcome back, welcome back . . ." The deep voice interrupted from over the waiter's shoulder. The owner of the "Ely Cathedral" was short, wide, brick-red faced and very dark, with a great blade of a nose flanked by twinkling, bright blue eyes.

"Hallo, Mark," Steed said, rising to his feet and introducing Emma. "Much of Mrs Peel's education was on the continent and in South America. I felt it my duty to demonstrate that we could still teach her something here—even if it was only in the culinary arts."

"Excellent, excellent," chuckled the man with the deep voice. "Though I take grave exception to that word 'only'. Now what are you going to have?" He leaned over the waiter's arm and scrutinised the order pencilled on his pad. "Ah, yes—the *poireaux*, trout with almonds . . . Good! . . . and the *Canard à la Rouennaise*. Fine."

"Mr Steed was about to initiate me into the mysteries of this dish," Emma said. "I'm afraid I don't know it at all."

"Why should you, dear lady? Why should you?" Lurchman said. "But however accomplished your host, this is a task I must arrogate to myself—you will permit me, Mr Steed?"

"Go ahead, Mark: you're the professional," Steed smiled. He

leaned back in his chair and looked idly at his fellow diners. There were several tables of solid, respectable-looking elderly folk—business people from Lincoln or Ely, or academics and their wives from Cambridge, he guessed. At the far end of the room, six lively young Italians were joking with the waiter heating their *shashlick* on skewers. A well-known television actor was psychoanalysing himself for the breathless benefit of a very young blonde. Two fat men talking French were slowly swilling Armagnac around the tulip glasses cupped in their hands. Nearer, two stridently "county" women in tweeds were extolling the virtues either of a stallion or a male acquaintance —Steed couldn't quite make out which. Their escorts stared mournfully at each other's moustaches across the white table-cloth.

Steed shifted his glance past the table next to his own—a tall man with glasses was sitting alone, wolfing a plateful of something covered in white sauce—to Lurchman and Emma. As an undercover man, one of those most special of agents not even assigned to a specific department, he was forced to use his man-of-the-world charm as a cloak for a particular type of ruthless dedication. To Steed, the end always justified the means—and if the means sometimes required a certain callousness, a certain unscrupulousness in the deployment of this charm to co-opt the assistance of such "amateur" help as Emma, well, that was all part of the game.

Even so, in those rare moments when he was, as it were, "off duty", Steed normally preserved an identical detachment to-wards his helpers. Tonight, though . . . he looked across at the square jawline, the imperious tilt of the triangular, pointed chin, the sensitivity of the wide mouth, as Emma listened, appreci-atively to Lurchman's peroration . . . tonight even Steed's iron nerves could not stifle a quickening of the pulse as his eye took in a voluptuous curve of the *lamé* jacket below the hollow of the shoulder, snatched a glimpse of a matching brassière between its open buttons, and lingered on a taut plane of suntanned flesh above the tight belt of the hipster trousers. Whichever way you looked at it—and it was equally pleasant any way!—Emma Peel was a very beautiful young woman . . .

". . . after it's been roasting twenty minutes," Mark Lurchman was saying, "you cut off the breast in long, thin slices, disjoint the legs and wings, and leave the whole shoot on one side while you attend to the carcass."

"I'm fascinated," Emma said, catching Steed's eye.

"That's when your special press comes in," Lurchman continued. "And that's why you'll rarely get the dish—or Duckling *á la Duclair* for that matter—in this country. You crush the carcass in this press and collect the blood, add the rest of the blood you have, deglaze it with red wine, and make a sauce with the blood, the duck's liver, and a couple of onions. Then, when the sauce has been reduced, you thicken it with butter and add the bits of the bird you've put on one side—simmering the lot until it's done."

"Fabulous. You can see why the English were always trying to take back Rouen from the French," Emma murmured.

The proprietor laughed his fat laugh again. "By the time we've put in our own stuffing and added the special *croutons*," he said, "you will see why Mr Steed enthuses. *Bon appetit, madame . . .*" He waved his hand and drifted across the dining room to talk to the Italians.

Later, when the exquisite trout was but a memory and the Tokay a tune vibrating in it, they watched with unconcealed interest as a waiter wheeled up a trolley and served Duck *à la Rouennaise* to the solitary man at the next table. His spectacles glinted greedily as he bent low over the spirit heater, drinking in every detail of the entrée dish sizzling on top of it. He inhaled appreciatively above the thick, rich, brown cargo of sauce, with its slivers of flesh savourily awash. He rubbed his hands with anticipation as the *croutons* were arranged on his plate and the contents of the dish reverently disbursed over them. And he exclaimed aloud with pleasure as the first morsel passed his lips.

Emma raised her eyebrows and turned back to Steed.

"Your proprietorial friend seems not to be the only enthusiast for the dish," she observed drily.

"Ours will be here in a moment; you'll see," Steed promised her with a grin. He waved away the wine waiter, who was offering to pour him a taste of the Grands Echézeaux. "I'm absolutely certain, my dear fellow," he said, "that Mark would never dream of charging *his* prices for anything that was less than perfect! You may pour . . ."

Emma sipped the lustrous Burgundy. "I must agree—it is rather gorgeous," she said reflectively. "Heavy and round-flavoured and rich. Now tell me, Steed: what are you up to? Why are we here?"

The undercover man rolled the wine around his mouth and

swallowed. "Perfect," he said. "Perfect. I've heard it described as having 'a violent bouquet of cherries and violets'. I can't say I can see that at all . . . To me, it simply tastes splendidly, beautifully, caressingly of *wine* ! What were you saying, my dear?"

"I asked you to come clean—and tell me why we're here."

"But to eat and drink, of course . . . Why else?"

"Oh, Steed ! Please ! Do I have to wait for the coffee?"

The faint, sardonic smile vanished from the agent's square-ish face. Above the impeccable dark suit, the clean lines of his features gathered under the crisp, dark hair into a frown. He looked for once slightly at a loss. "Mrs Peel," he began, "I do assure you—how can I convince . . . " He broke off, raised his eyes towards the ceiling, and started again. "Look," he said, "for once we're here *without* an ulterior motive ! Honestly. I just thought you'd like to try the food."

"I'm sorry, Steed. I simply do not believe you."

"But I give you my word—"

"In cases like this, your word's only as good as the next national emergency. Come on—what is it this time?"

"Oh, now *really*—" Steed began.

"Sorry, Mr Steed," a passing waiter called. "Be with you in a minute. Won't keep you another moment . . ."

"Quite all right," Steed called back. "We're not *pressés*, even if the duck is . . . Now look here, young woman—"

"It won't wash, Steed. It won't wash. I mean, I don't *mind* : it's just that I will not have my intelligence insulted."

"But I tell you . . ." The undercover man sat back with a sigh that was part amusement, part exasperation. "What can I say to you?"

"Just tell me *why* we're here," Emma said. "All right—the food is admirable; the wine is all you said it would be. But I simply cannot believe you'd come all this way for that alone. There must be another reason. Things have a habit of—happening, shall we say?—when you're around."

Exploding into the quiet sounds of dinner, a chair crashed over backwards. The tall man at the next table was on his feet, scrabbling at his chest with frenzied hands. A high, whinnying noise forced itself from his lips. He belched loudly and jacknifed forwards, to sprawl face downwards among the plates and glasses with an impact that shook the room.

"You see what I mean?" Emma Peel said.

# 3

## STEED SMELLS A RAT...

THE rain had stopped now and the East wind was scudding low clouds across the half moon. In the churned up mud of the car park, only Steed's vast vintage Bentley, Mark Lurchman's E-Type Jaguar and an old Austin belonging to the doctor remained under the dripping trees.

They had tried artificial respiration, they had tried injections, they had tried oxygen, coramine and other stimulants—but the tall man with the glasses was unmistakably, definitively and permanently dead. At last, the ambulance from Great Hornham had taken him away, leaving Emma Peel, Steed, Lurchman and the doctor grouped under the back porch of the "Ely Cathedral" rather like the bride and groom's parents after the honeymoon car has departed.

The doctor had actually been in the bar when the victim collapsed. He had been on the scene almost as soon as Steed had got the man lying flat and loosened his collar and tie. And he had sprinted over the bridge across the river, opened up the boot of his car and run back with the necessary equipment before a couple of minutes had passed.

But they had both known, as they worked together waiting for the ambulance, that it was too late.

"Obviously a sudden syncope—a cardiac failure," the doctor had said to Steed. He was a small man with a bald head and a stubby moustache. "Symptoms are obvious, so far as I can see: the clammy skin, the beads of perspiration, the cyanosed lips. Can't tell why, of course, as I wasn't here when it happened. Could be Angina. A coronary—no way of telling without some knowledge of the patient, whether there's a history of D.A.H., and so on . . ."

"D.A.H.?"

"Disorderly action of the heart," the little doctor explained.

"I see. Would anyone around here know about that?"

"Shouldn't think so. Fellow's a stranger, you see. Staying here for a few days. Just arrived in a cab from the station and took a room. Lurchman told me."

"What do you do about the Death Certificate, then?" Emma had asked.

"Do, young lady? Do? Why nothing, of course. Can't do a thing in the circumstances. Not enough to go on, you see. Have to do a P.M., have an inquest, contact the fellow's own G.P. and so on."

"And who'll conduct the post-mortem?"

"Well, as a matter of fact I shall have to. My name's Maltby, by the way. Gregory Maltby."

"How d'you do, Doctor Maltby? I'm Emma Peel. And this is John Steed."

They had murmured the usual inanities and then Steed had asked, in a conversational way, if Maltby encountered any difficulties in such cases with his local coroner. There had been an awkward pause. The doctor had coughed and reddened slightly.

"Well—it's an extraordinary thing," he had said at last, "but in fact I'm the coroner, too. Or at least I think so . . ."

"I don't quite understand."

"Well—er—it's Atherley . . . it *was* Atherley, I should have said. That is to say my colleague is—was—the coroner, but he was killed in an accident today."

"I'm sorry."

"So, as I'm the only other candidate around here, I suppose at least temporarily . . ." His voice had trailed off. And then : "But it's odd, damned odd," he had said. "I simply do not understand . . ."

"What don't you understand, Doctor Maltby?"

"Nothing, nothing . . . Never mind," the little man had said gruffly. And he had bustled off almost immediately afterwards on some pretext or other—something about getting the spelling of the dead man's name right from the hotel register.

The only thing was, the dead man hadn't signed the register. He had apparently arrived that afternoon, promised the receptionist that he would attend to the matter before dinner, and forgotten to do so. Odder still was the fact that among the effects in his clothes—watch, wallet, engagement diary, money, keys, cigarettes and lighter, a couple of circulars put out by local building societies—there was not a single item with a name or an address on it. Nor could Steed discover any when he slipped upstairs unseen and turned-over the dead man's room briefly but expertly while the body was being loaded into the ambulance. There were laundry marks and dry-cleaning codes on the clothes, of course. It would be a comparatively easy matter to identify the mysterious guest in time. But for the moment he would remain a corpse strictly anonymous. And it looked very much as though he himself had planned it that way.

"I suppose," Steed said now, as the four of them stood in the porch watching the lights of the ambulance fade away among the trees, "I suppose there isn't any remote chance that the food could have had anything to do with his death?"

"The *food*, Mr Steed!" Mark Lurchman sounded scandalised.

"Certainly not," Maltby snapped. "I told you : he died of a heart attack. Can't be sure which of the various cardiac conditions *caused* the failure, as I said. But there's no doubt at all that it *was* heart failure. None whatever." He turned abruptly and barged through the swing door into the interior of the inn.

"I didn't mean there was anything wrong with the food, Mark," Steed said mildly. "I was just wondering—I mean, perhaps some allergy . . . maybe some ingredient in one of the dishes . . . " He gestured vaguely. "The chap was certainly cramming it in at a prodigious rate of knots."

"So the waiter told me," Lurchman admitted, mollified.

"Would the remains of the food have been kept, Mark?" Steed persisted. "I mean, I know half the glasses and crockery were smashed when he fell, but what about the entrée dish itself, for example?"

The owner of the "Ely Cathedral" looked away. "No . . . No, I'm afraid not," he said evasively. "I tell you it was all thrown away. You can't blame the staff—it was chaos in there for a while. Naturally they cleared it all up. There were other guests to consider."

"All right, old lad. All right," Steed soothed. "I only wondered."

He turned and went back into the hotel, ushering Emma before him.

"Mr Steed, Mr Steed!" The head waiter was covered in confusion. "You were helping so much, you never get the rest of your meal. Please! Let me make something now for you and for Madame?"

"Thank you, Giorgio, I really don't think . . ." the undercover man began. Then he paused, struck by a thought. "Wait a minute, though," he said slowly. "The Duck *à la Rouennaise* that was being prepared for us. Presumably it's still there? Couldn't you heat that up for us?"

"Oh, Mr Steed, it wouldn't be the same. You know it wouldn't."

"Yes, Steed," Emma said quickly. "I really don't feel I could . . ."

"Have a look, Giorgio, will you?" the agent continued smoothly.

He waited, blandly aloof, until the man came back, a puzzled frown puckering his round, sallow face. "Is a funny thing, Mr Steed," he said. "It seems to have dissappear. Maybe one of the boys throw it out by mistake, eh?"

"Not by mistake, I fancy," Steed said softly. "But never mind. No—I wouldn't dream of having you make us another one, thank you. Come to think of it, I'm a bit off duck for to-night, anyway! Besides we must be getting back to town. On the other hand, there *is* the rest of that Echézeaux—I trust *that* hasn't been—er—thrown away?"

"Mr *Steed*!"

"No? I'm relieved to hear it, Giorgio . . . In that case, let us have some cheese—say a Chalaronne or a Géramont—and we'll polish it off."

But it was not until they were thundering home with the Bentley's touring hood up that he confided to Emma what he had seen from the window of the dead man's bedroom while he was searching it.

"It was still raining then," he said. "Absolutely pelting down. I happened to glance down into the garden as I crossed the room from the dressing table to the wardrobe—and there was this girl, waiting on the far side of the little bridge across the river."

"What kind of girl?" Emma asked, interested.

"The kind the Italians respectfully call *robusta*. You know— good, round arms, sturdy legs, billowy hips and tiny waist, with those huge, firm breasts that seem to go with that sort of figure."

"That must have been quite a glance."

Steed smiled. "You could hardly have avoided it," he said. "She was wearing a cheap cotton frock with no raincoat, and the material was plastered to that body by the rain and wind as though it was just drawn on."

"What kind of a face did she have? How old was she?"

"I only saw her for a moment, as somebody opened a door downstairs and she was outlined for a second in a shaft of light.

Besides, she had long hair and it was all stuck to her face by the weather. But she seemed to be the, you know, the sort of gypsy type."

"The proud animal, on equal terms with the elements?"

"Not quite as Mary Webb as that. Besides, she can't have been a day over nineteen. And she looked as scared as all get-out!"

"But what was she *doing* there, Steed?"

"I soon found that out. She was obviously waiting—but impatient to be away. Anyway, in a few seconds a man in a black slicker crept furtively along the path from the porch to the bridge, looked right and left, and then crossed the bridge to meet her."

"And then?"

"He pulled some kind of a package from under his raincoat, thrust it into her hands, and she vanished into the bushes like a dose of salts!"

"What did he do?"

"Hurried back to the pub as quickly as he could."

"Did you see who it was, Steed?"

"Yes. He crossed a bar of light from some window just before he reached the porch. It was Mark."

Emma gave a low whistle, clearly audible over the burble of the Bentley's two-and-a-half-inch exhaust as they rolled through Braintree. "I'm sorry I doubted your word earlier on, Steed," she said. "You're obviously as astonished by tonight's goings-on as I have been. What an odd sequence of events!"

"I think it's a bit more than odd, to tell the truth," Steed replied. "One way or another, I small a rat. A rat with wings . . ."

# 4

## HEARTS COME UP TRUMPS!

NEWSPAPERS were scattered all over the three wide stairs linking the two levels of Steed's sitting room when Emma Peel arrived at the flat in Westminster Mews the next morning. Her host, resplendent in a waisted lovat-green suit with a velvet collar, was perched on the edge of a wine-and-gold striped Regency settee, leaning forward with his forearms resting on his elegant knees as he gazed reflectively down at the litter of newsprint. Three items on a trio of separate pages were ringed in red marker pencil.

"Good morning, Steed," Emma called cheerfully. "The door was open, so I came up. What are you doing—trying your fancy for the two-thirty?"

Steed rose to his feet and helped his visitor off with her coat— a black wool affair braided in black and white, which concealed a white wool dress braided in black, rather like a photograph and its negative.

"Nothing so lively, I'm afraid," he replied with a smile. "All the subjects of this little investigation are strictly non-runners."

"These?" She indicated the papers on the steps. "Anything to do with our unfortunate friend last night?"

"Perhaps. I'm not quite sure yet," Steed said with a puzzled frown. "I went out to get the nationals and some locals, just in case. But the man from the 'Ely Cathedral' hasn't made any of them. On the other hand . . ." He paused, then picked up the three marked copies and handed them to her. "Have a look for yourself," he said soberly.

Emma glanced at each of the three papers in turn, then looked up enquiringly, her dark eyebrows raised.

"Don't you see anything odd about them?" Steed asked.

"One from the *Gazette,* one from the *East Anglian Echo,* one from the *Lincoln Mercury*—no, I don't think so." She examined the ringed stories in more detail. "Apart from the fact that they all report deaths in one way or another, nothing strikes me. They're all different people."

"But they don't all report deaths 'in one way or another'—they report deaths in the same way."

"Oh, surely not, Steed: one's a straight obituary; one's a news story about a man killed in a car crash; one's an announcement about a new speaker for a political meeting—mentioning by the way that the change has been occasioned by the death of the man originally down to talk."

"Yes, yes, my dear. The manner of *reporting's* different—but the *deaths*, the manner of death . . . What about that?"

"Oh. Yes—I see what you mean. All heart failure. And so?"

"And all taking place . . .?" Steed insisted.

Emma hesitated. She looked at the newspaper stories again. "That *is* strange," she admitted slowly at last. "The car crash at Bratby, the painter at Star Point, the orator at Great Hornham . . . and, of course, the poor chap we saw last night: they're all within a few miles of each other."

"Exactly."

"But that's not all, Steed!"

"What d'you mean—that's not all?"

The girl fumbled in her handbag. "Of course, it *may* be simply a coincidence," she said, "but I got a letter from my uncle this morning—yes, here we are!—and he mentioned that an old gamekeeper I used to be rather fond of had died during the past few days." She turned the pages, looking for the paragraph in question. "He had a heart attack, it seems . . ."

"Where was your uncle writing from?" Steed asked.

Emma looked at him. "The shooting box at Birningham," she said softly. "About five miles from the Wash."

Steed bent down abruptly and scooped up the newspapers. "I did ask you to drop in for an aperitif before lunch, my dear," he said. "In the circumstances, I feel something more substantial is called for, perhaps! There's a new Colombian blend from that chap in Duke Street by the grinder. John Jameson in the cupboard. Cream on the doorstep. D'you think you could possibly cope with an Irish coffee while I make a call . . .?"

While Emma busied herself with Moulinex and Cona machine, he dumped the papers on the rosewood desk, settled himself in a chair and drew the telephone towards him. First he dialled a number in three groups of three. The line was opened instantly, though no word was spoken at the other end. Steed immediately gave another number verbally—a number so secret that less than thirty people in the whole country knew it. There was a decisive click on the line, then the normal ringing tone. After three double burrs, a receiver was lifted and a man's voice said crisply:

"Control."

"Steed here," the undercover man said.

"Identification?"

"Played Portia in prep school *Merchant of Venice* in 1935. Three tries against Harrow Colts in 1937. Stroked the Head of the River boat in 1939."

"Go ahead, Steed. Thought you were resting."

"So did I. Something may have come up, though. Can you get L.7 at the Yard to do a spot check on area mortalities within the half hour—Grade One, three-day limit, computed against the Mean?"

"Of course, if it's necessary. What's on your mind?"

"I think it may be." Steed picked up the newspapers and read from them in turn. "Vanessa Arco, painter, 27, obituary in today's *Gazette*. Oliver Freesing, town councillor and prospective parliamentary candidate, 54, death mentioned in *Lincoln Mercury* announcement of change of speakers at political meeting tonight. Henry Atherley, doctor, 61, death in motor accident reported in today's *East Anglian Echo*. Got those?"

"Right."

"In addition, two more so far unreported: a gamekeeper at a village called Birningham a day or so ago; and a diner at a pub called the 'Ely Cathedral'—that's between Boston and Little Hornham—last night."

"Right, Steed. And the area?"

The undercover man picked up a large-scale atlas of the British Isles and read off a series of six-figure co-ordinates. "That should be wide enough for them to give a definitive figure," he said, "I'm at home. I'll expect your call in about half an hour, then?"

"In *exactly* thirty minutes," the impersonal voice said precisely.

The Napoleonic barrel clock on the desk was striking the half hour after eleven o'clock as Steed replaced the receiver on its cradle.

Soon afterwards, he was sitting cross-legged on his tiger-skin rug, the newspapers once again spread around him, as Emma spiralled the thick, slow cream over the back of a spoon on to the surface of the aromatic, whisky-laced coffee roasting in the steaming cups.

"You really think there's something here, don't you, Steed?" she asked as she curled up on the striped settee with her own cup and saucer in one hand.

"M'mmmm. Delicious, Mrs Peel. Delicious ! Yes—I've been convinced of it for years. One of the most invigorating drinks—"

"Steed !" Emma cried warningly.

"But I have, my dear. One shouldn't be chauvinistic about these things, you know. Of all the arts, gastronomy is the most cosmopolitan. Because the Whisky is Irish, the recipe French and the coffee South American, that's no reason at all to deny the excellence—"

"Steed ! I was speaking of heart failure, as you know very well."

"And so was I, Mrs Peel ! As I was saying, this splendid drink is a first-class stimulant—but you're leading me astray, talking about food ! If I may venture to change the subject, I'd like to get back to this affair of the deaths in East Anglia . . ."

Emma burst out laughing. "You really are incorrigible," she said. "Why *do* you do it?"

"Another kind of stimulation—using the female variety of logic *on* a lady," Steed grinned softly, rising to his feet and putting the empty cup and saucer on his desk. "Besides, the pink spots on your cheeks when you're angry are most becoming. Seriously, though—"

"*I* know," Emma interrupted again. "I'm doing a grand job. What I cannot see at the moment, is just where a job comes in to this at all. If you're right, that is, and there *is* something odd about these deaths . . . Unless"—she paused and eyed Steed suspiciously—"Unless you've known all along and are simply pretending to discover it stage by stage for my benefit. I wouldn't put it past you !"

Steed was contrite. "My dear Mrs Peel," he assured her, "you have my word on it that there's nothing going on—nothing at all—which you don't know as much about as I do."

"You're just playing an outsize hunch, then?"

"If you like to put it that way. You saw that man collapse last night. I wasn't entirely happy about the local GP's diagnosis. There were one or two things . . . But never mind. The point is that I happened to see these three newspaper reports this morning. And then you mentioned your father's letter—and the five deaths together suddenly seemed an awful lot to have occurred in the same way, in such a short space of time, in almost the same area."

"And so?"

"And so I've asked for a check. Just in case. At this moment, the girls in L.7, Scotland Yard's new liaison department, are doing a top priority run-down for me—correlating all deaths bearing any resemblance to these in a given area, during the past few days, and checking them against the national average."

"Of deaths from the same causes over the same period of time?"

"Exactly. I mean, see what we have already." Steed ticked them off on the fingers of his right hand. "One, a middle-aged man falls dead in the middle of a meal. Cause of death diagnosed as a heart attack. Two, an elderly doctor drives his car head-on into a horse trough. He is thought to have died of a heart attack before the actual crash. Three, an unconventional young woman, well known as a painter of birds—"

"Of course!" Emma exclaimed suddenly. "Birds! Vanessa Arco. She's the painter all the smart gossip columnists call The Beaknik!"

"That's the one," Steed smiled. "The Beaknik. She dies in an isolated studio—from a heart attack. And then there's your gamekeeper to make four, and the gentleman who never did make his speech at the political meeting coming in at number five . . ."

"And they're both heart cases too?"

"It seems like it. I know it could be coincidence, of course. But suppose it isn't—what on earth have all these people in common? Why should everyone suddenly start dying from heart failure in a corner of East Anglia?"

"But Steed, people die from heart failure all over the place, all the time . . ."

"Of course they do, my dear. It's just—how shall I say?— the . . . the *concentration* of it that seems a little odd to me in this case."

The barrel clock on the desk was striking twelve. Before it had got half way through its silvery pronouncement, the strident bell of the telephone was shrilling it into oblivion. Steed scooped up the receiver.

"Steed here."

"Identification; for mercy's sake."

"The quality of it's not strained. When you're at school, it droppeth like the gentle rain from heaven, upon—"

"All right, all right, all right. No need to show off, Steed. Some of us were on the science side. I have the gen you want."

"Splendid. Fire away."

"Within the coordinate and time limits, L.7 report nine deaths of this kind, including those you mentioned."

"*Nine?*"

"Nine. The plus percentage over the Mean is sixty-two. Six two."

"Thank you very much," Steed said. "Do you have details of the other four?"

"Of course. You have pencil and paper ready?"

"Of course."

But the undercover man did not write anything down as the voice dispassionately continued its report. He drew nine little men with glasses on the back of one of the newspapers, added moustaches to eight of them and breasts to the ninth, and finally doodled in what looked like a child's version of a seagull above the head of each. Eventually the voice stopped.

"Fine," Steed said. "Thanks very much again. Yes . . . yes, I see what you mean. *Quod erat demonstrandum,* as you chaps on the science side would have said . . ."

He put down the phone and turned to Emma Peel.

"In the last three days," he said, "nine people have died from unexplained heart failure in the neighbourhood we were in last night. Per hundred of the population, that's sixty-two per cent up on the national average for the same three days. And in six of the cases there was no history of cardiac trouble whatever."

In her turn, Emma whistled. "You *are* on to something, then, aren't you?" she asked.

"I'm afraid it does look like it."

"What about the previous figures for the area, though?" the girl pursued. "Perhaps there's a history of higher-than-usual cardiac failures for some reason."

"They were intelligent enough to check that, actually. Until these three days, it was dead normal, right on the average—for as far back as they were able to go in a half hour, that is."

"Then obviously you must be right—there's something . . . well, *wrong* about these deaths. We know about five of them; what did you find out about the other four?"

"A retired admiral dropped dead in his rose garden; a railway porter shuffled off this mortal coil between the 8.45 and the 9.15; a tramp was found stiff in a camp fire but wasn't burned; a 25-year-old insurance agent perished in his bed."

"And the places—the venues, as they say in show business?"

"Bratby, Little Hornham station, the roadside between Bratby and Flint's Dyke, and Boston," Steed said. He picked up the atlas from the desk again and opened it at the page showing the area they were discussing. "Let's mark in the nine fatal spots," he added. "Here, you take this red thing and ring the places as I call them out . . ."

"Well, I'll start with the Martello tower at Star Point," Emma said, making a neat circle on the printed page. "That's the furthest North. Then I'll do my gamekeeper at Birningham. That's the furthest South."

"Right," Steed said. "Then there's this long bit of straight road following the coast in between. That's where they found the tramp." He leaned over Emma's shoulder and indicated a spot on the map. "And a couple of circles at Bratby, a few miles further on. Those are for the doctor and the retired admiral. One at our pub, of course—that's ten miles or so inland and to the Northwest. And . . . let me see . . ."

"The Hornhams?" Emma prompted.

"Yes, of course. One at Little and one at Great, for the porter and the councillor. How many do you have now?"

"Eight."

"Well, that just leaves the insurance agent at Boston. Now, how does it look?"

Together they bent over the atlas and studied the pattern of red circles. "Seems as obvious as a signpost," Emma said at last. "You can't very well miss it, can you?"

"Absolutely not. Apart from that one-off example at Boston, all the rest are within a ten-mile radius of Bratby—and the concentration seems heavier as we get nearer to that village. Bratby has to be, as it were, the epicentre of the operation . . . whatever the operation is."

"Yes, Steed—but *why*; why should people begin dying off like flies around some obscure hamlet in the Fen District? If we accept that the deaths are deliberate, we still come back to that. What could anybody gain—what possible connection could there be—between the deaths of five professional men, a gamekeeper, a tramp and a lady painter?"

"That, my dear," Steed said grimly, "is what we have to find out."

"What d'you mean—*us*? It may be nothing to do with you, let alone me. It may be entirely a police matter, some local vendetta, an M.I.5 affair or a Special Branch party to do with . . . with—oh, drugs or black magic. Anything. There must be some common denominator that would give a pointer, the way the circles did on the map. Couldn't all the conceivable details be fed into a computer—?"

"I didn't say 'us'. I said 'we'," Steed corrected her drily. "And L.7 already *have* fed all the available data to a computer."

"Well?"

"Well, there *is* a common denominator—which is why I think we ought to be on our way to Bratby."

"For heaven's sake, Steed! Do I have to wait for next week's bumper issue before I get another thrilling instalment?"

Steed grinned suddenly. He reached for Emma's coat. "Mrs Peel," he said smoothly, "your culinary expertise entitles you to an immediate explanation. You shall have one at once."

"Steed! What on earth has my culinary—what do you mean?"

"The common denominator, my dear! The one linking factor. Like our friend at the 'Ely Cathedral', every single one of the other eight victims was eating—or had recently eaten—some kind of duck when he died . . ."

# 5

## "IT LOOKS LIKE ONE OF OURS"

STEED decided to motor up to Bratby alone and telephone Emma that evening when he had spied out the lay of the land a little. "I may want you to come up and lend a hand, one way or another," he said nonchalantly. "But I shall probably know about that tonight. Anyway, I'll let you know when I phone."

"Yes," Emma said. "There is one thing, though."

"Really, Mrs Peel? What is that?"

"I may decide not to come. I may not *want* to come. Even if I was asked properly instead of told."

"Nonsense, my dear," Steed said heartily. "A spot of the good old East Coast breeze'll do you the world of good. Blow all those cobwebs away!"

He handed her courteously into the low-slung, black and white Lotus Elan she had left outside the street door of his flat, and waved good-bye as the little car rocketed away down the mews with a crisp snarl of its exhaust. Then he opened the big double doors of his garage and went inside to operate the electric lock of the steel grille behind them which protected the Bentley. He had thrown an umbrella, a pair of bowler hats and a weekend case on to the back seat and was just raising the bonnet to flood the twin carburettors when there was the sound of tyres on the cobbles and a taxi rolled slowly to rest outside.

"Cab, sir?" a voice called persuasively. "Cab, Mr Steed?"

Steed didn't look up from the engine room of the Bentley. "I should have thought it was fairly obvious that I was just about to go out by car," he called back. "It does start, you know . . ."

"Not until after lunch, it doesn't," the voice said. "Not today."

The undercover man straightened up and sauntered towards the doors. "Just who the devil d'you think you're talking to," he began . . . and then he paused, a slow smile spreading across his face. "Why it's Benson," he said. "Didn't recognise you at first, my dear fellow. What are *you* doing here?"

The seamed little man crouching inside his overcoat on the

driving seat of the cab winked with a kind of reprehensible familiarity. "You better hop in, cock," he said hoarsely. "You got a lunch date."

Steed sighed. "O God," he complained, "not with—?"

"That's it, mate. Hole in one, as I daresay your posh friends'd say. His Nibs wants to see you."

"For lunch, you say? Not at—?"

"Right again, Mr Steed! At the club. Come on, now—orders are to get you there at half past, and it's nearly that now . . ."

"Hang on a moment, Benson. You'll have to turn that thing round: this is a cul-de-sac. I'll just nip upstairs for a couple of bicarbonate tablets while you do it."

Later, as the taxi threaded its way through a traffic jam on the short journey to St. James's, Steed slid aside the partition window, sat sideways on the collapsible, backward-facing occasional seat, and questioned the driver further. Benson had been batman to the Very Important Personage at whose command Steed was lunching—and had continued to work for him after the war as a kind of personal aide and courier in the Service. There was a strange *rapport* between the two men and the select band of agents who came into contact with His Nibs frequently found that the tough little Cockney was able to give them guidance on the way that unpredictable mind was working. And since it pleased His Nibs's schoolboyish sense of the dramatic to send his mandatory invitations to "lunch at the club" via Benson, the consequent taxi-rides usually saw a lot of fast talking. ("Though if you ask me, old man," an Harrovian colleague of Steed's once said, "there's no such bloody thing as a leak from that quarter. Every crumb of info that chap drops is dropped because H.N. has told him to drop it, you can depend on it.")

"So how is the old boy, then?" Steed enquired offhandedly, as the cab squeezed between two converging buses in Cockspur Street and shuddered to a halt at the zebra crossing at the bottom of Haymarket.

"Perishing old women!" Benson exclaimed. "Think the whole of the traffic all over bleeding London comes to an automatic halt immediately their toe touches the ruddy zebra!—His Nibs? Doesn't complain, Mr Steed. Doesn't complain; though we're none of us getting any younger, are we?"

"No," Steed said. "It's just that some of us are able to bear it more gracefully than others. You've no idea why he wants to see me, then?"

"Well, now, cock, I really couldn't say, could I? 'Xpect you'll find out when you're having your nosh-up with him. Talking of cock, though—and who isn't in this business!—I'd watch the poultry course, if I were you, cock ..."

Steed sat back with a sigh of relief. This transparent piece of obliqueness was as direct a hint as he was likely to get that the summons was at least in connection with the same mystery that was occupying his own thoughts. Though how the old man had got on to it he couldn't imagine.

Benson edged the taxi into the swirl of traffic that was bifurcating round the island at the entrance to St. James' Street. "*I* don't know," he complained resignedly. "These perishing one-way streets! Gets more like driving in Rome every day ..."

There was nothing Roman about the appointments of the club, however. That dismal building was notable only for the lack of imagination of its catering manager, and Steed and his host were able without any difficulty to find seats in splendid isolation at the end of one of the long tables in the funereal dining room.

"There we are, my boy," His Nibs said encouragingly. "Now what do we have today? Let's see ... Why, look at that! *Pommes de terre Monte Carlo*! Would you believe it! D'you get it, Steed? ... Monte Carlo—gambling—*chips* ... That's a fancy way of saying chips, you know. I call that jolly smart."

"Very droll, sir," Steed said dutifully.

"I think I'll have some. Doesn't do any harm to encourage these artistic fellers, what? And what about a spot of Lancashire hot-pot? I must say I like something substantial at luncheon. Feeds the inner man. D'you fancy some yourself, Steed?"

"Er—no. I think I'll ... I'm not really very hungry, sir, actually. Perhaps I could just have some bread and cheese?" Steed said hollowly.

"Nonsense, my boy. You need something filling under your belt. You people are supposed to keep in tip-top condition, you know. I'll order you some hot-pot too. Now what shall we drink? You like wine, don't you?"

The undercover man admitted faintly to this sybaritic taste.

"Thought so. Somebody told me you're quite an expert on wine."

"Well, I wouldn't go so far as to say—"

"Rubbish, rubbish. No need to be modest about it, Steed. I understand the carafe *rosé*'s very good value here ..."

And later, after Steed had listened to two golfing stories and a scabrous anecdote about a former head of Naval Intelligence, His Nibs shot a curiously penetrating glance at him from below the shaggy eyebrows and rapped out: "Now what's all this I hear about ducks?"

Steed told him. "I hope you don't think I'm trying to go into business on a freelance basis, sir," he added. "It was just that I wanted to be quite sure before I bothered you with it. I was going to drive up to Bratby this afternoon, as a matter of fact, to see what I could find out."

"That's all right, Steed. We encourage initiative, you know that. You did quite right. And I have an extra piece of information, I think, that will make your journey really necessary, as we used to say in the old days."

"I'm glad of that, sir. In a case like this, every little helps."

"What's that? Oh. Yes—well, I don't know if *you* know, but L.7 shoot me along a précis of any little query like yours that they get. Just in case it might interest me, you know. So does Control, for that matter."

"I didn't know, as a matter of fact, sir. I shall file the information away for possible use in the future."

His Nibs permitted himself a wintry smile. "No doubt. Well, it seemed to me that you might be on to something. So I told L.7 to keep on plugging—to take the thing as far back as they could before luncheon. They were able to continue your cross-check for a six-month period and feed the data into their blasted computer before I left the office to come here. And d'you know what they turned up, Steed?"

"No, sir."

The old man across the table paused for effect, relishing the dramatic possibilities of what he was about to say. He popped a faintly sweating cube of Cheddar cheese into his mouth. "They told me," he said, munching stickily, "that apart from the nine deaths you know about, there had been in the past six months no less than seven other fatalities of the same nature in the same area."

Steed raised his eyebrows.

"Now I know that hardly raises the figure above the normal average," His Nibs continued before the undercover man could speak. "Unexplained and unexpected heart failures are common enough, God knows. But there was just this other point—all seven of 'em took place at the dining table. And as far as L.7

could tell, the majority at least were eating, or had eaten, some kind of bird!"

"Good Lord! I see what you mean, sir."

"Yes. So I think we can safely say there's a case to investigate."

"The only thing is," Steed said thoughtfully, "that the case—such as it now is—may just be a police matter. It may not (if you'll forgive the phrase) be our pigeon at all. At the moment, one just can't tell."

"I don't think you need worry about that, my boy. From all the indications, and I've been in this game a long time, you know, this definitely looks like one of ours . . . And if it turns out that I'm wrong—well, you can always hand over the dossier to MacCorquodale, can't you?"

"Yes, of course." Steed said. "Well, since I have your approval, I think I'll get ahead with it right away, sir."

"Splendid. But won't you stay for a coffee?"

"Well, no—er—no, I really feel I should be on my way, sir, thank you. It's—er—there's quite a way to go, you know. Thanks just the same."

"Just as you like. What are those two white tablets you're taking, though—you're not going to tell me you're on some blasted quack's diet, Steed? Don't think I haven't noticed you've been off your food today."

"No, no, sir. The only quacks connected with this case are the ducks. These are . . . these are—just a couple of throat tablets, you know. Been a bit dry around the mouth for the past few days . . ."

"H'mm. Go easy on them, young feller. I don't hold with chaps in your line of country taking to drugs," His Nibs said disapprovingly. "Nothing like a good meal to put you right if you're feelin' out of sorts. Best tonic in the world, I always say."

"I couldn't agree with you more," Steed murmured, thankfully making his exit . . .

# 6

## THE CORPSE IN THE CARDBOARD
## COFFIN

AT six o'clock on the morning of the third day the single pane of glass which served as the cottage's front window erupted inwards with a noise like a bomb bursting. Steed was awake and out of bed with a golf club in his hand almost before the last jagged fragment had shivered to the brick floor. A large, smooth stone with a piece of paper wrapped round it was lying on top of the rickety table.

He snapped off the elastic holding it in place and smoothed out the cheap paper. Two lines in crudely printed ballpoint capitals sprawled across the surface:

WE DONT LIKE MEDDLERS ROUND HERE.
GET OUT OF BRATBY—FAST!—IF YOU WANT TO
STAY HELTHY ...

Steed crossed the room in three strides and jerked open the door. A figure in dark trousers and windcheater—he couldn't tell if it was a man or a woman—was just disappearing over the crest of the huge storm-beach. He ran across the stretch of balding turf and ploughed up the sweep of shingle as fast as he could. But by the time he reached the top there was nobody to be seen. The quarter of a mile of reed-covered saltings between the ridge and Bratby village could have concealed an army. Smiling slightly, he turned with a shrug and retraced his steps to the cottage.

The village was nearly a half mile from the sea. From the high ground of Star Point to the North, a long spit of land ran southwards for several miles, separated from the mainland proper by a shallow lagoon which had silted up and become overgrown with marsh vegetation at its inner end. The cottage Steed had rented— it was only a shack, really, with a single room and a primitive bathroom and kitchen—lay on the seaward side of the storm-beach which formed the backbone of the peninsula and protected the saltings beyond it from all but the most severe gales.

Lower down, the lagoon boasted patches of open water before it ran out into the sea via the disused harbour at Flint's Dyke. But up here the reeds and grasses were pretty dense. It was possible to walk across the marsh from the cottage to Bratby, but only the wildfowlers knew the paths: the rest of the world went round by the head of the inlet.

For Steed, the position was ideal. It was early Spring still, and very few people troubled to walk up to the point and down the spit to the handful of fishermen's shanties scattered along its length. Apart from his own, so far as he could tell only one other shack was inhabited—a rambling structure of tarred boards about a mile to the South. And even this he had deduced from the nets drying on the stones, the upturned boat on the beach, rather than because he had actually seen anybody.

On the other hand although he was thus isolated, from the top of the shingle ridge he himself could mount a permanent and invisible watch on Bratby and its surroundings.

For the greater part of two days, he had been lying flat on the stones, scanning the old brick and weatherboard buildings of the village through powerful Zeiss binoculars. Behind him, the grey waves sucked at the shingle and the wind scoured the rolls of seaweed piled along the high-water mark. In front, across the rippling tufts of the marsh, the everyday life of the hamlet pursued its distant routine. A trickle of people visited the few shops in the High Street, farmers drove in from outlying areas and parked in the square by the church, the three pubs opened and closed. There was a certain amount of through traffic—cars, lorries, vans, an occasional army convoy, using the road from Lincoln which swung seawards beyond Flint's Dyke and followed the coastline to the South in the shelter of the storm-beach. But on his side of the lagoon, hardly a soul passed. A gang of schoolboys brawled down the water's edge one afternoon, throwing stones at the sea. Coasters steamed slowly across the choppy horizon. Once he trained the glasses on a group of men, far down the spit, who seemed to be launching a boat.

There was a rough track bordering the marsh on the inner slope of the ridge, and in the late afternoons he bumped the Bentley up to the point, past the Martello tower, and round to the village to buy food. Later, posing as a journalist writing a series of features on wild life, he drank at the pubs and tried to strike up an acquaintance with the locals. But this was wildfowling country; most of the men had to do with birds and were taciturn in the extreme. Until this morning, nothing had happened to jar the sleepy routine of the place.

Now, however, as Steed swept up the broken glass from the cottage floor, there was an expression of pleased anticipation on his rakish features: his ostentatious enquiries had born fruit. The word had got around and somebody, somewhere, had been stung to action.

Perhaps, now, things would begin to happen . . .

*      *      *

Thirty-six hours later, Emma Peel stood with three men in the angle between a high stone wall and a macrocarpa hedge. Darkness had fallen and fitful gusts of wind snatched at the flames of the oil lamps where they stood behind a makeshift sacking screen. Over the cemetery wall, crosses, stone angels and the sombre shape of an elm etched themselves against the sky in the reflected light of the torch Emma held shielded in one hand.

The Home Office pathologist was conferring in low tones with his colleague as the girl directed the man with the spade.

"Just about there, I should say— it won't be very deep," she said quietly.

The man thrust the shining edge of the tool into the ground, put one foot on the shoulder of the blade, rested his weight on it, and levered at the handle, grunting, as a great clod of the clayey soil broke loose from the surrounding earth. He shovelled it to one side, sank the spade in again, and dug away another. The ground immediately over the grave had been stamped flat and hard, but it had been a hurried job: once the compounded topsoil had been removed, the shovel sank in easily enough— though it was heavy work levering away the sticky clods. In a few minutes, he had dug away about eighteen inches and Emma laid a hand on his arm.

"Go easy," she said. "It can't be far now."

The man prodded experimentally with the tip of the spade and struck something hard. The two men and the girl leaned over the shallow hole as he scraped away, gradually exposing the box. Finally, he drove the spade into the mound of discarded earth and prised the coffin loose with his bare hands.

"Right," the pathologist said. "That's the first part over with. Let's get it to the mortuary and see what we can find . . ."

They put the box in the back of the plain, dark green Home

Office van and went back to tidy up. The man with the spade shovelled the earth back into the grave and patted it roughly down as the others rolled up the sacking screen, pulled up the stakes which had supported it, and doused the lamps. Despite the chill in the night air, there was a heavy dew of perspiration on his brow when he had finished. He wiped his forearm across his face, shouldered the spade and followed them back to the van.

"All right, Horrocks," the pathologist said briskly. "I'll take the shovel in the back with us. You know where to go: make it as quick as you can. I'd like to get back to Town before it's too late."

"Very good, Sir Charles," the man said. He climbed into the driver's seat, started the engine, and drove slowly down the narrow lane until they reached the main road. A signpost showed briefly as the beam from their headlamps swept past while they were turning North. *Little Hornham* ½; *Boston* 11, the black lettering spelled out on the arm pointing in their direction. Behind them, the white finger indicated *Great Hornham* 3¼.

It was almost half an hour before the van pulled up in a covered yard behind high double gates. "Come on in," the pathologist called. "We can leave the—er—formalities to Horrocks and the attendants. I must apologise for having to bring you so far," he went on, "but this was the nearest mortuary the Home Office could suggest with the necessary laboratory facilities."

He led the way to a small, square room, tiled from floor to ceiling, comprehensively equipped with bench, sinks, flasks and retorts, Bunsen burners, racks of test tubes, microscopes, and shelves of brightly coloured reagents in glass jars. "Here you are, Wickham," he said to his colleague. "It's not very large, but I imagine you'll find everything here that you need. You're the analyst, though—what *will* you need?"

George Wickham was tubby, red-faced and moustached. Beside the lean elegance and grey-haired distinction of Sir Charles, he looked rather like an old-fashioned music-hall comedian trying out a new straight man.

"Well—ah—thank you, Sir Charles," he said. "Microscopes and slides, of course. The usual culture dishes, I suppose. Spectroscope. Our normal—ah—apparatus for reaction tests . . . But really, this is a little beyond my experience. Perhaps Mrs—ah—Peel could give us a more succinct idea of what's required?"

"If by any chance I'm right," Emma said, "none of your normal tests would reveal anything. I suggest that, instead of following the customary routine and methodically eliminating the possibilities one by one, we just try straight off for this one particular reaction."

"Just as you like, Mrs Peel," the pathologist agreed.

"It doesn't react like the alkaloids, you see. It's neutral to all the usual reagents. But if you know what to look for and you do suspect it, the test's as simple as you like. If it's what I think it is, all you'll need are a couple of slides and a test tube with a Bunsen."

"I must say this is beyond *my* experience, too," Sir Charles said. "It's most fortunate that you studied in Brazil, Mrs Peel. Were you reading toxicology at Rio university?"

"No, I was at Bahia. And I was doing pure mathematics," Emma said with a smile. "But I had friends in the biology department—and it's an absorbing subject . . ."

A few minutes later, white-coated and rubber-gloved, they were grouped around the chill slab of the autopsy table. Behind them, grey steel drawers—each bearing in its seven-foot length some grisly souvenir of terror and disaster—penetrated the cold-storage section. At one side of the table, Emma waited by a trolley of gleaming instruments, ready to assist Sir Charles; at the other, the analyst stood prepared to take notes. The corpse itself, laid out now awaiting their attention, looked small and somehow ineffably pathetic in the hard glare of the overhead lights.

". . . no obvious signs of violence," the pathologist was saying. "The neck's not broken. There is no evidence of any wounds, by shooting or otherwise. We're ruling out natural causes—at least for the purpose of this investigation. So we might as well carry on with the organs. I take it you'll be requiring vascular sections, Wickham?"

"Ah—yes, please, Sir Charles."

"I'll give you auricular and ventricular tissue, a bit of lung section, some liver—and you'll have to put up with whatever I can manage on contents. The time factor, you know; and the quantities . . ." He shook his head and sighed. "Want any kidney, by the way?"

The analyst looked across at Emma, his eyebrows raised enquiringly.

She shook her head. "Wouldn't be any use," she said. "And I

don't think you need bother too much about those contents: if it shows at all, it'll be in the heart or lungs, I think."

The pathologist grunted. "Thank God for small mercies," he commented. "Kidneys'd be devilish difficult in a case of this kind." Abruptly he gave a short bark of laughter.

The other two looked up, startled.

"I was just thinkin'—devilled kidneys," Sir Charles explained. "Now—if you'd kindly pass me the smallest of scalpels, Mrs Peel . . ."

The blade plunged into the livid flesh. Emma watched, fascinated, at the miraculous dexterity of the dissection, marvelling at the delicacy of touch which laid aside layer after layer of skin, muscle, nerve and tissue until the required region was laid bare—and then wondering anew at the precision with which the exposed organ was itself stripped down.

A half hour passed. From time to time, Wickham went into the laboratory to prepare his slides and stain his specimens. The pages of his notebook became gradually filled with spidery notations.

A door to one side of the cold-storage drawers opened and a fat man in blue overalls came in carrying a trayfull of steaming cups. "Perishing cold in here tonight, I must say," he observed. "I thought you might be glad of a nice cup of tea."

Sir Charles looked up. "That's very thoughtful of you," he said warmly. "Very. I could do with something hot . . . Mrs Peel: another clip, if you please."

A few minutes later he laid down his scalpel and stood back. "There we are," he said, "that's it. The rest's up to Wickham and to you. Now for that tea . . ."

While they were waiting for the analyst to complete his preparations, he walked meditatively around the slab looking at the remains laid on it. "What I can't understand," he said conversationally, "is how the stuff—if it's there—can have got there. You say it's only fatal if it's ingested in the bloodstream or actually consumed?"

Emma nodded.

"Then how the devil did this chap get it—if he did? . . . I say! Wait a minute . . . Look at this!" He indicated a tiny scratch on the flesh. "There's a cyanosed discoloration around the abrasion. Now I wonder . . ."

He picked up a limp leg and flexed it experimentally. "Yes,

look!" he said excitedly. "That metal anklet he's wearing: it could have made that scratch. See—the sharp edge here fits exactly! We'd better have it off him and take it in to old Wickham . . ."

He hurried in to the laboratory, with Emma at his heels. The analyst was sitting on a high stool bending over a microscope. "All negative or neutral," he said, "just as you thought, Mrs Peel. There's just your special test to do, if you could give me the stuff."

Emma produced a small phial of oily, green liquid, poured a few drops into a test tube, took the tube in a pair of crucible tongs and heated it in the flame from a Bunsen burner, agitating the fluid gently until it boiled. She laid the tube in a wooden rack, extracted a small amount with a pipette, and allowed a single drop to fall on to a section of tissue on a prepared slide labelled "Lung".

"According to the Moraes test," she said, handing the slide to Wickham, "a drop of Herskovit's Reagent added to this will turn the cells violet if the reaction is positive."

"And if it's negative?"

"There'll be no change."

The analyst nodded, clamped the slide in position and adjusted the eyepiece of the microscope. He reached out to one of the shelves, took down a bottle half full of pale yellow liquid, and decanted a little into a clean test tube. Then, picking up another pipette, he closed his forefinger over the open end and transferred a drop to the slide. After a moment, he grunted and leaned back on his stool, allowing the others room to peer into the eyepiece.

The complex cellular structure of the tissue, stained a vivid green by the first fluid, swam in Emma's vision as the globule of reagent, vastly magnified, spread slowly across it. The cells blurred, became muddy—and then suddenly cleared, all at once springing into relief in a hard and brilliant purple.

"Positive, by Jove!" the pathologist breathed. "So you *were* right."

Emma smiled. "I'm afraid so," she said. "One of the world's most deadly poisons—a rare derivative of *Curare* that's odourless, tasteless, soluble in water, and virtually undetectable unless you know what to look for. We'd better have a look at the others, just to make sure."

The slides marked "Stomach contents" and "Liver" gave

negative reactions, but sections taken from both sides of the heart were positive.

"Well—ah—that definitely settles it," Wickham said. "The poison was not consumed but entered the bloodstream directly, where it would quickly produce syncope and total paralysis of the muscles of the lungs. Death would follow almost at once—either through stoppage of the heart's action or through—ah—asphyxia."

"We think we know how it got into the bloodstream, too," Sir Charles said. "I wonder would you mind doing one more, my dear fellow?" With infinite care, he scraped a spatula against the inner surface of the metal anklet they had brought through from the mortuary. A few tiny grains of a white-ish, crystalline substance detached themselves from the metal and fell on to the filter paper he had placed beneath. Wickham re-heated the test-tube carrying Emma's green liquid, shook the contents of the filter paper into it, placed the tube in the flame once more, and then dropped in half a c.c. of the reagent.

The hot fluid frothed and became opaque, turning gradually to a dirty rust colour. Then abruptly the whole length of the tube was translucent again—in the same bright, glittering purple.

Sir Charles nodded his head several times. "Just as I thought," he said. "The poison was on that metal thing, and he scratched himself with it."

As they walked through the mortuary on their way out, he stopped by the corpse on the slab. "Not a bad bit of flesh on him," he said, patting it familiarly. "In happier circumstances, I wouldn't have minded sinking my teeth into that bird—provided he'd been roast, of course."

"It's just as well you didn't, Sir Charles," Emma said with a grim smile. "Who would there have been to have done the P.M. on *you*?"

She picked up the remains of the dead duck from the slab and shovelled them back into the shoe-box in which it had been buried.

# 7

## ENTER A GIRL WITH A SHOTGUN!

"What I cannot understand, Steed"—Emma Peel said—"is how you knew the duck would be there. I mean, what on earth made you think we'd find the body of a poisoned bird buried outside Little Hornham churchyard? And where did it come from?"

"It came from the 'Ely Cathedral'," the undercover man said. "It might even have been the one we were going to eat, for all I know. And there's really no mystery about how I knew where it was: Lurchman told me."

"But I still don't see—"

"I didn't think they were actually responsible for the man's death—at least not directly. But I knew there was something odd going on in that pub, so I drove across to see Mark the night before last and—er—put the screws on a bit," Steed said.

They were sitting on the shingle outside the rented cottage, lobbing pebbles at a tin floating a few yards offshore. The wind had dropped for once and the sea was calm. In another half hour, the sun would have set, but now there was still a faint warmth in the Spring afternoon.

"What did you find out from our late host, then?" Emma asked, scrambling to her feet to dust off the black leather trousers she wore beneath a severe overblouse in white twill.

"Well, he was very reluctant to tell me anything at all—kept on being evasive, saying he couldn't see what I was getting at, and so forth. But then I sort of—well, pointed out how suspicious it would look if ever the police did decide to investigate, or if the doctor wouldn't give a certificate, or if there was an exhumation. And finally he decided to come clean."

"Did you tell him you'd seen him hand that package over to the girl when you were looking out of the bedroom window?"

"Yes—that was the ace up my sleeve. After that, he began to talk."

"I suppose the dead duck was in the package?"

"And you're quite right; *ab*solutely *cor*rect," Steed said in mock fairground barker style. "Give the lady in leather pants a cigar . . ." He picked up a fistful of small stones and began to hurl them one after the other at the tin. "The whole point is—*Splash!*—that Mark has a tremendous reputation to keep up. Any breath of scandal—*Splash!*—attaching in any way to his food, or the way he gets it—*Splash!*—could ruin his business overnight. And it appears that the ducks he was using last night were poached—*Splash!*—and not only that: there was, I think, something wrong with them. Perhaps they were found dead or something of that sort—*Splash!*—so at the first hint of any trouble he naturally got rid of them fast. That's why he was so shifty while we were there—*Splash!*—and why the ducks that had already been cooked had all mysteriously been thrown away."

Emma bent down and gathered a handful of stones herself, which she began to shy at the tin alternately with Steed's. "In that case," she said, "who was the girl—*Plop!*—and why did Mark give the parcel to her?—*Plop!*—Couldn't he just have buried the ducks—*Plop!*—himself?"

"He didn't want any part of it—*Splash!*—If there was anything wrong with the birds, they mustn't be associated with his precious kitchen—*Splash!*—So the obvious thing was to shoot them back to the poacher who supplied them and let *him* cope—*Splash!*—But so far as the lady was concerned, he wouldn't say a thing. Bit of a romantic interest there—*Splash!*—I fancy."

"Then his girlfriend—*Plop!*—was a kind of go-between, a contact linking Lurchman and the poacher?—*Plop!*"

"Exactly—*Splash!*—And in a few minutes we're going to set off to pay an unexpected visit—*Clang!*—to the poaching gentleman."

The tin sank, bubbling, beneath the surface.

"This is a silly game," Emma said, dropping the rest of her pebbles to the beach. "It's getting cold. I'm going to fetch a jacket."

"Don't be discouraged, my dear," Steed said. "After all, I used to be reckoned a pretty fair cover-point at school . . ."

Later, as they walked down the landward slope of the ridge to a boat he had somehow got hold of and concealed in the reeds, she made a thoughtful re-cap on what they found out so far. "It seems we have a bird—or birds—fitted with a metal anklet in some way carrying this poison," she said. "And that the anklet made a small wound when the bird scratched itself—which let the poison into its bloodstream and killed it."

"That's right," Steed said.

"And that the dead bird was found, perhaps with others, by a poacher, who sold it to the 'Ely Cathedral'."

"Exactly."

"And that the pub, furthermore, cooked one of these ducks in all good faith, as they say, and served it to the man we saw die?"

"Yes, my dear. But—"

"Well there are two questions, Steed," Emma interrupted, "that we haven't answered: was there any intention on someone's part to kill this particular man? And how was he killed anyway? The poison was in the *duck's* bloodstream—why did the man die through eating its flesh?"

Steed parted a six-foot clump of reeds fringing the marsh and handed her into a flat-bottomed Carvel dinghy hidden behind them. "Your second question's a matter of gastronomy," he smiled, taking up a long pole and nosing the small craft slowly out into the dense vegetation. "The sauce for *Duck à la Rouennaise*, as Mark told you, is made from red wine, onions, the liver *and the blood of the bird, which is collected by crushing the carcass in a special press . . .*"

"Yes, of course," Emma said slowly. "And the poison doesn't break down or deteriorate either in storage or under heat."

"Quite. And so far as the mysterious guest is concerned, Mac-Corquodale has solved that one. Apparently he was a Lincoln solicitor, henpecked for years, whose wife—whom he loathed—had just died. And he couldn't resist celebrating . . . though he was careful to do it incognito, in case any of his clients should think it lacking in respect!"

"Some celebration!" Emma said grimly.

In the fading light, the dinghy forced its way laboriously along the choked lagoon. Clouds of mosquitoes hung in the dank air, hovering like smoke in the gaps between tall reeds. Sometimes the channel widened to several yards, only to narrow again as the rushes closed in above their heads and the hummocks of rank marsh grass scraped along the gunwale. The sea was inaudible. The only sounds to break the monotonous plop and drip of Steed's pole were the furtive movements of night creatures hidden in the foliage and an occasional gurgle from beneath the boat. Several times he was forced to back out from a passage that became impenetrable and find an alternative route. Once something heavy splashed into the water from a floating island and swam stealthily away into the dusk.

"If, as you say, this poacher lives further down the spit," Emma complained in a low voice, "why on earth couldn't we have walked?"

"On that shingle," Steed replied, "you can hear someone coming half a mile off. I want to make sure our friend's there—so I prefer to drop in unannounced. And talking of camouflage, my dear, your protective colouring's almost perfect!"

Emma shivered and wrapped her thigh-length snakeskin jacket more tightly around her. "Some of our problems solve themselves as we go along," she said quietly. "But the most important one remains: how does this poison get *on* the birds' anklets? And who puts it there, for Heaven's sake, and why?"

"The anklets are the normal rings put on migratory birds so that they can be identified and a check kept on their movements—"

"Yes, Steed, I know, I know. But the poison—that stuff's dynamite! It's a hundred times more virulent than Curare itself. And it's soluble in water. If one of those ducks had survived and landed on water that was going to be drunk—on a reservoir, say—why, the implications are terrifying . . ."

"I know," Steed said soberly. "There's something exceedingly malevolent going on around here. It's up to us to track it down —quickly."

"I mean we don't even know how many deaths have been caused already. *Are* all nine of the people you heard about poison victims, by the way?"

"We don't know for certain. Sir Charles checked on the solicitor, just to make sure, and of course *he* is. H.N. got exhumation orders on the Martello tower girl, the doctor, the tramp and the others. We should hear the results of the P.M.'s tomorrow. And they may dig up *one* of the earlier seven, as a sort of spot check. But I should think it's a hundred per cent a foregone conclusion."

"Yes, but if you're right, how did *they* get poisoned? They weren't all eating at the 'Ely Cathedral'."

"I hope we may know more about that after we've asked a few questions *chez* Monsieur Poacher," Steed said, motioning Emma suddenly to silence.

The reeds parted and the dinghy glided out on to a stretch of open water several hundred yards across. He gave half a dozen strong thrusts with the pole and then crouched down in the stern with the girl, allowing the boat to drift noiselessly onwards.

To their left, the shingle ridge humped blackly against the sky. Across to the right, they could dimly make out an irregular line of bushes marking the mainland boundary of the lagoon. Gradually losing way, the Carvel approached the southern end of the open space, its passage opening an ebony wake in the weed covering the surface. Just before the reeds closed in again, Steed took a paddle and dipped it twice deftly in the water to bring the dinghy to the bank on the seaward side. He jumped lightly ashore and hitched the painter to a rotting tree stump half buried in the marshy ground.

"Come on," he whispered, holding out his hand for Emma, "the place is just over the ridge." He gestured vaguely towards the long, low outline of a roof barely discernible beyond the slope.

They had gone perhaps a dozen yards when the voice spoke from behind and to the right.

"Put up your hands and turn slowly around," it said. "And don't try anything funny—there's *two* barrels to this gun . . ."

Arms obediently raised, Steed and Emma swung back to face the lake. Thigh-deep in the dark water, she stood over against the reeds—a commanding figure in rubber hip-waders and a gleaming oilskin blouse. The long-barrelled twelve-bore was rock-steady in her hands.

It was the girl in the rain whom Steed had seen from the bedroom window at the "Ely Cathedral".

# 8

## CONVERSATION WITH A POACHER

JIM REEVES was a gnarled little man with a nutcracker face and silver hair. He was sitting at a plain table squinting down the barrel of a shotgun when the girl kicked open the door of the shack and motioned Steed and Emma in with the twelve-bore.

"I found these two snooping about at the back, Pa," she said. Her voice was low and throaty, a disturbing trailer for the programme of soft intimacies which might lie concealed within the stiff confines of oilskin and waders.

Reeves put the gun down on the table, picked up a four-ten, broke it, and held the barrels up to the single electric bulb which lit the room. "All right Bella," he said, peering through each in turn, "bring 'em over into the light and let's have a look at 'em." One handed, he clapped a piece of four-by-two cotton waste across the neck of a small bottle of oil, inverted it to moisten the material, and then began to thread this through one end of a length of weighted wire.

"What's the weight of a pull-through?" Steed rapped unexpectedly as the girl shepherded them to the far side of the crudely furnished room.

"The piece of lead on the other end—" the poacher replied automatically, in a conditioned reflex to the old army tag. He broke off and looked up at Steed. A corner of his clamped-down mouth twitched briefly as he rose to his feet, the gun still in his hand. He was wearing faded blue trousers tucked in to gumboots and an old tweed jacket with huge patch pockets. Steed had no doubt that there were others, supported by shoulder straps, inside. From the brim of the battered trilby on his head, part of the greasy black ribbon dangled rakishly.

"Seems like you could be a sight too smart altogether, mister," he said mildly. "We're simple folk around here; we keep ourselves to ourselves. But we don't go too strong on strangers—and trespassin' can be downright dangerous, can't it, Bella?"

The girl's sullen face was hostile. Over the high storm collar of her oilskin, her dark eyes regarded Emma and Steed unwaveringly. "There's accidents happen sometimes," she said levelly. "A party shoots at a bird, say, and there's people behind the reeds that didn't have no right to be there. It's nobody's fault—but they're dead just the same."

"Wouldn't it be easier to shoot just the bird—and then give it to them to eat?" Steed drawled.

The girl's eyes blazed. "You've no call to say that," she cried hotly. "Mark didn't know a thing about—" She stopped abruptly in mid-sentence, realising what she was saying.

Steed laughed. "Believe me, Miss Reeves," he needled, "you don't have to kill anybody else if it's a murder charge you're looking for!"

"At the very least an accessory after the fact—and we're by no means the only people to know it," Emma added, piling on the advantage.

"Shut up!" Bella Reeves shouted. Her knuckles whitened on the stock and barrels of the twelve-bore, and the highlights across the breast of the tightly belted oilskin rose and fell agitatedly. "I didn't even *know* the man was murdered. Nor does Mar—Mr Lurchman. Who d'you think you are, skulking about behind people's homes, making accusations—"

"Stow it, Bella!" The poacher's voice was suddenly commanding. He lowered the weighted end of the wire through one of the barrels of his gun and then, shifting his grip, twisted it twice around an index finger and pulled the oil-soaked rag on the other end steadily through. "Now," he went on in a quieter voice, "I think we're due for an explanation, mister; and we aim to get one . . ."

Emma and Steed were standing—still with their hands raised above their heads—backed up against one of the room's board walls. Behind and to each side of them, a collection of antique guns was displayed on nails driven into the wood. An old fowling piece immediately behind him, Steed had noticed as they came in, was supported at two points only—through the trigger guard and under the long barrel. Throughout the exchange with Bella, he had been imperceptibly allowing his left arm to fall back towards the wall. Now as the back of his hand brushed the breech of the old gun, he inched it sideways until the knuckles touched the head of the nail projecting through the trigger guard. Stealthily, he separated the middle and index fingers and then closed them again over the nail, gripping the head between the lower joints. It was quite loose.

"Certainly you can have an explanation, Mr Reeves," he said easily, working at the nail with his knuckles. "There was no intention to offend, you know. I'm staying at the old cottage up at the other end of the spit, and I thought I'd show Mrs Peel here something of the wild life on the marsh, that's all."

"What's that got to do with threats about murder charges?" the old man asked gruffly. He began to feed the pull-through into the second barrel of the four-ten.

"Nothing, really," the undercover man said. Without moving his raised arm, he jerked his hand forward from the wrist, keeping the fingers pressed tightly together. Between them, the nail pulled out from the wall.

The fowling piece crashed to the floor.

As Bella Reeves and her father looked up, startled, Emma shot into action like an uncoiled spring. In one lithe bound she was at the table, seizing the edges in her hands and somersaulting across it in a forward roll. She came hurtling feet first off the far side before the girl had recovered from her astonishment, knocking up the barrel of the shotgun and wrapping her legs around Bella's waist in a scissors grip. One barrel of the twelve-bore discharged deafeningly, bringing down a shower of plaster from the ceiling, as they hit the boards together.

Before the poacher had time to reach for the gun on the table, Emma was on her feet again, the twelve-bore in her hands. "All right," she panted, "there's still one up the spout! Now—over there, the two of you, if you please . . ."

Bella Reeves got slowly to her feet, circled Emma warily, and joined her father over by the curtained window. Water, still beaded on the calves of her waders, slid down the heavy black rubber to leave a trail of damp footprints on the floor.

Steed hadn't moved. An elegant figure in charcoal trousers and a honey-coloured suede windbreaker with an olive green square at the neck, he was leaning against the wall with one ankle crossed over the other. Now he moved languidly over to Emma and took the gun. "Thank you, my dear," he said quietly. "That was most impressive . . . Mr Reeves, I assure you again that we didn't come here looking for trouble. We were in fact on our way up to knock on your door when your daughter—er—surprised us. We only wanted to talk to you for a moment."

"What do you want with me?" the old man asked suspiciously.

"I told you: to talk. And as a proof of our good faith"—he broke open the shotgun and extracted the spent and the unused cartridge—"I shall put this thing down for a start. You can't have a conversation over a gun, can you?"

He laid the gun on the table, picked up the four-ten and placed that beside it, and then collected the oil bottle, the pull-through and a handful of shells which had been scattered on the floor by Emma's exertions. "Now," he said, pulling up a kitchen chair, swinging one leg over it and seating himself astride with his arms resting on the back, "perhaps we can make ourselves comfortable for a few minutes?"

Reeves tried not to be impressed. He glanced from Steed to Emma and then back to the undercover man again. He moved unwillingly forward, tugging at his lower lip. "I don't know as I want to talk," he said reluctantly. "Anyway, it depends what you want to say."

"Don't talk to them, Pa," Bella said urgently. "No good'll come of it. They're only here to make trouble. You don't have to say a word."

The poacher absentmindedly retrieved the fowling piece from behind Steed's chair, accepted the nail from the agent's hand, and pressed it back into its hole in the wall, replacing the gun in its old position. "Now hold hard, child," he said, stepping back to scrutinise the effect. "No harm ever came just from talkin'. Maybe we ought to see what the gentleman has to say." He adjusted the position of the firearm fractionally and then sat down himself.

"You're perfectly right, Miss Reeves," Steed said reasonably. "Neither you nor your father have to say anything at all. But at least let me say what *I* have to say, and then you can answer or not as you please. But why don't you get out of those wet things —you'll catch your death?"

The girl glared at him for a second, and then sullenly began to strip off the waders and her oilskin. She was wearing jeans and a loose fisherman's sweater, beneath which her nubile young body moved easily. Emma hitched one slender hip on to the table and sat there, swinging a leg, as Steed spoke.

"I'll put it as briefly as I can," he said. "I'm not interested in how you make your living; it doesn't concern me in the least.

You're a wildfowler, let us say, and among other commissions you supply certain people around here with game; right?"

"Pa!"—it was Bella Reeves speaking—"Don't answer, *Please*."

"And if it's any help, Miss Reeves, I can tell you that in fact no breath of suspicion attaches to the landlord of the 'Ely Cathedral'. We know all we want to know about that affair. It's the others that interest us now."

Bella scowled. She jerked back the flimsy curtains and stood, arms folded, with her back to them, staring across the beach at the dark sea.

"What's it to you, anyway, mister?" the old man said. "Why should I tell you anything about my affairs?" He got up and began to pace nervously back and forth.

"For this reason," Steed said—and then, in a creditable imitation of a sergeant-major's parade ground voice: "That man . . . Att-en-*shun!*"

Reeves's limbs acted independently of the man himself. Before he realised what he was doing, the fingers straightened and the hands snapped back to a position just behind the trouser seams; the heels slammed together—and for an instant he stood ramrod stiff . . . then relaxed with a sheepish smile. "That's the second time," he said accusingly.

"Third time lucky!" Steed said lazily. "How long were you in the army, Reeves?"

"Twenty-five years, sir." There was pride in the man's voice.

"Whose lot were you with?"

"Eighth Army, sir. From Alamein on. With Colonel Trottson's unit."

"Parry Trottson? I saw him a couple of months ago, on leave from India. He's mapping the Himalayan foothills for the government, you know."

"Is he really, sir? He always was a one for the hard life. How is the old—how is the Colonel?"

"Blooming, Reeves. Blooming . . . If you were with the Colonel in North Africa, you must have been one of the Special Scouts—sabotaging Rommel's tanks, and all that?"

"That's right, sir. Fair old caper that was, and all."

"Yes, it must have been. I worked with Colonel Trottson myself, a little bit after that. In northern Italy, it was."

"Not with them eye-tie partisans in the Po marshes, kidnapping—"

"That's it, Reeves. But we don't talk about it now. The point is, I could do with an East Anglian partisan in these marshes here. Somebody's trying to set himself up as a sort of private Rommel, and it must be stopped."

There was respect tinged with admiration in the man's manner now. "You can count me in," he said. "What do you want me to do?"

"For the moment, wait until I call on you—but you can help a lot by answering these questions we were talking about."

"Pa, for the last time!" Bella Reeves burst out.

"Shut your mouth, girl. Why don't you do something useful instead of arguing all the time? Go get a broom and sweep up all that plaster from the floor there."

The girl flung out of the room with an angry toss of her head. After a glance at Steed, Emma followed. Soon, they heard the two voices—one furious, the other soothing and placatory—alternating from beyond the door.

"She's a good girl," the poacher continued, "but wild. Headstrong—that's what she is. Won't listen to reason. She was goin' on for a nurse, but she gave it up and come home to look after me when her Ma died three years ago. Not that she don't help me a lot in my work, mind . . . Still—what was it that you wanted to know, then?"

"Did you supply birds to many people around here?"

Reeves shifted from foot to foot. He looked embarrassed. "See here," he said. "I'm afraid I'll have to ask you to treat this as strictly confidential. The whole point of a connection like mine is the mutual *trust*—you know, *they* don't know you're poachin' 'em, and *you* don't know they're receivin', see?"

"I quite understand. You don't need to worry."

"Thank you, sir. Well, then—yes, I did. Most of the nobs."

"Doctor Atherley?"

"Oh, yes. Regular. He had something every week. And the old admiral—and David Oates at Hornham station. And the mayor. And the three pubs at Bratby. Oh, and that young lady up to the tower. Couldn't afford much, but she was nice . . ." He stopped, struck by a thought. "*Was* nice. I said it. And I just realised : half me clients are dead, aren't they. You don't think—?"

"I'm afraid I have to. D'you remember how many of these people bought birds you'd *found* dead—recently, that is?"

The poacher looked uncomfortable. "You understand, sir—

it's not the sort of thing I *usually* . . . I mean to say, I supply game; I go and shoot that game—or trap it or whatever. But in this case . . . well, it wasn't as if they'd died of some disease or other, or been killed by something else. Why, some of 'em were still *warm* when I found them! And it seemed a shame to waste them . . ."

"And you *do* remember?"

"Well, that's not to say—well, yes. Some of 'em. The mayor never. And the pubs never. But the bird at the tower, she had one. And so did the doctor and the admiral. Oh, and Lurchman, of course—he had several. As for the rest, I can't rightly tell. Difficult to sort 'em out, anyway, once they're in with those I got meself. There *were* others, though."

"They were all ducks, were they—the dead ones?"

"Couple of Teal. Rest were Mallard."

"Where did you find them, Reeves?"

"Ah, now, look, sir—you're asking me to give away the secrets of me trade. A free fowler—I don't hold with the word Poachin'—has to take his chances where he can get 'em. You wouldn't believe the number of busibodies, and gamekeepers, and enforcement officers, and police, and game laws you can run foul of up here. And then there's the nobs themselves—the mugs who *pay* for licences. What with this and that, a man keeps a good bit of territory to himself when he finds it."

"Remember Rommel, Reeves."

"Yes, sir. Well . . ." The man was obviously reluctant. ". . . Well, the most of 'em come from the old Mendip place, and that's the truth of it."

"The old Mendip place? Where is that?"

"It's a bit to the south'ard—mile or so beyond the Dyke."

"What is it, a farm?"

"Bless you, no. Bloody great red brick mansion, used to belong to old Sir Hugh Mendip when he was alive. It was built in his father's time, they say. Stands just off the coast road in about a hundred and fifty acres of saltings."

"Who does it belong to now?"

"Couple of right nut cases, if you ask me. One of 'em is a professor; name of Charnley—muckin' about all day and night in a ruddy laboratory they've built. The other one—it's him the place really belongs to—is Sir Albert Charles Frobisher Warbeck-Simner, no less. Too bloody blah for words! He's supposed to be an ornithol—orni—well, he's mad on birds, anyway."

"Ornithologist?"

"Yes, that's it. Well, he's got a bird museum there, and a whole zoo full of cages, with everything in 'em from a wren to an eagle. And the whole property, all of the marsh around the house, is a kind of bird sanctuary."

"And so you find it a very profitable—er—row to hoe?"

"Well, at least you don't get these idiots in plus-fours and moustaches banging off at everything in sight all day long! Got to be very careful, though: it's strictly night work, or just after dawn at the latest."

"Why do you say that?"

"They can see everything you do, otherwise. That's why. They got some kind of crazy camera in one of them turrets—at least, I think that's what it's called. And they see what goes on all over the saltings."

"Not a *camera obscura*, by any chance?"

"Yes. That's it. That's what it is."

"How delightfully *fin de siécle!* Shades of *The Eye In The Museum!* But you seem to be extremely well-informed about the place, Reeves."

The old man looked down. He coloured slightly. "Well, to tell the truth," he said, "my girl goes over there and does for the two old blokes. Bella's in service there, in a manner of speakin'."

"Biting the hand that feeds your daughter, eh?" Steed smiled. He got up and put the chair back against the wall. "We must go. I'll fetch Mrs Peel, if you'll permit me—and thanks for being so frank."

Jim Reeves thrust out his lower jaw and gnawed at his stubbly top lip. He appeared distressed. "Look, sir—all these people," he said. "I never *knew*; honest . . . I mean, I admit I pay no mind to the game laws, but that kind of lawbreakin's one thing; sellin' folks poisoned food's another. I never dreamed there was anything wrong with those bloody birds. Otherwise I'd never for a moment—"

"Don't you worry, Reeves," Steed interrupted, clapping him on the shoulder. "Nobody blames you for their deaths. I'm sure you acted in good faith—it wasn't your fault."

"Yes, but the poor sods are dead just the same, aren't they?"

Steed was adjusting his silk square in a cracked mirror that was hanging beside the door. "Don't blame yourself. *Somebody's* responsible—and I'm going to find out who it is," he said grimly.

Emma was helping the poacher's daughter to gut a small pile of fish in a scullery at the end of a passage with two tiny bedrooms leading off it. Bella kept her back resolutely turned as Steed and her father came in. Beyond her, in a sort of lean-to porch, a row of dead birds in assorted shapes and sizes hung from a rail. Small-mesh nets were looped on pegs driven in to one wall, fishing rods leaned in a corner, and on the brick floor a pile of gins, traps and snares gleamed faintly in the light from the scullery.

Steed wandered out on to the porch. Three sleek cats were lapping milk from an enamel bowl on the floor. A retriever curled up in a basket below a long bench opened an eye to look at him and then went back to sleep. Cages piled three deep on the bench held live rabbits, pigeons and ducklings. The pigeons were obviously the subject of some veterinary experiment, for—like temperature charts in a hospital—pieces of paper bearing scrawled notes and dates were pinned to each cage, while the rows themselves were labelled *"Ailing"*, *"Treating"* and *"Helthy."*

"Come, Mrs Peel," Steed called. "We must take our frail craft and steal softly away into the night . . . Goodnight, Miss Reeves. Thank you so much for having us." He unlatched the door leading out into the night, then paused, gesturing to the pigeon cages with their mis-spelled label. "Oh, and by the way," he added, "next time you want to send me a message—use one of these, would you? The East Anglian dawns get so cold with no glass in the windows . . ."

# 9

## BELLA GOES TO WORK

BELLA REEVES's one souvenir of life in the city was a Moulton bicycle. On four days a week, she collapsed this small-wheeled machine, ferried it across the marsh to the main road, tied up her boat, and then assembled the bicycle and rode South to the home of her employer. Turret House was several miles from Bratby: beyond Flint's Dyke and the end of the lagoon, past the long, straight stretch of road where the body of the tramp had been found, beyond the turning for Ely and the Hornhams —a good fifteen minutes ride.

Remote and isolated across the sweep of marshland, the building itself was half hidden in a grove of trees, only the four corner turrets and the central tower with its green copper cupola being visible from the road.

The girl arrived at five minutes to nine on the morning after Steed's visit. She dismounted by the massive brick gateposts flanking the drive and wheeled her bicycle towards the centre portion of the wrought iron gates. There was a small button inset in the metal. A second after she had pressed this, a sharp click presaged a crackling of static before a disembodied voice rasped:

"Who is it? What do you want, please?"

Bella leaned forward and spoke into the louvred steel box attached to the inner side of the gate. "It's Bella, Professor. Bella Reeves. It's my day today—alright to come in now?"

"Ah, Miss Reeves! Jolly good! You're very punctual, my dear; very. Yes—come up at once, do," the voice grated. "But be sure you pay attention to the old yellow line, what! It would never do if you were to actuate the alarm—cry havoc and let loose the dogs of war, eh?" The sentence ended in a little wheeze of laughter, followed by another loud click as the apparatus was cut off. An instant later there was a buzz from the mechanism controlling the lock, and Bella pushed open the gate and wheeled her machine inside.

Two hundred yards down the road, screened by the clump of

bushes masking a lay-by, Emma Peel sat on the roof of her Lotus and watched. Like the tree-lined causeway leading across the marsh to Turret House, the main road, too, ran along the top of a dyke here—and from her vantage point, Emma could easily follow the girl's progress through Steed's glasses.

The causeway was dead straight, and for about two hundred and fifty yards of its length, Bella pedalled steadily towards the house. With that peculiar, high-geared, loping movement imparted by the bicycle's rubber suspension, she appeared and disappeared behind the boles of the plane trees with monotonous regularity. Then, curiously, as the drive ran for a few yards between a line of white painted posts linked by chain, she lifted her legs to the handlebars and coasted, before dropping her feet to the pedals once more and cycling out of sight round the corner of a shrubbery fronting the building. For a moment more, Emma scanned the gothic chimneys, the turrets, the mesh tops of aviaries among the trees, and the roofs of outbuildings which showed behind the house. She noted that there was a thin spiral of smoke rising from the most northerly stack; that the turret windows and the few dormers she could see were uncurtained; and that there was something bright catching the early morning sun from the summit of the copper dome. Then she slid to the ground, put away the glasses, insinuated herself into the driving seat and drove back to report to Steed.

Bella traversed the gravelled sweep in front of the great portico, turned down the side of the house past a balustraded terrace, and rode into the brick-paved yard at the back. Bounded on two sides by the L-shaped block of the old stables—which now housed an extensive ornithological museum—the yard gave directly on to the kitchen quarters of the house itself. A long, low ferro-concrete construction in which lay the professor's laboratory completed the rectangle. Further back, the aviaries dotted what had once been a walled garden before the ground dropped away to the marsh.

At the laboratory entrance, Charnley was waiting: a spare little man with thin, pursed lips drooping at the corners, a beaky nose, and small, bright eyes behind oblong spectacle frames.

"Good morning, good morning, good morning," he cried cheerfully as Bella dismounted. "I wonder would you mind helping me tidy up the lab a bit before you do anything else today? Sir Albert doesn't want his coffee until eleven."

Bella didn't like the laboratory. Partitioned off at one end was what looked very much like a miniature operating theatre, with a steel table, chromium trolleys carrying gas cylinders looped with sinister corrugated tubing, and a rack full of shining syringes. Usually, there were hutches or crates full of live creatures—rats, guinea pigs, birds, and sometimes rabbits. Once, when the professor had been in there behind locked doors, she had heard a rat screaming like a baby.

Today, however, Charnley only wanted her help with what she thought of privately as the clinical part of the place. The tiled benches and porcelain sinks had to be cleaned; there were dozens of test tubes, retorts, flasks and crucibles to be washed; slides and culture dishes to sterilise; and complicated apparatus to dismantle and store away.

The scientist kept up a sporadic flow of chatter as he directed her efforts. He had a mercurial temperament, alternating periods of elation—when his schoolboyish enthusiasm bubbled over in bursts of gossipy trivia—with moods of depression when the least remark was liable to make him boorish and tetchy. Bella found him difficult to get on with and would much have preferred to do the work alone.

"It's getting on, the great work's getting on famously," he prattled. "My investigations will be completed—should be completed, that is: you never can tell with research, my dear—they *ought* to be finished by the time Sir Albert is ready . . . He's a very clever man, you know; a pioneer . . . That's it: put that flask on that shelf along with the others . . . He'll be jolly pleased, I can tell you . . . Sir Albert's a splendid fellow, really splendid. But he does like things to work out on schedule . . ."

"What's the great work going to be, then?" Bella asked idly, running the cold tap into a bell-jar misted over with an oily condensation.

"Oh . . . you know. Scientific research, my dear," Charnley said evasively. "You wouldn't understand—but it's going to make both of us jolly famous, I can tell you. People to be reckoned with . . . No. Don't touch that piece of apparatus: I haven't finished with it yet." He gestured towards an elaborate construction of distilling retorts and cooling towers of spiralled glass from which electrical leads snaked across the bench to a power plug on the wall. Bella reached out for a wide-necked flask nearby which appeared to be empty except for a mush of greyish crystals lining the bottom.

"*Leave that alone!*" the scientist snapped. "Really—why can't you *listen* and do what you're told? . . . Put it *back*, I say ! Now wash your hands. At once . . . That's it. Thoroughly . . . You want to be careful, you know. If you handle some of these things and then put your fingers in your mouth, you could get—you could make yourself ill." He looked quite white with anger, and there was a beading of perspiration on his upper lip.

At eleven o'clock, the girl made coffee in the great, bare, old-fashioned kitchen and took a tray into the study.

Charnley was slumped in a leather armchair, gnawing at an empty pipe. Bella drew up a low table, put the tray on it, and spoke to Sir Albert Warbeck-Simner, who was sitting behind a flat-topped desk covered with papers and books. "Would you like to pour yourself, today, sir?" she asked. "Or would you prefer me to do it?"

The ornithologist looked up. He was a big man, six foot two and heavily built, with a great, domed head innocent of hair except for a feathery tuft over each ear. His features were coarse in the manner of an 18th century aristocrat, with thick lips and insolently drooped eyelids. And his voice was deep and surprisingly mellifluous. Paradoxically—as Bella had often thought—it was the ornithologist who looked as though he could be a scientist, and Charnley, with his dry, hurrying voice and birdlike appearance, who could well have been an expert on the feathered world !

Bella repeated her question, as Warbeck-Simner had not replied and was still looking vaguely in her direction.

"Eh? What's that? What did you say?" he asked suddenly.

"The coffee, Sir Albert . . ."

"Ah, yes. Pour it out yourself, Reeves. My word, but that smells good, doesn't it Charnley?"

"Delicious," the scientist said perfunctorily. "You were about to say, my dear Sir Albert, that in a few days . . ?"

"That in a few days the balloon should be ready to go up. I've not decided finally which species—but it doesn't do to have everything too cut and dried, does it?"

"Oh, by no means, by no means . . . Ah—*three* lumps today, I think, thank you, my dear."

"I mean to say, it would never do if Worthington and his men got to hear of it too soon, would it?"

"No, no. It would never do if Worthington and his men got to hear of it," Charnley repeated with a gusty chuckle. The two old men giggled together like a pair of schoolboys, stirring their coffee and glancing slyly at the girl.

"How are your experiments with the birds going?" she asked conversationally, as she picked up the tray and prepared to leave.

"Birds, birds? What do *you* know about birds? Why don't you mind your own business? Your place is in the kitchen—not asking impertinent questions of your betters." The scientist was on his feet, trembling with rage.

Bella backed away, startled by the vehemence of the outburst. "I'm sorry . . . I didn't know—I mean, I thought . . ."

"You are not employed to think, Reeves," the ornithologist said severely. "Really, I can't think what the servant classes are coming to . . ."

An electric bell shrilled warningly in the hall outside.

". . . The gate," Warbeck-Simner said, breaking off his rebuke. "Go and see who it is, will you, Reeves?"

The girl turned and left the room. He stared pensively at the muscular movement of her haunches beneath the cheap cotton dress, at the twin bulges of taut flesh above and below the outline of her brassière strap. He sighed. "A comely creature," he said. "But a little too inquisitive, I fear. What did she mean about the birds? I trust you haven't been indiscreet, Charnley. I hope you haven't been talking out of turn to her. Because if you have . . ."

The Professor was pacing up and down in his agitation. "I, my dear chap? Most certainly not. Absolutely no. Really, I assure you . . . I suppose she must have a *certain* intelligence, after all. She sees the crates. She sees me working. *Experiments* is one of the few scientific words she knows—so I suppose, really, it's quite a natural, innocent question. It was perhaps foolish of me to become so upset."

"I suppose so," Warbeck-Simner mused. "I hope so. Because if it's . . . more than that—well, we shall have to . . . take steps."

Bella Reeves poked her head around the door. There was a sullen set to her full-lipped mouth and she still had a heightened colour. "It's the boy from Lorimer's with the fish," she said curtly.

"Very well," her employer said. "Tell him to leave it at the gate. Then go down and fetch it—and you can start some of the housework before you prepare it for luncheon."

They heard her speaking into the talk-back installation by the front door, relaying his instructions. Then, a few minutes later, she passed outside the window on her bicycle.

Meanwhile, Warbeck-Simner had crossed the room to the wall behind the door. Unlike the others—covered, apart from window embrasures, from floor to ceiling with books—this had a practical and mechanical air. At one side there was a complicated Ampex tape deck, vertically arranged with a dozen output channels, each boasting switches and rheostat controls. Next to this, amplifier, pre-amplifier and turntable of a high fidelity record-playing unit were neatly housed on tailored shelves. Discs and boxes of recorded tape were stacked on the far side, alongside a unit containing three separate television screens—one orthodox and two closed circuit. Twelve-inch speakers inclined downwards from the two top corners. And centrally placed, like an electronic desk jutting from the wall, was a console—a slanting surface crammed with dials and buttons and indicator lights from which all this apparatus could be controlled. Here were bass, treble, volume and filter controls for the hi-fi; three different sets of knobs for the televisions; an inset panel from which the Ampex could be worked; banks of warning bulbs in various colours, each labelled with coded letters and numerals—and a special raised deck marked *Camera*. This bore two switches— labelled *On/Off* and *Shutter*—and two wide knobs with milled edges. One was surrounded by a graduated scale calibrated in ten-degree units from zero to 360; the other was similar, but the pointer moved through an arc of only 45 degrees. They were marked respectively *Scan* and *Incline*.

The ornithologist had switched on one of the closed circuit televisions. As a picture assembled on the screen, he moved a pointer to a position marked F/G on the dial. The screen momentarily blacked out, then abruptly swam into focus. Wherever the concealed camera was, it showed from slightly above a close-up view of the main gates. A youth in an alpaca coat was staring through the tracery of wrought-iron towards the house. As they watched, he shrugged, put a package in a narrow space between two bars, tried the locked gates again, and then walked to a small delivery van, which he got into and drove away.

A moment later, Bella Reeves cycled into shot, dismounted, and reached for the package. Warbeck-Simner grunted, and moved the pointer to D/1. The picture changed to a ground-level shot of the drive about a hundred yards from the gates.

After a few seconds, the girl came into view on her return journey. The package was tucked under her arm.

The owner of Turret House clicked the knob once more. This time it stopped at position D/3—further up the drive, almost at the house now. Bella pedalled into shot, lifted her legs to the handlebars, steering carefully past the line of white posts, then cycled off-screen.

"Nothing wrong there, eh?" Charnley said. "Nothing wrong there."

"No—but it's better to be safe than sorry," Warbeck-Simner replied. He switched the circuit off and turned on the other set— a fixed view transmission relaying only what was appearing on the ground-glass observation screen of the *camera obscura* at the top of the central tower. Charnley moved over to operate the *Camera* panel.

He turned the switch to *On*, moved the *Shutter* control.

The dark screen became light as steel blinds rolled back from the mechanism five floors above them. Gradually, a picture of sun-dappled foliage emerged. The scientist twirled the two knobs complementarily, inclining the prisms downwards through five—ten—fifteen degrees until the ground at the foot of the trees was visible, then swivelling the whole apparatus in a wide arc to scan the property. Thus he was able, as it were, to pan from the avenue of trees bordering the causeway to the saltings—and then, by slightly lessening the angle of incline as he turned, to track out towards the dyke and the road running along it. Apart from clouds of birds rising and settling on the marsh, the only sign of life was the tradesman's van disappearing into a dip at the furthermost limit of the dyke.

"Really, I fear you are becoming *too* suspicious," Charnley chided. "Everything was in order, you see."

As he spoke, Bella Reeves's head and shoulders moved past the window outside as she returned from her expedition to the gates.

"This time, perhaps," Sir Albert was saying sombrely. "But you simply cannot trust the lower orders, old chap. I mean, look at that girl's rascally father, for instance: does the old fool really think I don't know he comes snooping around the saltings three times a week, stealing my birds at night? . . . As it happens, it—er—suits our plans for various reasons. But the moral's there just the same."

"Oh, I agree, I agree," Charnley said in his repetitive way.

"Just look at this wretched country. An empire thrown away in twenty years; thrown away. The government in the hands of middle-class illiterates and woolly-minded liberals—and the ruling classes, who by rights ought to be holding the reins, taxed almost out of existence! It's nothing short of monstrous, Charnley."

"Monstrous," the Professor agreed, his glasses glinting angrily. "And the intelligent men, the thinkers, the men of vision . . . reduced to the position of paid lackeys, hirelings of the civil servants."

Warbeck-Simner smiled. "Still," he said, "it won't be long now. When the Plan goes into operation, we'll show 'em, won't we? I bet there'll be a few red faces in Whitehall on *that* day!"

"You bet! Wouldn't it be super if only we could be there, though? Wouldn't you love to look out of the window of your town flat and *see* them? Wouldn't you like to see the *papers*?"

"No, no. Our place is out there at the despatching end. We'll come into it later . . . We can leave the rest to Worthington and his men!"

"Yes. Yes, of course. We can leave it to Worthington!"

And the two men burst into another fit of giggles.

"Come," the ornithologist said at last, dabbing his eyes with a handkerchief, "I want your help on these beastly anklets; perhaps if we used an *alloy* it would turn more smoothly . . . And you haven't told me how your experiments on the concentration are going . . ."

Chuckling, they walked out of the study arm in arm and made their way to Warbeck-Simner's workshop, which was housed in a corner of the museum. In the study, the closed circuit television screen continued to relay the eddying of birds on the marsh, the passage of an occasional vehicle picked up by the *camera obscura* in the central tower.

Bella was doing the housework. Apart from the viewing room at the top of the tower, the upper stories of Turret House were all unused, only the bedrooms and bathrooms on the first floor, and the dining room, drawing room, study and servants' quarters at ground level being furnished. The décor of the sleeping quarters was heavy and ornate, and it was over an hour before she had finished vacuuming the old-fashioned carpets, making the beds and dusting the intricately carved pieces and numerous cases of stuffed birds with which the rooms were strewn. As she

was shaking a duster from the landing window, the ornithologist and the Professor were crossing the yard below, deep in conversation, on their way from the museum to the aviaries.

"It's still a bit parky, despite the sun," Warbeck-Simner was
saying. "Gosh, won't it be wizard when we can put the Plan into
operation and enjoy a bit of real warmth!"

"Wonderful, wonderful," Charnley said. "I can't believe
we're really almost ready to go! I keep worrying that something
will turn up to stop us, you know."

"What could stop us? I hear there's some journalist fellow
from London nosing about in Bratby looking for material on
wildfowl migration—but he'll hardly come bothering *us,* I
imagine. And even if he did, the Trusty Retainers would jolly
soon send him packing with a flea in his ear," Sir Albert replied—his fifth form phraseology as always contrasting oddly
with his mature voice.

"True, true," the scientist was chuckling as the two men
passed out of earshot. "I think we can rely on the Retainers . . ."

Bella picked up the vacuum cleaner and carried it down the
broad central staircase. There was just time to do the study before she cooked the fish and called the two old men in for their
lunch.

She crossed the room to the power point behind the desk,
glancing casually at the closed-circuit television as she passed.
Bending down to thrust home the plug, suddenly she paused,
straightened, and turned back to stare at the screen and the area
of marsh it showed.

The road stretched emptily along the top of the dyke. Reeds
and rushes stirred in a breeze, oscillating their shadows across
the hummocks of grass. On the patches of open water, floating
birds preened themselves in the midday sun. There was nothing
else to see.

The girl shrugged her shoulders, a faint frown wrinkling her
forehead. Funny, she thought, bending down once more; she
must have been mistaken . . . But for an instant—in the split
second during which her travelling eye had swept the screen—
she could have sworn that a man with a bowler hat and an
umbrella had been sliding down the bank of the dyke into the
shelter of a clump of bushes!

# 10

## THE HOUSE ON THE MARSH

"Bowler hat, umbrella and dark suit?" Emma Peel had said. "To go crawling about a marsh in? At *night*? —You must be out of your mind!"

"On the contrary," Steed had replied urbanely. "Suppose I should be discovered by Sir Albert Whatsisname? It is after all the first call I'm paying—and I hear he's a stickler for the formalities. Did you know you had ended your second sentence with a preposition?"

"But, good grief—surely you can't be serious, Steed!"

"We Steeds rarely jest . . . except when it hurts. Besides—there are certain—er—advantages to this particular ensemble which must for the moment remain a closely guarded secret."

And with that, Emma had had to be content. Steed's exasperating flippancy often concealed an inflexibility of purpose which only appeared in retrospect, and she had long realised that when he appeared at his most facetious, he was as often as not deadly serious. Accordingly, she had let the subject drop and told him what she had been able to find out during her brief vigil on top of the Lotus.

"There's only one way to get to the house, unless you go through the marsh," she had said. "And that's along the causeway. There's a barbed wire fence as far as the saltings—probably tricked out with alarm wires. And the gates are iron, about ten feet high, and controlled by an electric lock—they operate with one of those talk-back things you get in blocks of flats. There's no back entrance: the marsh extends on either side of the place and sweeps round behind it as well."

"Is the marsh itself fenced off in any way?"

"No. It lies considerably below the level of the road—probably below sea level, too. It starts at the foot of the dyke on which the road is built."

"I see. Is the sea far away?"

"Just on the other side of the dyke. It's a sort of sea wall

really. There's a few bushes, a dozen yards or so of sea pinks
and moss and mud—and then the shingle."

"H'm. And you say this story about the whole place being
under the scrutiny of a *camera obscura* is true?"

"It could be. So far as I could see. There are four ghastly
turrets in the worst Scottish Baronial style—about 1840, I should
say—and this central tower, complete with cupola. There was
certainly something up there that moved and caught the sun like
a heliograph. If it *is* what you think, then absolutely everything
that moves on that marsh—and on most of the road and the
causeway, too—could be seen from the house."

Steed had sighed. "They do make things difficult, don't they?"
he had complained. "Did you manage to glean anything of
interest during your tête-à-tête over the fish guts with our rustic
beauty?"

"She's not a bad girl, really. We got quite friendly in the end."

"I know. Her father told me. It's just that she's—er—a trifle
on the headstrong side. Especially when she has a twelve-bore in
her claws."

"She's never seen anyone around the place but these two extraordinary old men. But apparently they keep mentioning somebody called Worthington. 'Worthington's men' are a frequent
subject of conversation—oh, and their 'trusty retainers', whoever they may be."

"Perhaps they have strong-arm men deployed around the
place at night. After all, Bella's only there during the daytime,
four days a week. And they could easily keep hidden while she's
there—especially if, as you think, the upper floors are unused.
Perhaps they are very clever old men."

"They could, of course, simply be two innocent old gentlemen who happen to cherish their privacy—no strong-arm men,
no camera, no nothing."

"No. These—if you will forgive the phrase—are our birds.
I'm convinced of it. It has to be them. What I cannot figure out is
*why*. Why should an ornithologist and a scientist shove poison
pellets into the anklets of ringed birds? Why should they let
them loose?—there have been far too many for it to have been
accident, you know. Why should they use wildfowl, if not because the stuff is soluble and wildfowl will get it to the water?"

"Steed—surely you can't mean . . . You don't think the poison's *supposed* to be dissolved in the water? Deliberately? That
if the ducks hadn't killed themselves . . .?"

"That tramp hadn't been eating duck—but he did die of the same poison. I contacted Sir Charles while you were on watch this morning. The poor chap had hardly begun his meal—he'd prepared some fish over a fire—but he had brewed up some tea and drunk that. Where did he get the water?"

"The marsh! But how dreadful, Steed."

"How dread-full. Literally. If I'm right, patches of that marsh may be as deadly as neat hydrocyanic acid . . . As a rule only migratory birds are ringed in a sanctuary like this. Imagine the Lea valley in North London, my dear—if your aesthetics can stand it. Think of the Lea Bridge Road and the huge reservoirs off it. Think of the others between Chingford and Waltham Cross. Birds migrate to those stretches of water every year—you can predict their arrival almost to the day."

"But, Steed—"

"Imagine yourself secure in Scandinavia, or sunny Africa, or wherever they come from," the undercover man had continued remorselessly. "The day before the pretty creatures leave, you pop in the pellets, the birds fly to the reservoirs, they settle and paddle about—and when the population turns on the tap to make the cup that cheers but does not inebriate . . . Hey Presto! Instant death!"

"But why not just drop in the pellets yourself?"

"Safety, my dear. How can *you* have done it when you're hundreds of miles away in another country? In other words, the perpetrators must be presumed to have the intention of coming forward and profiting in some way from the deed. But again how? And *why*? . . . I wonder . . . I wonder if these two old men are in some way the dupes of some organisation?"

"The familiar neo-fascist group—hoping to profit by the ensuing chaos?"

"The neo-fascist group indeed. Except that I don't know of one at the moment. Still—the mysterious Mr Worthington and his myrmidons, to say nothing of those retainers—they have a sinister ring to me."

"What can we do then?"

"As I said, I'm going to pay a social call on Turret House," Steed had said. "And then we'll see what happens . . ."

Now, having dropped from the rear doors of the fishmonger's delivery van as the young driver, suitably bribed, had slowed down behind the shelter of an alder thicket, the undercover man was preparing to sit it out until darkness fell.

He had figured that, if the road *was* under constant observation, the van might be watched until it was out of sight—but that the scrutiny might conceivably relax after that. He had therefore waited an hour in the shade of the thicket, and then slid quickly down the bank to conceal himself in a clump of reeds, where he proposed to remain until nightfall.

It was a strange world on the fringe of the marsh. The tops of the reeds rustled in the breeze, but down at ground level, completely sheltered by the dyke, not a stalk, not a leaf moved. The sun was quite hot, the air stagnant and heavy—and the whole atmosphere somehow brooding and oppressive. Behind him, the yellowed blades of last year's grasses spiked stiffly up the flank of the dyke. In front, through a curtain of ochre stems, he could peer at a segment of the saltings—alternating bands of coarse grass and mudflat punctuated by stretches of shallow water through which deeper channels occasionally carved their way. Here and there, patches of alder, whins and other marsh scrub islanded the desolate scene. Far off to the West, a line of trees signalled the existence of dry land, but closer at hand there was only the promontory of Turret House and its environs to break the monotony. Except, of course, for the birds—and they were everywhere.

Great flocks of Mallard and Pintail speckled the dun flats, rode in colonies on the water, and continually took off or landed on apparently urgent errands. Nearer to Steed, a gaggle of Greylag geese nattered among themselves. There were Teal, Sheldrakes, Tufted Ducks, Crested Grebes, and a pair of large birds that Steed thought were Goosanders—while among the rushes and grass around him he identified Reed Warblers, Buntings and a Water Rail.

For a long time he sat cross-legged on the ground, taking evident pleasure in the teeming life of the sanctuary. But at last he glanced at his watch, sighed, and picked up his umbrella—one of many in his collection which was not what it seemed. First he unscrewed the handle, an unusually fat one in curved malacca, from the lower end of which he removed a small cork. Next, he took off the wide ferrule, extracting from inside it a tiny beaker of stainless steel. This he filled with cognac from the hollow handle. He drank, refilled, and drank again. And finally he dismantled the entire parasol part of the umbrella, including the ribs, leaving himself holding just the shaft. This was in fact a slender but powerful spyglass: all he had to do to make it operational was to reach into his pocket for a small lens, which he screwed to one end, and a wide eyepiece, which he attached to the other. Then, cautiously parting the reeds, he put the device to one eye and aimed it across the marsh at Turret House.

A pair of Coots, which had become accustomed to the strange visitor and were paddling about in the water just beyond the stems, bobbed away with shrill cries of alarm. And a black, white and chestnut duck with a bright scarlet bill waddled angrily down from the hummock where it had been sleeping and flopped into the water.

The little telescope showed a small area but it was remarkably clear. Steed surveyed the shrubberies and copses between the causeway and the marsh. Nothing moved except the birds. He examined the two sides of the house that he could see. Many of the windows were obscured by foliage, but apart from a glimpse of Bella Reeves passing a ground-floor casement, those in view provided nothing interesting either. He scanned the turrets and the tower. The former were empty, but there definitely *was* a *camera obscura* in the latter: he could make out the prism and the 360 degree turntable on which it revolved, under a cap on top of the cupola. He couldn't see much to the rear of the building, there were too many trees in the way—but he caught sight once of two men, one short and one tall, crossing an open space between the stables and the house. Later, someone visited the aviaries. He was unable to tell whether it was one of the men he had seen before.

The afternoon wore on. The wildfowl maintained their ceaseless activity. Vehicles passed along the road in each direction. A bank of cirrus clouds appeared high in the western sky, temporarily shrouding the sun.

At five o'clock, the poacher's daughter appeared on her bicycle at the top of the drive. Steed watched her through the spyglass as she cycled to the gates—noticing the leg-lifting routine about which Emma had told him as the machine passed the row of white posts. A few minutes later, he heard the whirring of tyres above and behind him as she pedalled up the road.

At a quarter to six, when it was almost dusk, a light came on in two of the ground floor windows. Shortly afterwards, curtains were drawn across them. The sun, which had dropped into view below the cloudbank for a few minutes before it set, now flamed vermilion accents across the mackerel sky from below the horizon. The constant rising and circling and settling of the birds became more pronounced. As a long skein of Brent geese flew in over the marsh from the sea, Steed decided that the time had come for action. He reassembled his umbrella, adjusted the angle of his bowler and scrambled to his feet.

It was about a hundred and fifty yards from his hiding place to the junction of the dyke and the causeway. Since it would obviously be madness to attempt a crossing of the marsh in the darkness, he decided to edge his way along the foot of the dyke until he reached the wire fence protecting the entrance to the drive. From there, he would cut the corner to gain the higher ground on which it ran, and then work his way up to the house through the shrubberies bordering it. He had about two and a half hours before the moon rose—when he would have to leave to avoid the risk of detection, either directly from the windows or via the *camera obscura*.

The going was relatively easy at first. Stepping gingerly from hummock to hummock, testing every one with his toe before putting his weight on it, he advanced cautiously. Soon, the causeway trees rose blackly against the sky—shading now from the palest of greens along the western horizon to a deep violet in the East. He should run across the fence before long . . . Yes, here it was: an ugly tangle of spiked wire, attached to iron stakes cemented into the marshy ground. It ran from the gateposts to the beginning of the dyke, curved down the bank, and ended about a dozen yards along the flank of the causeway. The only thing was, Steed discovered when he tried to walk around the end of it, that there was a deep pool ideally placed to prevent such a manoeuvre. He decided to examine the wire—and for this the umbrella was once more pressed into service in yet another guise. Beneath the beaker, recessed in the deep rim of the ferrule, was a small electric bulb. Steed took a slim battery from his pocket, clipped it into place below the handle, pressed a button at the top of the shaft—and a pencil beam of light shone from the foot of the umbrella. He poked it in among the strands of the fence and clucked disapprovingly below his breath. Twisted in with the barbed wire at each level were filaments of small-gauge alarm wire—though whether they were of the electrical or mechanical type he was unable to tell. Without knowing this, and with the time neither to track the wires to their source nor to investigate their type, it was obvious that any attempt to disconnect them was out of the question. He would

have to retrace his steps, make a cast across the corner of the
marsh, and outflank both wire and pool.

Pointing the umbrella at the ground before his feet, he trod
carefully back a dozen yards, the thin ray of light illuminating
the rough terrain over which he had to travel. It was quite dark
now, windless and becoming cool. The faint, high humming of
insects had ceased and only the intermittent murmuring and
gabbling of wildfowl out on the marsh broke the silence.

Steed shouldered his way through the barrier of reeds and
began picking his way across the dark saltings. He jumped
lightly over a rivulet, stepped along a shelf of sedge that squelched underfoot, and traversed a firmer area humped with coarse
grass. Skirting a bed of rushes beneath which the ground was
sure to be waterlogged, he leaped another stream and then
turned at right angles to approach the causeway parallel with
the dyke. Once his foot slipped as an apparently firm tussock
sank beneath his weight; another time, he miscalculated and
plunged one leg into eighteen inches of icy water—but his water-
proof shoe and sock, bonded together and elasticised to the calf,
let none of the moisture in; and the fibres of his seemingly ordinary dark suit were siliconized to make the material as imper-
vious as an oilskin.

At last he approached the silhouette of the causeway once more.
He had cleared the pool and the end of the wire well enough.
But now there was another barrier : immediately before the firm
ground, water had carved a deep channel in the mud—and,
even if the marsh had permitted him to take a run at it, this
time it was too wide to leap . . .

He came to a halt, exasperated, and switched off the eye in the
umbrella. He looked to either side: the channel seemed to ex-
tend in each direction. Then, on an impulse, he looked up into
the air.

About five feet above his head, a branch from one of the big
trees on the far side of the water stretched darkly across the sky.

Steed pointed the umbrella at the dim shape and permitted
himself the briefest flick at the flashlight button. In the fraction
of a second that the beam lanced the night, he saw that the
branch, not yet in leaf, looked solid and sound. He reversed the
umbrella, gripping it by the ferrule, and then, holding it at arm's
length, stretched up on tiptoe and hooked the handle around the
branch. After a moment's hesitation, he reached up the other

hand, grasped the ferrule firmly and swung himself, Tarzan-like, out over the water . . .

He landed heavily on firm ground, the impetus of his fall pulling the umbrella away from the tree with a scattering of bark and small twigs. A Water Rail, startled from its sleep among the grasses at the edge of the channel, splashed noisily into the water and swam away with a *Quark!* of alarm.

Steed picked himself up and listened. There seemed to be no other reaction to his arrival so, after waiting a moment, he settled his hat more firmly on his head and moved up the bank into the grounds of Turret House proper. The causeway was about eighty yards wide, the drive running straight up the middle. There was therefore a sizeable strip of ground on each side, fairly densely covered with trees, shrubs and an occasional spinney—and it was through these that the undercover man intended to work his way towards the house.

He had no idea whether or not there might be watchdogs— animal or human—staked out around the house or available to come rushing at the call of an alarm. Either "Worthington's men" or the "retainers" could be swarming around him unseen. He must therefore proceed with great caution—and be extremely prudent in his use of the flashlight from now on.

Holding the umbrella, unlit, before him like a geiger counter, he inched forwards into the shrubbery. The ferrule quested this way and that, seeking obstructions that might impede his progress, roots over which he might trip. He had only gone a few yards when it brushed against something a few inches from the ground, not solid enough to be a branch, too resistant for leaves. He probed and prodded experimentally in the dark: it seemed to be some kind of cord or wire . . .

There was a metallic squeak somewhere above his head.

He jumped backwards as a cascade of liquid showered to the ground, splashing noisily on the hard earth and pattering off leaves. Had he not been holding the umbrella at an arm's length in front of him, he would have triggered off the trip-wire with his leg and got soaked!

Risking a flash from the light, he shone the bulb upwards. Yes— a simple schoolboy booby trap: a galvanised bucket pivoting on a rod supported by two branches. When the wire was displaced beyond a certain point, a counterweight tilted the bucket—which spilled its contents on whoever had actuated the wire. It was simple and harmless. But what on earth could

be the point of dowsing an intruder? Surely no burglar would
be discouraged simply by having a bucketful of cold water
poured on him?

Water? Steed sniffed. A peculiar choking smell drifted on the
night air. He held the umbrella down and pressed the torch
button again. Above the drenched ground, leaves were steaming.
From a narrow iron band encircling the ferrule, reflected light
showed him a curl of heavy brown smoke rising. With a stifled
exclamation, he crouched down, sniffed again, and reached out
to touch one of the wet leaves. He put his finger to his lips and
licked briefly at the moist fingertip. With a grimace, he spat and
then rubbed the finger hard on a patch of dry earth.

That was no water. The bucket had been filled with sulphuric-
acid!

All right, then, Steed said to himself grimly. At least we know
where we are now! The people who had rigged up that particular booby trap were no innocent old gentlemen guarding
their privacy . . .

Plunging the acid-splashed ferrule into the ground to cleanse
it, he gripped the umbrella more firmly and went on. He
crossed an open space under some trees and came to a thick
hedge of hawthorn. Treading with infinite care, he moved along
it towards the house until he came to a wicket gate. This time
he was taking no chances. Shielding the light with one hand, he
pressed the button and examined the gateway minutely. There
was no sign of any trip wire. He touched the gate itself. It swung
easily on oiled hinges, with no sign of squeaks or creaks. As he
pushed it open and went silently through, his toe caught on a
root and he instinctively lowered his head and looked down.

There was a vibrant metallic twang and a giant fist slammed
him on top of the crown.

Steed was knocked backwards by the force of the blow and
sat down heavily on the ground. His ears were ringing and for
the moment he didn't realise what had happened. Then, gingerly, he reached upwards and prised the bowler hat off his head.
It was a very special hat: both brim and crown were of bullet-
proof steel under the furry velour covering. ("But where on earth
did you *get* it?" Emma Peel had cried, the first time she saw it.
And Steed had replied, smiling: "An idea I picked up from a
film I saw—one of those preposterous spy things, you know.
But it's a good one for all that . . .")

Now, sitting in the darkness, he felt the hat all over. There was a dent, two inches across and an inch deep, in the steel crown. He whistled softly and felt around him for his umbrella. Before he found it, his groping fingers touched something else: an eighteen-inch shaft tipped with a murderous iron sphere about the size of a golf-ball.

It was the bolt from a crossbow—and if he hadn't been wearing the hat, or if he had not looked down, it would have gone straight through his head . . .

He crawled through the gate on hands and knees and located the weapon wedged in the fork of a tree. It was operated quite simply: the gate was of the self-closing variety, worked by a weight hanging down inside the hollow gatepost. When the weight rose as the gate was opened, it pulled a wire connected with the mechanism of the bow—and the bow was trained with deadly accuracy on the person using the gate.

Steed's nerves were steelier than most, but the next half hour was a nightmare, even for him.

Turret House was ringed with lethal variants of schoolboy booby traps. A magnesium flare erupted with a violence that seared his eyeballs while he was negotiating a thicket near the drive. Later, he was brought up against another hedge—pierced this time by a conveniently placed stile. He tested the four steps by prodding them with the umbrella. Both of those on the far side collapsed under the slightest pressure, hingeing forward so that the foot of anyone putting his weight on them would plunge downwards to be impaled on a row of wicked-looking steel spikes projecting from the ground below. Steed handled that one by retreating a few yards, taking three quick paces forward, placing the palm of one hand on the rail, and vaulting neatly over the stile.

His eyes had grown quite accustomed to the dark, but it was still extremely difficult to make out details under the trees bordering the drive. From the house, chinks of light still showed between the curtains of the downstairs room he had noticed from the marsh—but there was no other sign of activity, despite what had seemed to him the enormous noise made by the various devices he had actuated. And, of course, the nearer he got, the more careful he had to be with his own small light. He edged his way towards the drive—he was almost there now—between two rhododendrons.

"*All right Worthington: you move round behind. I'll take him here.*"

Steed froze. The penetrating whisper had come from somewhere on the far side of the bushes. He took a firmer grasp on his umbrella.

"*Will do. But don't hit too hard: we want to ask questions.*"

Steed whirled. This time the voice, a different voice, had come from behind. As he waited, tense, a low chuckle came from behind a clump of box hedge clipped into ornamental shapes on his right.

The undercover man took three quick paces backwards and dropped to the ground, lying flat on his face and hardly breathing.

Nothing happened.

The expected rush of feet did not materialise. No blow swished through the air, no flame stabbed the dark.

Steed's fingers had levered a stone loose from the mossy ground. Cautiously, soundlessly, he raised one shoulder so that his arm was free and lobbed the stone towards the rhododendrons. It crashed in amongst the leaves and dropped to the ground.

Silence.

Steed frowned. Slowly, he wormed his way along the ground towards the bushes. He had almost reached them when:

"*All right Worthington: you move round behind. I'll take him here*"—the whisper sounded exactly as before. For the first time that evening, Steed grinned. He did not turn round when the second voice repeated: "*Will do. But don't hit too hard: we want to ask questions*"; he took no notice of the second performance of the eerie chuckle. He got to his feet and walked boldly to the rhododendrons, poking the umbrella in among them and switching on the light.

A tiny loudspeaker was wired to one of the branches.

Obviously the voices were recorded on a tape loop, transmitted via three separate speakers. And the apparatus was set in motion every time anyone passed a certain point—probably by a contact concealed beneath the dead leaves on the ground . . .

Steed wasted no more time on it and stepped on to the driveway. Just to his right were the twin lines of white posts Emma had told him about. "Apparently there's a yellow line painted in the middle of the drive," she had said, "and Bella's told to get up a bit of speed, lift her feet, and coast while she's between the posts—but she must be very careful to steer exactly along the line. It's some kind of warning device, and they don't want it set off every time she comes or goes . . ."

Taking care not to pass in front of any posts, Steed examined the place carefully. Yes—there was the yellow line; just like a lane-line on an arterial road. And, as he had surmised, each post bore at the top, on the side facing the driveway, a disc something like a reflector. The discs were faintly luminescent and tilted slightly forwards. This must be a rather elaborate version of the "electronic eye"—a series of photo-electric cells which would actuate some kind of warning system if anything broke the circuit by passing through the invisible rays they emitted. Presumably they were beamed downwards so that there was a narrow "dead area", marked by the yellow line, not covered by the rays from either side. Anything wider than the line—a pedestrian, say, or a car—would be bound to cross one of the rays and set off the alarm. But, provided the feet were kept up off the pedals, the narrow tyres of a bicycle could pass along the line without breaking the circuit. This, however, was essentially a system to give advance warning of "legal" callers coming up the drive; it wasn't one of the anti-prowler series with which Steed had been wrestling! He shrugged and crossed the drive to the far side. Here at least there was a stretch of clear ground under the trees reaching almost to the house. Shouldering the umbrella, he tip-toed rapidly across it towards the lighted windows.

Suddenly he was falling.

The earth had given way beneath his feet and he dropped like a stone into a narrow hole. In a lightning reflex, he whipped the umbrella from his shoulder as he fell, put up his other hand to the sliding collar and opened it.

The erected canopy slammed down over the aperture like a stopper in a jar, bringing Steed up short with a jolt that shook the breath from his body. The special reinforced steel ribs groaned . . . but held. If they had given way, and his weight had pulled the umbrella inside out, he would have gone on down, taking the umbrella with him. As it was, he hung like a man on a parachute in pitch blackness—his own arm's length plus the length of the umbrella shaft below the surface.

For a moment he gasped to regain his breath. There was the dank smell of moist earth about him. Small pieces of soil and pebbles were still crumbling from the lip of the hole to plop into water somewhere below him. He kicked out with his legs until he found one of the sides of the shaft—then, redoubling his grip on the umbrella, he "walked" himself slowly upwards until his feet were on a level with his waist. From that position it was relatively simple to lower his back until it touched the opposite wall. Then, pressing with feet and shoulders, inch by inch he worked his way up to the top in the manner of a mountaineer negotiating a chimney.

It was only a matter of five or six feet, but the earth was soft and puddingy, giving nothing like the purchase to be obtained from rock. By the time he rolled over the lip of the hole to safety, he was covered in sweat.

He lay still until the hammering of his heart had quietened down, then sat up and reached for the umbrella. First he closed it up, then he unscrewed the handle and drained the remainder of its contents, and finally he tested the button to see if the flashlight was still working. It was. Lowering it into the hole, he saw, about fifteen feet below, the faint gleam of water—through which the points of a dozen stakes whittled to a needle sharpness thrust evilly upwards. At the edge, branches and leaves which had covered it lay scattered.

"A Pooh trap for Heffalumps, by Jove!" he breathed.

He rose to his feet, a scarecrow figure very different from the immaculate Steed who had left the cottage that morning. His shoes were caked with wet mud, his jacket was torn, both suit and shirt were stained with moss and earth and plastered with leaves, and his hat was dented . . .

He looked at the luminous dial of his watch. In twenty minutes time, the moon would be up. He could do nothing more now.

Turning to the dim outline of Turret House, he raised his battered bowler in a theatrical gesture.

"Very well, gentlemen," he apostrophised the unseen occupants. "Your round, I think! . . . But I shall try again tomorrow —though it'll be by a more socially acceptable route, I fancy!"

He clapped the hat back on his head, straightened his muddy tie, and headed back towards the marsh.

# 11

## A GHOST IN A BATTERED BOWLER...

EMMA PEEL was laughing. Under the low roof of the Lotus Elan, she hunched over the steering wheel trying hard to stifle the spasm of uncontrollable mirth which had seized her. From the big, twin dials of speedometer and tachometer subdued dashboard lighting picked out an occasional contour from her black jersey cat-suit and rippled the highlights dancing across the shiny *ciré* insert stretched over her shaking breasts.

"Oh, Steed!" she gasped. "Oh, Steed—one of the slowest entrances you ever made . . . and unquestionably one of the best!"

She had been five minutes early for their rendezvous at the lay-by from which she had watched Turret House that morning. But at the appointed time, there had been no sign of the undercover man. Five minutes had passed . . . ten . . . fifteen. And at last, far down the road, her anxious gaze had caught a movement among the bushes fringeing the dyke near the gates. A moment later, a nightmare figure had burst out on to the road. Like a badly designed ghost, it had been covered from head to foot in shining, dripping white. A white and dented bowler hat crowned its head; white plastered its face, clung to its jacket and coursed down its trousers; and from its albino shoes a trail of white footprints led, clown-like, to the foliage from which it had emerged. Slowly, this apparition squelched down the road towards the lay-by. At last, it drew to a livid halt by the car. In the ghastly mask of its face, matted eyebrows raised and Steed's eyes looked out.

"Enter," he said sepulchrally, "a man in a white suit."

And Emma, dropping her tawny head to the wheel, had collapsed. "Oh, dear . . . I *am* so sorry," she cried. "But really . . . you looked so . . . so *hysterical*—Goodness! My mascara's running!—No, but really, I mean . . ." And she burst into another peal of laughter.

"We are always pleased to be able to entertain," Steed said stiffly. "Perhaps if you could direct me to a convenient television station—commercial, of course—I might be able to turn an honest penny: I must be whiter even than that whiter-than-white fellow."

"Now you're adding brightness to whiteness," Emma said. "But what happened, Steed—what *happened*?"

"I managed to evade a boxful of lethal tricks and fell for a harmless one. Perhaps it's fortunate it wasn't the other way round."

"I don't follow you."

"Your innocent old gentlemen have a bizarre sense of humour, it seems. The place is crawling with booby traps."

"Not the explosive kind, I hope?"

"Not so far as I found out. That doesn't mean there aren't any, though. But concealed pits covered with dead leaves, showers of sulphuric acid, gates which set off crossbows and dummy stiles which impale you on spikes are enough for me. We Steeds can take a hint—and I received a definite impression that I wasn't welcome. Naturally, as a gentleman, I left immediately."

"You didn't penetrate the defences at all, then?"

"No. By the time I was at the house it was too late."

"You still haven't explained about the *white*, though!"

"I do beg your pardon; I had no intention of keeping a lady waiting," Steed said, sweeping off his hat with a theatrical gesture. A quantity of viscous white fluid showered from the brim and splatted on to the Lotus's bonnet.

He surveyed it for a moment. "It's whitewash," he said at last. "It'll wash off—me as well as the car, I hope ... No—I'd managed to avoid all their tricks, and perhaps I became a little careless on the way back. I went in on the far side of the drive, you know, and came back this side—so it was all new territory, as it were. And just as I got to the bank of the causeway and was thinking that at last I was clear ... I missed a trip wire and set off this blasted thing!"

"*What* blasted thing, for Heaven's sake?"

"Repeat performance of the Great Sulphuric Acid trick—as carried out before crowned heads throughout the civilised world; and parts, as they say, of Bratby."

"You mean there was another bucket ...?"

"Balanced on a plank this time. Full of whitewash. Didn't half fetch me a grievous blow on the shoulder, I can tell you!"

—5

Steed said, rubbing the injured area reflectively. "Anyone for tennis?"

Emma slid across the passenger seat and uncoiled her slim length from the Lotus. "But what are you going to do?" she asked. "I mean I don't wish to seem inhospitable, but—"

"Yes, I see what you mean. Whitewash can be sponged off me, and my clothes can be cleaned—but black leather upholstery's another thing, isn't it? To say nothing of black leather ladies."

"It's black *ciré*."

"Same thing, only less so . . . I tell you what, the only thing is, I'll have to strip."

"To the buff?"

"My *dear!* No—just the outer layer, you know. I'll take off me jacket, trousers, shirt, tie, hat and shoes—and bundle them all in the boot, if you don't mind."

"What will that leave you?" Emma asked curiously.

"Well, socks, of course. And . . ." Steed hesitated.

"Steed!" Emma laughed delightedly. "I do believe you're embarrassed. What is it? Are you wearing a darned vest?"

"No, it's not that, my dear. It's just . . ." The undercover man paused once more. "Well it's just that I thought I might be getting immersed in marshes and things. And so . . ."

"And so?"

"And so, recalling that it was cold for the time of the year, I thought it might be prudent to have something warm underneath. In short, I put on one of those long-legged sort of combination things that one wears under ski clothes. As a matter of fact they do look rather like ordinary combs," Steed said with elaborate nonchalance, "and I'd hate you to think . . ."

"I assure you, Steed," Emma replied gravely, "that *mentally* I shall see that lithe and muscular form clad in the briefest of singlets and jockey shorts . . . What colour are they?"

"Striped, actually. In violet and black."

While he peeled off his whitewash-soaked outer garments, Steed recounted in more detail the trials and tribulations he had suffered in the grounds of Turret House. Finally, before stowing the soggy bundle in the boot, he reached into the inside pocket of the jacket, took out a large gold cigarette case, opened it, and produced two smoked salmon sandwiches wrapped in grease-proof paper. Handing one to Emma and biting a large chunk out of the other himself, he sank gratefully into the Lotus's passenger seat and closed the door. "Now," he said, munching, "let's hear your own report. What have you been able to find out?"

"The undercover man indeed!" Emma said, looking admiringly at the horizontal stripes with which Steed was now ringed. She switched on the car's heater. "You'd better have this on, or you'll catch your death . . . Now, let's see. First, Sir Charles's findings. Doctor Atherley, the porter at the station, the admiral, the political speaker—all of these gave positive tests to the Moraes reaction. They were poisoned, in fact. The tramp you know about . . . Oh, yes—and the Beaknik."

"What about her?"

"Well, according to Sir Charles, that young lady was no better than she ought to be. The poor fellow they found on the Bratby road wasn't the only tramp in the case, it seems!"

"You mean she was pregnant?"

"Had been. An illegal operation was performed shortly— very shortly—before her death. A most *professional* job, Sir Charles said."

Steed whistled. "Maltby, of course!" he said. "No wonder he was scared if he'd just done an abortion and the girl died on him. How *did* she die, by the way? Was it poison again?"

"It was. Teal, this time. A sauce made with the giblets. But so far as Maltby is concerned, there's an additional reason for him to be frightened: according to my researches in the village, there's a three to one chance that he was the father as well. And he's a married man . . ."

"I see. The plot thickens . . . Anything else from Charles?"

"They exhumed one of the earlier seven: an old woman who used to be postmistress at Little Hornham. Positive again. But the insurance man at Boston and my gamekeeper were both negative—unquestionably natural causes, he said. I couldn't shake him on it."

"Don't worry. Statistically there have to be some 'genuine' deaths among them. Otherwise the area would be *below* the national average. And that would be just as odd! Besides, Boston's really outside the area, and Birningham's on its southerly fringe . . . Did you find out anything at all about our practical jokers?"

"Oh, yes. Your Special Branch friend, MacCorquodale, was a great help there. Warbeck-Simner's apparently quite a big noise in the ornithological world—writes books; contributes to *Field*, *Ornis*, *Zoologist*, *Ibis* and so on; reads papers before the Royal

Society and the French Academy of Natural History. That sort of thing."

"And the Professor?"

"Charnley has a doctorate in pharmaceutical chemistry. He studied at Berne and at Munich before the first war, and he had a chair at one of the red-bricks in the early thirties. But the interesting thing is that he took a degree in toxicology—in South America!"

"Did he, by Jove! Not at your old *alma mater* in Bahia, I suppose?"

"No, he was at Rio, as a matter of fact. But it's interesting—Munich could spell neo-fascist sympathies, couldn't it? And Toxicology in Brazil certainly smells of Curare to me."

"So much for your innocent old gentlemen," Steed said. "If I know old Mac, he'd never let you off the phone without telling you something about their personalities as well. Come on—give!"

Emma smiled. "He stressed that it was deduction and not fact," she said. "It seems that Sir Albert Thing comes from a Very Old Family. Apparently there was some legal tangle, years ago, about descent—and if he'd won he'd be the Earl of Bratby today. Only he didn't and he isn't."

"So he's got the dead needle to the rest of us because we're on the same level as he is—and he feels we ought to be below?"

"That's about it. Plus the fact that he has a thing about the divine right of people like him to govern the country."

"Any fascist, neo-fascist or Nazi connections?"

"No, MacCorquodale didn't think any of them were aristocratic enough."

"And the jolly old Prof?"

"Another embittered man. Originally he went to Brazil because he'd been passed over for some top executive job in favour of a civil servant. *He* thinks the eggheads and the boffins should run the world! Apparently Sir A took a fancy to him and set him up in this plushy lab in the grounds about three years ago."

"H'm. Toxicology, eh? Any fascist connections in his case?"

"Oddly enough, no. None whatever, despite the Munich period."

"And the organisations?"

"Blank. Special Branch have no knowledge of any group, overt or covert, calling themselves The Retainers or anything like it. They have no dossier on anyone called Worthington who might be linked up with our little battle. And they don't even have a file on any likelies."

"Well," Steed said with a sigh, "there's nothing for it but to press my *alter ego* into service."

"Your what?"

"My alias. As a journalist gathering material on migration, it's only reasonable that I should seek the help—and defer to the opinion—of one of the experts on the subject who's actually here. Tomorrow, I seek professional audience of Sir Albert Charles Frobisher Warbeck-Simner. And if he's as susceptible to flattery as your report suggests, it shouldn't be too difficult to get to him . . . But I shall want to borrow this car."

"What's wrong with the Bentley?"

"Nothing is *ever* wrong with the Bentley. It's part of the definition of a Bentley. But there is a special reason why a Lotus will be more suitable for this particular journey."

"What reason?"

"The fact," Steed said enigmatically, "that it is, in the words of a famous Kansas City blues, little and low and built up from the ground. You'll see what I mean tomorrow . . . In the meantime, there's tonight. That wasn't a very big sandwich. Do you fancy driving me back to my pad, waiting while I change, and then taking me to your inn for dinner?"

"I do wish," Emma said crossly, turning the ignition key to start the Lotus, "that you didn't find it necessary to be so infuriatingly *oblique* about things." She swung the wheel over and nosed the car out of the lay-by on to the road. Soon, they were humming along in the direction of Bratby. Just before they reached the gates of Turret House, Steed gave an exclamation of annoyance.

"Blast!" he said. "I've just remembered: I left my umbrella at the bottom of the bank while I was trying to fight my way out of the whitewash. Do you mind pulling up here for a second while I nip down and get it? It's one I'm rather fond of."

"You ended that sentence with a preposition," Emma called after him as he plunged through the bushes and down the bank out of sight.

About three minutes after he had gone, there was a swish of tyres and a large black Wolseley saloon cut in and stopped in front of the parked Lotus with a faint squeal of disc brakes. All four doors opened at once, as a spotlight on the roof swivelled to fix the sports car in its fierce glare. Four large men piled out and advanced on Emma.

Startled—for she had not heard the saloon approaching—the girl shielded her eyes against the blaze of light. For a moment she experienced a thrill of alarm. Then she saw that the men were dressed in police uniforms.

A heavy man wearing a sergeant's stripes on his sleeve came up to the driver's door. "All right, then—what are you doing here?" he began. And then, leaning down and seeing Emma for the first time: "Oh. Excuse me, miss. Routine check, you know . . . Do you mind giving me your name and address and showing me your driver's licence, please?"

"My name is Emma Peel. Mrs Emma Peel. And I'm staying at the 'Feathers' at Bratby," Emma replied, handing her licence through the window. "What's up? What are you checking, then?"

"Thank you, Miss . . . Madam, that is," the big man said in his soft East Coast burr, studying the little red book. 'We get a lot of poachin' around here, you know. Rascals with no regard for other people's property. You wouldn't believe some of the things people get up to. We just like to keep an eye on things." He handed back the licence. "D'you mind tellin' me what you're doin' here, Madam?"

"I'm—er—as a matter of fact I'm . . . waiting for a friend," Emma said, fighting back a desire to laugh hysterically.

There was a rustling in the bushes at the side of the road.

The four policemen swung round. A fifth, in the black saloon, turned the spotlight on to the foliage.

The leaves, silvered in the glare, became agitated. The rustling grew to a crashing. And finally the branches parted as Steed in his glory, dead on cue, appeared—first the chalky mask of his face just above the level of the road, then a hand grasping a piebald umbrella, and finally the splendid length of his combination-clad body, ringed in black and purple, as he climbed the steep bank and burst through on to level ground.

For a moment, he paused—an arresting sight. Then, walking towards the car, "I'm so sorry," he said to Emma. "I didn't realise that we had company."

There was a short silence.

"Would this be your . . . friend?" the sergeant asked heavily at last, with a helpless gesture in Steed's direction.

"Why, yes," Emma said weakly, dropping her head to the wheel once more, "there he is now!"

The sergeant coughed. "Good evening—Sir," he said, addressing himself to Steed. "I don't wish to appear unduly inquisitive, but might I ask exactly what you think *you're* doing?"

"Good evening, Sergeant. No trouble at all. I just came to fetch my umbrella, that's all."

The four policemen stared at Steed, eyeing him slowly from the top of his head to his stockinged feet. "Came to fetch your umbrella," the big man echoed at length. "Just so. I should have guessed, shouldn't I?"

"No, but really," Steed protested. "I happened to leave it here —on the marsh, that is—at the foot of the dyke, I should say. And then I remembered I'd forgotten it. So I came back for it ... Look!"

As though to prove his point, he lifted the umbrella and opened it. A cascade of whitewash splashed to the ground.

The fifth patrolman had climbed out of the police car and was standing with the others looking after them, Emma saw over her shoulder before the road took them into the dip at the far end of the dyke. The sergeant was still slowly shaking his head.

"All right, so I looked funny," Steed said later, as the little car drew up outside his rented cottage. "But I cannot see what you keep on laughing at."

"No, it's not that. It's just—it's just ... Oh, did you *see* that poor man's *face*," Emma cried. "And as for you, you don't look funny at all: you look as though you'd just been a ghost!"

# 12

## MATTERS OF MIGRATION

Sir Albert Charles Frobisher Warbeck-Simner placed the palms of his hands on the flat top of his desk. Below the domed forehead, his coarse featured face looked almost benign. "What school did you go to, Steed?" he asked.

Steed told him.

"I thought so," the ornithologist said, looking towards Professor Charnley. "Long after my time, of course. But you can tell, can't you?"

"Oh, yes, you can tell," echoed the scientist. "You can tell alright."

Looking as vacuous as he dared without making a lampoon of it, Steed perched diffidently on the edge of a straight-back chair. He wore horn-rimmed spectacles and his hair was parted at one side. A flat cap was stuffed into one of the huge patch pockets on the skirted tweed jacket he wore. His boots and his Norfolk breeches were linked by a pair of excessively hairy stockings.

"What a treat it is to see a man properly dressed," his host continued. "I can't imagine what a fellow with your advantages is doing messing about with journalism, though: it's hardly a gentleman's profession, is it? . . . Still—we mustn't be personal, Charnley, must we! Now . . . what can I do for you, young man?"

"Well, sir, I do hope you won't think it a frightful liberty," Steed said, shifting from side to side on his chair, "but I've been commissioned to do this series of pieces—articles, that is— for *Grandstand*—"

"*Grandstand*? That's the picture thing, isn't it? They did quite a decent colour picture of Ospreys at Loch Torridon a month or so ago."

"Yes, sir. That's the one. Well—I have to do this series on bird migrations, you see . . . and naturally Suffolk, the Fen District, and round here are the first ports of call, if you see what I mean . . . and while I'm here the obvious person to ask—I mean an ornithologist as famous as yourself—if an expert as well-known doesn't mind being quoted, that is . . ." Steed allowed his voice to tail away shyly.

"My dear boy. Of course I should be delighted. If there's anything I can usefully say, that is. Commander Scott's really *the* authority for this part of the world, you know."

"Yes, sir. Naturally we shall be paying tribute—but if you *would* be so kind, there are one or two things I imagine only you could tell us."

"H'm. Well tell me the general outline of your feature—the direction it's taking; so I'll know the level, so to speak, at which the audience is listening," Warbeck-Simner said, shooting an unexpectedly shrewd glance at Steed.

"Well, basically, the series is informative rather than discursive. That is to say, we presume a near-total ignorance on the part of the reader, and then fill him in on the—er—salient details."

"A fairly safe presumption in England today, I should imagine," Professor Charnley put in tartly.

"In other words," Steed continued, smiling politely, "we tell the reader that this extraordinary phenomenon exists, that the same birds return to the same summer or winter quarters every year, coming thousands of miles across the ocean without food or rest, to the very same pond or shed or hedge. And we give details of how they come and how all these things can be proved by ringing and so on. And how they come every year practically on the same *day*—and how they all get ready for the journey and leave together . . . all that sort of thing, you know."

"But that's the merest generalisation. Any encyclopaedia—"

"Yes, sir. I know, I know—Forgive me for interrupting you! —but that's just the background, as it were. Once they've been filled in we start on some of the more bizarre aspects of the thing. Then we tell them all about the fascinating research—the sort of thing in which you specialise, sir—and round off with as many —er—unusual stories on the subject as we can dig up. It's not exactly a scientific approach, I'm afraid . . ."

"No, it jolly well isn't! Really, I fail to see how I can help."

"If you could just perhaps answer a few questions . . ." Steed began desperately.

"Well, a man doesn't like to be churlish. What questions?"

"Well—let me see . . . I have it here somewhere, I know . . . now where can that piece of paper—Ah! Here it is! . . . Yes.

You have an actual sanctuary here. Do you find this means there is a greater variety of birds than on the normal Fenland salt-ings? . . . Do you find the fact that it's a sanctuary encourages birds to collect undisturbed before their migration? . . . Does the fact that it's uninterrupted encourage vagrants to stay here? . . . Can you tell me of any special techniques of observation you have developed here? . . . Do you think that winter—"

"Wait, wait, wait—wait a minute, old man!" Warbeck-Simner expostulated good-humouredly. "One at a time, yes? Your first point, now: variety. As a rule there's not too much difference in ordinary migrants. If an oddity *does* turn up, though—we're much more likely to get him."

"I saw something under that heading as I drove along."

"Did you really?" Charnley asked quickly. "What was that?"

"Well, that's what I mean: I couldn't place it. It looked like some kind of duck, but it had a bright red bill and the rest of it was black and white and a sort of auburn colour."

"Where did you see it?"

"Down on the marsh as I came along the dyke. There were two pairs paddling about—then one pair flew off. The wings look very white when they're in the air."

"Jolly good for you, Steed!" the ornithologist beamed de-lightedly. "Those *were* rather special, as it happens. We just have the two pairs this year—and we're lucky to have them, I suppose. That's *Netta Rufina* : the Red-Crested Pochard, no less."

Steed was scribbling in a small notebook. "Thank you, sir. Any more like that?"

"Well, first of all, you do realise that I specialise entirely in wildfowl, in water birds, do you? You'll hear nothing from me of Stints, or Sandpipers, or Dunlins, or Godwits, or Redshanks, or Buntings, though I am sure most of them are about, if you care to look for them. No—I'll talk to you about these birds, may-be tell you something about them; but I won't *examine* them Steed. I won't *investigate* them."

"What *are* your special interests then, sir?"

"You've been around here some days. You tell me," the old man said, with another penetrating look at the undercover man from beneath his shaggy brows.

"Well I've noticed Mallard and Pintail, of course. And Cur-lew. And Brent geese and Grey-lags and Pinkfeet. Grebes. Divers. Sheldrakes and Tufted Ducks . . . Let's see—Oh, yes.

and Wigeon and Teal. And I thought I saw a pair of Goosanders one evening."

"You *have* done your homework well, haven't you, Steed? But you saw no Goosanders here: those were Merganser—*Mergus Serrator*, you know. Still, it's a natural enough mistake, I suppose . . . You were asking about the blessed rarities we get. We have a few you *won't* have seen on the marsh at Bratby—Gadwall, for instance. Shovelers. Garganey and Smew. Even Hodder Ducks and Black Scoters."

"By Jove! One hadn't even heard of the last two!"

"Aha! They're both from the Order *Anseres*, you know—*Oidemia Nigra Nigra* and *Somateria Fuligula* in the Linnaeus classification. But whereas almost all the ducks and geese we get here are winter migrants—flying South from the Arctic to take advantage of our relatively mild winter—these two bracket themselves with the Swallows and Nightingales and other perchers: they're in fact *summer* migrants. They fly up here from North Africa to nest, because it's cooler!"

"But are they here already, then? Is there some kind of overlap?"

For a moment Sir Albert appeared to be disconcerted by the question. He exchanged a glance with Charnley, looked down at his hands on the desk top, and then said rather testily: "Yes, yes, of course there is bound to be a certain amount of overlap at times—not much, mind you, but a little. The earliest of the summer migrants have often arrived and started looking around for nests before the last stragglers have pulled themselves together and flown back to the North, you know."

"Was one correct in thinking you had said the Scoters and—Hodder Ducks, was it?—had in fact already arrived this year?"

"No, no, no. Certainly not." Warbeck-Simner looked quite cross. "I don't know what can have given you that idea at all."

"But one distinctly had the impression that you had *said*—" The vague man with the glasses appeared all of a sudden to have become persistent. The ornithologist cut him short.

"If anything I said gave you that impression, you were mistaken. They're not due for another week or two yet. Now—you were asking earlier about how we observed our visitors . . ." With the Professor following close behind, he led Steed up one carpeted and three bare and dusty flights of stairs to the observation room at the top of the tower. The second, third and fourth floors of Turret House, so far as Steed could see, stretched away on each side of the landings naked and unused. There was no sign in the dust which lay thick in the corridors of the footsteps either of the egregious Worthington and his men or of any retainers, trusty or otherwise.

The undercover man expressed admiration for the ingenuity of the Victorian forbears of Sir Hugh Mendip who had installed the *camera obscura*. He examined the great ground-glass screen and the little television camera trained forever upon it; he exclaimed at the fidelity of the inverted image swimming serenely in its greens and browns and yellows as the wind stirred the grasses on the marsh far below. He exclaimed in schoolboyish pleasure as Charnley spun the smooth iron wheels and inclined the oiled ratchets to control the prisms at the top of the dark tunnel leading from the observation screen to the open air above. "All the twist controls on the console in the study do," Charnley said, spinning the scanner wheel briskly, "is to duplicate what we're doing now—Look! There's your Pochard! You can pick out the scarlet beak even from here, can't you?—to duplicate what we are doing with rather less—er—effort."

"Even Worthington could hardly do better, could he?" Sir Albert chuckled, taking the scientist by the arm.

The Professor exploded into laughter, glancing slyly at Steed as he moved towards the stairs. "Oh, no," he wheezed. "Even Worthington would be hard put to it—very hard put to it—to better this!"

"Worthington?" Steed allowed a polite interest to tinge his voice.

"Oh, my dear chap!" Warbeck-Simner gasped, dabbing his eyes with a handkerchief. "A private joke. Just a little private jest. You really must forgive me—beastly rude in front of another fellow."

Later, when they had gone back downstairs and looked over part of Charnley's laboratory, the ornithologist succumbed once again to a fit of the giggles and kept nudging the scientist and digging him in the ribs as they conducted Steed over the bird museum.

The old stables and coachhouse had had a lot of money spent on them when Warbeck-Simner first installed his museum there. One wing of the L-shaped block was entirely given over to row upon row of glass cases displaying stuffed birds. Many of the displays were complicated and ingeniously arranged, the suggestions of the exhibits' habitat being especially well carried out.

Ducks, geese and other waterfowl predominated, but there was a considerable section on seabirds, another on land migrants from Africa, and a third devoted to the avifauna of the Mediterranean littoral. In the other wing were Warbeck-Simner's workshop, a fully equipped taxidermy room, a small cartographical section full of cabinets of flat drawers housing distribution maps and migration charts, and what he called the research department. Basically, this was a series of insulated glass compartments in which birds' behaviour could be observed and photographed while such variables as temperature, humidity and atmospheric pressure were manipulated by the experimenter. Beyond it were two more narrow doors, but neither of the two men made any move towards opening them or mentioning what they might hide.

Finally, Steed was shown the aviaries. These varied from small cages in which a tall man would have to stoop to vast, domed edifices thirty or forty feet high. They stretched in a haphazard pattern from the yard, across a neglected garden, and down a slope to the marsh—where a narrow boardwalk led for several hundred yards out across the flats.

"Many of them, as you see, are empty," Warbeck-Simner said. "This is because we do not as a rule reckon to have a permanent collection of foreign birds here—and the native ones you can see, after all, all around you. What we do when we want to —er—examine one of our guests from the sanctuary more closely is to walk out along the catwalk and secure him (or go and fetch him in the Carvel dinghy, for that matter), and then bring him back for a temporary spell in one of the aviaries. As soon as we have finished our researches, the doors are opened— and out he flies again . . ."

A number of the larger cages near the house were, nevertheless, reasonably well inhabited, Steed saw as they strolled back. He noticed Pelicans, Storks, Cranes, a variety of hawks and buzzards, and even a cage shared by a couple of bald, leathery looking birds on long legs and a small flock of Flamingos.

"This migration business now, Sir Albert," he said as they passed a pile of empty bird crates in a corner of the yard. "Tell me : if you went up, say, to the Lake District and netted some birds; if you brought those birds back here and kept them in an aviary; and if—when it was time for them to migrate—you crated them up and *took* them to wherever they come from . . .

when it was time for them to come back here the following year, would they fly here or to the Lake District?"

"To the Lake District, of course. Moreover, if I let them go here before it was time for them to migrate, they go back to the Lake District first. You can't mess them about, you know!"

"And if you kept them here *after* it was time for them to go?"

"As soon as you release them, they go. Right away. We've tried that one, Steed."

"And if you kept them right through the time they're usually away, crating them up and sending them back only a day or two before they would normally have been coming *back* again . . .?"

"They'd return here on the normal day, just as though nothing had happened—staying the necessary number of days—hours for that matter—in their other home until the time for departure came. But you'll be making your readers' brains reel with these technicalities . . . surely I've said enough? Come, let me fetch you a glass of sherry wine."

Back in the study, Warbeck-Simner produced a very tolerable *manzanilla*. Pouring a small amount into each of three elaborate and rather beautifully chased goblets, he turned to Steed and said conversationally: "You must forgive me attending to this myself; the servant only comes four times a week—and this is not one of her days. Just one more reflection of the sorry state of affairs things have been allowed to come to."

"Oh, you do feel that, too, sir, do you?" Steed picked up his cue adroitly.

"Feel it, Steed? Feel it? One cannot avoid feeling it: it is positively *hammered* into one at every turn, is it not? You and I, Steed—people out of the top drawer—and the brains like Charnley here . . . all the people with *class*, to use an unfashionable word—we're being driven to the wall. And there's not one chap with the beastly guts to do anything about it. Not one, is there, Charnley?"

"Not a single one."

"Oh, I do so concur," Steed said mendaciously. "I simply could not agree with you more. But really, why don't—I mean to say, surely . . . that is to say, couldn't one *do* something about it?"

"Aha! Never give up hope, my dear man. *Nil desperandum* Steed! Beneath the acquiescent surface, things are moving. I'm not at liberty to say more just now—but rest assured, *our* kind is going to come into its own again, mark my words. And when it does . . ."

"Yes, Sir Albert . . . when it does . . .?" Steed prompted.

"When it does," Charnley interposed glibly, "the balance will be redressed at last. By rights, Sir Albert should be the Earl of Bratby, you know. But small-minded people have denied him the rewards he deserves."

"The seventeenth Earl," Warbeck-Simner said, flushing a dull red. "There have been Warbecks and Simners at Bratby and Hornham for over four hundred years. And then, just because some common, cheap, jumped up little jack-in-office of a county court judge decides—" He broke off, choking with rage. "Some people have it in them to rule, to lead; it's bred in them," he added in a strangled voice. "But the majority of our masters today are totally unfitted for *any* kind of responsibility. If I had my way, I'd have half of them put down, destroyed, before I let them anywhere *near* a job where they exercised any control over other men's lives, really I would—I say, look here! My dear chap, your glass is empty! Do let me . . ."

"Very nice of you, sir," Steed said. "It's a delightful wine. Thank you . . . but aren't you taking some more yourself?"

"No, no. Charnley and I drink very little alcohol, you know. Bad for the wind—and we've got to keep in tip-top condition, really fit, for this game."

"I'm afraid I don't quite . . ."

"Out on the marsh, you know," the scientist explained. "We have to keep dashing along the jolly old catwalk to bag the chaps we want to examine."

"Yes—jumping over streams, too. And rowing the old boat about and going for tramps in the early morning. Takes it out of you at our age unless you're fighting fit, dash it all."

A few minutes later, Steed snapped shut his notebook, put it away in his pocket, and bade his hosts farewell with many protestations of gratitude.

"Not at all, not at all," Warbeck-Simner said affably, leading Steed to the front door while Charnley unobtrusively switched on the closed-circuit television set. "Only too glad to help, old chap. Besides, it's so seldom one sees one of *us*, these days . . . I say, what a funny little motor! What is it? Don't you find it terribly cramped in there?"

"It's a Lotus Elan, actually. I suppose it is rather small—but there's more room than you'd think inside. And it does have its—er—advantages, you know."

"I suppose so. Mind you, we're not frightfully well up in motors. For the few journeys we make into Cambridge or Ely, we find our old Austin"—he pronounced it Orsten—"perfectly satisfactory."

"Yes—well, thanks again. You chaps have been most awfully decent. See you again some time, I hope . . ."

And with a final wave of his hand, Steed ran down the steps of the great portico, strode across to where he had left the Lotus on the far side of the gravelled turning circle, and inserted his 74 inches behind the wheel.

Warbeck-Simner watched the car turn round. Tyres crunched on the gravel, then, with a crisp crackle from its exhaust, the Lotus swung out of sight behind the shrubbery masking the entrance to the drive. He waved again as it reappeared further down the causeway—but the low roof of the car, and his own elevated position standing at the top of the steps, prevented him from seeing if the gesture was returned. He turned and went back indoors to join Charnley at the monitor screen.

"There we are, then," the scientist said as the streamlined shape shot into vision, braked for the entrance, and then nosed slowly out on to the road through the open gates. "He's clear of the premises anyway!" He switched on the second circuit and watched as the *camera obscura* relayed the Lotus streaking along the dyke towards Bratby.

Warbeck-Simner grunted. "I hope the young ass doesn't break his neck," he said. "It seemed to me that the driver's door wasn't properly fastened when he left . . . Anyway, let's stroll down and shut the gates, shall we? We'd better have a look at the retainers, too—we haven't done the rounds today, don't forget."

"Good gracious me, so we haven't! Your young man quite put it from my mind. Yes, my dear fellow—let's go at once . . ."

But the door of the Lotus had been left unfastened deliberately. With the hand-throttle set and the gear lever in second, Steed had rolled neatly out of the car while it was momentarily hidden by the shrubbery, as Emma Peel—after waiting all morning curled up in the space behind the front seats—had slid across to take over the wheel. So far as Charnley and Warbeck-Simner were concerned, they had seen an expected guest step from an apparently empty vehicle; they had seen him get back into it when he left—and they had watched the vehicle itself leave the property. Since cars did not drive themselves, it was obviously a reasonable assumption that the driver had gone with it. And yet —the undercover man reflected—here he was, safely inside the ring of booby-trap defences, undetected and unsuspected. How fortunate that Mrs Peel should have chosen to buy a car whose roof-line was so low that a tall man standing on the steps of Turret House was unable to see who was driving it !

The two men passed within six feet of Steed's hiding place in a clump of laurel and went on towards the gates. A faint smile curved his lips as he watched the tall figure and the short one recede down the long drive. Then, rising silently to his feet, he moved wraith-like through the bushes and sprinted across the gravel towards the open front door.

# 13

## BELOW STAIRS FOR EMMA...
## ...AND STEED IN A CUPBOARD!

AFTER lunch, Emma Peel drove from her hotel at Bratby to the rented cottage on the shingle spit across the marsh, threading the little car expertly through the winding lanes, past the old Martello tower, and down the rough track behind the storm beach to where Steed's Bentley loomed monolithically against the reeds. She dumped a large paper sack full of provisions on the cottage table, unloaded a quantity of bottles from the Lotus's boot and checked them against a list in Steed's handwriting, and then tacked a big rectangle of thin cardboard over the broken pane in the window.

A thin drizzle was blowing in from the sea as she set off on foot towards the tarred board building where Bella and her father lived. Before she had trudged far through the shifting shingle, moisture was beading her eyebrows, plastering her hair across her face in long strands, and furring with small droplets the black and white concentric circles of a wool beret she had pulled down over one ear. Above black leather boots and trousers, a short white vinyl raincoat glistened as she walked.

Bella and the old man were doing something technical to a length of fine-gauge net draped along the rail of a ramshackle verandah running from back to front of the building. The sea had withdrawn into an oily calm and they must have heard her striding across the stones long before she reached them. But neither of them looked up until she had gained the shelter of the verandah.

Nevertheless, the girl bade her good afternoon civilly enough, and the poacher looked up momentarily to enquire what they could do for her.

"I thought you might like to know," Emma said, "that the results of the other post-mortems we told you about were—in the main—much as we feared they would be."

Reeves grunted. "Don't know why you bothered to come all

this way across the beach just to tell us that," he said. "What d'you expect us to do? Dance for bloody joy?"

"Oh, *Pa*!" Bella Reeves expostulated. "Don't take any notice of him: it's just because he's upset that anything like this could have happened through us, even indirectly."

"No, you miss my point," Emma said. "What I'm really here to say is that we're very much afraid—practically certain, really —that the *moral* responsibility for those deaths may belong to your employers at Turret House . . ."

"That doesn't surprise me. Forever messing about in that laboratory and then biting a person's head off when you ask a simple question! I *knew* there was something nasty going on there—and if it's ended in people getting killed, the police ought to be called in."

"You're off today: are you going back to Turret House to-morrow, Bella? Is it your day?"

"It's supposed to be. I'm meant to be there tomorrow. After yesterday, though, I'm not at all sure that I'm going to *be* there." The girl stood up and wiped her forehead with a sweatered fore-arm. Her dark eyes were blazing. "The way those two old monsters treated me, they'll be lucky if I *ever* go back to do their stinking work! Who do they think they are, anyway, treating people like dirt? What gives them the right to talk to you as if you were an idiot, I'd like to know?"

"You're thinking of—er—going on strike, as it were?"

"Yes, I am," the girl cried. "And serve them right, too, if I did!"

"You could help to serve them right quite literally," Emma said smoothly. "If you really wanted to. I mean help to make sure that they got what was coming to them."

"What do you mean?"

"Well, it's all to do with what Mr Steed was talking to your father about the other night, Bella. Mr Steed believes these men are up to no good and he's hoping to catch them red-handed while they're doing wrong."

"I don't see how I can help."

"It's a question of having somebody actually there—of being able to get a person in among them, as it were, to report on what's really going on in that house."

"But *I* couldn't do that. I wouldn't know—"

"No, Bella—listen. You could help by *not* being there—by actually going on strike tomorrow as you intended."

"I can't see how that would help."

"If you stay away and say nothing, just to spite them, all that will happen will be that you'll annoy them. And then you'll be out of a job . . . But if you do it my way, you can kill two birds with one stone."

"What's your way, then?"

"You stay away—but you telephone them and tell them you're awfully sorry, but you are ill. You say you feel very guilty about letting them down—would it be satisfactory if your cousin came on the same days until you were better again?"

"My cousin? But I don't *have* a cousin!"

"Your cousin Emma," said Emma Peel.

\*        \*        \*

At Turret House, Steed lay low while Warbeck-Simner and Charnley had a cold lunch. Afterwards, from one of the grimy, curtainless windows on the second floor, he watched them cross the yard to the laboratory. Half an hour later, Warbeck-Simner emerged and went into the museum—and in a few minutes Charnley joined him. For some time after that, the undercover man saw nothing of the two men. Then they began to make a series of journeys back and forth between the old stables and a corner of the yard, fetching bird crates and baskets from the stack Steed had noticed on his way back from the catwalk that morning.

They were too far away for him to hear what they were saying —but whatever task was occupying them appeared to be giving them a great deal of pleasure, for they were continually pausing to chuckle and slap one another on the shoulder. While they were thus safely engaged, Steed explored the whole of the second and third floors of Turret House. Not a door on them was locked —and not a single room was furnished, or gave any indication of having been used for decades.

Later, when he had seen the two men head away from the yard towards the aviaries, he ventured downstairs and discovered a small anteroom off the hallway which obviously acted as operations centre for the booby-trap defences surrounding the place at night. There were a number of small tape machines, each with a simple loop in place; there was an actuator fitted with code-labelled inputs marrying up with these; lockers housed measured and tagged lengths of wire in varying thickness, pulleys, guides, bolts for the crossbow, and so on; two huge carboys full of acid squatted in one corner; and there was a centrally placed indicator board equipped with coloured lights. These—duplicated in both the bedrooms upstairs, Steed discovered—corresponded to rooms in the house and various strategic points adjacent to it. The "magic eye" beams must be well placed and cleverly concealed ... for, as he saw with rueful admiration, his own progress from room to room and floor to floor had been duly charted by the different coloured illuminations winking their testimony from the wall. Fortunately there was a master re-set switch, and before he slipped unobtrusively from the house to make his unseen way to the museum, he had erased these electronic witnesses to his visit.

In the old coach house, he found a pile of glass-fronted cabinets awaiting repair and concealed himself behind these to keep watch. The drizzle which had been blowing inland across the marsh in great clouds earlier had now given way to heavy rain, and for the greater part of the afternoon the monotonous drumming of this on the raftered roof far above his head was the only sound Steed heard. There was a small window near his hiding place, and through this he could see a segment of the rear of the property. Charnley and the ornithologist made several appearances on this restricted screen—carrying flat pans of food out to the aviaries, fetching more crates from the far end of the old walled garden, and once—resplendent in oilskins and sou' westers—walking far out along the board path, to return bearing two protesting Mallard, professionally held by the legs. Presumably these had been taken to the laboratory, for when the two men went through the museum later to Warbeck-Simner's workshop, they were again empty-handed.

Steed heard the rise and fall of their voices from the workshop, but he was too far away to make out the subject of the conversation. He was just about to risk a foray to seek a hiding place within earshot, when the workshop door opened and both men came out.

". . . really has got rid of the irritation problem and they don't scratch themselves," Charnley was saying, "then it seems we're past the final hurdle after all."

"Yes. It's just a matter of selecting the species and correlating the dates," Warbeck-Simner said. "The new alloy will be splendid, you can depend on it. But don't tell Worthington!"

Charnley erupted into the usual high-pitched giggle that this name always produced. "On no account," he wheezed. "After all, secrecy and surprise—those are the two elementary factors on which the entire . . ." The remainder of his words were lost as they went through one of the twin doors flanking the workshop and closed it behind them. Before the voices died away into a featureless mumble, Steed had a momentary impression of heat and light and movement as the door opened and closed—then he was once more alone with the rows of stuffed birds looking knowingly out from behind the glass with their beady eyes.

He would have to have a look behind those doors—the doors whose purpose was so ostentatiously not mentioned when he was shown over the museum earlier in the day. But there was already one thing he had found out in the comparatively short time he had been on the watch: Worthingtons and retainers notwithstanding, there wasn't a living soul billeted in the Turret House demesne except for Warbeck-Simner himself and Charnley . . .

\* \* \*

"So, you see, it'll be quite easy, really," Emma said to Bella Reeves. "I'll write down what you have to say on the telephone—then all you have to do is to lend me your bicycle."

"All right, then," the girl said dubiously. "What are you, then, anyway—a detective or something?"

"Not exactly a detective, but something after that sort of thing," Emma replied with a smile. "Kind of semi-official, shall we say?—Which means, by the way, that I shall be handing over intact whatever the old boys owe me for however long I'm there. You can keep the money, just as though you were there yourself."

"But I can't do that. It wouldn't be fair. After all, it's you who'll be doing the work!"

"Not at all, Bella. *You* are doing *me* a favour by giving me the chance to get in there. And naturally, I couldn't dream of offering to pay you for a favour—but the least I can do is let you keep the money you'd be earning if you *hadn't* done that favour!"

"I still think you ought to—"

"Besides which," Emma interrupted with a flash of inspiration, "I wouldn't be allowed to keep the money myself, anyway."

"Why ever not?"

"Regulations," Emma said mysteriously.

"Oh. Oh, I see. . . . Well, in that case . . . If you're sure . . ."

"Of course I'm sure. I insist. Apart from which, you'll be helping your boyfriend, you know."

"Mark?"

"Yes. Naturally he wants to get to the bottom of all this business of the tainted ducks. He could have been ruined over it, couldn't he?—Well, I mean, look at your own reactions when you thought *we* were after him!"

Bella laughed. It was the first time Emma had ever seen her face animated. Under the full, dark lips, her teeth were even and startlingly white. Her nose wrinkled at each side and a network of fine lines appeared at the corner of her eyes. She was, Emma suddenly realised, quite amazingly beautiful. "It *was* a bit strong, I must admit," she said. "But I didn't realise you were friends of Mark's . . . All right, let's call it a deal. You come down here some time after eight tomorrow morning, and I'll let you have the bike. Now I must be getting along—Mark and I have a date in a half hour."

"I'll run you out there in the car," Emma said. "It's a filthy night for cycling—and you can phone from my hotel on the way."

"Oh, is that the little Lotus? Is that yours?" Bella asked, her eyes shining. "I'd like that very much indeed."

She pulled on a pair of heavy wellingtons and buckled herself into the oilskin blouse she had been wearing when she surprised Emma and Steed disembarking from the dinghy. "If we dash up to the top of the shingle bank and then down the landward side," she said, "we can get a bit of shelter for the walk to your friend's cottage. It's murder along the beach when the wind blows rain in from the East . . ."

Reeves himself having departed on some secret and nocturnal mission some time before, she locked the plank door before turning her storm collar up round her ears, smiling at Emma, and stepping out into the weather. Together the two girls, the white and the black—Emma lean and elegant as a greyhound, Bella as voluptuous as a ripe apricot—bent their heads against the stinging rain and ran across the shining stones. Behind them, through the dusk, wind now tumbled the sea in jagged lines of ivory as the waves broke along the shore.

\* \* \*

It was nearly seven o'clock before Steed could satisfy himself that his unwitting hosts were safely at dinner. In the notebook

he had used during his interview with Sir Alfred that morning, he had also copied from the indicator board the disposition
of all the "magic eye" beams guarding the approaches to the
house. With this to guide him, he was able to work out a route
by which he could flit between the laboratory, the museum and
house, without revealing his presence, while Charnley and the
ornithologist were engaged elsewhere.

The two old men should be at least an hour over dinner, he
estimated. This should give him time to investigate those doors
near the workshop at the far end of the museum. He jumped
down from the window ledge from which he had seen the meal
begin, slipped across the wet cobbles of the yard, and re-entered
the museum, brushing the damp from his tweedy suit. Two
large stacks of crates, each labelled with the name of some bird,
now ranked themselves against the wall outside the doors—and
the doors themselves were open. Both of them, to his surprise,
led to a common lobby—and from this a flight of stairs led
downwards to the most astonishing of all Turret House's sur-
prises. On each side of a small office/anteroom, enormous display windows gave on to two zoological "natural habitat" rooms
—and both of them were seething with hundreds and hundreds
of live wildfowl.

The rooms were vast—far bigger than Steed would have
imagined possible, even with the excavations which must have
taken place. There was a strange and dreamlike quality about
them, an other-worldliness and an almost science-fiction *ambi-
ence* which divorced them from the drab realities of the wet
evening above as effectively as the armour-plated glass partitioned off their controlled atmospheres from the raw chill of
the old stables. Heat and light blazed behind the glass of the
left-hand room; between sand and rock, deep-channelled water
fringed with exotic flora teemed with bird life—there appeared
to be dozens and dozens of them. Several colonies of goose-like
creatures stood about at the edge of the water, wagging their
stumpy tails from side to side and nattering; two varieties of
duck—one with a distinctive blue-black head and a bright crimson bill—waddled up and down the shelving sand or floated
somnolently upon the surface; and seeded in among these were
a number of tall and elegant wading birds, beautiful black and
white shapes with long, upturned and curved beaks. On the
outside of the glass, in the fashion adopted by aquaria and
museums, small cards identified the species within—although

there was of course no means of marrying a particular card with any one of the many birds in sight.

There were four cards. One, headed *Order: Anseres*, read: GARGANEY ("Sarcelle d'éte"). *Anas Querquedula*—and carried underneath the legend *Lea Valley/Clapton/Hoddesdon/Fairhaven . . . 3-6/IV*. There were two cards headed *Genus: Oidemia*. One was labelled BLACK SCOTER ("Macreuse"). *Oidemia Nigra Nigra*; and the other HODDER DUCK ("Canard Quiroule"). *Somateria Fuligula*. Both of these captions carried a superior classification again reading: *Order—Anseres*. A fourth was labelled *Order—Limicolae*, with underneath the words: AVOCET. *Recurvirostra Avosetta*. The distribution legend beneath said *Halvergate Island/Birningham . . . 29/III*. Both Hodder and Scoter ducks was identified as from *Ely/Waltham/Boston/Fairhaven/Tummel*. And the date in each case was given as *31/III—5/IV*.

Grey was the colour predominating in the right hand room. The vegetation and décor was that of the tundra—mudbanks, sedge, reeds and thin channels of cold-looking water. Steed was able to recognise all four species of ducks massed along the water's edge: Gadwall, Teal, Pintail and Common Pochard. The labels outside the glass added the information that the Teal complemented the Garganey inasmuch as it was known in France as "Sarcelle d'hiver"; that the Pochard was of the genus *Nyroca*; and that all four species were to be found in localities described as *Lea Valley/Clapton/Waltham/Tummel/Bristol/Walberswick/Ely*.

Steed whistled softly as he read the legends, copied the names, dates and other data into his book, and studied the panels outside each room which controlled the temperature, pressure, humidity and air movement inside. He was just about to climb the stairs and make his way back to the house when the door of the museum opened. Footsteps crossed the floor, another door was opened—and feet began to descend the stairway to the two "conditioning" rooms. Steed glanced around him desperately. Although he had no misgivings about handling the two old men, both together if necessary, it was absolutely vital that he should not be discovered at this stage of the game. His eye fell at last on a tall, steel stationery cupboard beside a desk placed to command both rooms. It was unlocked—and beneath the lowest shelf there was a sizeable space. In a flash, he was in, crouching down, and pulling the door shut from the inside.

Whoever it was coming down the stairs reached the bottom, hesitated by the observation windows, and then crossed the room to the desk. There was a shuffling of papers, the squeaky scratch of a pen. In a few minutes, more footsteps descended the stairs and a low-voiced conversation began.

Only a few sentences had been spoken before Steed realised for the first time that Sir Albert Warbeck-Simner—and probably Professor Charnley, too, for that matter—was hopelessly insane.

After about ten minutes of talk, both men went back upstairs and out into the wet darkness "to take a dekko at the traps," as Sir Albert said. As soon as he heard the outer door close, Steed slid out from the stationery cupboard and made his way back to the ground floor. There was—he was almost sure he remembered—a telephone on the bench in Warbeck-Simner's workshop. If only it should prove to be an outside line . . .

He was in luck: the number in the centre of the dial was different to that in the study; the workshop did have a separate line. Smiling slightly, he pulled the instrument towards him, lifted the receiver, and asked the operator in a low voice for a London number.

*     *     *

Bella arrived in Mark Lurchman's private suite at the "Ely Cathedral" as black and as glistening and as frisky as a seal. The hotelier was standing looking out of the big double windows at the rain when she burst in. He swung his short, broad-shouldered body round and held out his arms as she hurled herself across the room at him. "Oh, Mark!" she exclaimed. "Oh, darling, it's good to see you! How are you? What have you been doing? Is everything all right? Has there been any more trouble about—"

"Just a minute, just a minute, just a minute!" Lurchman laughed, holding her off at arms' length. "One thing at a time, Bella. Hold hard and give us a chance to kiss you Hello, then!" Placing his strong, square hands one either side of the cold, slippery stiffness of the oilskin, he drew her slowly towards him again and kissed her warmly on the mouth.

"Oh, never mind about my silly questions, Mark," the girl said, leaning back and staring at his face. "Just let me look at you and hear you say everything's going to be all right." She seized his hands, held them together with her own, and laid her flushed and rain-wet cheek against the dark hairs outlining the backs of his fingers.

"Of course everything's going to be all right," he said gently. "I can't see what you're worried about . . . Oh, Bella darling! Really you are the most beautiful—quite the most beautiful creature . . ."

He brushed the drenched hair back from her forehead with one hand and then cupped her face in his palms as he gazed long and intensely into her smouldering eyes.

"You're earlier than I expected. Who was it gave you a lift in that sports car?" he said possessively at last.

"That was Mrs Peel—you remember, darling: the girl who came to dinner here with that man Steed on that awful evening—"

"Of course. I saw Steed yesterday, as a matter of fact. There's —er—something he'd like us to do for him."

"Us?"

"Well, yes. You and me—more strictly, perhaps, the society."

"The film society? What on earth has the Boston and Hornham Amateur Film Society to do with Steed? Why doesn't he leave us alone? I've already helped Mrs Peel . . . probably more than I should. Mark—I don't want us to get mixed up in this, whatever it is."

"Bella, we haven't much choice. Or at least I haven't."

"Why not?"

"Well—Steed did me a favour once, years ago. A very big favour, as a matter of fact. And he's been good to me about this wretched affair of the duck. You don't think we wouldn't have had a lot more trouble from the police if he hadn't pulled strings, do you?"

"I suppose not. But—"

"Darling, I have to help him. *You* don't have to if you don't want to—the decision's entirely yours."

"If you're in it, Mark, so am I. It's us as a *thing* that I don't want involved—not me personally . . . Anyway, what do we have to do?"

"Very little, actually. It will be good practice for us—and it *should* have the extra advantage of ridding the neighbourhood of something very nasty indeed . . . if Steed's right. And if it does come off."

"Yes, but what *is* it, Mark? What will be good practice?"

Lurchman laughed his deep laugh, his blue eyes twinkling

brightly behind the great blade of his nose. "We simply have to set a little scene," he said. "Very good exercise in ingenuity. We have to create an atmosphere, to arrange a set—and make it one hundred per cent convincing . . ."

"What scene? What atmosphere?" Bella asked, interested in spite of herself.

"Steed's got to let me know. But it'll almost certainly involve the use of all the arc lights we have, the limes—and we may even have to take The Brute."

"The *Brute*! What on earth's that?"

"It's the in-group name for that enormous bloody spotlight thing we bought second-hand from the film studios last month."

"Oh, *that* . . . Well, what do we have to do with all these?"

"Transport them across some ridiculously difficult terrain and set them up secretly on location—and then play out a little scene as extras. It's not going to be at all easy."

"It begins to sound fun, Mark. Tell me more—and who's going to be in on it? Not the whole society, surely?"

"Good God, no! That's what's going to make it difficult. Just you and me—and your father . . . Steed's apparently got round him some way or another! . . . and a bloke Steed's bringing up from London to help work the lights when we've got them all in place. Plus Steed himself and Mrs Peel, of course."

"What do we have to do as extras? And who are the principals?"

"Depends on the scene Steed wants set. Just loll about in the middle distance and lend local colour, as far as I know. So far as the principals are concerned, these are going to be your—er—employers, though they won't know it, and me!"

"You?"

"Yes. Apparently I shall have to find some excuse to persuade the old boys to take a drink with me—several drinks in fact! Pure type-casting, of course: I shall simply be playing myself!"

"But Mark, it sounds fascinating! What about Steed, though? Where does he fit in? Do tell me more."

"I fancy he prefers to hover about in the background—in effect he'll be directing, as it were. I can't tell you any more, because I honestly don't know what in hell it's all about."

"Well, what shall *I* have to do, then?"

"So far as I know, I think you have to sit about looking glamorous in a bikini—a part you're *well* qualified to play, my pet. Talking of which, for God's sake get out of those things!

Our dinner'll be almost ready—and what's the point of your keeping sprauncy clothes here if you're not going to wear 'em?"

Bella grinned. She unbuckled the glistening oilskin and hung it up behind the door. "Help me off with these boots, Mark," she said, "and then I can dress in a fitting way for your food. May I use your bedroom?"

"Be my guest."

He crossed the comfortably furnished room to a heavy sideboard, poured himself a whisky from a cut-glass Waterford decanter, pulled a cord to draw the floor-length curtains across the windows, and stood sipping reflectively as he listened to the rain hammering at the panes.

"Hook me up, darling?" Bella Reeves was back in the room, unconcernedly manhandling one full breast into the cup of a black satin brassière. She held the edges of the garment together behind her back against the pull of the elastic, backing up to Lurchman so that he could manipulate the fastener. From the waist downwards, a crimson tie-silk dress lasciviously hugged her heavy thighs, its scanty top falling forwards while she fixed the bra. Lurchman set down his glass and took the two elasticated edges from her fingers, his pulses quickening as he pulled the material against the swell of her moist, cool flesh. Minutely, his eyes followed a cascade of tiny black hairs tracing the course of her spine. And suddenly he released the brassière, his hands snaking round to the front of her body to cup the breasts as they quivered free. The nipples were hard against his palms as he spun her round to face him and sunk his mouth on hers. Her tongue flickered between parted lips and her hands came up behind his shoulders to cradle the back of his head as she swung herself against him.

"Oh, Mark," she breathed. "Oh, Mark—don't do this to me ... the dinner—we'll be late for your dinner!"

"Don't worry," he panted, kissing her on her upturned eyes, "in honour of the coming Spring, both the first two courses are cold ..."

\* \* \*

By eleven o'clock, most of the ageing members of The Club—that gloomy establishment hiding behind the Nash portico near Prunier's in St. James's Street—had tottered down the curving staircase and sent the porter in search of a cab. One reading lamp still cast a pool of light into a corner of the funereal smoking room, however. Into it, from two of the shabby leather armchairs with which the room was dotted, there projected two pairs of legs—each pair stretched out, crossed at the ankle, and clothed in dark blue trousering bearing a faint chalk stripe. The rounded toecaps of two pairs of black shoes winked brightly under the electric bulb.

"Extraordinary thing," the august voice of the man called His Nibs said from the shadows behind one pair of legs. "Most extraordinary—in fact I'd never have believed it if I hadn't heard it from young Steed meself. Extraordinary!"

There was a deep sigh from somewhere on the far side of the pool of light. And in a thick Highland accent, on the exhalation of the breath, the single syllable:

"Aye."

"I mean to say, it's all very well, Mackinlay," His Nibs continued in an aggrieved tone, "but if these two old fools were to get away with their crackbrained scheme, there'd be the very devil to pay. The very devil."

"Aye."

"Young Steed's just told me—had him on the telephone not more than an hour ago—he's told me the whole story. Mind you, I knew something very fishy was up as soon as we heard the first reports on all these so-called heart attacks. But I never realised it'd be quite as bad as this."

"No. Ye'd hardly be realisin' that."

"D'you know what these two rascals are planning, Mackinlay?"

General Mackinlay was Head of Security, from which exalted but elastic position he had the twin tasks of keeping the country sane and on even keel—and carrying out the wishes of His Nibs. "Ye did mention it over tea," he said drily now. "But likely ye'll be givin' it a wee bit goin' over again."

"That rogue Charnley has synthesised this vicious derivative of Curare and evolved a soluble, crystalline form that can be moulded into pellets . . ."

"Aye."

". . . And they're going to stow pellets in the ankle rings on these damn birds when the birds are due to fly here from wherever it is, and the blasted creatures'll fly over and land in our reservoirs and paddle about—and the poison'll dissolve, and . . . and Bob's your uncle!"

One pair of ankles in the lamplight uncrossed themselves,

then recrossed the other way over. "How can they tell the birds'll fly to our reservoirs?" General Mackinlay asked. "From over there, I mean."

"Because they've nabbed the birds over here while they're *on* the blasted reservoirs, that's why, Mackinlay. They visit a reservoir they want to poison, just before the migrants are due to leave for, say, Morocco—or Stavanger, for that matter. And they bag these birds and *keep* 'em here all the time they would normally be in Morocco or Stavanger or wherever—keeping them in artificially simulated conditions matching whichever of those places they come from. Then, just before the birds are due to fly *back* here, they ship 'em out home and let 'em loose. Sure enough, promptly on schedule, the birds'll fly over—and there you are."

"Why not go out there and prime the birds with poison just before they left, instead of keeping them here all winter?"

"Because, you great loon, they couldn't identify which of the millions of birds there were coming *here*! It's only by getting them from the target area, as it were, that they can be sure of hitting it again. They go to and from the same places every year, you know."

"Aye, I know. Forbye—"

"The only other thing they could do would be to put the poison in place just before they *left* here—but it would never last all the while they were away: it'd merely poison all the people in Norway or Morocco. And the aim of the operation, Steed says, is to poison all the people in London. And Birmingham. And Glasgow and Edinburgh and Chester."

"Aye."

"I must say, that fellow Warbeck-Simner was pretty damned odd at school. He was years junior to me, of course—but one heard things, you know. They filtered up . . . Still, I never thought it'd come to this!"

"Likely ye'll be wantin' a platoon of men to go in and clean the place up then?"

"Well, no—not yet."

"But for why?"

"Various reasons. Steed says—and I agree with him—that it's no earthly use just nabbing them both. That would stop them going off with one set of birds—but would it necessarily end the operation? We don't know. There may be confederates,

here or abroad. There may be other birds, more poison, somewhere else . . ."

"Aye. I suppose so."

"Steed wants to trick them into giving away the whole crack-
pot plan—catch 'em red-handed, as it were—so that we *know*,
absolutely, that we've got the whole shebang in the bag. Apparently the balloon's due to go up any time now—and his own
scheme's mad enough to work, in theory at least. It's the only
kind that would, I fancy—because both these chaps are batty;
absolutely barmy, the pair of them. Must be."

"Aye. But ye've no told me just *why* we've all to die from
the poisonin' like this. What's to be gained? Whose cause are
they advancin'?"

The second pair of feet moved : they jerked abruptly back out
of the circle of lamplight as His Nibs sat forward in his chair
and rested his forearms on his knees. A gnarled hand with a pipe
in it appeared in the radiance. "That's just it, Mackinlay," he said
vehemently, stabbing the stem towards the lean, lined face he
could barely see in the shadows. "We simply do not know. We
have no idea, and that's the truth of it. This is why I've agreed
to allow Steed to go ahead with his plan to expose the whole
dratted thing."

"Aye. Maybe . . . But would it no be better—"

"The only leads we have to possible accomplices or organisations have both resulted in dead ends. There's nothing else we
can do. Perhaps I'll be asking you later for your platoon—even
if it's only to stand by. For the moment, I'm sending Benson up
to help Steed, and that's it."

General Mackinlay sighed again. "Aye," he said. "But I still
have a mind—"

"Oh, Mackers, for Heaven's sake dry up!" His Nibs said
crossly. "The trouble with you, my dear chap, is that you talk
too much . . . Now come on : leave it to me and have one for
the road. *Parsons!*—Two more large whiskies, please . . ."

\*　　　\*　　　\*

At five minutes to nine the following morning Jim Reeves loaded
a quantity of dead birds into the panniers of an ancient motor
cycle; Benson swore moodily as he waited to thread a Land
Rover through a blocked roundabout on the North Circular
Road; Bella Reeves turned warmly over in bed and bit Mark

Lurchman on the shoulder—and Emma Peel arrived outside Turret House on a bicycle.

She dismounted by the massive brick posts flanking the drive and wheeled her machine towards the centre portion of the wrought-iron gates. There was a small button inset in the metal. A second after she had pressed this, a sharp click presaged a crackling of static before a disembodied voice rasped: "What is it? What do you want, please?"

Emma leaned forward and spoke into the louvred steel box attached to the inner side of the gate. "It's Emma Peel, sir. Miss Peel who's cousin to Bella Reeves—I'm deputising for her while she's ill and it's her day today. I think she's telephoned you about me. May I come in now?"

"Ah, Miss Peel! Yes, of course, Bella did telephone about you. Most kind of you to help us out. Most kind . . . You're—ah —very punctual, my dear; very. Yes—come up at once, come up. Did Bella tell you about the yellow line? . . . She did? . . . Splendid! In you come then . . ."

An instant later there was a buzz from the mechanism controlling the lock, and Emma pushed open the gate and wheeled the bicycle inside.

Two hundred yards down the road, screened by the bushes masking a lay-by and out of range of the *camera obscura*, Steed yawned, stretched, and rose from the back seat of the Bentley where he had been sleeping since he had emerged from the bird sanctuary just after midnight. He sat on the wide running board and reached for his binocular case. From the velvet-lined interior, he removed, instead of a pair of field-glasses, two cylindrical packages wrapped in brown paper . . .

Opening the first of these, he took out a miniature thermos flask filled with hot coffee. When he had undone the second, two hard boiled eggs in greaseproof paper, a buttered *brioche* and a twist of blue paper containing salt were revealed. Finally, he fished in his pocket and produced a small leather case about the size of a packet of cigarettes. He placed this beside him on the running board and turned a milled wheel projecting through the hide. ". . . o'clock News," a voice said softly within the case. "*There has been another rail disaster in Arizona. At Chequers last night, the Prime Minister received members of the cabinet, following . . .*"

Smiling contentedly, Steed began to peel an egg.

# 14

## EXIT A JOURNALIST!

AFTER finishing his breakfast, Steed plugged an electric razor
into a socket on the Bentley's dashboard and shaved. The wind
had freshened during the night and blown away the rain clouds.
Now beneath the high, pale sky the cold breath from the East
scoured the shingle and spilled over the dyke to undulate the
reeds and grasses of the marsh in long ripples. From the lay-by,
over the thrashing tops of the bushes which formed his own
protective screen, he could see branches tossing in the grove of
trees around Turret House.

He unlocked the long mahogany box below the Bentley's
nearside running board. This had originally been designed to
house a superior tool chest, but like certain other parts of the
old car had been somewhat modified by its present owner! From
the lengthy cavity within, he drew out a fitted dressing case
which had been specially made to measure, snapped open the
clasps, and took from it a carefully folded charcoal suit, socks,
tie, underwear, shoes, and a self-striped silk shirt in cream. It
was not yet ten o'clock and traffic on the road was light. Behind
the angular bulk of the Vanden Plas body with its erected touring hood, he was easily able to change in the lay-by. When he
was completely dressed, he packed away the clothes he had been
wearing before, took a high-crowned bowler hat and an umbrella from the back of the car, and re-locked the wooden box
below the running board. Finally, he took down the hood,
zipped the tonneau-cover over the Bentley's open body, pad-
locked the zipper tag to a ring on the scuttle, and walked, whistling, towards the gates of Turret House two hundred yards
down the road.

At first there was no answer when he pressed the metal button
in the gate. He paced up and down, clasping his umbrella behind
his back and listening to the roaring of the wind in the treetops,
while he wondered whether to have another go. He was just
approaching the gate for the second time when he heard the
familiar crackle, followed by Emma Peel's voice:

"Yes? Who is it please? Whom did you want?"

Steed leaned down towards the louvres. "My name is Steed. I am a journalist. Sir Albert kindly granted me an interview yesterday. I was wondering—as I had discovered a couple of supplementary questions—whether he would have the great courtesy to grant me another five minutes of his time?"

"Just a moment, please, Mr Steed. I'll enquire." There was the sound of distant voices mumbling, and then:

"Hallo? Steed? This is Charnley here. I'm afraid Sir Albert is not available for a few minutes, but I'm sure he'd be only too —er—delighted to see you. Why don't you come along in and wait?"

"Thank you very much, Professor: that's frightfully decent of you. It'll take me several minutes to get up to the house anyway, as I'm on foot."

"What did you say?"

"That I'm on foot."

"God bless my soul. On foot. Well, well, well."

There was a buzz from the lock and Steed pushed open the heavy iron gate and walked on to the causeway. Considering the amount of lethal machines concealed in its narrow width, it was amazing how innocent the strip of shrubbery and trees on each side of the driveway looked, he reflected as he tramped, swinging his umbrella, up towards the house.

Charnley had said nothing about yellow lines, so presuming he was supposed to be innocent of any knowledge of alarm systems, he walked deliberately to one side of the road when he came up to the double line of white posts linked by chain.

He had no sooner passed the first post than complete bedlam broke out all around him. The noise of Bloodhounds baying ullulated deafeningly from the shrubbery on all sides; frenetic yappings and the deep, growling barks of a Doberman sounded from nearer the house; there was a determined crashing in the undergrowth behind him; and over all, from all quarters of the compass, came the sound of a confused and unintelligible shouting. It was really most effective. Had he not known that the whole performance was simply a series of pre-recorded tapes set off by a "magic eye" beam and relayed through different speakers dotted about the grounds, Steed felt, he might well have been tempted to flee!

Charnley was waiting for him at the top of the steps. "My

dear young chap," he exclaimed, shaking hands, "you really must forgive me. I completely forgot to switch off the dogs of war. Must have given you a devil of a shock."

"The dogs of war?"

"Cry havoc, you know, and let loose the same. Just a little private joke—but come in, come in. I do hope you weren't scared."

"Not at all. Just a little surprised—especially as I could see no dogs, bellicose or otherwise."

"Ha, ha. Bellicose is good. Very good. I must tell Sir Albert. He'll be down in a moment, by the way. In the meantime, is there anything I can perhaps help you with?"

Steed had decided to pay this second visit in his rôle as journalist simply to see if he could possibly surprise some hint from one of the inmates of Turret House about their intentions. Birds of the summer migration were due to start arriving at any time now—and if they intended to crate any of those he had seen in the rooms below the museum, and take them either to North Africa or the North in time to release them for the flight back to England, they would have to be packing up and leaving in the immediate future. But it was vital to Steed to know when they were to leave, which place they were going to, and what species they had decided to use. Only with this information—in the event that he failed to spring the whole plan first—could he deduce the probable dates of arrival of birds carrying the poisoned pellets; for each species arrived each year on precisely the same date. And only with this information could he work out, from the notes he had taken in the conditioning rooms, which reservoirs the chosen birds would be likely to land on when they did come. He had therefore nothing to lose—and perhaps something to gain—by "stirring things up." So he replied to Charnley's query by saying:

"Not in connection with migration, thank you: there are just a couple of simple questions I have to ask Sir Albert. But you might be able to help me—or rather a friend of mine—on another matter."

"Really?" the Professor said warily. "What is that?"

"I believe you are a toxicologist of some note, sir, and that you studied in Brazil?"

"That is so. But I fail to see—"

"This friend of mine is a doctor, sir. He has diagnosed no

less than seven recent deaths in this neighbourhood as being due to a poison deriving from South America."

Charnley had gone quite pale. "Really, Mr Steed, I cannot for the life of me think why you should imagine I could be of any help," he stammered.

"If you studied toxicology in Rio, Professor," Steed continued remorselessly, his vague and diffident manner suddenly evaporating, "I imagine you must be familiar with Curare?"

"Indeed. Yes, of course I am familiar with it. An Indian drug."

"What would you say were its main characteristics?"

"Well . . . I—I . . . Well, I suppose that it totally paralyses all muscular activity, especially of the diaphragm and thorax—"

"Thus inhibiting the circulation and the action of the lungs so that the victim dies very quickly of asphyxia?"

"Er—precisely. Without losing consciousness, as it happens. The French have often used it as an extra anaesthetic in surgery. Its advantage is that it can aid surgery by making the patient *totally* relax the muscles—of the stomach, for example—and thus facilitate incision and manipulation."

"And its disadvantages?"

"That it is difficult to calculate accurately the very small amounts required—and that it is possible, without realising it, to operate on a *conscious* patient, since he cannot move a muscle to tell you of the agonies he is suffering . . . But what on earth has this to do with your friend and his diagnoses?"

"Does the word Helimanthine mean anything to you, Professor?"

Charnley had gone a ghastly colour. Beads of perspiration stood out on his upper lip and his forehead. "What—what—how dare you cross-examine me, sir!" he blustered "What, pray, do you know of Curare and—and Helimanthine?"

"I'll tell you," Steed said affably. "I know that Curare was discovered by Europeans soon after the discovery of South America in the late fifteenth century. I know something very like it was mentioned by Homer in the *Odyssey*. I know that it is an extract of the juices of a diversity of plants, the exact blend of which is a carefully guarded secret. And I know that Humbold saw it being prepared in 1800. Do you know about Humbold, Professor?"

"He said it was a mixture of vegetable juices and saps, cooked together and evaporated, filtered through a cone of banana leaves and then concentrated again," the scientist said sullenly. "And he also reported that the natives found the resulting concentrate too—er—runny, I suppose you'd say—for their purposes, so that they had to mix it with some bituminous substance to make it stick to the heads of their killing arrows and darts."

"Exactly. And because all the Curare we got in Europe was this sticky, bituminous concentrate, it was awfully difficult for the medical johnnies to separate out the active ingredients or measure accurate doses for clinical purposes. Until Bohm isolated Curarine—the active constituent of Curare—in 1912; and then proceeded to synthesise it chemically, so the profession no longer needed to rely on the import of supplies from Brazilian witch-doctors who wouldn't let them into the secret of its manufacture."

"So you can read an encyclopaedia, Mr Steed. I fail to see what this has to do with me, or why you should presume to come here—"

"I mentioned Helimanthine, Professor. How would you define that?"

"It's a—a—a synthesised drug. It's in effect a highly intensified version of Curarine . . . a hundred times more deadly and with the added advantage that it's soluble in water. But it's enormously difficult to make because several of the ingredients themselves never occur in a natural state and have to be synthesised first. Why—why are you so interested in this rare substance, Mr Steed?"

"Because the seven deaths my friend diagnosed were all due to the ingestion of Helimanthine, Professor . . ."

"Very well, Charnley: tell Mr Steed all about it!"—The voice boomed out from the doorway, where Warbeck-Simner's tall figure stood outlined against the light—"Tell him the truth: that you and you alone succeeded in synthesising Helimanthine where all the others failed; that we have succeeded, again, in manufacturing it in crystalline form; and that, via our friends the birds, we intend to use it to relieve this beautiful island of ours of many of the vermin at present infesting it . . ."

Steed swung round in his chair. "That's a very challenging statement, Sir Albert," he said. "It could almost be taken, by those with mass homicide on their minds, as a veiled threat."

"I'm a challenging man, Steed, as I should have thought you

might have realised by now. But I uttered no threat: merely a statement of fact."

"I'm afraid I don't quite understand."

"I think you understand very well. Nevertheless, I am prepared to dot the i's and cross the t's if you wish. First, though, let us take some coffee." He crossed the study to a hanging bell cord and pulled it. In a suspiciously short length of time, Emma —wearing a white vinyl apron over a simple black jersey dress, with no make-up and her auburn hair caught back in an Alice band—was standing in the doorway.

"Ah, Peel. We'll have the coffee now, if you please," Sir Albert said. "There will be one extra, as you see."

Emma bobbed down in a curiously old-fashioned parody of a curtsey and turned to leave, as Steed became the sudden victim of an apparent attack of coughing. The tray must have been waiting immediately outside the study door, for she reappeared instantly and began to hand round the cups and saucers.

"Thank you, Peel," Steed said gravely. "That smells very good."

"Thank *you*, sir."

"Very well, Peel: that will be all. You may go," Warbeck-Simner called, stirring his coffee as he moved across to his desk. "Now, Steed—you wish me to commit myself, no doubt?"

"I didn't say so. I was merely dashed curious about that remark of yours concerning the vermin, you know. If I were a news man instead of a feature writer—"

"*If* you were a journalist at all, Mr Steed. I think we can drop the pretence, if you don't mind. It will save you the embarrassment of trotting out your beastly little vacuities in an attempt to convince me that you are less intelligent than is the case; and it will spare Charnley and myself the tedium of watching you make a fool of yourself."

Steed made no reply. He sat, relaxed and well back in the chair to which Charnley had shown him, with his eyes fixed on the ornithologist's face. His umbrella stood between his knees and his hands were crossed over its handle. The bowler hat lay on the floor beside his chair.

"Were you a journalist," Warbeck-Simner continued evenly, "you would indeed have a story fit for a news department. For I tell you categorically that I intend to destroy the population of the greater part of London—and that of many other cities and areas as well."

"Why?"

"As a lesson. The fools have permitted the reins to fall into the wrong hands. Those whose mission it is to rule, to govern, to direct the lesser ones into paths where their meagre talents may most usefully be employed—they have been pushed aside. And the time has come to redress the balance. But first there must be a drastic purging, a cleansing, before I move in to assume responsibility."

"You're mad. Quite mad. You do realise that?"

"Madness is relative, Steed," the big man said coolly. "What was insane yesterday is normal practice today; what is madness to you and the great majority of unimportant people is perfectly sane to me. Besides, that is a quibble, a matter of semantics—what matters is the *fact* that I shall do as I planned."

"I see. It would, as you say, be a very good story. What makes you imagine that—even if I am not a journalist myself—I won't use it?"

"The fact that you will not be leaving here alive."

"Oh. Might one ask why?"

Warbeck-Simner picked up a photograph from the desk. "You're a fool, Steed, as I said. I confess I'm most disappointed in you. I had thought from your conversation at our first meeting that we might have much in common—but now I see that I was deceived, wilfully deceived. You have been poking and prying and peering into things which do not concern you—and like all nosey parkers, you must pay the penalty. Regrettably, Charnley and I had been dilatory in going the rounds of our little—ah—protective devices on the occasion of your first visit. Otherwise we would have known that some intruder had been blundering about on my property, and the evidence of your duplicity would have been to hand."

"Evidence?"

The ornithologist turned over the photograph in his hand so that Steed could see what it portrayed. The background was totally dark and the foreground was blurred with a moving branch—but between the two, arrested in a pose of astonishment, a man in a dark suit and bowler hat faced the lens with an umbrella held like a sword. Unmistakably, it was Steed himself.

The subject of the picture now smiled faintly. "Not a very good likeness, I'm afraid," he said. "The flash was in my eyes . . . I suppose the camera was automatically exposed when the trip wire set off that magnesium flare?"

"Certainly it was." It was Charnley speaking now "There's not a device in the grounds that doesn't have a purpose. You don't suppose the flare's put there just to startle you, do you?"

"I suppose not. Silly of me not to realise that. I should have guessed from the quality of the other—er—devices."

"The whole episode was silly—a reckless and immoral escapade which is going to cost you your life," Warbeck-Simner said severely. "I will not tolerate trespassers violating my property. I will not tolerate interference with my plans. And most of all I will not tolerate deceit."

"Assuming that one has been found guilty on those charges, is a condemned man allowed a last wish?"

"Condemnation, charges, guilty—these are terms implying a court, a trial, fixed penalties for a particular verdict arrived at by a given set of rules. There's no question of that in my system. I just decide if a given person is to be punished—and if so, how."

"'I'll be judge, I'll be jury, said cunning old Fury; I'll try the whole cause and condemn you to death'," Steed quoted softly.

"Precisely. You make my earlier point for me: much of Lewis Carroll's so-called nonsense is in fact profoundly sensible if looked at from the right point of view."

"The point of view of a monomaniac or a madman, for instance?"

"Relative terms again, Steed. You will not succeed in needling me. I have, after all, every card . . ."

"Then surely you'll not miss one. Deal it to me and grant that last wish—it's only for a piece of information. And you did promise to dot the i's and cross the t's, you know."

"What is it, then?"

"Tell me which species you are going to—er—honour with the task of being the harbingers of your brave new world. Which birds'll be the carriers of death?"

"I haven't made up my mind."

"Ask me another! Very well, then—who is Worthington?"

Charnley gave a little crow of laughter. He exchanged glances with Warbeck-Simner—and for a moment the big man, too, allowed a brief smile to soften his arrogant features.

"Worthington, Mr Steed?" he said. "Why *you* are Worthington. It's a private code name we invented for Them—for all the meddlesome, shortsighted and narrowminded fools who try to thwart the beneficial designs of superior intelligences such as Charnley here and myself. But, as you see, the day of reckoning

for the Worthingtons is at hand. So far as you yourself are concerned, we have a pair of nesting eagles in a rather special aviary.
They are vicious and ruthless in defence of their young—and
they have been kept, I regret to say, hungry. What a pity such an
engaging fellow should stray into their cage during a trespass-
ing expedition!"

"I'm not too hot on the straying, actually," Steed drawled
lazily. "You'll have to get me there, you know."

"Fortunately that contingency has been—er—provided for,"
Warbeck-Simner replied. "You presumed a moment ago to
bandy a quotation with me. Here is one for you. *Thou wretched,
rash, intruding fool*—farewell!"

As he spoke the last word, he pressed a button set in a platen
on his desk.

For Steed, the room and the two old men in it abruptly
whirled down to his feet and spun away into darkness as the
armchair in which he was sitting tipped silently backwards on
a hidden trapdoor and precipitated him down a slanting chute.

There was a brief rush of darkness, sensations of bruising at
elbow, head and knee, and then he was brought up on level
ground with a jolt that knocked the breath from his body. As he
scrambled automatically to his feet in bright light, he heard from
somewhere above the soft thud of the trapdoor swinging back
home.

"*Hamlet*, Act III, Scene IV, by Jove," he murmured as he
looked about him. He was on the floor of an underground aviary
—an earthed area about twelve feet by twelve which formed the
bottom of a shaft more than twenty feet deep. There were steel
bars lining the sides of the shaft, and these continued up beyond
its lip, forming a dome of about the same depth which projected
into the open air. At one side of this, there was obviously a caged
passage communicating with another aviary—for through an
opening as Steed gazed upwards a giant bird hurtled with a scaly
flapping of wings. It was indeed an eagle—and at that moment,
seeing him, it plunged downwards into the shaft with a scream
of rage . . .

The umbrella that the undercover man found himself still
grasping was his only weapon—and although it was steel shafted
and steel handled, in other respects it was perfectly normal.

He backed against the steel bars of the cage, his eyes fixed on
the descending bird, his mind, ice cold, drained of everything
but the vital necessity of keeping at a distance from it. A single

blow from one of its wings could break a limb, a twist of that cruel beak would lay flesh open to the bone, a convulsion of its claws could rip through sinew and tissue as easily as a butcher's cleaver through a hanging carcass.

Against the solid, barred wall of the shaft, he was a difficult target. For a moment, the eagle hovered, flapping, and then it struck downwards with claws outstretched. Steed was waiting. Delaying it until the last moment, he thrust violently and rapidly upwards with the ferrule of the umbrella, between the bird's rigid legs. The steel shaft struck the softest part of its belly, just below the breastbone—and while it was too blunt to penetrate the covering of strong feathers, the force of the blow, plus the enormous momentum of the eagle's striking descent, made an impact sufficient to send Steed sprawling to the ground and the bird reeling to the far side of the shaft, squawking its dismay. The secret agent was on his feet like a cat. In one fluid flow of movement he had hurled himself across the floor of the cage and leaped on the eagle before it could flounder into the air again. There was a brief maelstrom of movement, a flurry of arms, wings, feathers and legs—and then the steel handle of the umbrella had been crooked around the bird's neck, the shaft twisted once sharply in a certain way . . . and the great bird was no more a menace than the examples of the taxidermist's art which enlivened the corridors of the museum above.

Steed turned from the inert bundle of feathers to meet the attack of the eagle's mate, which was now winging with cries of fury from the opening leading into the aviary above. He could not use the same defence a second time, for the collision had buckled the long tip of the umbrella and it was no longer sufficiently inflexible to have the same effect. As the bird dropped down the shaft, he crouched in the angle of wall and floor, erecting the umbrella and holding it shield-wise above his head and shoulders.

The outstretched talons struck the taut nylon like a thunderbolt.

The whole of the umbrella's canopy vanished instantly in a criss-cross of black tatters. Steed was holding onto the shaft like grim death, however, and the charge did not succeed in wresting it from his hands.

The eagle wheeled in a tight circle and came in again. Again the shock of the impact almost knocked Steed to the ground. But, as before, the construction of the umbrella prevented the bird from getting to close quarters. When it struck for the third time, Steed adopted a different tactic. Rising slightly on his toes, he jammed the umbrella upwards as the wicked talons hurtled down towards its battered frame. Then, just as the iron-hard claws penetrated the remaining shreds of fabric, he twirled the shaft to entangle the curved toes and heels in the complications of the umbrella's ribs.

The ruse worked. The eagle's feet were fast caught in the damaged framework of the umbrella. With a great beating of wings, it sought to gain height. It was immensely strong—so powerful that its efforts nearly lifted the undercover man from the ground and the two of them, the man and the bird linked by the ruined umbrella, bounded from side to side of the shaft in a kind of grotesque slow-motion ballet. Finally, Steed could hold on no longer: he released the shaft and dropped his aching arms.

Freed of his weight, the bird bobbed upwards, flapping its wings thunderously as it fought to free its talons from the mesh of steel spokes.

Steed gasped for breath and reeled against the wall—then suddenly saw, to his astonishment, a length of hawser which had certainly not been there before dangling down the opposite wall of the shaft. It came into view over the lip of the hole into which the aviary was sunk, and reached almost to the floor. And it was still spiralling slowly from side to side, so it must only just have been dropped.

With a wary eye on the floundering eagle, he edged round the side of the cage until he reached the rope. Then, bracing his legs against the wall, he shinned up hand over hand. The bird was still blundering about all over the aviary, but it was obviously more interested in freeing its feet than in attacking him.

As he drew himself up to the lip of the shaft, he came face to face with the anxious countenance of Emma.

"Thank goodness!" she exclaimed as she opened a small wire door in the side of the cage and helped Steed through. "I was afraid we'd never get you out!"

Steed was dusting off the knees, elbows and shoulders of his suit. "I'm much obliged," he said formally. "Just where are those two murderous old rogues now?"

"Quite happy to leave you to a fate worse than whatever. They informed me that you had left and then went over to the laboratory."

Steed looked around him. The domed aviary from which he

had just emerged was one of a group of several isolated cages off to one side of Turret House. He had not particularly noticed it when he had been shown round the property the day before. Not far off, the old walled garden sloped down to the marsh.

"Does the laboratory have any windows facing the back of the property?" he asked.

"No, it doesn't."

"Good. Then I can make my way to the board-walk that leads out across the marsh without being seen."

"Yes—but hurry, Steed. They may be booby-trap-minded, but they do have duck guns, you know! If you run out right to the end of the catwalk, you'll find an old dinghy there. Don't try to get back to the dyke road; forget about the Bentley. You can collect it later. Head straight away from the house—there's quite a deep channel and the marsh isn't nearly so extensive that way. The old boys use it whenever they fetch supplies: it brings you to a landing stage just off the Ely Road."

"Splendid. Next time they can swim for it, then!"

"And Steed—what about *this*?" Emma said, gesturing towards the aviary and the giant bird still flapping inside it.

"Oh—leave the doors open and let him go. He's earned his freedom. Then our hosts can either think I'm Superman, or that he was a super eagle who's taken me off to his mountain eyrie. You can alibi yourself all right for my—er—miraculous escape, can you?"

"Yes, yes. I'll telephone you if anything at all seems likely to break . . . I assume the plan we arranged still goes through?"

"Of course, my dear. And I've a little chore to keep you amused while you wait for our friends to make up their minds."

"Really? What's that?"

"There was a rather splendid limerick which began with the challenging lines: *A vice both bizarre and unsavoury / Was that of the Bishop of Avery* . . . I've forgotten the middle bit, but it ended up with something concerning an underground aviary. In view of recent experience, I was wondering whether you might not bend your talents towards the composition of a version that was a little more—shall we say?—topical," Steed said lightly. He waved his hand gaily and ran down the path between the cages towards the marsh.

# 15

## OPERATION WORTHINGTON

For four days after Steed's escape from the eagle, nothing happened. Deliberately, in case she might be under surveillance, he kept away from Emma during the time she was not working at Turret House. Across the marsh, life in Bratby followed its sleepy routine. Benson arrived in the Land Rover and put up at the "Ely Cathedral" with Mark Lurchman. And Steed himself lay very low, not knowing what channels of information Warbeck-Simner and Charnley might have in the village. Most of the time he spent on top of the storm beach with his field glasses—a position from which he could command most of the surrounding area visually and yet still hear the telephone in the cottage if it rang. He saw Reeves and Bella several times down at the far end of the spit, busy recaulking and painting a boat, attending to their nets, and performing mysterious services for a variety of birds and beasts running about outside their shack. Benson and Lurchman bumped down the track in the Land Rover one afternoon to discuss certain arrangements with him. And a fierce gale blew up from the North in the night, dragging great breakers up from the shallow sea and pounding the shingle beach so that the darkness was filled with the thunder of waves and the rattle of receding stones.

The telephone rang just after lunch the following day. The wind had died down but the sky was overcast and lines of white capped rollers still marched in obliquely to the shore from the North. Steed was actually in the cottage and had scooped up the receiver before it had had time to shrill twice. Emma's voice sounded strained and anxious.

"Steed? It's on. They leave tomorrow morning."

"Ah! Peel, isn't it? I trust you're liking it in service."

"Look, Steed, don't—we don't have time for pleasantries. I've been given my notice and paid off. I'm supposed to be leaving right away and I can't find any excuses to stay here—I may have to put down the phone at any time if one of them comes back into the house. Alright?"

"Right, my dear." His voice was all at once alert and crisp. "Tell me what you can. Where are they going, first?"

"Morocco. They've put it about that they're going on holiday to Tunisia, but I managed to get a look at the air tickets. They're travelling by one of the charter lines—and they've booked two dozen crates of livestock as freight on the same plane."

"Have they indeed! If it's Morocco, then those crates will contain one or all of the species in the hot-room under the museum . . . No sign which one, I suppose?"

"No, none. But it'll hardly be all. The hot-room birds are all crated up—and there are *seven* dozen crates! I think they still haven't made up their minds which to take . . . But the birds from the cold-room have already been let loose—I can't *tell* you what a confloption that made!"

"One can imagine! . . . All right. We'll put Operation Worthington into action—starting, as the Americans say, as of now. You leave as soon as you like and cycle to your pub. I'll pick you up there later on . . . You did manage to execute all those little—er—commissions about the house that I dreamed up, did you?"

"Yes, I did."

"Excellent. Do you know what time tomorrow—"

"Steed!" Emma's voice was low, urgent and hurried. "There's someone coming. I must go now . . ." the receiver was quietly replaced.

The undercover man hung up and hurried out to the Bentley. There was a great deal to do—and not much time in which to do it. His plan to find out which species were to be used was daring and crazy. But it might work—so long as the wind held off and it didn't rain . . .

Half a dozen miles away across the flat countryside, two hands —one small and feminine, the other, on top of it, large and masculine—pressed down on the telephone receiver in the study of Turret House.

"I was too late to hear whom you were telephoning, Miss Peel," Sir Albert Warbeck-Simner said menacingly, "but I think you and I had better have a little talk . . ."

\* \* \*

At dusk that evening, a strange convoy set out from "The Ely Cathedral." In the lead, Steed's vintage Bentley carried beneath the cover zipped over the rear seats an inflatable rubber dinghy, a couple of duck guns, two suitcases full of certain "props", and a half dozen cardboard boxes containing seven-inch spools of tape. In the passenger seat beside the undercover man Jim Reeves sat with his hands nervously clasped around his knees. Behind them, still wrapped in overcoat and muffler, Benson piloted the Land Rover with Bella Reeves beside him. The back of the vehicle was loaded to the axles with studio flood- and spot-lights on telescopic stands with cast-iron bases, a jointed framework for a semi-cyclorama, a huge roll of nylon for the screen itself, a 35 mm. film projector and three cans of stock, and a quantity of semi-tropical plants in pots. Bringing up the rear, Mark Lurchman's E-type Jaguar—which carried only a case of Champagne apart from its owner—seemed almost dull by comparison.

The three vehicles headed South until they reached the left turn for Bratby at Little Hornham church, when Steed pulled in to the side of the road and waved the others down. He got out of the Bentley and walked back to the Land Rover.

"This is where we part company for the time being, Benson," he said, leaning in at the window. "Mr Lurchman and I turn off for Bratby and the road along the East side of the marsh here. You carry straight on until you hit the Ely road—and that skirts the West of the marsh."

Benson sighed heavily. "I suppose you do know what you're doing, Mr Steed," he said. "His Nibs said to give you every help. But if you ask me . . . all right, all right; I know you *don't* ask me ! . . . if you did ask me, I'd say it was the most harebrained scheme—even for you—that I'd ever heard of ! It's crackers ! It's bloody mad . . ."

"Madness is best met with madness," Steed said. "You've viewed your unloading place, haven't you? It's pretty well sheltered there, so you shouldn't be bothered—but if anyone does ask, you're a second unit from a film company, on location, right?"

"I suppose so, Mr S."

"Right. Now you know what to do when you get there. We'll rendezvous with you at exactly eight fiftyfive. Mr Lurchman goes in at nine prompt. And we start the ball rolling by signal at twenty past."

"I can't for the life of me see what you can gain by it, sir," Benson said morosely. "Mark my words, no good'll come of it; it'll never work. Not in a hundred years."

"Come, Benson—let not your honest countenance be sicklied

o'er with the pale cast of thought. Yours not to reason why and all that jazz."

"That's as may be, Mr Steed. But I owe it to His Nibs to—Oh, well . . . never mind. It's all water under the bridge, I suppose . . ."

"That's my boy! If there *is* any doubt—geographically, I mean—Miss Reeves'll put you right . . . All set, Bella? You're quite happy about your doubling role, are you?"

"All right, I suppose. But not to say *happy*," Bella Reeves said, leaning across from the passenger seat to look up at Steed. She was a striking sight—white teeth flashing in a face made swarthy with three careful applications of She-Tan. "What I'm worried about is 'Mrs Peel. You still haven't heard anything?"

"Not a word. We shall call in at her hotel as we go through Bratby—just in case. But I'm very much afraid our hosts for tonight must have become in some way suspicious. In which case she's no doubt still lodged at Turret house . . ."

"Oh, but how awful!"

"It's a risk one takes," Steed said seriously. "She knows very well how to take care of herself. All the same, I'd be much happier if I knew she was out of there . . . if, indeed, she's ever going to get out of there now," he added half to himself in a low voice.

"It seems somehow . . . wrong—to be setting out like this, I mean—when we've no idea what's happened to her," Bella said.

"Believe me, Miss Reeves, our little expedition is much more likely to help her than sitting back and just waiting—but don't worry before you need to: I shall probably find her sitting in the 'Feathers' scolding me for being late!"

There was no sign of Emma Peel at the inn in Bratby, however; nor had they any message from her. Reluctantly, feeling very much more despondent than he cared to show, Steed clambered back into the Bentley and pointed its aristocratic radiator in the direction of Turret House.

He pulled up under a clump of trees just before the road ran out on to the dyke. Lurchman's E-type coasted to a halt behind.

"We're taking off from here, Mark," Steed said. "Reeves says it's the best place, despite the distance from the causeway. I suggest you push off and wait in that lay-by I told you about. It's—let's see—yes: it's eight twenty now. Give us an hour. If you arrive at nine as expected, that'll give you twenty minutes to set the stage . . ."

As the twin tail-lights of the Jaguar dwindled away down the straight road, Steed and the poacher stripped and changed into lightweight, black rubber frogmen's suits. They darkened their faces and pulled on black gloves. Then, having inflated the dinghy, they piled into it the boxes of tape, the guns, the suitcases and their clothes, before taking one side each and carrying it off through the trees.

"I'm sure you know this marsh like the back of your hand," Steed said as they negotiated a stretch of Alder bushes on the far side of the trees, "but is it really the quickest way of getting to the house, starting right out here?"

"Bless you, yes," the old man replied. "You go in near the causeway, where you did the other day, and you get swamp, you get reeds, you get waterlogged sedge, you get your grassroots all undermined and boggy. Takes you hours to get anywhere . . . But you go in this end, you'll see, you can *use* the boat ! There's a fair channel, you see—for them as knows where to find it—which takes you right out to the middle of the marsh from here. You can get to within a hundred yards of the house. Mind, the last bit's tricky, but you're practically home by the time you reach it, aren't you?"

They were walking down a slope now, stumbling on the rough ground and hoisting the laden dinghy over low scrub with some difficulty. The night was windless and cool, the stars hidden by a high overcast. The waning moon was not due to rise for several hours. Steed found it almost impossible to see, but the poacher appeared to be familiar with every bush and each clump of grass.

"Mind, now ! Let her down a second," he said after they had gone another fifty yards. "Shouldn't be far from here."

They lowered the rubber boat to the ground and Reeves dropped to a crouching position to line up some private landmark with what meagre lightening was afforded by the night sky. After a moment he grunted. "Thought so. We should be another ten yards or so to the left . . ."

Picking up the boat again, they moved across slowly. Then again he halted, listening. Quite clearly, Steed heard the sighing of the waves on the shore, away on the far side of the dyke. "Right. We'll let her down, then, if you're ready," Reeves was whispering. For a moment the undercover man couldn't see what he meant—then gradually he realised that, immediately before their feet, the ground fell away to a grassy lip. And that under the lip, sombre and mysterious, was water.

The dinghy rocked giddily as they stepped down into it through a screen of bare branches, but as soon as they had pushed it out from under the overhanging trees, it lay very steadily on the channel. Steed sat in the stern while Reeves, who had unclipped a paddle from the bulbous gunwale, crouched at the other end sensing his way across the marsh.

It was an eerie experience. Steed felt no sense of motion at all. The poacher dipped the paddle and directed the craft with uncanny delicacy. Patches of deeper blackness loomed up, passed and dropped astern as they threaded their way through banks of reeds and islands of floating vegetation. At one point the channel widened into a small lake and Reeves waited for several minutes, apparently listening. It was very still. But from every side, Steed gradually became aware, there rose a low sussurrus of noise, a constant ebbing and flowing of staccato gutturals just above the threshold of audibility. It was the gabbling of the innumerable wildfowl across the sanctuary as they settled for the night.

Eventually, the poacher stiffened, craning towards the bow of the dinghy. "Got 'em!" he whispered. "I was listenin' for the Pinkfeet. We have to keep to the left of the mudflat they're on. Hear 'em rabbiting away out there?"

Steed obediently listened—but he could hear nothing ahead of them which distinguished the nasal muttering of hundreds of birds from that behind or to either side. How Reeves could not only identify a particular species but use the noise it made as a direction beacon to "home" on was beyond his comprehension.

The old man sank his paddle noiselessly into the water again —and sure enough a long, low bank of mud soon drew alongside the starboard quarter of the dinghy. Steed could dimly make out the bulk of the big geese, shifting and twitching, as they glided past. A few minutes later, a whisper of sound in the air resolved itself into the rush of wings just above their heads. Hundreds of birds, flying very low and very fast, streamed over uttering a strange *whee-oooo* call as they went—a wild, unbirdlike noise which exploded out of the night like the shrill whistle of a rifle bullet. Steed's hands itched for the duck guns stacked in the bow.

"Wigeon," the poacher commented laconically. "Flighting inland to their feedin' grounds. They're late tonight. Must have been a long way out . . ."

Above the dark mass of a reed bed to their right, the head-lamps of a car lanced the sky over towards the Ely road. Some-where a long way away, a dog was barking fretfully. And then—startlingly close—there sounded the piercing and mournful cry of a Curlew.

"Ah, that'll be Bella," Reeves exclaimed with satisfaction. "It's the signal. Means they've landed the first load successfully. I'll just confirm that we're doing all right, too." He cupped his hands and raised them to his mouth.

For the second time, the haunting call floated out over the desolate marsh.

\*       \*       \*

"Oh, good—that'll be Pa. They must be between the Pinkfeet and the Pintail," Bella Reeves panted. "Do you think this old tub'll take the rest of the stuff in one more load?"

"I'm sure I couldn't say, miss. As you know, I regard the whole bleeding enterprise with . . . misgivin'. That's what: misgivin'." Benson scratched his head and looked at the broad-beamed rowing boat tied up at the outer end of the board walk leading to Turret House. "We'll have a shot at it, anyway," he said dubiously. "Anything rather than have to make a third journey!"

They had had no trouble so far. The boat had still been at the landing stage where Steed had left it after his escape from the aviary. Benson had managed to get the Land Rover to within a few feet of the rotting wooden jetty. And they had contrived to load aboard all the lights but one for the first trip, filling in the gaps with the potted plants and the cans of film. Bella had poled the boat across the channel and successfully found the end of the catwalk in the dark. And they had laboriously manhandled the equipment along the narrow board pathway to dry land. It was parked now at the lowest limit of the old walled garden which sloped down to the marsh at the back of Turret House—and all that remained before they started Phase Two of their task was to bring across the remaining spotlight, the projector, and the cyclorama and its framework. Benson, however, having stepped off the board walk in the dark while he was carrying a heavy lamp base and soaked his trouser leg to the knee, was disposed to find difficulties where none existed.

In the event, the rest of the stuff fitted quite easily into the boat and they managed the crossing without incident. It took them a long time to manoeuvre the projector along the narrow walk—

but at last it was done, and they relaxed, breathing hard, with all their cargo safely landed.

Phase Two consisted simply in carting the equipment up past the aviaries and the laboratory, through the yard, and to a flagged terrace which ran along the south side of the house. This was more a matter of time and care than anything else, for Bella knew which route to take to avoid the trip-wires and "magic eyes", and the whole route was along brick paths which were relatively flat. "All right, then," she said at last. "It's twelve minutes to nine. We'd better get started . . ."

\* \* \*

The lights of Turret House were showing through the screen of trees which surrounded the property when Steed and Reeves got to what the poacher called "the difficult part" of the journey. Here, the channel they had been following twisted away to the West to join the one leading up to the end of the board walk further out in the marsh. To get to the dry ground of the causeway, they had now to cross an open swamp—a boggy area completely waterlogged, but with the liquid only just covering the saturated ground, too shallow to float even the flat-bottomed rubber dinghy.

"Walking's the only way, I'm afraid," the old man said with a sigh. "And it's as mucky as all get-out—that's why I insisted we had these frogman things. Follow me over the side . . . but don't be alarmed when you sink in: the bog only goes down to about mid-thigh depth at the most. It's good and hard beneath that. And the best part of it's only about eighteen inches . . ."

The swamp was only about fifty yards across. But, as Steed soon found out, the poacher was right in considering it the worst part of the whole journey. As soon as he had climbed over the side of the boat and put his weight on his foot, it sank slowly into the quagmire, to fetch up against solid ground when the surface was at his knee. To take a step, it was necessary to haul leg and foot out of the sucking bog, raise it up above the surface, and then plunge it squelching in again a pace away. The consistency was far too thick for wading—and progress was thus analogous to stepping over an interminable series of hip-high hurdles . . . with the suction of the swamp as an added obstacle to rapid movement. In addition, since the surface moisture was too shallow for towing the dinghy, even without their weight in it, they had perforce to drag it bodily across the tangle of sub-

merged grasses and waterlogged sedge. By the time they reached
the far side, their muscles were shuddering with fatigue and they
were slopping with sweat inside the rubber suits.

Between the swamp and the high ground on which the house
was built lay a pool. They pushed the dinghy across, wading
through the water to clean off some of the heavy mud which
clung to their legs from ankle to hip. The pressure of the cold
water creeping up the skin-tight latex struck clammily against
their heated pores and they were glad to start work on dry land
again to stave off the effects of the chill night air on the flimsy
suits.

Methodically and in silence, they hauled the boat out of the
water, stowed its paddle, and vanished into the trees with the
guns, the suitcases and the boxes of tape.

They had landed very near to the house : only a dozen yards
separated them from the gravelled sweep before the front door.
Steed now took charge. He had been content to leave everything
to Reeves while they were crossing the marsh : the man was a
genius in his field—but now that he was back in his own métier,
he automatically assumed command. "Keep right clear of that
shrubbery—and avoid all bushes like the plague," he whispered.
"You'll be okay if you keep to that clear patch down the centre.
But watch the gravel. And don't pass between the portico and
the edge of that outbuilding : there's a 'magic eye' beam connected to an alarm guarding it . . ."

Between them they achieved a lot in a very short time. Under
Steed's direction they disconnected a number of booby traps and
trip wires, dismantled several loudspeakers and re-hung them
in different positions nearer to the house, Reeves paying out wire
from a field telephone spool to connect them up with the old
installations—and finally approached the building itself, where
Steed made various strategic alterations to some of the alarm
wiring. Mainly, this consisted of running tap wires to an earth
peg which he pushed into the ground at the foot of the wall. As
soon as it was finished, he turned to Reeves.

"They should be all set on the other side of the house," he
said. "Would you like to check, just to make sure?"

The poacher nodded. He cupped his hands again and dropped
his mouth to the thumbs. This time, it was the mewing cry of a
Little Owl which split the air. And almost immediately it was
returned—a sharp sliver of sound piercing the night from somewhere over the roof.

"Splendid!" Steed breathed. "As they seem to be there without incident, I gather Mrs Peel must have been able to attend to certain things I asked her to, before she was surprised by our hosts. In which case it should be safe for us to tiptoe round and join them . . ."

Noiselessly as shadows, the two men slipped around the corner of the house and across the yard behind, their shining black suits and dark faces virtually invisible against the sombre bulk of the building. On the far side of the house from the study, the flagged terrace was reached by a flight of shallow steps. It ran the width of the place, bordered by a stone balustrade, and below it was a lawn formally sectioned by gravel paths. It was here on the terrace, and in the space between the balustrade and the trees at the far side of the lawn, that Operation Worthington was to be staged . . .

Bella Reeves and Benson were waiting for them at one end of the terrace, the equipment neatly stacked along one wall.

Steed drew the party together and briefed them. "Everything's fine so far," he said crisply. "But we've a hell of a lot to do now in a very short time indeed. Let me take your tasks in order. Bella—you go to the museum and get the birds. Flamingo, Ibis, Egret, Hoopoe, Mediterranean Shearwater, Phalarope, and that little display of Crossbills and Desert Bullfinch . . . Right?—Mrs Peel should have left the various cases unlocked for you. When you've brought them, arrange them and the plants in the way we discussed. Then wait here for me and I'll let you indoors to change . . .

"Benson—you arrange the lights as planned. You'll see that the French windows leading to this terrace are bowed, and have a small balcony over them. After I've gone in, I'll come out to the balcony and you can hand me up the projector and The Brute, which I shall install on the balustrade. At the same time, I'll lower you a lead from the room inside—it's a guest room, fortunately!—so that you can hitch up the junction box and activate the whole works.

"Reeves—you'll find an outhouse across the lawn. Mrs Peel will have left it unlocked. Bring up all the wrought iron garden furniture you can find stacked in there and arrange it here on the terrace, right?

"I shall erect the cyclorama screen and then go in to make certain arrangements and leave these spools of tape in place of those already there. Then I'm going to fix the things on the balcony. And finally—thank God!—Reeves and I will get out of these wet things and we'll all get into drag for the party! ... Any questions?"

"Yes." It was Bella speaking. "What about Mrs Peel?"

"I've arranged that with Mr Lurchman. As soon as he possibly can, he's going to try and find out if she's a prisoner here. If he can, and she is—and she's still alive—he's going to give a signal from the study window, which your father will be watching for. And as soon as I get that signal the operation proceeds as arranged. If anything has happened to her, or if she's in immediate danger, he'll give a different signal, and I shall take off on my own. But the rest of you carry on as planned in either case. Any more?"

"Any chance of testing our lights, Mr Steed, before we're *on*, as it were?" Benson asked.

"Absolutely not. *Nothing* must be tried—nothing at all—until we get the word from Lurchman that they've gone under. Then we'll have ten minutes at the most to get the set-up perfect."

"How long do we continue working it? How do we know when to stop?"

"We'll have to play that by ear, Benson. Just carry on. I'll contrive to get any messages necessary to you."

The group broke up and went about its various duties. In a short time the wintry-looking terrace was transformed—insofar as anything could be seen at all before the moon was up. White-painted garden chairs and tables were dotted about in front of the balustrade; exotic plants bloomed by the French windows, down the steps and in a semicircle across the lawn; a length of red-and-white striped blind material with scalloped edges hung down from the balcony—and above it were the arc light and the projector, aimed at the big curve of screen which Steed had erected behind the flowers and shrubs on the lawn. Between this and the balustrade—and indeed on the terrace itself—sub-tropical birds were visible in arrested motion.

Steed, who seemed to have had no difficulty in forcing the lock of the French windows, handed down a length of flex from the balcony, and Benson set about hitching up the light standards to a square, wooden junction box he had stowed at one side of the terrace. The little chauffeur then went through the French windows to where Bella and Reeves were busied about the two suitcases Steed had brought with him in the dinghy. They seemed to be full of clothes.

In a moment, Steed was with them again. Silently, he led Benson from the room, through the hallway of Turret House and up the stairs to the guest bedroom leading on to the balcony. "Since you're the only one not changing," he whispered, "you might as well get settled in now. See you later—I hope!" He left the little man loading film into the projector and stole back downstairs. There was a rumble of voices from behind the closed door to the study, and a crack of light showed below the old-fashioned curtain that hung across it. But neither Charnley nor Warbeck-Simner showed any sign of having heard the trespassers who were violating their privacy.

Of Emma Peel there was no trace at all. Steed searched as far as he dared in the minimal time at his disposal, but the timing of his plan was so critical that it was impossible to pursue the quest. He must simply hope ...

Back in the room leading out to the terrace—it was in fact the house's drawing room—he stripped the damp frogman's suit from his body and dropped it on top of the quivering heap that had been Reeves's. From the suitcase, he took a collection of heavy, cream-coloured robes and put them on, adding an arab headpiece which almost completely covered his face when he bent forward. Reeves—now staked out on the far side of the house awaiting Lurchman's signal—should be similarly dressed. Bella had retired to the kitchens to await her cue.

Steed scooped up the rubber suits and the empty valises and stowed them out of sight beyond the terrace. He rolled up the carpet from the drawing room floor and exposed the narrow boards. Then, after removing certain bibelots and rearranging some of the furniture, he went out on to the terrace to wait.

Across the marsh floating on the still air, faintly he heard the clock on Little Hornham church tower striking the quarters, and then the nine solemn strokes of the hour.

As though in answer, there was a burst of sound from the twin exhausts of Mark Lurchman's Jaguar as it drew up by the gates at the far end of the drive. A door opened in the interior and voices called. Footsteps strode through to the front door. Then, probing into the dark sky like fingers, Steed saw through the trees the lights of the E-type moving slowly up the causeway towards the house.

# 16

## A TOUCH OF THE SUN

STEED's plan was bold, simple—and as lunatic as the men it was designed to catch. It consisted of nothing less than tricking them into believing that they were already in North Africa. After which, Steed hoped, they could be persuaded to insert the poison pellets and thus identify the birds they were about to release as messengers of death on their "migration" to Britain!

Lurchman, ostensibly having heard that two old clients were about to go abroad, had telephoned and begged them to accept a case of Champagne as a *bon voyage* gift. He would bring it across himself that evening and crack a bottle with them.

Since they rarely drank, it was reasonable to assume that Mark could fairly easily persuade them to have a little too much —and while they were in that position, he was to introduce into their drinks two small capsules provided by Steed. "Nothing harmful, old boy," the undercover man had assured him. "Just a temporary knock-out drop allied with a mild hallucinogen. The former will give us the required break in time—we could never put it across just taking them as it were from a room in England to a room in Africa, however sloshed they were. But if they *wake up* and find themselves 'in Africa'—well, that's a different thing, isn't it? The memory's never as reliable as a continuous experience. And the hallucinogen?—That's to help them believe what they see, or think they see, when they do wake up."

"How on earth does that work, then?" Mark had asked.

"It's a derivative of *Cannabis Hallucinatrix*—a relative of *Cannabis Indicus* or Marijuana. In this form it doesn't of itself induce specific hallucinations, but it does have the property of making the person under its influence believe—or be more likely to believe—what is *suggested* to him. And I'm hoping that this suggestibility, plus the fact that they'll be a tiny little bit plastered, plus the *trompe l'oeil* we're going to put on for them, will do the trick . . ."

The optical illusion of course was in reality crude, and wouldn't for a moment have deceived a sane or a sober man.

What Steed was doing, in effect, was to create a film set outside the drawing room windows of Turret House and bring the owners into it. A blaze of arc lamps was to create "sunshine" on the terrace, while carefully deployed props and a projector casting a colour film on to the cyclorama were to sustain the deception. Four factors could upset the illusion: if the "sun blind" hung outside the French windows did not mask the top of the cyclorama screen from the view of those inside the drawing room; if the semi-circle of plants and shrubs did not conceal the junction of the foot of the screen and the lawn; if the two old men at any time realised that the room from which they saw these things was their own drawing room; and if they were unable to get the thing finished before the moon rose. Completely dark surroundings would not obtrude—but moonlight on the marshes would hardly fit in with hot North African sunshine, and middle-distance features in the landscape certainly would show once the moon was up! Similarly, if the striped awning did not hide the top of the screen, whatever scene was shown on it, would apparently be "cut off" half way up the sky . . .

Thinking of all these preparations frantically going on unseen within a few yards of him, Lurchman smiled inwardly as he went through the formalities with his hosts and prepared to open a bottle of Champagne for them. ("Pile it on," Steed had said. "There is no flattery too blatant, no sycophancy too obvious to swell the ego and feed the gullibility of monomaniacs like these!")

"We are distressed indeed, gentlemen," the hotelier said as he poured the frothing liquid into their glasses, "that two such eminent—I was going to say great—men are leaving us, even if only temporarily. I am sure I speak for the rest of my fellow townsfolk when I say: please come back soon—we cannot afford to lose our two most eminent citizens . . . the world's foremost ornithologist and—er—the world's most—er—distinguished scientist!" Feeling slightly ridiculous, he raised his glass to each of the old men in turn. But the exaggerated phraseology and the absurd praise obviously raised no doubts in the minds of his hearers.

"Very civil of you, Lurchman. Very civil," Warbeck-Simner said. "I speak both for my colleague and myself in accepting your good wishes. Your loyalty and that of the townsfolk will be —er—remembered."

Now came the difficult part, Lurchman thought. He tried to

remember the exact words in which Steed had coached him. "It is always a pleasure to associate oneself—however humbly—with men of vision," he said carefully. "And we are only too glad to lend our support—our *unqualified* support—where others have been perhaps . . . ungenerous."

"Disloyal," Charnley snapped. "One might almost say treasonable."

"*Treasonable!*" Lurchman gasped in spite of himself.

"Certainly. By rights Sir Albert is the *seigneur* of this district. Failure to show the proper respect can fairly be described as treasonable, I fancy. Especially since Sir Albert's authority will so shortly be so very much—"

"That's enough, Professor, I think," Warbeck-Simner said. "Let me simply say, Lurchman, that those less wise than yourself may soon have cause to regret it."

"A very good thing too," Mark said emphatically. "We have had enough trouble with people not prepared to recognise your —er—greatness. Why only this week—"

"Yes, yes—what were you going to say?"

"Well, there was a busibody—some fellow from London who claimed to be a journalist—who was shooting off his mouth in the local inns in a most disrespectful manner. The villagers soon shut him up and packed him off home with a flea in his ear!"

"Was his name Steed?"

"I believe it was, now that you mention it."

"Ah. I had arranged a lesson, a most salutary lesson, for that impertinent young man—but unfortunately he was blessed with the luck that sometimes attends that kind of beastly insolence, and he ran off."

"Well," Lurchman said, "he's run off altogether now . . . And then there was that young woman . . ."

"Young woman?" Charnley queried sharply.

"Yes—she was a cousin to Bella Reeves, the poacher's girl, you know. And again—not by any means as respectful as one would wish. Still—I haven't seen her for a day or so. Perhaps she's gone, too."

"Oh, no," Charnley burst out. "*She* hasn't gone—at least not yet, you know—"

"*Charnley!* . . . No, the young woman you mention was—is —indeed a cousin of Miss Reeves. She came to work for me for a short while. But, as you rightly say, she was disrespectful as well as being a busibody. I was forced to discipline her. As a matter of fact she's outside now—er—waiting until I decide what to do with her."

"I'm certain that whatever you decide will be just," Mark said, advancing with the Champagne bottle. He prepared to pour.

"No, no, thank you," Warbeck-Simner protested, raising his hand. "We rarely take alcohol, you know—and we have a long journey before us tomorrow."

"At least allow me to toast the confusion of your enemies!"

"Ah, well—if you put it like that. Just a little—no, really. It really is most agreeable of you to bring us this—this libation to attend our wanderings, Lurchman. We shall be grateful to you when we're out there, you know . . . Your good health!"

"And yours, sir," Mark said, raising his glass and wandering over to the windows. Expertly he opened another bottle of Champagne. "Allow me to add a refreshening draught . . ."

"No, no, no, no, no. My dear fellow. Really, we're really not drinkers, you know. Really. No, I insist . . ."

"It's not much use drinking to the downfall of those who would thwart you, if we don't also toast the success of those ventures which should follow their defeat," Lurchman said sententiously.

"A point. That's indeed a point," Charnley said a little thickly. "Don't you feel, my dear Sir Albert—the fellow's right: no earthly use . . . no use at all getting rid of *them* if we don't *succeed!*"

"Perhaps you're right. Well, perhaps just a *little* . . ."

Lurchman poured again, raised his own glass, drank, and placed a cigarette in his mouth. "I hope the weather will keep fine for your flight," he said conversationally. "I think the clouds were finally passing over, as I drove across the marsh. And the wind has definitely dropped . . ." Casually, he raised the curtain and looked out and up at the sky. He produced a lighter from his pocket and lit the cigarette.

"Yes, gentlemen: I think you're all set for a fine day tomorrow," he said, dropping the curtain and moving back into the centre of the room with Steed's four capsules concealed in his hand. "Now—one final sip for the road, as we say: it would be a pity to leave any in the bottle, would it not . . .?"

Out in the garden, Reeves hurtled round the corner of the terrace and caught hold of Steed's arm. "It's all right," he panted. "Mr Lurchman gave the signal. He lit the cigarette—and he was looking up at the sky. They've swallowed the bait . . . and Mrs Peel's still there unharmed . . . !"

Steed sighed with relief. "Thank God for that," he said fervently. "Can you hear me, Benson?"

"Loud and clear, Mr Steed," a voice drifted down from somewhere above the striped awning.

"All right, then," Steed called. "I'm nipping upstairs to look out some tropical clothing from our pigeons' luggage while they sleep off their ten-minute Mickey Finns. In the meantime— *Lights! Action! Camera! . . .*"

*        *        *

Raymond Charnley struggled awake. His mouth was dry and there was a slight ache behind his eyes. Really, he felt almost as though he had a hangover ! But that was absurd . . .

Was it absurd, though? He sat up in the easy chair in which he had been slumped. There was a half full Champagne bottle in a silver bucket just beside him—and on an occasional table by his knee an empty glass. Most puzzling. He looked around him. Warbeck-Simner lay back in a similar chair across the room, his mouth open, snoring. There was a bottle and a glass by him, too. Beyond, double doors opened on to the terrace. The terrace? . . . Well, *a* terrace . . . On the far side of the shadow cast by the striped sun blind, the warm stones were drenched in heat and light . . . Light, light, light shimmered and danced from the blooms of Fuchsia, Bougainvillea, Geranium and Salvia which cascaded over the balustrade and down the steps to the lawn; it gilded the leaves of the tubbed Jasmine whose insidious perfume drifted into the room on the warm breeze; and it scintillated among the jagged spikes of Agave, Yucca and Cactus which fringed the cliff-top at the far end of the hotel garden.

The hotel . . .? Charnley rubbed his eyes. *What* hotel, to be sure? He simply could not recall the rest of the place; nor what he had done last night, for that matter. It was all most odd . . . He looked out of the window again. Beyond the garden, apparently far below, he saw the sea, blue and intense, stretching sun-dappled to the horizon. Beyond parallel lines of white rollers advancing on the invisible shore, a speedboat towed a water-skier in a vee of foam—and surely that was a felucca sailing slowly towards the . . . the what? . . . the East? Or the West? . . . Charnley shook his head. He was consumed by a great thirst. Reaching for the champagne bottle almost automatically, he poured himself a glassful. To his astonishment, the amber liquid was not the flat and stale souvenir of an evening gone by that he expected: it was ice-cold and sparkling.

"The wine, she is not to your liking, sir?"

A waiter in a white jacket—a squat, wide fellow with bright blue eyes behind a blade of a nose, and a huge black moustache—came into the room from the terrace. He dusted off the white wrought-iron table and chairs set just inside the French windows and looked enquiringly across at the scientist.

"Oh—I—I—why, yes, thank you. Very nice. Very good indeed," Charnley stammered, draining the glass and pouring himself some more. "It's—how long has it been here, d'you know?"

The waiter raised his eyebrows. "Why ten minutes, sir," he said. "Since you ordered it."

"I—er—ordered this Champagne ten minutes ago?"

"But yes—you say she is the only wine to drink before the *petit déjeuner*, so I delay your breakfas' while you drink. The girl bring your coffee and *croissants* in a minute."

Charnley put his hand up to his forehead. Of *course* he had ordered the wine a few minutes ago. He must have done . . . yet he couldn't recall actually saying the words. Nevertheless, the waiter was familiar enough. Definitely, he *had* been talking to him a few minutes before. And yet . . . and yet . . .

*Was* this the Hotel Armorica in Rabat, where they had booked? Certainly that looked like Mazagan Bay out there—and there was some Arab fellow pottering about among the birds in the garden—There was an Ibis ! . . . Really his head felt most curious . . . Still, it was strange that he couldn't remember the journey at all . . . Sir Albert was sitting up and pouring himself a drink.

"Morning, Charnley," he said breezily. "Gorgeous day, isn't it. I must say, I could do with a spot of the jolly old coffee, though. Got a thirst on me like a dredger—this is first-class bubbly, though. Clever of you to think of it."

The ornithologist's hand was unsteady. He spilled a quantity of Champagne down the front of his honey-coloured alpaca jacket. Charnley looked suddenly down at his own clothes. White duck trousers and jacket. Rather creased. They *must* be in Morocco !

There was the tapping of high heels on the terrace. A girl in a black dress with a frilled apron and cap walked up to their table with a tray and begun unloading cups, saucers, cutlery and coffee. "Good morning, gentlemen," she smiled. "I hope you enjoy your little trip last night."

"Little trip?" Warbeck-Simner asked uncertainly. "Last night?"

"But yes. You go to a nightclub in Casbah, no?"

Again, Charnley shook his head. He supposed they must have done. Good God, yes! He could actually hear—beyond the sound of the distant breakers, which he had not noticed until now—the gargling noises of Arab voices raised in argument. There must be a native market place just around the corner. And from the other side of the terrace, carrying clearly on the warm air, the voice of a priest calling the *muzzein* floated. "Most enjoyable," he said, looking at Sir Albert.

The girl poured out coffee. Her hair was looped up in a big chignon and her eyes were heavily made up. From her face—it was quite exceptionally dark—white teeth flashed in a blinding smile. There was something about her that was disturbingly familiar, Charnley felt, eyeing the ripe figure bulging in the tight little dress. Never mind—he would have just one more drink before he tackled the coffee. My word! This Champagne *was* nice . . . Over the rim of his glass, he watched the girl primp away down the terrace.

Bella had really achieved a remarkable transformation. Now, out of sight around the corner, she stripped off the maid's uniform and revealed herself in a brief two-piece swimsuit of citron yellow satin—an ensemble particularly suited to contrast the rotundities of breast and hip with the concave depths of darkened skin at her waist. Steed approached as she picked up a striped beach towel and slid her feet into sandals. "You're doing splendidly, my dear," he whispered. "Just walk across the garden as though you were expecting to be discovered by a film producer . . . Yes, Reeves, what is it?"

The poacher was tugging at his sleeve on the other side. "Mr Benson's worried about the time element, sir," he said. "Unless you can create some diversion, the reel will run out in a few minutes and there'll be no more sea and sky until another is loaded."

"I'll do what I can," the undercover man said. "If nothing has happened, tell him to reverse it and run back—I suppose their imagination can stand waves rolling slowly *out* to sea and speedboats towed by water-skiers going backwards! How's the sobriety stakes?"

"The little one's practically on his ear. I'm not sure about the other—he's a funny customer, that one. But they're both digging into the fizz."

Just inside the French windows, Warbeck-Simner and Charnley sat at their table, toying with Champagne, *croissants* and coffee. "I say, there's a dashed attractive gel on her way down to bathe," Sir Albert observed, catching sight of Bella—whose hair now streamed in a dark wave down her back—sauntering across the lawn.

"Yes, yes—most curvac . . . curvace . . . most agreeable," the Professor giggled. "But look here, don't you think—I mean isn't she—don't you think she's rather like Reeves?"

"Certainly not. She's much taller for one thing."

"Oh, I don't know . . . Perhaps one ought to—bit of a closer look, you know. Feel like a bit of a constitu'n'l, don't you? Why'n't we just amble down to the . . ." He got up from the table, swaying slightly.

"No, no, Charnley, old boy. You go by all means if you want to. To tell the truth I feel dashed odd this morning . . . can't seem to rem'mber anything before—why, I can't even rem'mber getting *up*! . . ." He began to laugh: a deep chuckle interspersed with an occasional hiccough. But Charnley was up and away. With an excited cry of "*Look*! Flamingos! In the garden!" he had bounded down the steps and was on the lawn before anyone could move to stop him. As he approached a group of three Flamingos posed before the line of cacti, the Arab gardener who had crossed the lawn earlier moved quickly in his direction. He appeared to be carrying a small billhook. Just before he reached the birds, the scientist appeared to stumble— and an instant later he gave a sharp cry and began to flap one of his hands up and down in the air. "Blasted bird pecked me," he complained, running back up the steps to Warbeck-Simner. "I was only going to have a look . . . Blast it!" The back of his hand was bleeding.

"Treacherous birds," the ornithologist said. "Yes, my good fellow? What do you want now?" The waiter was by his side again.

"Excuse me, sir," he said, bowing and turning to the wall. "You do not have your calendar improved for today." He removed the top sheet of a United Arab Airlines daily tear-away calendar.

Warbeck-Simner sat up at the table. He rubbed his eyes. "Good gracious me, Charnley," he exclaimed. "Look! No—

leave your wretched hand alone, man. You're not dying! Look! Look at the *date* . . ."

"I—well, really, I . . . Oh! My goodness! The *birds* . . ."

"Certainly the birds. It's *today*. They must be released!"

"Then let us . . . But just a minute, Sir Albert. Where *are* the birds?"

"Where are they? Why, don't be ridiculous, they're in the . . . in the . . . yes, by gad : where *are* they, indeed?"

"In the la-borrrr-atorr-y, *effendi* : let me show you the way," a tall Arab in burnouse, djellabi and Jermyn Street socks called from the French windows. This was the crucial moment. If either of the two drunken old men thought to query the familiar laboratory in a context of "Moroccan" splendour, the entire exercise was wasted.

But Charnley got up and stood unsteadily by the table without displaying any doubts. "We'd better go, then. Mustn't keep the jolly ol' birds waiting, what!" he cried in slurred tones. "But what about you, my dear S'r Albert? Aren't you coming—or would you like me to—would you like me to cope?"

"No, no, Charnley," Warbeck-Simner waved the scientist away. "I really feel most—*would* you mind? . . . Just to prepare the pellets and slip them in place and . . . and . . . and I'll come along later and see them fly. The Hodder ducks, you know. Just the Hodders . . ." He sank back into his chair and dropped his head into his hands as Charnley shambled off in the wake of the tall Arab. If only his head would stop spinning; if things could stop swinging away from him for a moment . . . And there was a curious, distant whirring noise all the time, which reminded him strongly of something . . . He lifted his head and stared out across the garden. The girl in the swimsuit was walking back towards the terrace. Apparently she hadn't bathed, for her costume was still dry. He watched approvingly as her shadow undulated over the grass, across the spiky leaves of Agave, out over the rollers towards the horizon and then up into the sky . . . *Over the sea and into the sky? A shadow?* Warbeck-Simner leaped to his feet with a shout of fury. "Charnley! Charnley! Stop! Come back!" he screamed. "We've been tricked. There's something wrong . . ."

And at that moment there was a loud snap followed by a hectic slithering, flapping noise, as the entire panorama—waves, sea, sky and shipping—vanished into total darkness.

The film in the projector had broken . . .

# 17

## MRS PEEL PASSES OUT

OF ALL the events in the macabre charade which took place that evening at Turret House, Lurchman was to remember best the moment when Steed made his reappearance on the scene: with his Arab robes held up around his waist like the skirts of a fastidious woman crossing a stream, and his elegantly trousered legs pumping up and down like pistons, the undercover man whistled round the corner of the terrace and sprinted across the lawn in pursuit of Charnley—who had himself clattered into view an instant before in the middle of a flurry of squawking birds. Brightly coloured ducks and drakes were still flapping agitatedly across the flagstones as Steed pelted through the display of stuffed birds and sent them spinning right and left in his wake.

"Stop him!" he called urgently as the scientist streaked across the open space and vanished among the trees on the far side. "He's still got the pellets on him!"

Lurchman and Reeves both moved into action to cut Charnley off, but the little man commanded a fair turn of speed and he was out of sight before they had crossed the area behind the cyclorama screen. Steed waved them down as they reached the edge of the wood between the driveway and the marsh. A false moustache hung drunkenly from one side of his upper lip.

"Leave it," he panted. "We'll have to take it slowly now he's out of sight. Reeves—you're the one with the woodcraft, after all; you follow on after him. If he lies low, wait until he makes a move and then nab him. If he makes a break and goes for the gates—head him off. But keep your mouth shut. Literally. Those pellets are lethal . . ."

As the poacher melted into the shadows beneath the trees, Steed and the hotelier turned back towards the terrace and the house. "We've got to get to Mrs Peel," Steed said roughly. "From what you tell me, she's probably alright. Probably. But I shan't be satisfied until I'm sure—and until we've got her out of

wherever she is . . . What we have to do now is to—er—persuade that insane villain to tell us *where*. Either that or—" He
broke off suddenly.

The inner door to the drawing room—that stage so carefully
set as part of a Moroccan hotel—was swinging open. And
through it they saw the mundane hallway of Turret House,
with the stairway rising to the upper floors.

But of Sir Albert Warbeck-Simner there was no sign.

"We'd better separate and search the place floor by floor,"
Lurchman began. He stopped and looked round him. "Where's
Bella?" he cried wildly. "Where's Bella gone? My God, if that
lunatic has harmed her . . ." He dashed from the room and made
for the stairs. For the girl, too, appeared to have vanished.

In three strides, Steed was beside him, laying a restraining
hand on his arm. "Hold it, Mark," he said quietly. "Nothing to
be gained by rushing off without thinking. Let's just recap, shall
we? Tell me exactly what happened while I was away?"

"Well, I—I—let's see . . . You went off with Charnley to—to
get the birds, right?"

"Yes?"

"And then—well, the film broke. At least, I think that's what
happened. And the next moment, the madman was on his feet
shouting after you and the Professor . . . shouting that they'd
been tricked, and that he must come back."

"In fact he had tumbled?"

"Yes—but it's odd. For I'm pretty certain that he was on his
feet screaming blue murder just *before* the film broke. Bella was
walking back across the lawn at the time, I remember."

"He probably saw something that tipped him off. Perhaps
he recognised her."

"I don't think so, Mr Steed. But I don't suppose it matters
now. Anyway, Charnley came roaring around the corner with
you close behind a moment later, so I guess I forgot all about
the boss. Until you called me over, that is, and we began to think
about it . . . What happened over there in the stables, by the
way?"

"Well, it was all going to plan, very nicely, as a matter of fact.
Pity he had to cotton on just that little bit too soon. We so nearly
managed it. Still—I'd done what I meant to. Charnley led me
straight to the birds he'd decided to use as his beastly messengers
of death: the Hodder ducks . . . all crated up ready to go. He

went across to the lab to get his poison—one small jar full of the stuff, all ready rolled into pellets."

"Did you find out if that was all there was?"

"Oh, yes—that was more than half the aim of the operation. Otherwise we could just have taken them quietly in yesterday. But we had to get them, not knowing who we were, to show us the extent of the stocks."

"And one jar was all?"

"Yes. Apparently it's very difficult to synthesise—Curare itself is—and he hadn't had so much time since he'd first succeeded in isolating it. This was all he'd had time to make."

"What happened then?"

"Well, apparently it hadn't struck him as odd that, although he was in a hotel in Morocco, he went to the old stables at Bratby to get the ducks—and he was quite happy to accept me as an Arab layabout! Part of the hired help laid on to assist. So he asked me to help him get the ducks out while he put the stuff in place."

"He must have been pretty far gone!"

"On his ear . . . Then I heard Warbeck-Simner yelling his head off—and unfortunately so did the professor. I'd no idea if the—er—facts would percolate through the haze of drink and hallucinogen, so I acted just in case."

"You let the birds loose?"

"Well, shall we say that the crates kind of—er—capsized as I was helping to reach in for the birds? I knew it might tip him off, but I had to get them out of the way: they were the only ones fitted with anklets of the right type, you see. Once they were gone, neither Charnley nor Simner could use any—" He broke off.

A woman's scream had shivered the silence of the huge house. It rose sobbingly into the night air, cracked on a high note and hung eerily in the echoing stairwell.

"*Bella!*" Lurchman was half way up the stairs before Steed moved.

The girl was standing on the first floor landing, knuckles showing white through the trembling hands bunched under her chin. 'I—I'm sorry," she said weakly. "S-silly of me, I know. B-b-but it was so—so unexpected, you see. And it's . . . oh, so *beastly* in this house!" The hotelier had his arms around her. He caught Steed's glance over Bella's bowed head and flicked his eyes towards a door on the left.

Benson was hidden behind the bed. He was lying on his face with his arms outflung. Blood oozed from a swelling below the grizzled hairs at the back of his head. Steed's probing fingers were gentle. "He'll be all right," he called. "It's a nasty crack but it looks worse than it is. He'll be walking about with a headache and a foul temper in half an hour . . ."

"But what can we do?" Bella asked.

"We haven't time to do anything. I've laid him on the bed. What happened?"

"Well, when Sir Albert started to shout, naturally I looked up, and I saw him turn round and rush indoors. So, as there wasn't anybody else around, I thought I'd better follow him . . . but by the time I got upstairs, he'd disappeared."

"That was very courageous of you."

"It wasn't, really. I didn't stop to think. I tiptoed about, and then I heard Sir Albert stamping down the back stairs. I was coming to the window to call you when I tripped over . . . when I saw . . ." She gestured to the room where Benson lay.

"I understand. Was Sir Albert carrying anything? —Did you *see* him going down the back stairs? —Did he see you? Did he say anything? Think, Bella."

"He was carrying on like anything, muttering to himself all the time: that's how I finally knew where he was. I saw him rush out of that small store-room near his bedroom with a little bottle in his hand—"

"A bottle?"

"Yes—one of those medicine bottles with grooves down the sides. I don't think he saw me."

"What colour was the bottle?"

"It was dark green. And he was mumbling something about that was that; now he knew what to do. He'd get a syringe and the busibodies—"

"A syringe!" Steed interrupted brusquely. He looked at Lurchman. *"The lab!"* he cried suddenly. *"There's a vivisection theatre at the far end. Come on!"*

Seizing Bella by the arm, he took the stairs two at a time and ran through the kitchens to the back entrance with the hotelier close behind.

They raced across the yard and burst into the long, low building opposite the museum. At the far end was the room which Bella had always thought looked like a small operating theatre. The door was locked.

Steed and Lurchman exchanged glances, then together they hurled themselves at the flush-fitting wood. The door shivered but held. From within came an inarticulate shout of rage. They shouldered it again. And once more the panels shuddered but refused to give way. Lurchman laid a hand on Steed's arm. "Let me," he said quietly—and he withdrew several paces, ran forward, and launched himself at the door with one foot held before him like a battering ram. His heel slammed into the door just below the handle, with all his weight behind it. There was a splintering crash and the door burst open.

Emma Peel lay bent backwards over the steel vivisection table. Her long, slim legs dangled over the edge nearest the door and her arms were drawn down over the sides at the far end. Her wrists and ankles were strapped to the tubular legs. They could not see her face as her head was dropped back over the edge of the small table—but below the pointed chin a pulse was beating faintly. Behind, Warbeck-Simner crouched by an anaesthetic trolley laden with heavy gas cylinders, his eyes wild and furious. In one hand he held a gleaming hypodermic.

"Get away," he snarled. "Keep out of this or it will be the worse for you—and for her." He swung the operating table around on its castored wheels and drew it towards him, thrusting the trolley down towards the door with a push from his foot at the same time. Now that she was broadside on, they could see that Emma appeared to be unconscious.

"By God, Simner," Steed said thickly, "if anything's happened to her . . ."

He moved forward purposefully into the small room. Mark and Bella stayed one at each side of the door.

"*Stop!*" The ornithologist was behind the vivisection table with its inert human cargo, his syringe held menacingly above her vulnerable neck. "Nothing has happened to her. She's under sedation while I decide how to punish her impertinence." He stared at them balefully, his crazed eyes glittering. "But if you come a step nearer, the needle goes into her throat—and I need hardly specify, Mr Clever Steed, with what the syringe is filled . . ."

"You dangerous imbecile, *drop that syringe.*" Steed's voice was like a whiplash.

Warbeck-Simner's face crumpled. "You mustn't talk to me like that," he said. "You're supposed to respect me. *I* am the important one here; *I* give the orders. How dare you flout my authority!"

"*Your* authority!" Steed was still advancing slowly, his features a mask of contempt. "The authority of a madman, an outrageous lunatic who has already killed at least sixteen innocent people—for no reason other than the feeding of his own monstrous ego."

"If you mean the fools who died because they ate ducks which had been poisoned by Helimanthine, don't waste your sympathy. They were dispensable. If they were idiot enough to buy illegally poached game, they deserved all they got. It's not my fault if people get hurt poking their noses in—besides, we had to have practical experiments; we couldn't do it *all* on paper: it's not reasonable to expect us to. We had to have a few trial runs before we could justify the expense of taking the birds all the way . . ." He stopped speaking suddenly, his gaze fixed on Steed, who was still wearing the remains of his Arab costume. "Yes," he said softly. "All the way to Morocco. Only we didn't go, did we? Mr Clever Steed was too bright by half: he brought Morocco to us by an underhand, sneaking, despicable, cowardly trick that would have disgraced the lowest guttersnipe in the Civil Service. Well, Mr Brilliant Steed"—his voice, which had been steadily rising as he spoke, now cracked on a note of hysteria and fury—"Well, Mr Brilliant Steed, you're so good at fixing things, see how you can fix *this*!"

With a lightning-like movement, he twitched up the hem of Emma's black skirt to reveal her thighs and plunged the hypodermic needle deep into the soft white flesh which showed above the tops of her stockings.

Before Steed could hurl himself across the room or Mark Lurchman reach the table, he had thumbed home the plunger to inject the contents of the syringe into Emma's veins and swung the wheeled table round to keep it between himself and the two men. Then, with a brusque movement of his arms he shoved it towards them and dodged towards the door. He plucked Bella Reeves away from the doorpost and spun her into the path of Lurchman to confuse the pursuit, and was through the door and away down the long aisles between the laboratory benches before they had realised what he was doing.

Once more Steed took command. "After him, Mark," he cried tightly. "Bring him back alive if you can. But kill him if necessary—like a mad dog, he'll have to be destroyed if he can't be contained." Before Lurchman had wheeled to set off after the madman, he was beside the table, thumbing back Emma's eyelid. His face was very grave.

"All right, Bella," he rapped. "This is up to us. You used to be a nurse. Concentrate—and *remember*. Forget all about the lunatics, forget about what we've been doing, forget about the birds and the marsh. The only thing you must think about is saving Mrs Peel's life. If it's possible, we'll do it."

"What did he inject?" Bella asked.

"Helimanthine, I think. I'm not sure, but we'll have to take a chance—thank God I forsaw something of this kind might happen."

"What can we do?"

"Find me a clean syringe on that rack—No, no. Don't bother to sterilise it. We haven't time." He reached into his pocket as the girl ranged along the wooden fixture, seeking a hypodermic of suitable size, and took out a small phial.

"That'll do," he called. "Hand it over. Quick. Right."

He snatched the gleaming instrument from her hand and jabbed the needle upwards into the rubber bung of the inverted phial.

"What is it, Mr Steed?" Bella asked as he withdrew the plunger to fill the syringe.

The undercover man was pinching up a fold of flesh in the bend of Emma's elbow. "Prostigmine," he replied without looking up. "It's the antidote to Curare—and Helimanthine's a more powerful derivative of Curare—so I'm hoping that it may work."

"Suppose it wasn't Curare that he gave her? What effect will the antidote have?"

Steed plunged home the piston and held the hypodermic in place. "I don't know," he said soberly. "I just don't know."

He straightened up, handing the syringe back to Bella. "Now we have to work," he said. "Do you know the effect of Curare?"

"Only that it relaxes you. They use it in surgery sometimes."

"It relaxes by completely paralysing the muscles, so that you've no control over them whatever, conscious *or unconscious*. In minute doses this helps surgeons: it stops patients under anaesthetic from involuntarily contracting their muscles while incisions are made. But in large doses it's fatal because it stops the muscles of the heart and lungs working and the victim suffocates."

"What does the antidote do?"

"I don't know," Steed said frankly. "All I know is that it acts fairly quickly, but that you've got to give it time to chase round the circulatory system until it catches up, as it were, the poison. Then it has a chance to do its work." He had been anxiously watching Emma's face as he spoke, and now he leaned down and scrutinised her features. "Bella," he said sharply. "One of those trolleys must carry oxygen cylinders. Please locate it and bring it over."

The girl darted over to the opposite wall, spinning the rejected trolleys out of the way as she sought the one Steed required. "Nitrous Oxide," she muttered, "Chloral Hydrate, Ether, Chloroform—surely there must be . . . Ah! It's the one he shoved at the door!" She wheeled the heavy carriage with its twin cylinders and corrugated loops of rubber tubing over to Steed.

"We'll have to use this, Bella," he said tensely. "The drug's acting too quickly. Look—the breathing's getting shallower and shallower. The muscles of the lungs are packing up."

"Shall I untie her hands and feet?"

"No. We haven't time. Put the mask over her face. Quick— we'll have to help her breathe until the antidote's had time to work." In the silence of the laboratory, the rubber bag beneath the face mask filled and emptied itself pathetically slowly, the creases in the quartered container inflating and deflating with a desultory pop. Soon, the flow of breath was reduced to a flutter.

"More oxygen," Steed said tightly. "The movement of the lungs has practically stopped . . . Bella—watch the rhythm of her breathing and take over."

"What do you mean?"

"Reverse the tap so that the gas fills the bag, and then force it into the lungs by squeezing the bag with your hands . . . yes, that's it. Slowly. Keep the same rhythm as the breathing . . . Good. Keep her going while I give her another injection of Prostigmine . . ."

Intent about their tasks, the man and the girl busied themselves around the inert figure on the operating table. As Bella palped the breathing bag and kept the mask firmly jammed over Emma's unconscious face, Steed leaned his weight on and off her rib cage, willing the paralysed lungs to work in time with the incoming oxygen. At last there was a tremor, an answering movement beneath his hands. The marbled eyelids shivered; the nostrils dilated. There was a faint rattling at the back of the throat as air began to be drawn back into the mouth.

The antidote was beginning to work.

Several things happened at once then. There was a sudden confused noise of shouting outside the building. Footsteps pounded on the cobbles of the yard. Clearly into the night air the sound of two shots reverberated—the flat, ringing crack of an automatic followed by the deeper boom of a shotgun. Steed sprang for the door. "Look after her, Bella," he called. "She should be all right now—but keep a close watch. I must go out and help . . ."

He sprinted through the laboratory and out into the open air. The moon was up now, etching ebony shadows behind the pale, flat cutouts of turret and wall. On the terrace and across the lawn, the debris of the evening's masquerade was strewn oddly in the silver light. Someone had put out the arc lights and these, like metal birds roosting on their gantries, presided over the tangle of cables on which stuffed Flamingos and live ducks lay scattered and bemused. At one corner of the balustrade, Reeves crouched, the barrel of his duck gun glinting in the moonlight.

He was facing the yard, head cocked forward and eyes strained to pierce the shadows at the foot of the steps. And round the corner of the house behind him—having circled the building undetected—Charnley stole step by step across the flags with a pistol at the ready.

Before Steed could open his mouth to shout a warning, there was a blur of movement from the balcony above the scientist's head, and something dark and amorphous swept down to envelope his head and shoulders in its folds. The poacher swung round and closed with the struggling man, his long arm tweaking the gun from his adversary's grasp before Charnley realised what had happened. There was a brief tussle on the terrace, but by the time Steed had run up the steps to lend a hand, Reeves had the scientist in an arm lock and the battle was over. "Thanks, mate," the poacher called, panting, with a glance upwards at the balcony. And then Steed saw that Benson, recovered from the blow which had knocked him out, was leaning over the edge by the silent projector.

"Have you seen the other one, Benson?" Steed asked.

"Not a sign, Mr S . . . Came to after that crack on me nut and looked out to see Reeves and Dr Who down there doin' a duel in the moon, and that's all. I did hear footsteps—*There he is!*"

The little man was pointing excitedly towards the drive. Reeves swung the captive Charnley, still with the coat Benson had dropped over his head, in that direction and they all stared towards the front of the house. The substitute tape recordings Steed had lodged earlier in the evening were still relaying the sounds of waves breaking and oriental voices bargaining in the market. Against this bizarre background Warbeck-Simner's appearance was lent a grotesque quality which momentarily froze them to the spot.

The master of Turret House was dressed in full peer's regalia, ermine robes and all. A coronet sat rakishly upon his domed head. There was some kind of mayoral chain of office around his neck and in his hand he carried what looked remarkably like a mace. In the bright moonlight he strode towards the house gesturing with his free hand, his eyes glaring and his lips flecked with foam.

"Strewth!" Benson said from above. "He's gone right round the bend now . . . off his rocker completely!"

"I think we're seeing the first appearance of the new Earl of Bratby—and probably the Gauleiter of all England in his own crazy mind," Steed murmured. "He's going to get a bit of a shock, though, if he comes much further."

"What, them white posts with the magic eyes?"

"Yes—but they won't actuate a tape of dogs barking. I—er—altered the programme for tonight . . ."

Warbeck-Simner was approaching the double row of posts. Before he reached them, Charnley twisted eel-like from Reeves's grasp, threw off the coat, and dashed towards his chief. "My lord," he was shouting, "your humble subjects prepare to demonstrate their loyalty . . ."

Warbeck-Simner passed the first pair of white posts.

There was a screech of multiple jets, the roar of a heavy aircraft diving immediately overhead. The noise was appalling.

The ornithologist halted in his tracks, gave one terrified glance upwards—and then broke for the cover of the trees. At the other end of the line of posts Charnley, too, stared at the deafening noise in the sky before running in panic from the road. On converging diagonals, the two madmen rushed towards each other through the bushes.

*"Simner! Stop,"* Steed cried suddenly, starting forward. *"Look out, you fool. Charnley's going to run across—"*

He broke off. The roar of the tape-recorded airplane died away in the distance, and clearly in the ringing silence which replaced it they heard the squeak of the gate as Charnley hurled himself through the wicket. There was a dreadful, vibrant twang and the crash of something heavy among the Rhododendrons. Then the scientist's footsteps receding among the dead leaves under the trees.

Steed and Reeves hurried across the drive as Benson ran down the stairs inside the house to join them. Warbeck-Simner lay on his face. The murderous bolt from the crossbow had caught him between the shoulder blades and now only the tip of the steel shaft gleamed incongruously in the bright moonlight above the crumpled crimson of his robe. Below him, a deeper crimson seeped stealthily among the leaves.

\*         \*         \*

It was a half hour later. Emma had quite recovered and was sitting in one of the wrought iron chairs by the French windows, with Bella standing protectively behind her. Steed, Benson and the poacher were sampling a bottle of brandy which Reeves had found in the dining room cupboard, and Mark Lurchman was standing guard over a sullen Charnley. The scientist had run full tilt into him while he was still trying to locate Warbeck-Simner and the struggle which followed had been short but decisive. The jar of poison pellets stood isolated in the centre of the table.

The body of the master of Turret House had been decently recovered and now, as they waited for the police to arrive from Bratby, they looked at each other wondering what to say.

The six of them presented an odd sight: Bella with a bath robe flung over the yellow bikini and her darkened flesh; Steed and the poacher still swarthy beneath their Arab robes; Mark wearing a white jacket and a false moustache; Benson in ordinary clothes—and Emma looking prim and proper in the black and white uniform of a housemaid . . .

It was Emma who broke the silence first. She burst out laughing. "Well, I don't know about Double-Oh-Seven," she said, "but if this was an espionage operation, at least we could claim to be the Double-Ee-Three!"

"I'm sorry to be slow on the uptake, my dear," Steed said, looking at her dubiously, "but I don't quite . . ."

"You and Bella and myself," Emma said, laughing weakly again. "Steed, Reeves, Peel—the three names, don't you see? They all have double ee . . . Oh, never mind! Perhaps Heliman-thine makes you light headed . . ."

"It's not that, miss." It was Benson speaking. "There's a perfectly good reason here for the whole shoot. Look!"

He was pointing to the calendar which Mark had altered to show the date on which the Hodder ducks were due to leave Morocco. The heavy black lettering spelled out the words *APRIL 1st.*

# 18

## YOU CAN ALWAYS DUCK...

"Pretty gel. Got a fine pair of legs on her." His Nibs was not noted for the prodigality of his praise when the distaff side was under review. Across the low table General Mackinlay lay back in his armchair and nodded his head several times.

"Aye," he said at last.

"I mean to say, I don't hold with all this modern flummery and women drivin' motors an' all that. But young Steed's at least picked a gel to help him on this do who knows how to hold herself. Bet she's a tolerable seat on a horse, too."

"Aye."

"Mind you, Mackinlay, these things are best left to men. But I'm not saying she wasn't of use. We'd never have known about their batty plans at all if she hadn't been staked out inside the place, would we?"

The general leaned forward and lifted his glass of whisky from the table. He sipped and considered. "No," he said at length. "No, ye would not indeed."

His Nibs reflected a moment longer on their recently departed guests. "All the same," he said, "I shall never really understand these young people. Just look at their behaviour at luncheon." He picked up his own glass and drained it.

"Ye're no suggestin', forbye—"

"I'm suggesting nothing, Mackinlay. But you'd think after all that gadding about in the open air that they'd have worked up something of an appetite, wouldn't you?—Not a bit of it. They left practically all of that duck pâté. Both of them. Extraordinary people! I'm surprised at young Steed ..."

He picked up his copy of *The Times* and rattled it disapprovingly.

"It's all finished, then? Ye'll no be needin' the platoon I was offerin' ye?"

"No, no, thank you very much, Mackinlay. MacCorquodale's men have combed the place out and taken away all the interesting stuff from the lab. The poison's accounted for and so are all the birds. Charnley'll get ten years on the conspiracy charge alone. It's all over now, thank God."

"Aye . . . 'Twas a queer case just the same. A weird one."

"Nonsense, Mackinlay." His Nibs settled down behind his paper once more. "Not half so queer as some of the things these newspaper fellers would have us believe." His voice growled on petulantly. "What do they take us for? A lot of blessed idiots or what? . . . Just listen to this—here's some feller says an *eagle* has been seen over the beach at Ostend carrying an umbrella . . . I mean, I ask you! An eagle. With an *umbrella*!"

"At Ostend?"

"Yes . . . I daresay you're right there, Mackinlay. They're a pretty odd lot, these continentals. Even so, fancy expecting us to believe a story like that . . ."

Edward F. Meade

# REMEMBER ME

Introduction - Norman Shrive

General Editor - Malcolm Ross

New Canadian Library No. 47

MCCLELLAND AND STEWART LIMITED

The following dedication
appeared in the original edition:


To Winifred


This book was first published by
Faber and Faber Limited, England, in 1946

*The Canadian Publishers*
*McClelland and Stewart Limited*
*25 Hollinger Road, Toronto 16*


PRINTED AND BOUND IN ENGLAND BY
HAZELL WATSON AND VINEY LTD
AYLESBURY, BUCKS

"We who have trod the borderlands of death,
   Where courage high walks hand in hand with fear,
   Shall we not hearken what the Spirit saith :
   'All ye were brothers there, be brothers here'.

"Let us draw closer in these narrower years,
   Before us still the eternal visions spread;
   We who outmastered death, and all its fears,
   Are one great army still, living and dead."

*Canon Scott*

*All the characters
in this novel
are fictitious*

# INTRODUCTION

PROBABLY sometime in 1918, perhaps shortly before he was killed in action on November 4, Wilfred Owen hastily scribbled a Preface to the little collection of poems that was to make him, with his fellow soldier Sassoon, the most notable of the so-called "war poets." In those less than twenty lines, most of them abrupt, even elliptic, statements, Owen warned his readers that his book was not about heroes but about war and the pity of war. And the poetry, he said, was "in the pity."

Remember Me is a "war novel" in the same way that Owen's poetry is "war poetry." It points up, in fact, how such classifications are merely convenient, how they may, indeed, by their implications, be inaccurate. For it is not about heroes in the traditional sense, unless the Canadians at Caen can be considered as a single person. And certainly O'Rourke, the central figure of the story, is not at all concerned with glory, honour and deeds of valour, as were, for example, Crane's Henry Fleming or even Hemingway's Frederick Henry. For although Fleming learned that the days of Homeric struggle and waving banners were gone, he also discovered that he could still attain his red badge of courage. And Henry, although he came to realize that "the words sacred, glorious and sacrifice" were "embarrassing," even "obscene," wants us to believe that a man can achieve the most heroic act of all—to opt out of the war, to make a separate peace. But Meade's soldier is neither of these. He is closer to Owen's, even though he is of another generation, of another country, and fighting in another war. Meade believes as Owen believed—as Hemingway ultimately did—that war is the abscess of the human condition, that when it breaks, people like O'Rourke are committed, and that the battle is not so much against the opposing army as against the festering sore of evil that threatens to infect all sides. As O'Rourke, almost sickened by the sight and stench of the shattered German bodies, views the aftermath of heavy bombardment, he realizes that here too "a poppy will grow." This is about as close as he ever comes to expressing his feelings about war in general; he is not the sensitively articulate speaker of Owen's poems. But O'Rourke is representative of his time and place, the individual who despises the war and the wreck it makes of human lives but who, albeit sorrowfully, accepts its apparent inevitability and his own necessary involvement. And it is Meade's poignant awareness of the role of O'Rourke and the legions of others like him that makes us realize, as we turn the lovingly written last pages of this book, what the title means. For then we know, as perhaps never before, the significance of the time-worn phrase "lest we forget."

Then we know. And then we know too, if we think about it, how we have been prepared throughout the novel, subtly but assuredly, for its conclusion. The title, in fact, is given early to us in the thoughts of O'Rourke's wife as she stands on the platform long after the regiment has pulled away from the little prairie station :

> He will remember me when he hungers for love, and when he is tired and thinks of warm sleep. He will think of me when he sees the sun on quiet fields or hears a bird sing at dawn. He will not remember me when he is fighting, nor in the mud and rain. He will remember me only at times when he is quiet, when he thinks of joy and love and happy days. And that is enough . . . .

But despite the emphasis upon the individual human sensibility conveyed by such lines and others like them, the dominant impression of at least the first third of the book is rather that of the documentary film, the subject in this case being a young Canadian going to war; one can imagine, indeed, that he is reading a National Film Board script, much elaborated but simply entitled "Bob O'Rourke, First Division." There is an abstract, almost generalizing, character about these pages in their delineation of the long trip to Halifax, the poker games and the letter-writing, the "east coast port" and the troopship ("the greatest liner afloat"). It is this quality of objectivity in presentation, both of scene and of men, that will make such chapters so vividly realistic to those who with thousands of others embarked on that greatest adventure of their lives, those who might identify O'Rourke with now almost-forgotten figures in battle-dress, even with themselves as they were part of an army. We do not learn O'Rourke's first name until we are many pages into the book; there were many Barbaras in London ("Someone else had undoubtedly taken his place. Life makes its own laws and finds its own justification"); every company had its ingenious Finkle; more than one had a Private Snowden, a

Captain Brodin. Major Brest who finds it expedient, for the sake of his career, to take away O'Rourke's stripes and, for the sake of his conscience, to offer them back, was (and probably still is) a recognizable figure in the squirrel cage of service politics. And O'Rourke who, "had he lived in another age . . . , might have been a pirate or a buccaneer or rebel leader or frontiersman," was "still one of the earth's little men."

And yet by such means Meade deftly gains our confidence and commitment. The pace of the novel is like that of the war itself, or more appropriately, the war as it was to those who for months, even years, waited in their H-huts and Nissens, played their serious games of war on the fields and coasts of Britain, grew to love the beauty of its landscape and the character of its people, and then at last met the enemy in the hell of Normandy. There are risks involved in such depiction, even when varied by anecdote and warmed by glimpses of individual personality, for it is largely dependent upon and limited by the historical facts. The novelist has to make the long time of waiting meaningful to his reader in reference to demands quite different from those that are enjoined on the military historian. And so Meade not only runs a thread of narrative through those months from December 1940 to June 1944—a thread insufficient in itself to warrant the term "novel" other than in the most technical sense—but he also gradually evokes from the relation of their passing, one after another, the enriching note of compassion that will eventually dominate the novel at its conclusion. It is this evocation that turns the story into a novel; to paraphrase Owen, the novel is in the pity.

And here the part contributing most significantly, and perhaps almost solely, to Meade's purpose is that played by Canada itself. *Remember Me* is a novel about war and the tragedy of war, but it is also a novel about Canada and the love of Canada. In O'Rourke's longings for home there is "a passionate, wild, unutterable love for the things which he had thought forgotten but which returned now, fixed forever in time because he had lived in them, been wrought out of them, and would return to them." In the snow that falls upon an English village "a thousand voices seemed to whisper . . . 'Canada! Canada! Canada!' " and to carry to the ecstatic men "a symphony of wind in wilderness," a music once heard and long forgotten but now returning O'Rourke to the winter night of his marriage, the sleigh ride home from the church, the parting on the snow-covered platform. And the plaintive "Red River Valley," sung around a fire that casts shadows upon a burnt-out Tiger tank, evokes memories "of the rich and powerful land of home, of the mighty slow-winding rivers of the prairies, of the solitary, lonely man upon the vast curvature of the earth."

The yearning of O'Rourke for home and love becomes almost agonizing after he kills the young German, and in a poignantly paradoxical sense its tender but fervent power is ultimately responsible for his being able to transcend time and space and to go home at last. From a field of yellow mustard in Normandy he is transported to Yellow Prairie, and his life has come full circle. A train had carried him away, long years ago, on that first day of winter. Now another train "was heading into the West," to "the fabulous land," to "the land of rich inheritance." And there, in the golden radiance of the harvest, O'Rourke returns to his father's house.

NORMAN SHRIVE

*McMaster University*
March 1964

# 1

I

THE station at Yellow Prairie at three o'clock in the afternoon presented a gala appearance. The platform was thronged with people : soldiers, women, children and civilian menfolk. At one end of the platform a military band played old, nostalgic war tunes such as "Tipperary," "Auld Lang Syne," "Roll Out the Barrell" and "Wish Me Luck." The music blared into the cold sharp air and mingled with the hum of voices. No one paid any attention to it. No one really heard it, except perhaps one or two girls who, withdrawn from the crowd, heard the slow even swing of "Auld Lang Syne" and cried gently, trying to suppress their tears while their menfolk, enormous in greatcoats and full kit, stood awkwardly by attempting to console them.

The crowd had gathered into tiny knots of four or five people, between which there was a constant weaving as friends went from one group to another, and of others searching for familiar faces. Each tiny group had as its centre a departing soldier upon whom mothers, sisters, sweethearts or wives were bestowing those eternal sentiments which are given in the last moments of departure to loved ones—sentiments of abiding love and anxiety clothed in admonitions, instructions and generalities.

The scene was jocular. As the Colonel expressed it later to his officers in the mess : "It went off well." Yet, withal, there was a dark melancholy undertone, a sense of heaviness in the atmosphere. The women looked at their sons, lovers and husbands as though to capture and hold forever the sweet familiarity of their faces, the known expressions, the last image. In the hearts of many there lay the dread, cold fear that this was the final parting. As though to hide their sentiments before the gaze of kinsmen and strangers alike they indulged in banal remarks about wearing apparel, comfort, and health, and glanced down the tracks as though to halt the approaching train.

On the second track in front of the station five cars had

been drawn up by a switch engine. They were old wooden coaches of the type in common use between mainline divisional points thirty years ago, but nowadays in use only on small branch line trains. The exigencies of war, however, had forced the railways to call out every available piece of serviceable equipment. There they stood, the once fine paintwork faded and chipped, the windows dirty, the plush seats dusty and worn, the under-carriage and trucks ridiculously light for modern locomotive power and speed. These cars awaited the troops who thronged the station platform with their relatives and friends.

But now the atmosphere of the scene had changed. From afar came the long whistle of the approaching train. The crowd heard it and was quiet a moment, and in that lull could be heard the sharp, staccato roar of a nearby yard engine. Then a wave of agitation gripped the crowd, and the din of voices and the shuffling of feet rose above the blare of the band. Final farewells were said by relatives and friends. People began to move back from the platform against the station front, leaving the soldiers with their next of kin—their wives, sweethearts and mothers. And these, grasping at the last few moments of farewell, began to speak the concern of their hearts. "Take care of yourself, son" . . . "I'll miss you, darling" . . . "Will you think of me often?" . . . "I'll be waiting for you, dear."

Against the baggage-room doors a young corporal and his wife stood gazing into each other's eyes, their hands clasped. She wore a brown coat with fur on the collar, which was open at the throat. Her head was thrown back as she looked up at him. Her lips were parted as though to speak, but instead her eyes filled with tears—great, slow tears. Hurriedly she dried them, turning her head away from him.

"Silly of me, darling," she said, smiling. "Forgive me."

She looked up at him again, with a bright smile that held back the tears. 'I mustn't cry, I mustn't,' she thought. 'He's leaving me. . . . In another minute he'll be gone. Oh, darling, you have given me so much happiness, so much life. You'll never know what you are to me. Never!'

"Bob," she said, aloud, turning her head to one side in a manner that he knew so well, "Bob, I just now thought . . . I'll have a great big apple pie and a fresh chocolate cake waiting for you when you come back. I'll put them in the oven the moment I hear you're coming. There, now!"

She bit her lip suddenly. Into her eyes there came a look of infinite sadness. There were no words, no expression that could convey to him the nameless wonder of her love and happiness. He was to go and carry with him only the certainty of her love locked within him. She was no more to him than that—a certainty of love, a faith, a belief—a nameless yet precious thing which he was to carry away with him to the battlefields of Europe, and that was to remain with him like a beacon to the end of his days. That and no more, and yet it was all.

Now the train was pulling into the station. The great engine thundered past the crowded platform and the multitude of eyes turned to it had a glimpse of the engineer in the cab, a small, grey-haired man with a sharp chin and nose and goggles over his eyes, who sat at his window looking ahead down the track, one hand raised to his controls.

The train came to a stop with the last car near the end of the platform. It had hardly stopped when a nearby switch engine coupled on to the five empty coaches on the next track and, with a tremendous roar and belch of smoke and steam, began to drag them off down the yards to a switch connected to the mainline track. In a few minutes it came back, pushing the coaches before it, and with a sharp clatter that passed successively through each car, coupled the coaches to the train.

O'Rourke took his wife's face in his hands and gazed at her a moment. "I've got to help get the men aboard, darling. Stay right here. I'll be back in a few minutes." He kissed her lips quickly and, turning, strode off to help the sergeant herd the men aboard. As he weaved through the crowd he heard the sergeant's voice above the din, issuing sharp orders to the men who were straggling behind. On the whole the men were embarking with very little trouble.

As soon as the cars had been coupled to the train, there had been a general rush to obtain the best seats at the windows. Many intended to find seats, shed their equipment on them, then return to the platform for a last hurried farewell with wives and sweethearts. The sergeant had anticipated this. He had posted pickets at all the doors. Once having climbed aboard no one was allowed off. Farewells were being shouted from the car windows and doors. The men waved their arms and shouted to friends and relatives, and these in turn called back last-minute endearments and words of courage. The band, playing "Tipperary" again, swung into "Auld Lang Syne," and some of the crowd joined in.

Meanwhile Corporal O'Rourke and the sergeant worked their way through the crowd getting the stragglers aboard. By the time they had reached the end of the platform every man had been put on board, the pickets stood by the doors barring the way down the crowded steps and the crowd, still singing with the band, pushed across the platform to the side of the train.

The sergeant took off his cap and wiped his forehead on his sleeve.

"Whoo," he exclaimed, "that's that! Went off easier than I expected. Let's see now. . . ." He looked at his watch. "We've got a minute and a half. Has your wife gone?"

"Not yet."

"Well, run over and catch a quick one, and then aboard. I'll stay here till we begin to move."

He watched the corporal shouldering his way roughly through the crowd. "Lucky bugger," he said aloud. His own wife was not there to see him off. She didn't believe in scenes and had said her farewell at home that morning. It had left a bitterness in him that he could not argue away. He consoled himself that he had left her well provided for, anyway. A soldier could do no more than that.

O'Rourke found his wife in a little clearing in front of the baggage-room doors. Her hands, grasping her purse, were crossed in front of her, and her eyes searched the people whose backs were now toward her. As she caught sight of her husband shouldering his way through the crowd, her face lit up with a radiant smile and she ran a few steps to meet him. Their arms were about each other and she gave herself to his kiss, fiercely. The train whistled; silence for a moment descended upon the crowd; then, effortlessly, without the usual roar of gathering power, the train began to move. She broke from his embrace.

"Darling, darling, the train is moving! Oh, darling!"

He drew her to him again, but now their kiss was not fierce, wild and spending; it was ineffably soft and gentle, and seemed to fuse them into one being. For a brief moment he stood away from her, holding her at arm's length, gazing into her eyes. Then he turned and was lost in the crowd. She had a glimpse of him as he sprang on to the steps of the last car as it drew past the platform. She raised her arm limply and waved as everyone was waving. But she could not see him in the crowd of faces and waving arms. She saw the roof of the last car above the crowd and for a moment saw the whole train down the tracks where it drew past the grain elevators. The windows and doors of the train were crowded with faces, shoulders and waving arms, and he was there, one of them, but she could not see him.

She stood for a long time on the platform with her eyes fixed upon the dark trail of train-smoke against the sky. A heavy snow had begun to fall, muffling the sounds about the station. Large, light flakes fell on her hair and about her shoulders, melting on her face with the softness of a caress. Gradually there stole over her the sensation that her spirit, the flame of her life, had left her, and she was only a shell. To her the surrounding voices came faintly as from a great distance. She felt cold and utterly empty.

Thoughts came to her from afar, from beyond the curtain of falling snow. And she thought: 'I am like a cup that he has emptied and set down upon a table in a cold room, which he has left, closing the door after him. He will remember me when he hungers for love, and when he is tired and thinks of warm sleep. He will think of me when he sees the sun on quiet fields or hears a bird sing at dawn. He will not remember me when he is fighting, nor in the mud and rain. He will remember me only at times when he is quiet, when he thinks of joy and love and happy days. And that is enough. . . .'

The sounds of her surroundings came back to her. She started and looked about her. Only a few people were left upon the platform. The express man, pulling a wagon load of rattling milk cans, shouted to the loiterers, "Gangway! gangway!"

She turned slowly, and walked up the main street of the town. People spoke to her in passing, but she did not hear them. At her door she stood for a long time, with her eyes fixed upon a fresh footprint in the snow, gazing at it until the soft, falling flakes obliterated its sharp pressed outline. Then she turned and let herself in and climbed the stairs to their room.

She stood in the opened door and looked around the room at the soft, bright quilt upon the bed, the pictures, the chair, the geraniums on the window-sill. Wearily she walked over to the chair and sat on the edge of it with her knees pressed together, her hands clenched in her lap. She sat there a long time in the gathering darkness, listening to the silence of the room.

2

The town of Yellow Prairie had hardly disappeared below the horizon when the soldiers began their preparations for the long journey to the seaboard.

Each of the cars contained twenty-four sections, each section to berth four soldiers—two upper and two lower. The problem of who was to sleep in the hard upper berths and who was to sleep in the bumpy lowers arose.

The men first argued, cursed and attempted to settle possession by main strength. But since the majority were of more or less equal tenacity, this course was soon dropped for more hopeful means of settlement. Some settled the problem by flipping coins, some by taking precedence by length of service, some by an agreement to alternate the positions nightly; some bought the lower berth preferences, and others simply took them. Within a very few miles it was all settled.

By the time Corporal O'Rourke began his first tour of duty through the cars the men had to some degree "settled down." The upper berths had been pulled down and loaded with greatcoats, packs, webbing, and all the sundry equipment worn by the men. They sat in the seats, playing poker on improvised tables or arguing or looking thoughtfully out of the windows at the dying day. In one of the cars O'Rourke stopped for a moment to watch a poker game. One of the men looked up at him.

"Where do we eat, Corporal?" he asked.

O'Rourke shrugged his shoulders. "Winnipeg, probably."

"Does anyone know?"

O'Rourke shrugged again. "It'll be looked after," he said, and passed on down the swaying car.

The soldier who had asked the question looked at his comrades, then, suddenly, he threw his cards across the table.

"There you go," he cried. "The same old line. IT'LL BE LOOKED AFTER. By who? Godamighty, I suppose. He's going to meet us at Winnipeg Depot with a mobile canteen and we'll have soup and chicken and nuts. That's how you get to be a corporal—by trusting somebody else to look after things."

"Hell, let's get on with the game."

"Yeh," someone else added. "Quit your beefing and play. We'll eat some time—we always do."

The game got under way again and the meal was forgotten.

Corporal O'Rourke reached the end of the last car and stepped out on the vestibule. The swirling snow carried in the wake of the speeding train drove against his face with the force of driven sand. The sway of the car, the roar of the wheels upon the tracks, the rush of wind, steam and blinding snow sent his spirit soaring with a sense of immense power and winged destiny. It lasted only a moment and was gone. The falling snow and gathering dark descended upon the prairie landscape like a curtain being lowered between the past and the future, shutting him off from the sight of his beloved homeland. There came to him, suddenly, the realization that out of all the substance of his life he had but a few imperishable memories—the sight of his mother making cookies on the kitchen table, a great tree standing alone upon the land, the picture of his father's door, the worn step, the open gate, the image of his wife's face.

'I must write Gerda,' he thought. 'I must tell her how wonderful she has been, how much she means to me.' There were a thousand things he had not said, had never told her. Now, in an instant, he was overwhelmed with a great desire to drain his soul to her, to express in writing all that he had left unsaid. He turned quickly and re-entered the car and picked his way down the crowded aisle, resolved to begin the letter at once while his mind was full of the things he had to say.

But he did not write the letter that night, nor the next night. Instead he got into a poker game and in five hours made ten dollars in cash and sixteen in IOUs. He did not write the letter until they sailed; then he wrote it, with the writing pad on his knees, sitting on the maindeck staircase of the troopship.

DEAR GERDA,

I have thought of many things I wanted to tell you—small things that, had you known, might have made you happier while I was gone. But now I come to write them down I find I haven't the words to express them, and I know that I never will be able to tell you. I wish I could tell you how much you mean to me, how much I love you. But there aren't words for that.

We've been married only a short while, and all that time you've had to share me with the army. And you must have known all the time that one day I would leave you. Yet you never spoke a word about it, never showed what you must have dreaded most. You have been a wonderful wife. I want you to know that I have loved only you, and that I always will. I'll try to come back just the same as you knew me.

Yours,

BOB.

When he had finished it he re-read it. It was only an ordinary letter. It said so little of what he wanted to say.

"Perhaps I'll be able to tell her later," he said to himself, and sealed the letter and posted it in the ship's orderly room. It was carried across the Atlantic and back again, and was delivered to his wife seven weeks after the day he sailed.

# 2

I

In the afternoon of the fifth day the troop train pulled onto
a siding in a small town near the sea coast. The men were
ordered out, and formed up beside their coaches. One squad
after another, they were led off at the double for a run of
exercise around the town. They had taken these exercising runs
at two or three stops in their long journey. The first had been
in the cold dawn of a rocky Ontario town; then once in the
deep snow around a mountainous Quebec village. That time it
had been fun, for the air was fresh and crisp and the sunlight
on the new snow roused their drowsy spirits and sent the blood
quickening through their veins.

Afterwards the men were herded back on the train. As
soon as they had taken their places again they settled down to
the endless games of poker, dice and bridge by which they had
amused themselves daily in the confined life of the train. Those
who had already lost their money had become spectators.
Money had changed hands a dozen times: the fortunes of the
players had waned and risen and waned again so that by now,
only the best gamblers, the barrack-room sharks, had the
money to continue, and these, like wolves waiting for the kill,
were closing in for the "take." In the beginning they had not
shown themselves, waiting, wisely, for the dimes and quarters
and dollars to collect in the pockets of the lucky winners, who
now, flush from their long streak of luck, gladly accepted the
challenge of the quiet sharks. Stakes were high. Later, during
the Atlantic crossing the sharks would settle among themselves
the eventual and final winner.

All afternoon and evening the train lay on the siding.
Speculation as to the reasons for the long wait ran rife and, as
in all such situations, it gave rise to false and impossible rum-
ours. Someone had talked to the engineer and learned of a wreck
ahead. Another person had spoken to an officer who had talked

with the O.C. of the train who attributed the delay to a mysterious change of plans.

A few hours before midnight the train pulled out of the siding and began to crawl toward the coast. The spirits of the men rose; they joined in well-known songs, songs of war, of love, of lost ladies and loose ladies—barrack-room ballads of endless verses. And so the train, creeping across the dark countryside, drew upon the coast and the great maze of tracks that fronted the docks of the port.

At length it drew into a long, vaulted shed that reverberated with the noise of ten thousand voices, the endless shuffle of feet, and the mumble of army lorries coming and going with loads of equipment and supplies. In the approximate centre of this vast shed a small group of officers sat at a huddle of improvised desks, sorting out piles of records, berthing and mess cards. From this desk, in a continuous rush of activity, a stream of runners kept constant contact with the arriving units. At first sight the floor of the shed resembled a section suddenly removed from a beehive, with its multitudinous and feverish activity. But order and control did exist there, set to a frenzied, high-speed tempo. From the group of intent officers in the centre of the shed emanated the chain of orders which moved the great body of soldiers from their arriving trains into the waiting ship docked alongside.

The small group to which Corporal O'Rourke belonged passed out of the train and down the shed by slow stages. Few of them had ever before been on board a big liner—few indeed had ever seen one. Their first impression was an overwhelming sense of unreality that deepened as they were led by a maze of passages and stairs, up through the ship, deck after deck, until they eventually were brought to their assigned quarters on the boat deck. The cabins opening on to this deck had been stripped of their luxurious furnishings and filled with two-decker iron beds of the type common to army barrack-rooms. The beds had been lined into the cabins so closely that there was only enough room to squeeze between them. Each bed contained a straw mattress and was numbered. The small spaces of the walls not covered by the beds, were plastered with innumerable signs and notices, warnings of careless talk, fire, emergency signals and enemy actions.

All night a continuous stream of men poured into the great ship : the winches on the forward deck rattled and groaned. The mighty leviathan, once proud beauty of a great fleet, moved imperceptibly on the rising tide and only the occasional tug and strain of her hawsers showed that she obeyed the tidal surge entering the harbour. From her engine-room ventilators on deck rose the dull throb and pound that is the sound of a ship making up steam. Up on her enormous bridge, shaped like a hunter's bow, the officer on duty paced back and forth, stopping now and then to peer down upon the men loading on the forward deck. Every part of the ship throbbed with life. A sort of infectious excitement swept through every deck and the thousands of men moved aimlessly about under its impulse. No one slept, nor made any attempt to sleep. Every available inch of space on the decks, in the lounges and even on the stairs was filled by a continuous surge of men. Only the promenade deck and the sun deck were out of bounds. There the anti-aircraft guns were manned for immediate action, as they were to be throughout the voyage.

Corporal O'Rourke, having put his equipment on to the cot allotted to him, had fallen in with the crowd milling through the ship and had, for an hour or so, explored the passageways and stairways with an interest as intense and avid as any aboard. But eventually he tired of it and found a sheltered place behind one of the piles of life rafts. He sat there in the lee of the life rafts until morning thinking out the pattern of his life, and thinking of the war. War was only a word of terror for something as yet unencountered. Try as he did, he could not bring himself to the conception of it.

When day dawned, cold and grey and damp upon the harbour, he knew that he did not want to go to war. He knew that he had left behind him the most precious things of his life and that there was slim chance of ever recapturing them. He was no coward. He had enlisted as a volunteer long before there was any talk of drafting men for service. He was ready to fight, and he knew it had to be done. But he did not want to go to war. There were at that time a hundred million other men who kept him company in thought.

2

At eight o'clock that morning the great ship sailed. A fleet of tiny tugs nosed her out into the harbour and turned her bow toward the open sea. At slow speed she passed through the gate in the submarine net. Workmen along the docks had a last, memorable sight of her as she steamed out to sea, sweeping past the headland in a gathering surge of speed. She stood for a moment against the grey expanse of ocean, and in that moment the watchers ashore saw the vision of her monstrous form. She was the greatest liner afloat, the supreme achievement of a mighty nation of shipbuilders, the last word in luxurious ocean travel. Now in war-time, her fine white paint was covered over with ominous navy grey. Gone were her luxurious fittings, gone the pampering service of a thousand stewards and stewardesses, gone the superlative cuisine. Now, soldiers thronged the once exclusive lounge, ran for exercise along the promenade deck. The great library held three hundred hammocks, and the rosewood shelves lining the walls were adorned with tin helmets, respirators, mess tins, chocolate bars and peanuts, and extra rolls of toilet paper belonging to the men.

The sergeant of the Yellow Prairie draft had completely disappeared. O'Rourke thought of looking for him when it was time for the breakfast parade. But he changed his mind finally and paraded the men to breakfast himself. Even if he had found him, O'Rourke would have had to do the job himself. No sergeant will work so long as he can delegate a corporal for the job. So, at 9.30, O'Rourke formed the men up in the passageway outside their cabins and counted noses. There were five missing. No matter, he thought; it's their own bloody fault and they'd have an empty belly by nightfall.

He got his men to the vicinity of the mess doors. A great crowd from other units had already gathered there. They waited with a surly attitude for the doors to open. They were all hungry. It was clear that two meals a day were not going to content them. O'Rourke elbowed his way into a corner next to a doorway and lit a smoke. He was hungry and the cigarette tasted like weed in his mouth.

He heard gongs ringing far off. Some signal, he supposed, and went on puffing his cigarette, growling to himself at his hunger. Then, all at once, the whole ship was filled with the ringing of gongs, sharp and insistent. Officers and N.C.O.s began to appear out of doors and stairways, and pushed their way roughly through the throng of waiting men.

A fat captain rushed out of the crowd and past O'Rourke. In a moment he was back. His face was flushed and he was still buttoning up his tunic. O'Rourke sprang to attention.

"What are you doing here, Corporal?" he asked, trying to control his breathing.

"Waiting, sir. Waiting for breakfast." O'Rourke indicated the crowd around the mess doors with a sweep of his hand. The captain rubbed his chin with one hand while he worked a button with the other. "Hm. Well, never mind that now. Get up to the boat deck. Report to station number sixteen." And then, impatiently he shouted, "Now! On the double!"

O'Rourke went. He already knew enough about the ship to know that the boat deck was where "they kept the boats," as he put it. At last, out of breath, he came to it, and raced along a passage-way until he arrived at a door leading out on to the deck. He stopped for a moment to study the boat station indicating signs, and found that number sixteen was on the starboard side.

"It wouldn't be where I was," he grumbled, and ran through the ship to the other side.

When he got to station sixteen he found everything in order. A number of men were lined up opposite each lifeboat, along the deck. A naval officer moved down the line, checking off the stations against a list in his hand. He was a small man, and looked bad tempered. O'Rourke eased himself into the line of men, and they, to accommodate him, shuffled along to make room. It was this movement that drew the officer's attention. He looked up from his list, and his hard grey eyes took in the shuffling and came to rest on O'Rourke.

"You! Corporal!" His voice was like the cut of a whip.

O'Rourke stiffened. "Yes, sir."

"Where have you been?"

"Well, sir I . . ." O'Rourke began to explain.

"Never mind your damned excuses. You're in charge of this station. Remember that. This is no picnic. What is your name?"

"Corporal O'Rourke."

"O'Rourke what?"

"O'Rourke, sir."

The officer scribbled on his list.

"Report to me after drill. . . . Ship's orderly room."

"Yes, sir."

The officer turned and moved down the line. The sun flashed momentarily on the gold bands on his arm.

"I'm buggered now," O'Rourke whispered to the private standing next to him. "And for breakfast, too."

The naval officer had finished his inspection of the stations. He took up a position at the forward end of the boat deck. From where O'Rourke stood he looked like a small, wooden figure fixed to the deck—a grim and forbidding totem. Then, suddenly, out of nowhere, but filling the boat deck with its slow and distinctive overtone, an English voice spoke calmly, with measured words.

"You are the men of the starboard boat-deck crews. During the entire voyage, night or day, wherever you are throughout the ship, whatever you are doing, when you hear the continuous ringing of the gongs you will proceed immediately to the stations you now occupy. You will take up your position at your boat station as you now stand. You will remain in that position until further orders from the deck officer. On the command from the deck officer you will take your places calmly in the boat to which you have been assigned. Each boat will then be loaded to its limit and lowered. The senior officer or non-commissioned officer in each boat will be in charge of that boat. Should he be unable to carry out his duties the next of rank to him will take charge. That is all."

The boat deck crew broke off. O'Rourke moved under the bow of a lifeboat. It was impossible to tell where the sea ended and the sky began. Overhead the sun shone, but far away the sea and sky were grey. He looked astern. The land had disappeared.

"We're on our own now, right enough," he thought. "We can run away from a U-boat, but not from a cruiser." He scanned the arc of the sea intently. Where was the Bismarck or the Tirpitz? They had others, too. They were out on the hunt, somewhere on these waters.

"Well, anyway, I'm too bloody hungry right now to worry about it," he said aloud. "That's what the high-priced help is for."

He swung off down the deck, his mind intent on finding something to eat. He had no idea where he would find it, still less where to look. But he knew that "he would do all right." This certainty came from that period of his life when he had first run away from home and become a hobo.

As he strode the deck those years of hobo wandering came back to him with all the pent-up force that had carried him careening across the great continent, those years when he sought out danger, when he had fought, sweated, whored, swaggered and loved his way across the land, asking nothing of life but freedom, giving nothing but the substance of his wild, riotous youth. And he remembered his old dictum of those days—that he who lives dangerously lives well. In that time he had never wanted for anything. Things always came along. He always ate; not regularly, to be sure, but then that would have been rather boring. And he always slept well, out in the jungles. People didn't approve of that sort of thing;

frowned on it heavily, in fact. Still, they paid a lot of money and went to a great deal of trouble to simulate it on vacations . . . called it the outdoor life.

Outdoors. Christ! He'd had the whole continent, from the Atlantic seaboard to the Pacific, from James Bay to the Gulf of Mexico. All his, once. He was not old now, by any means. Just thirty. Age was all in the way you looked at life, and what you put into living. Go at it in a riotous sort of way, burn up all you've got in you for each day and you didn't notice time sifting through your fingers. Still there was something to be said for the settled life—good food well cooked, a fine, firm-fleshed wife who always worried about you. That was nice. He had had that, too. Come to think of it, he had tasted of everything.

Before he had gone far along the deck he found himself swaggering a little, with the same old cock-sureness of years ago. He felt suddenly the same person he had been as a hobo— confident, strong, reckless and ready for anything the world had to offer. The war became, on the instant, a great adventure to look forward to, rather than, as it had been, the dreaded cause of separation from his wife and all the comforts that he had come to know. With the old surge of hobo adventure and restlessness stirring within him, he wanted now action and combat with the enemy as fierce and wild as the surging spirit within him. Many men, in the hour of combat, have felt this wild surge and thirst for battle that is the unutterable battle cry out of dark time and the ancient forests. Those who have felt the wild battle cry in their throats and lived, have lived as heroes. Out of time and the dark forests, across the wasteland steppes, that spirit has rolled onward through the centuries with the thunder of battle. It has fenced the earth, conquered frontiers, cut pathways into the wilderness, laid waste the dreams and ambitions of proud kings and despots. Yet it has never built a village, laid a stone nor lit a beacon upon the shore, and its flight across the dark of time is a stream of crimson blood girdling the earth.

O'Rourke did not feel in the least heroic as he strode the deck with his sharp eyes on the lookout for some sign that would lead him to food. Nevertheless he was rather amazed at how marvellous a man could feel on an empty stomach once he got the bit between his teeth again, as he expressed it to himself. Then, of course, there was that matter of reporting to the ship's orderly room to catch hell from that snotty-nosed naval officer. He wasn't worrying greatly about that. That could come later. Time enough for trouble after he had found something to eat.

He decided to go below decks and see what he could dig up around the kitchens. In the first kitchen he tried he found a very indifferent welcome from the cooks. They were busy with their mid-morning preparations and wanted no conversation in exchange for food. But on his second attempt, he had better luck. Here he found an enormous negro cook, one of those black, smiling, slow-moving giants often found around kitchens. O'Rourke instantly knew his man. He knew negroes, had often travelled with them. In a few minutes he was seated at a white scoured table near one of the stoves with a plate of tender fried chicken, french fried potatoes, hot cornmeal biscuits and a cup of good coffee before him, while the negro, with a great french knife in one hand, stood watching over him, grinning from ear to ear.

Afterwards he reported to the ship's orderly room. The officer was not there, however, nor did any of the staff on duty know anything about the incident on the boat deck. The officer had apparently forgotten about it, or had forgotten O'Rourke's name. There was no charge against him, anyway; that was the important thing. With his stomach satisfied, his outlook upon the world an exciting prospect, he went back to his cabin and stretched himself out on his bunk. In a few minutes he was sound asleep, dreaming that he was home and that his wife was baking corn-meal biscuits for him. He did not feel the slight roll that came to the mighty ship as it surged eastward onto the vast ocean. He shared no part, knew no consciousness of the tense alertness and vigil of the ship's crew as they entered the submarine-infested zone—that two thousand mile stretch of mid-Atlantic in which the enemy U-boats lay in packs, like wolves, waiting for the kill. He slept on, snoring a little now and then, dreaming of his wife's corn-meal biscuits.

3

The days passed uneventfully. The great ship steered a constantly changing course, sometimes veering southward into the sun for hours, then swinging east and north again. Each sunset found her with hundreds of miles easting made good. Each morning brought her nearer her destination and the protection of shore-based aircraft escort. She ran the gauntlet of the submarine infested ocean alone, relying solely on her tremendous speed to outrun any submarine or raider that chanced upon her course. And she had the speed. She charged across the ocean like a destroyer, but with the formidable and mighty power of a battleship. The great seas struck at her. But her bow knifed the waves and cast them aside with a grand disdain. Spray, driven on the howling wind, reached high to her top decks and stung the faces of the gun crews. Yet the seas that beat against her hardly moved her at all. Now and then she rose to them, but it was a great, long, slow lifting, as though she were gathering greater power for a new surge of speed. And out upon the limitless waste of ocean all was turmoil, wind and fury, and at night unutterable darkness and the mighty voice of the storm.

On the morning of the fifth day the men awoke to discover the ship lying at anchor between two hilly shores. For a few minutes the decks were crowded with an immovable throng. Excitement ran high. They had ARRIVED, safe and sound. Cheers and songs rolled across the broad waters to the shores.

What the men saw was not by any means an inviting sight. The hills were shrouded in a thin fog, through which appeared a sombre-coloured patchwork of ploughed fields and pastures. It seemed such a cold and inhospitable land that it provoked doubts in the minds of the Canadians. They had quite different conceptions of what Scotland and England really should look like. In the minds of all, the mighty, small island was something like a geography school-book description. It was like the "Old Country" calendar pictures; like those quaint embossed Christmas card scenes, brightly coloured and glimmering with mica snow, that distant relatives sent to their "kin in Canada." England and Scotland, but particularly England, was ever to remain in the minds of the Canadian soldiers exactly true to the memory pictures formed since childhood by scenes depicted on Christmas calendars and bright cards. Even when the towns and villages and historic monuments, the ale houses and bridges and canals and moorlands and vast estates had become known and familiar to them in time to come, as moving from camp to camp, they explored and traversed the dense web of the land, they saw in everything a magical similarity, an immediate and pleasurable recognition, between the reality and the pictorial impression formed so long ago.

At noonday the great ship up-anchored and moved slowly up the Clyde. The soldiers stared with open-mouthed wonderment at the tiny, dense villages along the shores, at the ever-opening mountainous land that was at once mysterious, remote

nd incredibly beautiful. The ship passed through the narrow
ate in the submarine net, and entered the great river of her
irth.

In the middle of the afternoon she came to anchor in
he centre of the stream, opposite a great port. With one long,
mperious blast of her whistle she summoned a whole fleet of
mall craft-tenders, supply ships, barges and a great assortment
f lesser craft which came puffing out to wait attendance upon
ier. The great business of debarkation was about to begin. She
wung slowly about on her anchor chains, and the fleet of little
hips followed her about like over-anxious and zealous suitors.

# 3

---

THE sun was a ball of flame in the sky. Over the vast harbour lay a thin veil of smoke. High, high above the great river and the city, barrage balloons floated majestically and gave off sharp glints of silver as they swung lazily in the breeze.

A strange horde of men came out to invade the ship, swarming over everything. They set to work unloading the cargo into the waiting barges. The winches rattled and snorted; the men cursed and jabbered among themselves. They were very belligerent and often fought, but they laughed suddenly, too, and worked like fiends. The cargo came up, slingload after slingload. The deck was a bewildering maze of gear. In silent admiration the soldiers watched the accuracy of the winchmen, as they dropped the slings into the holds or brought them up full speed and swung them over the side with a hair's breadth of clearance.

While all this was going on, the great draft of soldiers was being sent ashore by ferries. Some of these ferries were Dutch, some French, some Norwegian—all had escaped from the mainland of Europe at the outbreak of war and now flew the blue ensign. Even in their drab navy-grey they had, somehow, a gay and carefree appearance. It was not hard to imagine their decks thronged with holiday-goers in happier times, and upon their home waters.

All through the day the unloading of cargo and the debarkation of the soldiers went on. The sun sank behind the mountains. For a long time it left its light upon the world. Then the shadows deepened and spread across the water. Ships lying at anchor loomed mysterious in the dusk. A cold wind sprang up and whistled in the high rigging of the great liner. Obediently she swung about to face the wind and the night. When it was completely dark, the winches on the forward deck stopped suddenly and for a time the workmen stood in a group talking and smoking, while the wind and escaping steam from the machines carried their voices away. Then, one by one, they disappeared down a hatchway into the ship's bowels.

At dawn the unloading began again. For those who waited to go ashore there was a fascinating world to watch— the tugs, tenders and ferries to study, the service ships that passed up and down the mighty harbour, and all the host of sea-borne traffic, the infinite variety of ships, putting to sea or entering from long mysterious voyages. Once, about midday, a naval flotilla passed outward bound, grim and deadly in appearance.

The draft to which Corporal O'Rourke belonged debarked at sunset. The ferry warped itself in against the crowded dock and the men marched ashore, two abreast. They were herded onto a waiting train. There was a considerable amount of shouting and scurrying back and forth by officers, then came a shrill whistling along the length of the platform accompanied by the slamming of carriage doors. The train, without any audible signal, without the slightest apparent effort, began to move.

In a few seconds it was hurtling along the tracks at express speed between two rows of solid-packed tenement buildings, the windows of which opened onto the tracks. Between these walls of human squalor, begrimed and filthy with the smoke and soot of ages, the train rocketed and the noise of its passing reverberated back and forth amid the still buildings and the tragic waste of bombed-out areas. Dirty children and tired-looking housewives paused to watch the train dash by. Workmen engaged in repairing the lines straightened up to look and wave a greeting to the multitude of eager and excited faces pressed to the windows of the train.

To the Canadians, who stared from the windows as the train sped along, the great city seemed full of wonder, awe and something of pity, for there flashed before their eyes vast and unimaginable stretches of brick buildings so densely packed, so sombre, dark and forbidding, that it appeared to them, despite the people they saw moving about, like a deserted city. No light of life shone forth from any home, no corner light warmed the gloom of the streets. An oppressive veil of gathering dark half hid the city. Acres of bombed-out ruins flashed past—stretches of utter ruin so sad, so desolate, lonely and tragic in the dusk of night, that it evoked a sense of unspeakable horror and pity, forever to be remembered, forever etched upon the inward mind. Then the train, sweeping around a great long bend, plunged out of the city and out upon the body of the land—the land of to-morrow's discovery.

The soldiers settled down to the journey. Soiled packs of cards were produced, improvised tables set up between the seats and penny-ante poker games began. The stakes were not high, to be sure, for it was long since the last pay-day. Still, the games passed the time while the train sped along through the night, across the unknown land. Some slept, some argued, a few engaged in mild yarns and exchange of love adventures.

2

At four-thirty in the morning the darkness was heavy, and ominous. A mist, thin and shifting, gave the air a penetrating chill. The group of officers and men who stood on the station platform huddled into their greatcoats. A little beyond the end of the platform a signal tower burned its green and red lights into the dark.

From the black wall of the R.T.O.'s office next to the station a light flickered momentarily as the door was opened and shut quickly: then the sound of sharp steel heels striking the platform in hurried steps.

One of the officers flicked his flashlight.

"Here! What is it?"

"They'll be in in about five minutes," came a voice from the dark.

"Right. Thanks."

They saw the stab of light from the opened door as the R.T.O.'s man went back to watch his phone and read the book he had left opened on the table—*A Tall Ship* by Bartimeus. The office was warm and secure, and the book kept him awake.

Out on the platform the officers listened intently for the sound of the oncoming train. All they could hear was a faint rumble, not in the least associated with a speeding train. Then, close by, they heard a clear "click," and turning, saw that one of the semaphores on the signal tower over the tracks had changed position.

"Be along in a minute now," one of the officers commented.

"And none too soon, either," came a reply. "I'm damn near dead with cold."

"Cup of coffee would go good now," another observed.

"I'll settle for tea—without sugar."

There was feeble laughter over this remark.

"Here she is now. Come along, fellows."

The train came roaring into the station and glided to a stop. The carriages were emptied. Orders were shouted into the night. The officers shouldered their way through the milling, bewildered crowd of new arrivals who wandered about in the unaccustomed darkness. Gradually the drafts for the various units were segregated but some still wandered the length of the platform, calling the names of their friends until they received an answering "hello" out of the dark. Within a few minutes the newcomers had been told off into the waiting lorries, the tail gates were swung up and made fast, and the drivers stood by, waiting the order to move.

The officer in charge of the convoy stood a few paces out from the lead lorry and shone a feeble light upon the ground at his feet to indicate his position to the waiting drivers. He raised a whistle to his lips to blow the signal, and even as the shrill note cut through the dark, another sound filled the air—the screaming wail of a siren. In that first instant of utter surprise it was like the echo of the whistle caught and amplified a thousand times. The siren screamed and died and screamed again and again.

The drivers jumped into their cabs and switched off the lights. The crack of light that had marked the bottom of the R.T.O.'s office door disappeared. The train, which until now had been standing in front of the platform while the engine crew ate their sandwiches and talked, suddenly gave out a trembling whistle and began to move out of the station. The last note of the siren died gradually. From afar away could be heard the dying notes of other sirens falling in the night. And then another sound came to the ears of the waiting men. At first it was like the light ominous whisper of a gathering wind. It died, and came again, louder.

Then suddenly the roar of engines filled the void of night. The men looked up, trying to locate the direction of the planes. In the next instant they were overhead, wave after wave of them.

Not a man spoke. Through the mind of every one ran the one question: "Are they OURS?" The passing seconds gave no answer save the ever-growing roar of dread.

Out of the thundering darkness came a sharp, rising scream that was like the hollow whistle of wind through a tube. A few hundred yards from the station a great flash of lightning struck the earth, followed in a split second by an explosion that rocked the standing lorries. The drivers crouched by their vehicles; the officers ran for the nearest shelter, a wall, a lorry. Some fell flat upon the ground. All held their breath. Bombs rained on top of the railway embankment opposite the station. The flashes revealed the trees trembling and swaying, lit with a burst of yellow fire.

Suddenly one of the drivers gave out a surprised groan, spun around and leaned against the mudguard of his lorry. In the flash of another bursting bomb, the driver of the next lorry saw his friend sliding off the mudguard to a sitting position. He ran to him and put his arms about his shoulders and together they huddled beside the wheel of the lorry.

Above the noise of the falling debris, an officer shouted with cold vehemence, "The bastards! The dirty, miserable bastards!"

Brick and stone and flying timber settled. The earth seemed to moan. The air was filled with a sharp acrid smell. A tiny fang of flame appeared across the station yard. It fingered about in the dark for a while, and then grew bolder and rose up in the blackness, burning fiercely around a heap of rubble. The whole scene danced about in the night.

The planes had passed. In the sky to the north-west a dozen searchlights swept the heavens like fingers desperately trying to part the low-moving clouds into which the raiders had disappeared. But the raiders went free. They flew northward toward the Midlands. They did their easy job of destruction and then turned homeward to their hated land. Only a little flak was thrown up at them as they came, night after night. Only a few fighters rose into the sky to do battle. Easy! It was the winter of 1940–41, the fateful year of Dunkirk and the Battle of Britain. There simply weren't the planes or the guns. Not yet. That was the truth—the simple, terrible truth that dwelt with ten million people in shelters, basements, subways and holes. NOT YET! NOT YET!

3

O'Rourke had had his baptism of fire. He was a little shattered by it. It was not an experience he could assimilate easily. He saw at once that it was not something which the individual spirit of a man could cope with. It mocked the belief in a personal divinity which guaranteed safety and immunity on the basis of an adherence to a righteous, moral, decent code. It could and did strike anywhere. To hell with who it was: whether they wore diamonds and silk underwear, a derby hat or a dirty cap, whether they carried a pornographic novel, a Bible or a school book.

O'Rourke was one of those in the lorry whose driver had been wounded. Some pieces of shrapnel had struck his shoulder bone and smashed it. He was placed in the lorry among the men and another driver substituted. The convoy moved off, out of the station yard, past the blazing firelight among the ruins. It crawled up the steep grade to the main road, then through the town and out beyond to the open countryside.

The soldier who crouched on his knees supporting the injured driver swayed as the vehicle swept around a sharp bend, and for a moment he lost his balance and fell against the injured man. The man groaned.

"Christ! Take it easy on him, Biff," one of the men remonstrated.

Biff looked up. Only the whites of his eyes showed in the dark.

"What the hell do you think I'm doing, you big lug?" he snarled. "Do you think this is a cinch, squatting here?"

He moved to relieve the strain on his legs. "Here, Chuck. Give us a hand, will you?" he asked.

The fellow addressed bent down and took the weight of the injured man's shoulder on his arms.

O'Rourke, who had followed all this without interest, as one watches people adjusting themselves in a railway coach, spoke up,

"That's no way to handle him. Take off your greatcoat, Biff. Fold it up and put it under his good shoulder. There! That's the idea. Now turn him a little so he can rest on it. That's it."

He bent down to the driver.

"How do you feel now, fellow?" he asked.

"Ugh . . . Better, thanks."

"Hurt much?"

"Now and then. Mostly now," was the answer.

"Jeese! Wasn't that some show?" asked a fellow standing behind the others. "Thought we were all going for a ride there for a while."

"Some welcome," commented another, and added fatuously, "Merry England!"

"Have you been in many raids?" someone asked the injured driver.

"Four," he replied. The word was dry and husky, spoken with far-away indifference.

"It doesn't make much difference how many raids you've been in. The first is the worst: the rest of them are like nightmares that come back again. It's nothing to worry about. If your number is on one of those bombs, it's yours right enough, and all the dodging in the world won't help you. Yeh . . . If it's got your number on it, it's yours."

It came to O'Rourke suddenly, that those words held the kernel of truth. It was the unreasonable law of gambled chance that governed the destiny of man in wars. It was not a thing he liked to accept. There should be some more predestined and logically acceptable answer to the dark mystery of death. And yet there it was, and he had no other answer. He accepted it, after all, because it liberated the mind from remorses of the kind that lead a man to question whether the governing impulse in his life had been one of good or evil; whether, from such, or in spite of such, he was to pay a penalty with premature and ungentle death upon the scene of grizzled war.

Curiously, he felt a pleasure in this fatalistic explanation. It solved so many things. Above all, it freed him from the necessity of worrying further about it, since, if his number was called, there wasn't anything he could do about it, except at the last moment (if even that fragmentary glimpse of bright and all-seeing eternity were granted him) to reckon his millionth chance of cheating the gods and getting off with only a few parts missing. And if his number wasn't on it, then of course he needn't worry about that either.

No man ever went to war who did not, at some time, reckon on his chances of casualty and escape. In some cases it becomes an obsession out of which fear, like a slow poison, eats into a man's mind so that he is but the walking semblance of a warrior bold and brave. But in most men, and particularly those slow-minded, heavy and groping thinkers, who are called the salt of the earth, this contemplation of the chances of war produces a complete acceptance of fatalistic chance that turns them loose to do the dirty work of battle with an utter disregard for their own safety.

in the barnyard well, and how, as a boy, he used to lift off a board from the well cover and peer down into the dark shaft. When he did that in the middle of a hot afternoon there came up to him a water-cold current of air that tingled his face and bare arms, and sent a sensuous shiver through his body. And he thought of the thick, dew-soaked carpet of the pastures in the early morning against his bare feet, the sight of the smoke of the breakfast fire rising into the sunlight, the smell of coffee drifting out into the yard.

All these things came to him, a whole host of poignant memories. As they walked along the road the thread of enchanting and dream-haunted memory held him bound in its magic until he was filled with a passionate, wild, unutterable love for the things which he had thought forgotten but which returned now, fixed forever in time, because he had lived in them, been wrought out of them, and would return to them. Though he were to die upon a tank-scarred field in Europe, or across a rusting wire entanglement in some forgotten wood— no matter if, or how, or where he were to die—he would return to those things which transfixed his mind, would be forever his.

And what were these things?

They were the things that brought back to him the whole blazing glory of his land—the vast, illimitable land, the cruel and lonely and poignant land, the land of passionate beauty, power and wealth. They brought to him a vision of a bounteous land wrested from the wilderness, built upon the bones and sinews of grizzled pathfinders, the ploughmen of the virgin earth who had fought the Indian, felled the forests, cut the sod, wrestled and endured and in the end triumphed over the pitiless winters and the desert heat and waste of summers.

They brought to him a vision of the great waterways of the land—the great lakes and the majestic rivers whose mighty magic-sounding names clamoured in his mind: Lake Superior, Lake Michigan, Erie, Huron, Manitoba, Winnipegosis, Lake of the Woods, Great Bear, Great Slave, the lakes of Ontario, the lakes of the plains, the lakes of the far-western mountains; and the rivers, the mighty flowing rivers that threaded the land— the noble St. Lawrence, mother of them all, the Ottawa, the Winnipeg, the Red, the Assiniboine, the Saskatchewan, the Coppermine, the Mackenzie, the Thompson, the Fraser, the Columbia.

They brought to him the memory of untold numbers of granaries of the west, of a hundred thousand miles of wheat lands, of fine herds of cattle upon the western ranges, of the oceans and rivers of fish, of mineral wealth brought out of the magic earth, of forests, primeval, vast, silent and haunted forever with a time-sorcery, the silence and magic of dark time. And of the people, HIS people, Canadians all—the Irish, Scottish English, French-Canadians, the Galicians, the Roumanians, the Germans, the Italians, the Greeks, Jews, Poles, Scandinavians, the Danes, Canadians all. Dark, swarthy, fair-skinned; toilers, parasites, trouble-makers, glowing patriots—all Canadians: the conglomerate of Europe's overflow, the inheritors of the rich and powerful land that is Canada.

Out of the flood of dream-haunted memory there seemed to rise the murmur of a chorus of voices from the long-dead and forgotten men of his land. They murmured like a soft wind at night, and he listened to them.

"Who said these little men of to-day are the inheritors of what we left? Have they our vision? Have they our capacity for sweat and unreward and merciless toil? Have they? They have taken our earth. They plough our dust and the grain grows heavier where we lie. The tiger lily grows upon the scorched plain and no one sees. We lie along our forgotten trails beside the bleached skull of the buffalo, and daisies grow betwixt us, and no one sees.

"Why? Is our dust not rich enough to grow the grain? We could grow elms and ash and even oak. They grew here once. Is a brutal shave of the feller's axe all the forest hillsides mean to you? Our dust lies there, too. Wheels sing upon the roads and stir our dust. Goldenrod grows through the spokes of our broken cart wheels. We are forgotten.

"Who tills the soil, who builds a bridge, who plants a tree, who gives to the land his sweat and sperm, who fights for a cause of freedom, is our true inheritor," the voices whispered. "Others are impostors. They shout for land and freedom and mouth empty words of high patriotism. But do they sweat and toil? Do they reap the grain? Do they break the wilderness where our bones lie? Do they fight tyranny to mankind, or do they hide in their high houses of pretence when danger comes?

"They shall answer yet, to us. We are dead and forgotten but we survive in the blood of our inheritors. Our vision was fixed to a star and will endure through time. The grain shall flow in the sun, the acorn shall root and flourish in the wilderness. Only now endure, and freedom shall prevail, for we planted its seed in our dust."

The voices ended; the dream-magic faded. Their steel capped heels struck hard upon the road and gave out a thin high metallic ring. The earth sang a languorous song in the bright winter sun, and the myriad unseen birds join in.

Once, rounding a turn in the road, they saw a tiny cottage amid a circle of ancient and gnarled trees. The roof of the cottage sagged and the tiny gabled windows seemed to have been pressed small under the weight above them. Sunlight played brightly upon the bricks, upon the tiled roof, and touched the wandering ivy that crept around the cottage. The naked, ancient trees seemed to stand in a protective circle around the place. Meeker, looking at it, remarked thoughtfully:

"Hm . . I begin to see now where all those calendar pictures of the English country-side came from. Take that cottage there. It's exactly as we've always imagined an English cottage to look. It's familiar. But the tiled roof doesn't belong. It should have a thatched roof. And look now! The trees standing around aren't just right. They should be behind the cottage or to one side, to give the effect of planned background. Then in front of the cottage you'd have tall hollyhocks growing to the eaves and window-boxes full of flowers."

"Then, what's your point? By your argument that cottage isn't at all like our picture of an English cottage. And yet it's something like it, to me."

"Yes, yes. Of course it is. And that's exactly the point I'm driving at. It's something like our idea of an English cottage —SOMETHING like it—and the rest—the thatched roof, the hollyhocks, the garden—are all borrowed from other cottages. D'ye see?"

"I'm damned if I do. Are you suggesting the English borrow a bit of scenery from here and there and put it together into a composite picture and call it an English cottage? Gawdamighty! And then YOU suggest they print it for the export trade and say, 'Look now, you colonial Canadians—here's what a bit of England looks like. You fellows haven't got EVERYTHING'."

Meeker raised a hand in objection. "No, no, corporal," he cried with heat, "it isn't as deliberate as that. If it were, it wouldn't be English. That's certain. The point I'm driving at is this—that their pastoral art is representative, whereas ours, so far as we have any art at all, strives to be graphic—visually honest, or interpretive."

"So?"

Meeker had no answer for a moment. He paused, collecting his thoughts. Then, suddenly, he continued.

"So? So they're fakes. Fakes to us and to themselves."

Bob laughed at his friend's warmth and conviction.

"But what's the harm? Maybe the whole thing is screwy, according to our values. But then, you see, they aren't our values. And that's the thing to remember."

"Oh, I'll remember, all right," Meeker agreed with mock humility. "I'll remember that they still call us a colony. They've got some high and mighty ways all right."

Bob laughed. "You've got it bad, Jimmy. What did the English ever do to you?"

"Nothing," Jimmy snarled, "Absolutely nothing. That's just the trouble—they never did anything to ANYBODY, and they never did anything FOR anybody. They just sit on this pile of mud over here and dictate to the whole bloody world."

"But, Jimmy, they don't dictate. They just try to impress everybody that they and what they have and what they make is the best in the whole world."

"You know," he continued, "it's our fault as much as theirs. They don't see our side of it, and we don't understand theirs."

Bob had no love for the Englishman himself. That was something inborn and which, he knew, was shared by countless of his countrymen. But it was this very knowledge which instinctively warned him to tread softly about the subject of national differences. After all, he reasoned, the English wouldn't give a damn whether he liked or hated them. But it would make a difference to his own enjoyment of the country. And that was important if, as rumour had it, they were to be stationed there a long time.

Conversation could not be revived. Meeker sat silent, puffing at his cigarette, his face thoughtful and brooding. His sharp chin and hooked nose were thrust forward, his jaw set. Bob saw that his resentment was directed not so much against the English, nor the country itself, but, unknowingly, against the circumstances which had brought him from his old, known, sure world of swagger and cocky assurance and left him stranded upon an alien shore, to orient himself or sink into oblivion.

They came, in time, into a tiny village—a place hidden and lost in the soft stillness of the hills. Time had passed it by; it stood as it had for three hundred years. On one side of the road was an ancient leaning pub of yellow brick and oak lacings. Directly across from the pub, which was closed, stood an equally ancient tea shop wedged between a harness maker's shop and a draper's. The door to the tea shop was low, the step worn and concaved. There was a small, hand-lettered card in the window bearing the words: "Morning Coffee." It seemed to have been placed there as a sort of afterthought by the proprietress when she unlocked her door that morning.

O'Rourke and his friend entered, stooping low through the door. They found themselves in a cool, darkened room filled with the dying tinkle of the door bell. As their eyes grew accustomed to the semi-darkness, they saw the heavy tables and bench seats along the walls, the old hunting prints above the wainscoting and the small glowing fire of coals in the fireplace. They heard the shuffle of feet and then the creaking of a door. A woman came in, old and enormously round, with a mop of grey hair capped by a sort of bonnet of the same pale gingham stuff as her dress. Her arms were crossed on her ample bosom, her head cocked a little to one side. She smiled a broad, broken-toothed smile, at once disarming and friendly, yet shrewdly appraising.

"Good morning," O'Rourke greeted her, feeling suddenly awkward and very tall before this little, round woman.

"'Tis a good morning, though a heavy frost last night," she replied.

The two soldiers took off their wedge caps and sat on a bench near the window.

"Could we have coffee, ma'am?" O'Rourke asked, presently.

The woman did not reply. Instead she walked slowly over to them, and rubbing her eyes with the hem of her apron, bent and studied the sleeve patch on O'Rourke's battledress blouse.

"Ah," she said, straightening with an audible outlet of breath, "So! You are Canadians. Of course you want coffee." Her voice was sharp, abrupt. There was a throaty gurgle as she inhaled again. "I'd wager you'd like something besides coffee, eh?"

At that she turned, and with a series of short, shuffling steps, disappeared behind the dark, heavy-hinged door that led to the kitchen.

To O'Rourke the room brought a sense of peace and graciousness. He saw the host of villagers and travellers from the road who had taken tea in this dark, panelled room in generations past. How often had it been filled with the chatter of voices, the noisy arrival of travellers, mingled with the aroma of steeping tea, fire smoke, cooked food, and the flash of table silver in the candle light of evening.

Now bright sunshine stole in through the leaded windows. It lay upon the worn table top in latticed squares of warm gold. The war seemed far away, almost as though it did not exist at all. O'Rourke thought of the sign in the window: "Morning Coffee," and then he thought of his wife Gerda. How charmed she would be with this tea room. The image of her came before his mind's eye with a sudden flood of remembrance. He saw her as clear and real as at any moment in the past when she had been with him. And he knew, all at once, feeling her nearness and reality, that she would always be with him in this way, whenever he was quiet and at peace with himself. He pictured her "little girl" delight at the sight of the tea shop; he could see her grow serious and pensive at thought of all the stilled voices of the place; he could even feel her hand on his arm, see the sudden flood of happiness in her soft, brown eyes.

The door from the kitchen opened and the little woman came in with a large wicker tray which she supported on her bosom. She put it down on the corner of the table and began to set two places.

"You gents must be hungry," she said, in her cheery, sharp voice, with an audible outlet of breath as she spoke. "Now try a bit of this bacon—it's our own. My man was good for nought, but one thing he did before he passed on was to put in a good bit of bacon. Must 'ave known—he . . . Can't get it nowadays, I must say. And there's an egg each, lightly done just as I do for myself. The toast is 'ot, though I likes it 'ard myself."

"There!" she concluded, and stepped back, watching them as they gazed at the food so invitingly laid before them on brown-patterned plates.

"Great," said Meeker, rubbing his hands enthusiastically. "Marvellous! Bacon and egg and coffee! What a discovery!"

O'Rourke looked at the little woman and saw her broken-toothed smile of pleasure, so simple and childlike.

"This is grand, really. We had no idea we'd ever get eggs —anywhere. We'd never have asked for them."

"Oh, you mustn't say a word about them. Not a word, mind. I'm not allowed them . . . give me proper hell, they would. . . . They're special for you Canadians."

She pronounced the word "Canadian" with a soft roll, as though it contained a mystery for her. Her pronunciation of the word was so different from the usual English pronunciation. As a rule "Canadian" was pronounced "Can-y-deen": and this was true not only of Cockneys, but with slight dialectal variations of most places in England. In the area of the camp, but a few miles away, O'Rourke had noticed that the British soldiers thereabouts pronounced it something like "Can-y-dian," giving the word a sort of sing-song inflexion that sounded to him like mockery. He remembered hearing it spoken on a station platform through which the troop train had passed—heard it pronounced "Cyn-y-deen," shortened thus and called out in a sing-song manner above the harsh babble of voices. And he remembered, too, the soft, throaty burring sound the Scottish dockyard workers had given to the pronunciation of the language as they landed from the troopship.

"It's awfully nice of you, ma'am," said O'Rourke. Meeker nodded his head in agreement, chewing the while. "We don't want to get you in any trouble, though."

"Ha-hah-hah," cried the little woman. "Trouble? Not likely—that. Only the hens out back and I know what they give . . . Hah-hah. . . . And sometimes . . . sometimes THEY aren't sure" And she laughed, shaking, and wiped her eyes with the hem of her apron.

"Now," she cried in the tone of an accomplice to a dark crime, "just call if you want anything more. I'll only be out back."

At that she turned and disappeared into the kitchen.

They ate voraciously and drank the coffee that did not taste quite like coffee. They heard her busy in the kitchen—heard the slamming of the oven door, the tinkle of glass, the soft mewing of a cat, the woman's voice speaking caressingly . . . Bad Tabby. Bad Tabby. Where have you been? . . . Where?

They finished the meal in silence and lit cigarettes. Their smoke drifted through the shafts of sunlight playing in the window and laid a curtain of contentment in the room.

"That," remarked Meeker, stretching, "that changes my impressions of England a little."

O'Rourke snorted impatiently. "Your impressions change easily. Wonderful what a full belly can do."

He no longer felt drawn toward Meeker. He even resented him a little. He preferred his own company: it agreed with him completely. He had always been alone: the only person he had ever admitted into his life was his wife. Now he wanted to be alone, not to have to listen to Meeker's inane conversation. There was peace in this moment, and he wanted it to himself.

When they were ready to leave the woman came out of the kitchen and stood by the door.

"How much do we owe you?" O'Rourke asked.

And the woman, without a moment's thought, replied, "Tuppence each, please."

"But we must owe you more than that. Why, that's only four cents."

She shook her head firmly. "Tuppence only, please. You ordered coffee. The bacon and eggs are . . . are from me."

Impulsively she put a hand on O'Rourke's arm. The gesture was sudden, timid and embarrassed.

"Last war Canadians came here. I liked them . . . you you come again to help us."

And with that she led them to the door, and watched them go, nodding her head and waving away their thanks.

O'Rourke never forgot the place. He went back there every Sunday for many weeks, in the morning if there was no church parade, in the afternoon for tea when he could not get away earlier. He never took Meeker with him again. The little woman always had an egg for him, or some special treat, such as honey, a jam turnover, or scones with country butter and jam. He kept the place a secret from the others at the camp.

They developed quite a friendship. There was seldom anyone else in the shop, for Sunday was a quiet day and she was much alone. She answered all his eager questions about the country, about the people, the habits, customs, quirks of the farming folk in the neighbourhood. She gave him a picture of the life of the village, and the land; and this picture, put together piece by piece on successive visits, opened to his mind a panorama of the whole great country. He came to see it as few visitors ever did.

He saw that the true glory and greatness of the country existed within the villages, the roadside cottages, and not in the great country homes, the select schools, the mansions of the rich and powerful. The little man was the great man of England: the man who had left his cottage and his father's door to serve under Drake: who had read Nelson's signal and fired the cannon, had fought at Waterloo and Balaclava, the Somme, Passchendaele and Mons; who was not a warrior and did not like to fight, but was one of the greatest fighters on earth. This was the man who at Dunkirk read his nation's destiny in the flaming skies, and afterwards went up into the heavens alone to battle a horde, knowing he was going to meet his death, and met it with the same quiet resolve with which he had done the ten thousand little every-day operations of his life, each little thing to endure—done, finished, and complete. This was the little man of England, who had long ago found in his father's image his common clay.

And seeing this, feeling it grow within him as the weeks went by, O'Rourke came to look upon the people he met in the village streets, on the roads and in the shops, with a curiosity and admiration which he could never quite define. It seemed incredible that such a people, who so zealously preserved their history and tradition, could be so bland, so DISINTERESTED about it, could look so little like a great and powerful people. Sometimes, of an afternoon, he would see innumerable women pushing prams containing very expressionless and unlovely babies, and the women were all dull, expressionless, entirely without beauty or warmth, without any visible sign that they were interested in their children, the weather, the war, or themselves. And seeing them, he would wonder anew at the secret of a people who by every sign were ordinary, plain and dull, yet who had such strength, courage and fortitude, who had survived through time to greatness.

He came to admire England, to love it at times, but he came to loathe and hate it too, in varying moods of intensity. There was so much to admire and yet so much that was stupid, mawkish and senseless, that he was filled with a seething and bitter hatred for the country and everything that was in it. He could not define this. It overwhelmed him with blind and un-reasoning bitterness at times, so that for days at a stretch, he would not go beyond the boundaries of the camp, but did his work, and at night in the dimness of the hut wrote long letters of complaint to his wife about the country, the people and the climate. Then, suddenly, this mood would pass and he would live through a period, brief and charmed by the magic of dis-covery, wherein all he saw was admirable, beautiful and of such intensity that he felt he could not contain it to himself.

2

It was in this mood of mingled admiration, bitterness and loathing for his surroundings that he passed the weeks before Christmas.

The training syllabus of the Reinforcement camp to which he had been posted, and from which he would eventually go out to a unit in the field, was not strenuous. Actually he found it boring. He had covered most of the training before. But it was regarded as necessary refresher training for new reinforcements arriving overseas. It did serve to discover weaknesses in home training which could be rectified before the soldier went to a unit fully mobilized in the field. Culls and weak sisters could be discovered, too, during this period, and there had been set up an elaborate system of "placing" the men according to their natural talents, their fighting efficiency, their weaknesses and physical capabilities. From the point of view of the army the system was highly efficient. From the point of view of the individual soldiers it often presented a monstrous disregard for the value he placed in himself. The army took the long view, and in the end the individual soldier, no matter how misplaced he felt himself to be, conformed to it, if not by wholehearted agreement.

O'Rourke was not, therefore, in the least dismayed when he read on daily orders that he had been posted to the Motor Transport training wing of the camp. On the surface it seemed ridiculous, since he had never been an M.T. man, but such are the infinite and wondrous ways of the army. He fitted himself into his new role with a wry smile.

# 5

IT was at this time, just before Christmas, that O'Rourke received his first mail from Gerda. When he heard his name called out at noon parade and had been given a handful of letters, he stood like a man who had been shaken by a bomb burst. How many nights after "lights out" had he lain wide eyed in the dark, thinking of her, wanting her, hoping for her mail. In his mind, so often, he had conjured up the things she might write him, wondering if she would be able to span the distance that lay between them, and bring to him, in her letters, some fragments of the life that had been theirs together.

He put the letters in the inside pocket of his battledress blouse and went off to lunch. He went through the hours of that afternoon filled with a sense of exultancy. From time to time he would put his hand over the pocket in which the letters lay, and the desire to open them would become so strong that it was only the knowledge that he would not be able to read one completely through without interruption that made him defer opening them until evening. It was then, in the hut, when most of the men had gone off to their search of a night's pleasure, that he opened them one by one, opening first the one bearing the earliest post date, and so on until he had read them all and had fixed in his mind a picture of Gerda's life and activities covering a period of ten days—the first ten days after his departure from Yellow Prairie.

They were the grandest letters he had ever received. In them he read the endearing phrases she had always used, the apt turn of expression, the lilt and hidden merriment. But they were letters from a Gerda he did not know, too. Under the surface of her sentences there lay the suggestion of a heaviness, a great longing. It was not in what she said. Not by one word did she express what their separation meant to her. It was, rather, by her effort at lightness and the things which she must have felt and thought and left unsaid, that gave him this knowledge. There was some quality in her letters, something which had escaped unknown from her, that showed a maturity she had not possessed before.

She wrote of the things that were theirs. She had re-arranged their room: she had put the blue vase upon the table now, the couch in the far corner by the window, his cup and saucer upon the mantle, his picture near the window light. She planned new curtains. She told him where she had visited, gave him word of their friends. She told him when she thought of him most often—at mealtimes and at night when she lay wait-ing for sleep. She wished often that he had given her a child, but since it had not been, perhaps they would have one out of their reunion, and it would surely be a fat and happy baby—a boy. She bubbled over with things she wanted to tell him. "If you were here," she wrote, "I should talk on and on, all through the night—about our dreams and hopes, the fun we'll have and the work we'll do and of our life together. But, of course, I can't talk of such things to anyone else. So I'm bottling myself up—except for what I can put into letters." And she concluded with a turn that was happy and more intimate than anything else she could have said. "Do look after my husband, and tell him that his wife waits his return with all the impatience and love in her whole body. Since waiting is her job now, she would rather wait than be Queen of England."

He sat for some time on the edge of his cot, staring at the floor, and his thoughts moved restlessly. The more he thought of Gerda, of home, of the land and skies and space, and the quiet peace and contentment of his marriage, the more homesick he became. It grew in him and filled him with a hope-less raging hatred for the army and the inactivity of his life. If only, he thought, if only he could get AT the war! If only he could get his hands on the fight—get INTO it—and get it over with!

He put Gerda's letters away and stomped off to a nearby pub for a pint of bitter. Anything would be a relief—anything at all to get away from his thoughts, to escape the memories, the longing.

It was a moonless night, the stars brilliant in the black immensity. He stood for a while outside the pub door and looked up, seeking the known stars, Polaris, the Dipper, Cas-siopeia. As he looked he heard the soft, far-off drone of planes rising and falling and rising again. Instinctively he raised his arm skywards, with his thumb upthrust. "Here's to you, boys," he said aloud. "Give the bastards hell for me."

The pub was warm and filled with the smells of beer, tobacco and damp clothes. O'Rourke took his pint of bitter to a table in the corner. He sat watching the men playing their games, and listened to their voices, trying to catch the way they spoke, to discover how they pronounced their soft "r's", the way they ended a sentence on a rising inflection that was almost nasal and sharp. He found himself repeating certain words he heard to himself, trying to get the same sounds from them.

Over beyond the fireplace a group played darts. It was apparently a close game. There were moments when the teams stood silent and intent while a player poised a dart in front of him, then, with a sharp thrust sent it flying. A florid-faced man in a tweed jacket sat with a slate and kept score in a way that was undecipherable to O'Rourke.

The atmosphere was one of warm and homely fellowship. Here were the men of the village—the labourers, the clerks, the small shopkeepers—calling each other Tom and Harry and Ted and Jack—all friends from boyhood. They sat there every Saturday night, leaving their "missus" at home with the ironing and the kids. There was fat John Bull, with pouchy cheeks, and Harry, the stonemason; there, Ted the clerk, and Horace the butcher, and Walter, who used to pitch well as a boy, and old Mason "the bloody gripe", and Jimmy the carpenter, a little tipsy, and Bill, whose "missus" was in the family way again (and at her age)—all there, with the brand of beer they liked, the quiet bartender, the smells, the homeliness, the warm familiarity. As O'Rourke watched them, he could not help envying England's "little man", who went off to the pub of a Saturday night, with the missus busy at home. He fancied, somehow, that she did not mind being left out of it.

When he went out of the pub, finally, he passed a woman the only one there, who was sitting with folded hands waiting for her man to go home. He thought again of Gerda, with a pang of sudden remorse, for it occurred to him that she waited, even as this woman did, for her man to finish with the foolish business of "man's play", waited for him to come home —to the known door, the familiar step. He felt like speaking to the woman. He wanted to be kind and gentle a moment, to explain the foolish ways of men. But then he saw that she was quietly happy, sitting there, and he did not speak but went out into the night where searchlights knifed the sky and great motors throbbed in the dark immensity.

As he walked along the street the sound of planes grew louder. One swept low overhead, then another and another. Their whistle and scream filled the night until there was nothing else.

'Ours,' he thought to himself. 'They're going up to meet Jerry.'

Instinctively he moved a little faster. He walked closer to the high brick wall that ran along the sidewalk. He felt the quickening of his blood-beat. The sense of danger tensed his nerves. He was in the middle of a raid. He had not heard the sirens.

He passed a soldier and a girl. The girl tripped quickly along beside the soldier, her arm in his, her face upturned to the sky. He heard her laugh, a gay, rich little laugh. And she said, casually, lightly: "I'm never nervous in a raid, until I hear the bombs whistling. And then, of course, it's too late to be nervous . . . I remember . . ." Her voice trailed away.

The pause of hushed expectancy deepened. The planes droned and screamed in the sky amid the sweeping shafts of the searchlights, but on the earth, in the streets, all was suddenly silent, tensed, waiting.

Everything told O'Rourke to take cover, to hide, yet he moved along gingerly, step by step. He passed the opening of a lane and saw a small group of people huddled in the shadows, their faces upturned to the sky. They seemed to sway and waver, like something caught in the path of a whirlwind. He walked on, rounded a corner and came suddenly upon the town square. Here he was halted by an incredible sight. Out of nowhere, yet from everywhere, every doorway, alleyway and street, people streamed into the square. They were like columns of ants running for the safety of the anthill. Now and then a body broke from the moving columns, but it was quickly drawn back again. The shuffle of feet, the low nervous murmur of a multitude rushed like a wind through the square. In the spectral light from the sweeping searchlights amid the phantasmal shadows, these columns of people converged upon the centre of the square and disappeared into the mounds that were shelters. Suddenly the square was empty, still and desolate in the eerie light.

Now O'Rourke felt a terrific compulsion to hurry. He almost ran past the still and shuttered buildings. He cast a glance into the dark yawning doorways of the shelters, but no power on earth could have turned him into one of them. Beyond the square, in a narrow street, he came upon a small queue of people at a bus stop. The buses had apparently ceased running, for O'Rourke had seen none since leaving the pub, but these few people were hopeful that they could still get out of town before the raid.

It had taken him only a few minutes to arrive at this point from the pub. In that brief time the searchlight batteries had been synchronized, interceptors had taken to the air to turn back the raiders, and the entire population of the town had gone to the shelters. Ack-ack guns began to fire. A battery on the southern edge of the town opened up : Bofors, he thought, by the sound of them. Two other batteries opened up immediately after, as if in answer. Then he could not tell how many were firing, for the bark and crack of them filled the streets and rocked the buildings.

Strangely, it was not the whistle of bombs that first warned him of immediate danger, but the sound of splintering glass. It came so unexpectedly, without any apparent cause. He heard the glass break and tinkle as the pieces fell to the pavement. It was immediately after that that the rising whistle of the bombs came to him. For a moment he stopped and turned about in the street, searching for shelter. Then he dropped upon the pavement, beside a high brick wall, with his legs together, his face pressed against the stone. For a second more he heard the whistling and whir of a bomb falling.

"Jees," he said to himself, and heard his voice a long way off. A thought flashed across his mind then. "If this is it, I may as well see it." He raised his head a little and looked across the street.

The people who had been standing in the queue were crouched together in a mass, their bodies bent and their heads downthrust to ward off the terror. In the next instant there came a terrific explosion, and then another which felt right beside him. He clawed at the pavement for support. He was thrown prone along the side of the wall and found himself spread-eagled across the sidewalk. The earth rocked, and broken brick and rubble rained upon him. He buried his head deeper in his shoulders and held his breath.

He waited a minute while the falling debris settled. Then he raised his head cautiously and looked about him. The wall beside him had a gaping, half-moon crescent blown out of it. In the centre of the roadway a shell crater smoked. Across it a great length of iron pipe had been hurled from nowhere. On the other side of the crater, he saw the huddle of people who had been waiting for the bus. They were flattened now, one upon the other, and lay motionless. Above them, the brick building was pock-marked by a dozen holes, and the windows were blasted and the wooden frames hung out over the street.

At that moment he heard the soft whine and plop of a missile in the street, further down. He ducked his head again. But in a moment he knew it was not a bomb, for the world, even through his closed eyelids, became startlingly bright. He looked up again and saw an incendiary bomb burning intense and white in the centre of the roadway. He saw men running out to it. The light was so bright their bodies were without shadows.

He lay as he was and did not move, but slowly he began to think of escape. His eyes probed the length of the street, lighted brightly now by the incendiary and the searchlights overhead.

He saw a stir of movement in the huddled group across the street. A woman lifted herself from the others, and stood a moment wavering back and forth unsteadily with her arms outstretched for support. Then she took a step, suddenly grasped her belly low down, and holding herself thus, she bent doubled with pain. O'Rourke heard her scream. All at once he saw that she was far pregnant. Still screaming, she moved, blindly out into the roadway. She wavered on the edge of the bomb crater, and then staggered away from it. Finally she could go no farther. She stopped in the road, bent over. Her screams died. Slowly she sank to the pavement, still clutching the weight of her belly.

O'Rourke ran out into the road, and bent over the woman. He turned her upon her back and felt for the pulse in her throat. It beat strongly under his fingers. She raised a hand and, groping, caught hold of his wrist. Her grip was astonishingly fierce. She moaned and writhed, "Dick! Dick! Help me now! Dick! Help me, please . . . Oh . . . please!" She cried pitifully, yet there were no tears.

He had to twist his wrist to break her grip. He picked her up and started down the street in search of a first-aid post. When he came to an intersection he had to stop and rest, leaning against a concrete tank block beside the kerb. He could see no F.A.P. sign. When he had caught his breath he went on, past a pub whose sign had been knocked into the gutter, past a draper's shop, past a building of flats. When he had passed this building, he suddenly realized that he had seen an F.A.P. sign over a basement stairway. Gingerly, feeling for each step, he descended. At the bottom, in the pitch black, he bumped against a door. He kicked at it with his foot. He was about to kick it again when it opened wide and he stepped into a hallway lit with a dim bulb. A nurse led him into a room opening off the hall, and he laid his burden upon the floor between two other wounded women who lay with blankets over them.

The room was filled with injured people. There were several children, two very old women sitting on the floor against the wall sipping something from mugs, some men, old, too. It was a small room. At one end a doctor sat by a table on which lay heaps of bottles, instruments, dressings of all kinds, and case cards.

The nurse who had let him in came back from the table with a case card in her hand.

"Do you know her?" she asked him, nodding toward the pregnant woman.

O'Rourke shook his head.

"I picked her up in the street near the bus stop," he replied, and started to indicate with his arm the direction he had come from. It was quite useless. What did it matter?

The nurse bent over the woman, and made a swift, cursory examination.

"Doctor," she called.

"Yes," the man at the table answered. He did not look up from what he was doing.

"Will you please look at this woman?"

"Right," he replied, but there was a weariness and strain in his voice.

He picked up his stethoscope and came over and knelt to the woman. O'Rourke could not see what he was doing, but he heard the doctor breathing hard in the still room and saw the look of intenseness on the nurse's face as she watched him. Presently the doctor straightened up and took off his spectacles and wiped them on his handkerchief.

"Miss Niser, phone for the ambulance. This woman will have to go to hospital right away. A rather bad case. The child is already half born. It is dead."

He put his glasses in his breast pocket and went back to the table. The nurse picked up the phone and began to speak.

"Tell them it is an urgent case," the doctor said.

"I'll be getting along now," O'Rourke told the nurse. "Good night."

"Good night," she said, turning from the phone. "Good night, Canada."

He climbed the steps to the street and leaning against the railing, lit a cigarette. As he put the packet back in his pocket he felt a wetness against his hand. He raised it to the glow of his cigarette and examined it. It was blood. The front of his tunic and trousers were wet with it. Why, he wondered, would a pregnant woman, so far gone, be out on the street in a raid? Maybe she had been on her way to the hospital, or to a friend for help. . . . Husband away on the night shift, or fire fighting, or out in the Middle East, or God knows where. Well!

He threw the cigarette away and started back for camp. The sky over the far edge of town was bright yellow from a burning fire and smoke clouds. But the earth was still now : no sound came from the skies : only, faint and far away, the crackle of burning wood and the smell of smoke and brick dust, and another smell, acrid and suggestive of fire, that he could not identify.

Many were late into barracks, for everyone had taken shelter during the raid. Nothing was said when O'Rourke showed his paybook and passed into the camp. The hut was in darkness but no one was asleep. The men lay in the dark, smoking and talking about the raid, and how Jerry had tried to get the camp and missed.

O'Rourke listened to the talk while he undressed. It was the old barrack-room argument and opinion, with every man clamouring to be heard. It was good stuff for morale, usually; let every man have his say and get the steam off his chest. But tonight it galled him.

He was dead tired, but he could not sleep. His mind turned back to the pregnant woman in the middle of the road, clutching at the weight of her womb with both hands and screaming like a doomed animal into the night. And over and through this ran the chatter of voices in argument and exposition. Finally he could bear it no longer. He sat bolt upright on his cot.

"Listen," he snapped into the dark. "Listen, you goddam bedtime warriors. If Jerry wanted to get this camp he'd have got it and you'd be food for the daisies now. He wanted to get the town, and he got it. This is his innings, right now. Ours is next. But one of these days you're going to meet up with him, and if the whole bloody lot of you don't shut up and get some sleep you aren't going to be quite as good as he is when that day arrives. Now shut up and go to sleep."

The noise subsided. There were some faint whisperings, but no one spoke aloud. He was, after all, the hut corporal. He was in a bad mood, no doubt about it. He was also tough.

# 6

O'Rourke finished supper and took his mess tins back to his hut. As he walked down the lane he felt the new rain on his face. He cursed aloud. It was his duty night: his section was to go out on convoy.

In the hut the fellows were busy "dolling up" to go out, to the pub, a dance, or a show. There was a bustle of activity, whistling and singing. Boots were polished, faces scrubbed, hair combed and slicked down.

O'Rourke wished he were going along with them, instead of out into the bloody rain on a motor bike. What a night for a run, and a bunch of new drivers at that!

"God," he said, "I wish I was going with you fellows. It's starting to rain."

"Rain won't stop what I'm going to do," someone said.

Everyone laughed.

A corporal at the far end of the hut snorted.

"You wouldn't come with us if you could, O'Rourke. You never have yet."

"Yeh. What do you do with yourself, Corporal? Got something on the quiet?"

"We never see you out at night," another added.

O'Rourke laughed, and did not answer.

A little fellow with a Romeo moustache and wavy hair looked at himself in a bit of cracked mirror, very satisfied with what he saw.

"What the hell are you chasing tonight, Gable," his friend in the next bed asked. He did not look up from paring his toe nails to ask the question.

"Don't know," the Romeo answered. "I met her in the dark the other night. She wouldn't tell me her name."

"Maybe she didn't like you getting personal."

"What's in a name, anyway."

"Personally, I like to see what they look like, anyway," someone remarked dryly. "No pig in a poke for me."

"A body in a blackout is good enough, I guess. But I like

a little loving with mine. And God! I like to see what I'm loving."

The barrack-room Romeo went out, slamming the door. The room rocked with laughter.

O'Rourke changed, putting on his riding breeches, his high-topped boots, his leather jerkin, and over that a water-proof issue jacket. Then he wound his watch, picked up his crash helmet and left the hut.

"Happy landings," someone called as the door closed.

Across the parade square he saw the vehicles, a dark indistinguishable line, darker than the night. Great pools of water had formed on the square: he felt the splashes against his boots as he waded through them.

"This is what it will be like some day," he thought. "The real thing—rain, darkness, cold."

He crossed the square and came upon the dispatch office. A feeble crack of orange light showed beneath the door. He opened it and stepped quickly inside. The office was crowded with men—drivers and learner drivers, N.C.O.s and a few officers. On the wall was pinned a whole series of map sheets, forming one large map of the south of England.

"All right," an officer snapped. "All D.R.s over here. Here are your route cards. Read them, study the maps, memorize the route."

He passed a slip of paper to each Dispatch Rider. The D.R.s crowded around the map. Each man in turn began to trace the route out with his finger, reading each map reference from his route card, road junction to crossroads, to fork, to turn. Slowly, each memorized the route.

"Where is our first halt, sir?" one of the D.R.s asked, turning from the map.

"I'll give the warning of it in time. It will be somewhere along the Sunningvale road—on that long straight stretch before you enter the hills. I can't attempt to spot-point it now. There might be another convoy ahead of us when we get there."

"Any other questions?"

"All right, then. Speed, fifteen miles per hour. Interval seventy-five yards. Twenty-minute halt before every even hour. Fall out, everybody."

Out in the darkness, in front of the vehicles, the cor-porals assembled their sections, counted bodies in the dark, gave the orders to mount the vehicles, start up. Then came the officer's whistle, and the convoy moved out on to the highway. Only the front sidelights burned—two pinpoints of yellow light in the blackout—and in the rear a white disc of light played upon the white-painted differentials and gave the position of each lorry to the driver following.

O'Rourke, on his motor-bike, fell in beside his section. For a time he rode out in the road along the centre white line, checking the intervals between each of the lorries in his section. When he had got them spaced to approximately seventy-five yards, he picked up the section-corporal ahead and the two rode along together, side by side. They often did this. Though the noise of the convoy and of their own machines made conversation impossible, there was a sense of companionship in being thus together. Their boots were soaked, their water-wet socks numbed their feet. Their driving gauntlets were wet before they started and they had to beat their hands against their thighs to keep their blood circulating.

O'Rourke took over the point controls in his turn and checked the route off in his mind as the convoy progressed. As he sat upon his machine at a road corner watching the vehicles roar by, he would have given anything to have been able to trade places with one of the drivers, to enjoy for a few minutes the warmth of the cab. When the D.R. from the following section relieved him of the point control, they looked at each other over their machines and grinned in the blinding rain.

"That you, O'Rourke?" yelled the other, switching off his engine.

"It's his body," O'Rourke growled. "I left the better half of him back in camp—in a warm bed."

The other laughed.

"Only a horse's arse would be out on a night like this."

"And even a horse's arse has at least got a tail to keep it dry," O'Rourke replied.

"Well, it won't last forever, I guess. Some day we'll be through with it—and then home. Oh, boy!"

"Say," he yelled, as O'Rourke started his machine "see me at the next halt. I know where we can get late tea."

When the halt was made O'Rourke went down the convoy to find him, and together they slipped away for a few minutes, unnoticed. The place he led O'Rourke to was not a teashop, but the dwelling of a friend, who, months before, had asked him in for a cup of tea. It was a standing invitation. The cottage stood behind a stone wall. A gateway led to the inner yard. They pushed their machines inside the gate so they would not be discovered by any passing provost.

Their knock on the door was answered by a little, white-haired woman. As soon as she recognized the D.R. she drew them inside and welcomed them warmly. While they took off their crash helmets and jackets she went to the stairs and, in a voice surprisingly coarse and croaking, called into the upper darkness:

"William! William! The Canadian is here again. Come down now!"

She took them into a room crowded with an amazing assortment of furniture, bric-à-brac, pictures and collections of magazines—the accumulated treasures of a poor man's lifetime. O'Rourke saw his friend slip the woman a package, press it firmly, secretly into her hand.

"You must be frozen, poor things," she said. "The kettle's boiling. I'll have a cup of tea for you in half a jiffy. You'll have no more time than usual, I suppose?"

"No, mother. We're in a rush as always. The convoy's out on the road. Some time I'll come and spend a whole day with you. How's that?"

But the little woman had disappeared into the back of the house.

"I always call her mother," the fellow volunteered. "Pleases her, you know. And I always bring her a bit of tea when I'm coming this way."

O'Rourke wondered where he got the tea. Out of the camp kitchen, probably—bribed the cook for it with a package of cigarettes.

The door opened and an old man stood framed in the darkness of the hall. He gazed at them without a sign of recognition.

"Hello, Pops. We parked just down the road, and I said to O'Rourke here: 'Now, I know the spot for a hot cup of tea, a good old couple you should meet!' And here we are! We didn't get you out of bed, did we? Honest now—did we?"

For answer the old man came shuffling into the room, one hand holding up his trousers, while the other, outstretched as though to ward off a blow, trembled violently. Even the hand that held up his trousers trembled so that they shook on his bent legs. He grunted his way across the room to an old hideously carved sideboard, and from the half-open drawer drew out a letter. He was just on the point of giving this to O'Rourke when his wife came in with a tray of tea things.

"Now, William!" she croaked at him. "William! You're giving it to the wrong gentleman. Give it to Mr. Martin." Quickly she put the tray on the table, snatched the letter from his hand and gave it to O'Rourke's friend.

As she poured the tea, she remarked, in a bitter and wounded tone: "It's from our boy. The first word we've had of him since Dunkirk. . . . A long time, mind you. But, thank God, he's well and safe, as it says.

"He's a prisoner in Germany," she added, looking up at O'Rourke. "We are very proud of him."

The letter was passed to O'Rourke. He read the stiff, almost illiterate writing: "I am very well, Mother. I don't need things. I will see you soon, I hope. Love. DAVID."

It said so little and yet obviously it meant so much to the old couple. It was probably the single remaining thread of life they had.

He folded the letter and handed it back to the old man. And then, suddenly, he saw that the old man was not even looking at him, but beyond him to the wall with the empty gaze of the blind.

They had their tea—tea without sugar, but hot and instantly invigorating—gulping it down hurriedly while the old woman talked on and on about her son, giving them a detailed recital of his behaviour as a small boy. While she talked a black cat came into the room and sprang up on the table in front of her and rubbed its body against her resting hand.

Then, hurriedly backing out, apologizing for their haste, offering their thanks, they left the old couple standing under the gas lamp in the room, both bent a little, tired and worn. Out in the yard, as they pushed their bikes into the street again, Martin said solemnly:

"You know . . . every time I see them they look older. I never saw people grow old so fast. They were blitzed out of London. You can see what it did to them. Must have been hell. I don't drop in just for the tea. . . . I've an idea it helps them somehow.

"But Jees!' he added, "how I needed that tea to-night."

They rejoined the convoy. They had not been missed, or if they had no one had squealed on them. The lead D.R. was riding down the column sounding his horn as a signal to start. When he came back up the column he fell in beside O'Rourke for a moment.

"We'll be halting again before we get to the Thames," he said. "That's my guess, anyway. A Limey D.R. coming through told me the river has flooded the road.'

"They might have a diversion route laid out by the time we get there."

The other laughed bitterly.

"The British don't work THAT fast as a rule. We'll have our work cut out for us, finding a route."

"Damned if I know the country around the river," O'Rourke said.

"Me too!" the other replied, and sped away into the dark.

One by one the vehicles moved off, holding their interval. Rain lashed at the vehicles and swept across the road in wind-driven torrents. There were moments when O'Rourke thought he would be blown off the road. Every time the wind lulled suddenly, he felt himself over-balanced and his rear wheel skidded on the wet pavement as he sought to right himself. His hands were numb with cold; they had no life in them to control the throttle. He dared not use his brakes, for the slightest grip of the tires would have sent him spinning headlong. Every ounce of his energy was concentrated on keeping the machine upright. For the rest he trusted to luck.

"Some day," he thought, "someone will give the D.R. his due. They ought to put up a statue to him—a great bronze statue in a public square. . . . The hero. . . . The poor bloody fool!"

He had been riding beside one of the lorries, keeping close to the white centre line of the road for guidance. Gradually he became aware that the lorry was pulling over to the edge of the road. He noticed by the fact that the driver was allowing him more room than he needed. "There he goes," he thought, and was powerless to stop him. The lorry lurched off the road, careened on its side over the edge of the ditch. He heard the driver shout and gun his engine, and then the vehicle veered round in the ditch and came to a sudden stop. O'Rourke stopped his bike and turned round. He saw the two pin points of light from the following lorry advancing. It was following the other along the side of the road, being guided by the rear light. It, too, crashed into the ditch and rolled over. The next driver had the wit to stop when he felt his vehicle moving on soft gravel. The rest of the column halted. Cab doors were banged, men shouted questions.

A section corporal from the rear came up to O'Rourke.

"Some fun!" he yelled, grinning. "Why don't you build a corral for some of your drivers? D'you want breakfast sent out?" He threw back his head and roared with laughter.

"Cut it," O'Rourke growled.

He surveyed the situation. Far ahead on the road he saw the tiny, feeble spot of light of the last vehicle receding into the darkness.

"Look, Walters! I'll keep two vehicles. Take your section and the balance of mine and pick up the convoy. Then report to Mr. Melville up in the lead. Tell him I'll stay here to get these bastards out. Will you do that for me?"

"Sure thing, Bob," Walters replied.

He wheeled around and went off down the road. In a few minutes he came back with the rest of the convoy. As he passed he waved his hand and O'Rourke saw the flash of his grin.

Bob O'Rourke parked his bike off the road and examined the lorries. The first one had literally buried itself in the mud of the ditch. It would be a job to get it out. But no mechanical damage had been done so far as he could determine. The second lorry was in deep on its side, but it lay straight in the ditch.

They set to work. Using one of the lorries still on the road, they secured two lengths of towing cable and made it fast to the overturned frame of the ditched vehicle. It came back on to its wheels without difficulty, although it stood with a precarious list. Finally, they towed it up the steep ascent to the road.

Now O'Rourke had three vehicles on the road. With the power of these, and using all the cables, he hoped to drag the other out of its mudhole. But this proved impossible. It had driven so deeply into the mud that its wheels and undercarriage were completely buried. There was nothing for it but to dig it out. He sent the men into the ditch with the spades. Two of them had to lie on their bellies to free the mud from the undercarriage while the others worked to free the wheels and cut a path up out of the ditch.

They lost count of time. Dawn came like a grey shroud across the land. The men shivered as they worked. They did not talk: fatigue and hunger made them silent and morose. And at last they got the lorry out. It stood upon the road, a ruin of mud, hardly recognizable. The men, too, were covered in mud: their clothes were caked with it, their bodies soaked and half-frozen.

O'Rourke herded the vehicles back to camp by a series of short-cuts across the country. He completely disregarded the route card, striking boldly due south. They made good time, though he suspected the vehicles at times ran by themselves, for the men were half-asleep with fatigue. The rain ceased before they reached camp and his clothes dried hard and cold in the wind. He brought the vehicles into the parade square, watched them line up under the naked and consumptive row of elm trees beside the square. One by one the drivers left their vehicles and straggled across the square to their huts. Still he sat upon his bike where he had halted. He sat there, asleep, for a long time. It was the guard who finally stirred him.

He started up his bike and drove it over to the dispatch office and reported in. The clerk behind the table was not interested. He was reading a sex magazine and seemed very engrossed. There was no one else about. When he had left the office, O'Rourke realized that everyone had gone away on short leave. It was the day before Christmas! He walked slowly to his hut, empty save for the hut orderly, who was whistling as he swept the floor. As he took off his wet boots, he thought of Gerda. How nice to crawl into the warmth of her bed now! There would be the sweet body smell and warmth of her sleep still upon the sheets. To lie beside her, and rest his head in the warm, swelling firmness of her breasts. To sleep . . . sleep . . . sleep for ever.

He pulled back the rough blankets of his palliasse and crawled in. Even as he sank into sleep, a feeling of warmth and languor flowed through his body at the thought of his wife's loveliness. She was, at that moment, closer to him than she had ever been in their separation.

# 7

## I

It was almost midday when O'Rourke's train, bringing him to London on leave, entered the environs of the city. The suddenness of the train's entry into the suburbs, and the instant and overwhelming recognition that it was the magic city, made him sit bolt-upright in his seat. He fixed his eyes upon the scene with unspeakable fascination.

The train hurtled along, at roof-top height upon a viaduct. Objects in the immediate foreground blurred and became indistinguishable. His gaze focused upon the more distant view, on the far and incredible stretch of roof-tops, chimneys, smoked-yellow and grey brick buildings—the wastes of the forgotten man, the desolation of the slum areas.

You cannot gaze upon this desolation without becoming a part of it.

Your being feels a weighted sorrow and strange pity : the air becomes oppressive, stifling. You feel that it must soon end, that you must escape, put it forever behind you and never see it again. It draws you to it, with sorrow, pity and haunting loneliness, and immediately you want to escape from it forever. Yet as the train speeds onward the desolation opens, spreads and deepens to the view, and all that you have ever seen of proud and noble cities, of treed avenues, of children playing upon a vacant lot, of peace, hope and ordered life, fades from the mind, and you gaze upon this desert of smoke-yellow brick and dirt-grey rooftops and wonder : Why! Why!

In all that illimitable tenement of man-swarming life there is no beauty, no call to the wandering heart, but only an overwhelming sorrow. The endless rows of buildings stand against each other : the grey threads of streets bear no sign of life : the million chimneys rise smokeless in a waste of slate-grey, smeared desolation.

O'Rourke saw it all and turned away to the opposite side of the train. It was there, too. He had been looking at but half the circle. Far as the eye could see lay the dwellings of the poor. And suddenly he saw the ruins left by the great raids. They had been there, since the train first entered the city, but he had not noticed them because they did not in any way break or disrupt the unending desolation. Now he leaned closer to the window and shook his head involuntarily. He saw whole blocks and streets laid waste. The rubble lay everywhere, great piles of brick and stone and slate the same colour as the surrounding buildings. In some places he saw sections of buildings still standing, the walls bombed out, revealing a run of stairs still clinging to the wall, a toilet poised upon a ledge of torn floor, a chimney here rising from out the ruins, here only a door and the door closed, here the front of a dwelling standing alone upon a ruined street and a wisp of curtain fluttering from a splintered window.

Bombs had straddled the whole vast area, missing whole streets, yet laying low a section perhaps half a mile in area. As the train came closer into the city's core he saw that most of the slate roofs had been destroyed completely or damaged. He caught glimpses of charred rafters in the gaping holes of roofs, of gutted, blackened buildings. Once, in a flashing glimpse, he caught sight of a twisted gnarled tree flourishing in a ruined street. All about lay heaps of rubble, yet the tree stood, incredible and beautiful in its first flush of springtime green.

And, suddenly, the train was into Waterloo Station. The carriage doors opened, the people streamed out. O'Rourke found himself carried along in the crowd, through the barrier where a tough-looking woman snatched the ticket from his hand and yelled into his ear some words he could not understand. Still carried by the crowd, he let himself be propelled through the vast station into the underground entrance and down the great escalators.

He emerged upon the surface of the city at Trafalgar Square with a sense that he had escaped, by no effort of his own, from a subterranean world of mad movement and blind migration. He could not have said how it was accomplished, but he did arive at his destination.

It was a glorious spring day. High over the city the barrage balloons rode the breeze majestically. The sky was cloudless blue. All about him he saw the great buildings and monuments, a welter and weaving of traffic. There was even a jaunty air to the people who rushed about. In the Square the pigeons strutted, cocky and sure of their audience of loiterers.

O'Rourke went to a service club and found it filled. He ate a poor lunch in a restaurant and spent the afternoon wan-

dering from place to place. Afterwards he could not have retraced his course, yet street by street, landmark by monument,
district by district, the city unfolded itself to him. Somehow,
vaguely, he felt that he had seen it all before—the old, en-
chanted city of dreams. It was altogether an overwhelming
experience.

He walked many miles, driven on by a hunger to explore the city, to rend it apart and know it forever in his mind.
He saw the bombed theatres, the derelict churches in a wilderness of ruin, the empty, hollow buildings. A sombre people
swarmed restlessly through the streets. Posters, pasted on
gutted walls, upon board fencing around ruins, proclaimed the
might of Empire, exhorted the people to invest in war, cau-
tioned them on safety measures, conservation, needless spending, and guided them toward national hygiene. Eros in Piccadilly was boarded up and the boards displayed posters of
Britain's war effort. Shops with shattered fronts showed signs
such as "Business as usual", "Blitz prices", "Still here". And
British humour, never uproarious at best, chuckled wryly at its
own discomfort and found new inspiration for witticisms.

Late in the afternoon he asked a Bobby if he knew where
he could find a room. The Bobby shook his head hopelessly, and
then, on a sudden inspiration, directed him to a small, third-
class hotel high up in the Strand. O'Rourke hurried along to
the place. It was an upstairs hotel, dingy, evil-smelling and
packed with people who had been bombed out of their homes.
They had one room left, at fourteen shillings a night, bed and
breakfast. Desperate, he took it and was guided up the stairs
to a tiny room that contained a single bed, an old Victorian
wardrobe and a sink. He took off his tunic and flung himself
upon the bed and slept.

2

That night, along the south coast in the vicinity of
Beachy Head, the crew of an ack-ack battery heard the high,
faint, far-away drone and throb of aircraft. Almost simultaneously the crew of a direction-finder station a few hundred yards
away caught it and went into action. Within a few seconds
they picked up the bearing of the planes and held it. There
followed, then, within the space of a minute, a whole series of

relay messages spanning the whole coastline from Ramsgate to Weymouth.

The report of the approaching planes, with their bearing, was phoned through to a central command office where the times of departure and return of all our own planes were listed. A glance determined the fact that the approaching planes were not Allied. And so, from this command office, went the coastal warning to batteries—ack-ack, searchlight and direction-finder stations. The entire coast defences stood at the alert within a minute of the first report.

Simultaneously, all southern cities, towns and villages were given the alert. One after another, the sirens wailed along the coast; people started for their shelters, and the vast intricate civilian organization of fire-fighters, A.R.P., first-aid personnel, fire-spotters and auxiliary volunteers—all turned out for action. Meanwhile the command in London had been notified. Here several things occurred. On a great plotting board the approach of the enemy planes was charted, and their speed calculated. The height of the planes, too, was estimated, and accordingly squadrons already warned of the alert were dispatched into the air.

All this had taken place in minutes. London sirens sounded their chorusing wail over the huge dark city. The people shook themselves from sleep and made their preparations. Out of the city's ten or twelve million souls, several thousand had, by some unfathomable divination, anticipated a raid that night, and had already taken themselves and their bundles of precious belongings into shelters and tube stations when the alert sounded. Curiously, most of these were women.

The sirens wailed far off and O'Rourke stirred in his sleep. He wakened, wide-eyed and tense, a minute later when the sirens shrieked nearby. The crowded buildings took up the sound, absorbing the scream. It filled every alleyway, every entrance; it rushed in through every window, scream upon scream, and with it, beating an accompaniment of terror, came the sound of a multitude on the move before disaster. He heard this sound of people : it ran like a gathering whisper through the hotel. And then his mind swung into focus : sounds distinguishable and familiar came to him from the corridor. He heard a door slam; someone fell heavily against the wall; in the next room he heard a girl cry: "I can't go out like this ! Wait a moment!" There came the thud of racing footsteps upon the stairs, a shout, the swish-swish of feet along the carpeted corridor.

The sirens stopped. He put on his jacket and stood by

the window buttoning it up. Now he could hear the sound of the city—tense, terrifying. It seemed to rise up from the streets, the vortex of every sound of human anguish, terror and blind groping, of running feet, a policeman's whistle, the lumbering agony of a climbing lorry. As he listened to this monstrous and single tongue of terror, he felt that he too must escape it, run from it with the mob into the bowels of the earth.

He dashed along the corridor, and down the stairs. Everyone had already disappeared—everyone but the manager of the hotel and his wife. The manager was bent over his ledger and did not look up. His wife was sitting near a small grate fire, knitting, with a cat lying asleep across her ample knees. So unexpected was this sight that O'Rourke stopped short and felt unaccountably foolish to be running out to safety. It sobered him instantly. Feeling sick with himself, he walked the rest of the way to the street slowly.

He stood a while by the hotel door and watched the passing crowds, the growling taxicabs, the lumbering lorries pushing up the street. From the depths of a passing cab that slowed along the kerb he caught an instant glimpse of a beautiful woman half turned to a man beside her who held a tiny bright light to her cigarette.

Down near the corner, on the opposite side, he saw the faintly illuminated "S" for Shelter sign. A stream of people were going toward it and being swallowed up in the dark. He waited for a bus to pass, then crossed over. The street was filled with the shuffle and whisper of people, but no one rushed, no one shouted. At the entrance to the shelter he stopped and watched a group of women going down. They all carried little bundles. One had a child over her shoulder, another by the hand.

"This always happens when I get in bed," he heard a woman say.

"My God. I don't know when I'll ever get a bit of rest. You chase all day for food and worry about your man all night. . . . North Africa, he is . . . and me alone." The voice was a whine.

"Luck, m'girl. And you don't know it! Me, I've got two and one to come."

"Mrs Smithers! Mrs Smithers!" someone called down the entrance to a woman already inside. "Keep a seat for me."

O'Rourke walked away from the shelter and started down the Strand. He did not know where he was going, but he knew he would not go underground.

Halfway down the block he heard the high hum of the

planes. He stopped to listen. They were near and high and coming over the city in waves. He turned and went on a few paces. Then, in an instant, terror and havoc was loosed on the city. The bombs came whistling down. Thunder rolled through the streets. A bomb dropped through a big building across from O'Rourke. Another struck the pavement just ahead of him.

He was never sure what happened to him. He felt himself being lifted in the air and engulfed in a tornado of air blast. It seemed minutes that he was in the air, yet it could only have been a few seconds. He felt his bowels tighten with sharp and intense pain, saw light, blazing white and fierce before his eyes, and heard only a loud hollow roar.

He was thrown down into the gutter. He was still conscious. The fierce white light was still in the street, but a thick cloud of dust was overhead and he could not see the buildings. Something fell on his chest. Rubble was falling all around him; he heard it beating on the pavement.

"Now take it easy . . . Easy . . . You can get out of this all right . . . Got to !"

Slowly he raised himself. His left hand rested on broken glass and he snatched it away. He got to his knees, one hand on the kerb and the other in the gutter. Then another great explosion rocked the street and a terrific wind blast swept past him. He ducked his head between his shoulders and hugged the kerb. A shower of dust and rubble rained down.

Something struck him on the back and knocked him flat. He tried to hold on to the pavement but there was nothing to cling to. A piece of stone or brick struck the heel of his boot. There was no pain.

When the bomb blast swept past and the shower of rubble stopped, he raised his head a little and looked for shelter. Across the sidewalk a few feet in front of him he saw a darkened doorway. Still lying flat upon his belly he crawled on all fours to it. The door stood in from the street a little, affording a small shelter. In this he crouched, pressed against the wooden panel of the door.

How long he crouched there he did not know. It might have been ten minutes or half an hour. Fire blazed in a big block across the street. He read a printer's sign over the door as clearly as if it had been lit by neon. There must have been large paper stocks in the building, for, in a sudden blast, the whole of the top floor ignited and the flames roared down past the windows. The heat was intense.

He got to his feet. As he straightened up he felt a sharp pain in the small of his back. Gingerly he put his hand inside his

trousers and felt the spot. It was very tender, but he felt n
blood. He decided it didn't hurt so much then.

A fire truck came down the street, the bell clanging. He
heard it only for an instant as it passed the doorway. Immediately it had gone past, three incendiaries broke upon the road
and began to sizzle and splutter and then flared up with an
intense white fire.

He moved out to the shop front, holding himself flat
against the store. The fire engine had stopped beyond the print-
ing building and the firemen were running about dragging
lengths of hose that looked incredibly white and new in the
glare. Two of the firemen pulled a length of the hose down the
street past him and he saw that it was very old and dirty. The
faces of the men, too, had looked very white and clean as they
came toward him, but when they were close he saw the dirt
and grime on them streaked with sweat. They dragged the hose
down past the row of burning buildings to the hydrant. Then
one of them yelled through his cupped hands to the engine
crew.

A stream of water sprang up into the blazing building.
In a few minutes four hoses were going. They poured tons of
water into the buildings but the fire raged unabated. No one
put out the incendiaries in the roadway; all the firemen were
busy. They did not seem in the least concerned with the falling
bombs and incendiaries. Amid the roar of the flames and the
continuous bark and thunder of the ack-ack guns they worked
stoically.

O'Rourke took courage from them. As he moved along
the pavement, still tense and alert and ready to duck into the
nearest doorway, he remembered a remark made during his first
raid, on the night of his arrival: "If it's got your number on it,
it's yours."

The raiders came over London in droves. It was not so
much a raid as a massed attack, and in its furious intensity and
savage destruction paralleled the great raids of September 1940.

The south and centre were the worst hit. Fire bombs lit
the targets—shops, warehouses, hospitals, churches, and communication centres. Then came the rain of super-heavy bombs
into the burning areas. More fire-bombs—more H.E. bombs. Firemen worked like madmen. No sooner was a fire under control
than another bomb flared it up again. No sooner had they one
area smothered than a rain of fire bombs ignited it again. Hoses
stretched throughout the streets were ripped up by bomb
blasts or peppered with flying debris. Fire brigades were buried
beneath falling walls. One brigade that had fought a fire con-

men and first-aid parties worked among the
, climbed among the perilous heaps of masonry
and crumpled floors to rescue the trapped inhabitants. First-aid
posts were swamped with patients. Girl ambulance drivers
drove through the street furnaces hauling away the wounded,
or sat in their vehicles under the rain of bombs waiting for
their casualties to be brought out of the fires.

The city burned and rocked with the thunder of exploding thousand-pounders; death screamed from the skies, fire
roared through the streets; ack-ack barked curtains of flak up
against the raiders. And still they came, drove after drove.

Holborn Circus was a fiery furnace. Southwark was as
bright as day. A hundred fires burned in Pimlico. Fires raged
in Vauxhall, Kennington, Walworth, and across the river in
Soho, Bloomsbury, Clerkenwell and Finsbury. The Houses of
Parliament were hit, and the Law Courts. St Paul's received a
direct hit. A dozen telephone exchanges, eighteen hospitals,
thirteen churches, sixty public buildings, and hundreds of
shops, warehouses, flats and dwellings fell in ruins and the ruins
burned.

While all this havoc raged a hundred thousand people
took refuge beneath the ground, in the big tube shelters—
Waterloo, Trafalgar, Elephant and Castle, Charing Cross, London Bridge, and in the big street shelters. They lay packed
together in the ghostly light and slept, fitfully, and were safe.
And in the suburbs, countless tens of thousands took shelter in
backyard Andersons and sat the night through.

3

O'Rourke came to a corner where a direct hit had blasted
a tall building into the street. The roadway was blocked with
a high pile of debris. Behind this a twenty-foot stretch of pavement had been torn up, and in this yawning fissure escaping
gas from the mains had ignited to form a pit of roaring flame.
Part of the wall of the building stood and behind it fire raged
over the debris. The wall stood poised, as though about to crash
down into the street over the men who worked to clear a path
for vehicles through the rubble.

He stood for a minute watching the men shovelling

feverishly to make an entrance for a fire brigade to enter the street. Their efforts seemed to make no headway into the pile of rubble. Over near the gas fire burning in the torn pavement, he noticed a little man stop to rest and wipe his brow with the sleeve of his jacket. The fellow bent again to his shovel and worked like a madman for perhaps a minute and then had to rest again. O'Rourke noticed that he hadn't the strength to fill his shovel: all he picked up was a few bricks and dust, and as he threw these aside he teetered unsteadily on his feet.

"Here! Let me spell you off," O'Rourke offered, reaching to take the shovel.

"No. It's all right. . . . I'll . . . I'll be fine when I get . . . get my wind," the little man panted.

O'Rourke slapped him across the shoulder.

"Sure, I know, Pops. But just take a breather for a few minutes and I'll warm this shovel up for you."

The man gave up his shovel, and as he turned away O'Rourke saw the hair on the back of his neck was quite grey.

When he had been working for several minutes alongside the others, he heard a shout from the far pavement where a warden was watching the height of standing wall.

"Run, lads! She's coming down!"

They scurried like rats over the pile of debris and ran across the street corner. Out of range they stopped and looked back. The wall was already falling. The upper floors held together, but at the base it crumbled. It seemed to take a long time falling; it straddled the pavement like something lying down slowly. Seconds after its fall came a roaring crash and an enormous cloud of dust.

They went back to work again. The fallen wall made a second obstruction they had to clear. Meanwhile, a fire brigade had set up at the corner and was playing three jets over the heads of the working men into the furnace of debris. All but one of the buildings in the block were ablaze, but the firemen could not reach them from the corner and the whole area for blocks around was impassable. Whole streets burned: bomb craters and rubble blocked the streets. There was no other way in than to dig a passage-way through the ruins.

After a half-hour's work they succeeded in making an opening through the rubble, perhaps ten feet in width. The fire crews ran out their hoses and the truck worked its way through the passage, past the roaring flare of the broken gas main, and set to work halfway down the block. In a few minutes another brigade came through to reinforce them, and together the two crews tackled the solid walls of flame on either side. The water supply continued. The firemen held their ground. The men who stood by their pumps kept one eye and ear alert to the sound of falling bombs. But the men who worked the branches, bending low over the nozzles to get relief from the blazing heat by the draught of air created by the stream of water, could not watch for bombs or falling debris. They held their branches, straining against the pressure and could not move.

For hours O'Rourke worked with the shovel gang under the directions of a warden, digging out lanes of approach in the streets of the neighbourhood. No sooner had they cleared a path through one obstruction than they were given another. But finally, a little before 3.00 a.m. the area was again open to police cars, ambulances, fire brigades and rescue squads.

One of the first vehicles to come into the area was a Sally Ann mobile canteen. The men laid down their shovels and greeted the canteen girls with a shout. Firemen came, and police and rescue workers and the shovel gang—all begrimed, scratched, tired and unnerved, but still ready to continue the fight. There were hours of work ahead yet; no sign of let-up. Though there was a lull in the bombing, and the ack-acks fell silent one by one, the all-clear had not sounded, and everyone knew that more was to come.

4

The men drank the tea silently and when they had finished went back to work.

"What do we do now?" O'Rourke asked a tall, thin man, who looked like an accountant or business manager, as they walked away from the tea wagon.

"Oh," the fellow replied. "I daresay the warden can find something for us. Come along! We'll hunt him up."

He spoke in the clipped, matter-of-fact way, neither friendly nor cold, that Englishmen reserve for strangers, and which gives no indication whatever of his thoughts.

They found the warden in the basement of a burning building. A bomb had collapsed the ground floor, trapping a family who lived in the basement. The rescue squad were working an old man through one of the windows into the well that was half-filled with rubble and torn timber. O'Rourke could not tell if he was alive or dead.

The warden turned to the accountant and O'Rourke. His

ear was bleeding and the blood had run down and congealed over a long scratch on his cheek.

"Can we help here?' the accountant asked.

"We can manage, right enough," the warden replied, and wiped his nose across the back of his hand, then his hand across the seat of his trousers. "Up Long Acre way they need help. Ask the lass in the tea wagon if she's going over that way from here."

The accountant went over and talked with the canteen girl. O'Rourke saw her shake her head vigorously. He watched the firemen playing streams of water into the top-floor windows. When he looked around again the man had disappeared.

"The bloody sod. Now, how am I going to get over to that place? I don't even know where it is."

He lit a cigarette and stared up the street with his hands deep in his pockets. He turned right at the corner and found himself approaching Waterloo Bridge. He stopped on the bridge and leaned back against the side.

"How the hell did I get here?" he said aloud. "I figured if I turned right back there it would lead me up town." He shrugged.

"This is the screwiest place. Everything's screwy tonight, including me, I guess."

From where he stood on the approaches to the bridge the whole city upon the north bank seemed to be burning. The buildings backing upon the Enbankment hid the fires, but behind them, against the clouds of smoke, the flames showed bright yellow. At one place not far away the fire was particularly intense, for the smoke cloud above it was lit high into the sky and covered a great area.

And then, suddenly, the ack-ack guns opened up again.

"This is no place for me," he said to himself.

For a moment he hesitated whether to cross the river or retrace his steps. He decided upon the latter course. Across the bridge lay an area he knew nothing about.

He turned right up the Strand. He passed a tube station and came to a corner. Standing there, undecided, he heard bombs dropping across the river, and one of them dropped nearby with a great swishing noise, and immediately he felt a heavy thud. A terrific air blast swirled past him, but he did not know where the bomb had landed.

He retraced his steps to the underground entrance and ducked in. The platforms were jammed with people, lying, sitting and standing. Those who were lying down were so close together that legs crossed bodies, heads lay upon suitcases and bundles of clothing. Children lay between parents. The scene was one of indescribable confusion. Not a soul moved. No one spoke. Those who slept, slept deeply in exhaustion. Those who were awake stared sightlessly at the posters along the far wall. The hands of the clock hanging in the ceiling pointed to 4.15.

O'Rourke walked the length of the platform before he found a place to sit down. He sat between two women. One of them was turned to him, asleep, with her legs drawn up. The other lay turned away. She was covered with a thin black coat.

He sat down and took off his boots. His feet burned and he rubbed them through his socks. After a while he stretched out and stared up at the curved ceiling. The cement platform was the hardest thing he had ever lain on. Sleep was impossible, and yet everywhere people slept. Somewhere in the crowd a man snored fitfully.

Lying there it seemed fantastic that overhead fires raged through the streets, bombs were demolishing the work of centuries, people were dying, being maimed or buried alive. Yet, here in the subterranean cavern was safety and quiet and, for some, sleep.

He took off his tunic and folded it into a bundle and put it beneath his head.

Once, as a very small boy, when his parents were returning from a holiday trip, he had got lost from them in an enormous railway depot, and a burly Irish policeman with a red nose had sat him in a quiet corner on the stone floor and left him there a while. The smell of the depot came back to him now out of that long-forgotten memory. It was the same smell as in the underground station—an odour of faint disinfectant mingled with a warm, cloying smell of bodies and a mysterious odour of something like burnt carbon. And then he remembered the raw silk blouse he had been wearing that day long ago, and how he always liked to put his chin against his shoulder to feel the cool freshness of the silk against his face.

A great clap of thunder roared through the length of the station. The lights flickered but did not go out. Bits of plaster and dust fell upon the people. The thunder died slowly. For a long time it faded in the tunnel like wind moaning far away.

A girl under a black coat beside O'Rourke raised herself on one elbow and brushed the hair from her forehead. She looked at him with a slow, sleep-heavy gaze.

"Bit close, that one," he said.

She looked at him for several moments without reply.

He felt squashed. She did not look like the sort of girl one could just meet by casual conversation. Finally she said:

"Not very. Sounds close when you're underground, though."

She sat up and began to comb her hair, turning her head away from him. When she had finished she put her comb into her bag and snapped it shut, then turned to him with a smile.

"When did you come in?" she asked.

"Just a while ago. Not long."

"And do you intend to sleep? It's almost time for the all-clear. They usually turn for home about this time."

"I'm not sleepy," he said. "I wouldn't mind a wash and a cup of coffee, though."

She laughed. "You look as though you need more than a wash. What were you doing?"

"Shovelling rubble."

She stood up, straightened her skirt, and tucked her blouse in. He saw that she was quite beautiful. When she had put on her coat, she turned and faced him a moment. Her gaze was direct. Then she turned and walked slowly down the platform past the sleeping forms.

Though no word had been spoken, he knew she had invited him to follow. He flung himself into his jacket and hurriedly laced his boots.

At the tube entrance he fell into step beside her. Dawn was creeping into the street. The pavement and the shop fronts were faintly light, but the upper storeys of the buildings were still dark and dead, screened in a thick, greyish layer of smoke.

A fire truck passed them, travelling slowly. The men looked straight ahead, unseeing. An old hag crouched in her rags in a doorway. She showed her teeth and murmured something unintelligble as they passed.

"I wonder where she came from at this hour," O'Rourke remarked.

The girl turned around and looked back at the hag without stopping.

"Up from her hole, I suppose. She knows the raid is over."

"But how? The all-clear hasn't sounded yet."

"Oh, her kind know. They know a raid is coming before anyone else does and they know when it's over. I don't know how. They just do."

They walked for a time in silence. Finally, she stopped and asked: "What's your name? I can see you're Canadian, so you don't have to tell me that."

"I'm Bob O'Rourke."

"And I'm just Barbara."

"Well, Barbara, do you know where we are going at five o'clock in the morning?"

Impulsively she took his arm. "We're going to my place. That is—if it's still there, and you still want a cup of coffee."

They turned into a narrow lane. She led him into a dark hallway and up a flight of stairs. She unlocked her door and switched on the light. The room was small, warm and crowded. The windows were covered with heavy black-out curtains.

He stood by the door and looked around.

"Nice. Where do you sleep and eat?"

"Oh," she laughed low. "Of course a man would ask that."

She threw aside a curtain showing a narrow hallway.

"The first is the bath, then the bedroom. On the other side the kitchen. It's small."

She left him and went into the bedroom. He heard her open a drawer. After a while he followed her. She was standing in front of the mirror. She had taken off her coat and hat. They lay across the end of the bed.

He looked at her in the mirror. Her green blouse clung to her body, showing the rise of her breasts. Her hair was darker under the light, somehow. She smiled at him, a nervous smile. Gently he put his arms around her. She turned swiftly and clung to him. And all at once he drew his head down and kissed her fiercely. He felt her whole body soften into his and felt her thighs pressing against him. She pressed her mouth to his again and with a little cry, fiercely bit his lip. He sprang back from her and put his hand to his mouth.

Coolly she straightened her skirt.

"I'll make the coffee," she said.

In the hallway she looked back at him with a mocking smile.

"Sugar and milk?" she asked.

"Yes," he said, not looking at her.

He examined his lip in the mirror. "A hellcat," he said to himself and wiped the blood off on his sleeve.

He went into the bathroom and washed. Returning to the bedroom, he lay down on the bed. His body sank a long way down into the soft mattress. Warmth and soft feminine odours enveloped him. He fell asleep without knowing it.

A few minutes later he woke with a start. Barbara was shaking him gently.

"Here's your coffee, Bob."

She poured him a cup, pouring in the coffee and the hot milk at the same time. He didn't like coffee that way, and he wished he had asked for tea instead.

"This is what you need," she said, handing him the cup.

She sat on the edge of the bed and sipped her coffee, glancing sideways now and then, with a dark, veiled expression. The sweet, warm, maddening woman scent of her so close roused him. He reached out and grasped her arm.

"To hell with the coffee," he said. "It's you I need."

She gave a little bitter laugh and shook her head. "You don't need me," she said. "It's just a woman you want. Because you're on leave and the raid is over, and because, strangely enough, you're in my bed. It just happens to be me."

"So what?" he demanded. "What about you?"

She shrugged. It was a tired, hopeless gesture.

"What does it matter? I could be a duchess or a whore from Piccadilly. My need is the same. I'm sick of war and fear, and rationing and running for shelter, night after night. And I'm sick of being alone."

She spread her hands and locked her fingers, desperately.

"Do you know what it means? Do you? Can't we— can't we for a moment be together, not ask questions? Not wonder why, or what we are?"

He reached for her then, and took her in his arms, tenderly. As she sank beside him in the bed, he knew their need for each other was the same. Yet their worlds remained apart. Ten thousand miles and two worlds separated them. Yet for the morning that was breaking, the day to come, they were together, bound by a desperate need.

"Be gentle, Bob," she murmured. "Please be kind."

He held her fiercely in his arms, their bodies moulded together, and while he waited for his desire to rise, he caressed her and listened to her wild breathing. Gradually he knew that there was no desire in him. His experiences of the night had seared his soul and left his body dead with fatigue. Even as he held her, he felt himself slipping into sleep, and he did not try to resist it.

Hours later he awoke with a start. He could not remember where he was. He sat up in bed and looked at the luminous dial of his watch: 2.30. Then he remembered that it was afternoon. The world had been turned upside down.

He got up and drew the curtains a few inches. A shaft of light fell upon the bed and cut across the figure of Barbara. She lay on her side. Sometime during his sleep she must have thrown a cover over them, for it lay over her body and was curled under her arm. In the strong, sudden light he saw her breasts full and faintly pink with the dark circles of the nipples surprisingly large.

He left the curtain partly drawn and went into the kitchen. He had a great hunger. He made himself some coffee—made it his own way—and found some potted meat for a sandwich. He ate two sandwiches and drank all the coffee. Then he went back into the bedroom and lit a cigarette and sat on a chair by the window. Barbara slept soundly, her breast rising and falling.

Obeying an irresistible urge, he moved quietly over to the bed and lifted the cover off her. She turned a little, but did not wake. He went back to the chair and sat smoking, looking at her fine body in sleep.

Once, at home, he remembered, he had come in off the range at dawn, cold and wet, and had made himself breakfast, and then he had gone into Gerda's bedroom and sat on the edge of the bed and lifted the covers from her and gazed at her naked beauty and the mystery of her, gazed at her until he felt there was no longer a mystery of woman's beauty and the hidden secret of her loving.

His gaze awoke Barbara. She opened her eyes slowly. She made no attempt to cover herself, but turned on her back and, with her eyes upon his nakedness and strength, patted the sheet beside her.

"Come, Bob," she said quietly.

He rose from the window and went to her.

5

In the evening the city seemed at its quietest. To be sure, considerable traffic darted about—mostly grinding taxi-cabs, lumbering buses, army lorries and staff cars. But in side streets all was peace and quietness. A wan, misty light touched the smoked brick and dirty cream plaster look of the buildings and for an hour lent them an atmosphere of strange, indefinable charm and warmth.

O'Rourke walked alone toward the Embankment. He passed two dirty children playing in a street off Leicester Square. After he had passed them he realized that they were the first children he had seen in London streets. On a corner he saw a cabby eating his supper behind the wheel. The cabby glowered at him as he came up, until he realized that O'Rourke did not want a cab. Then he tore an enormous and vicious bite from his sandwich and winked at him as he passed.

In Trafalgar Square the pigeons strutted beneath the indifferent lions and a small group of people tossed crumbs to them. No one, for the moment, was concerned about the war, the raid of last night, nor the prospect of the night already gathering. Nelson, on high, seemed to keep an eye on the washed-blue sky speckled with silver balloons, and the other on the square below him. For an hour at least all was quiet and serene.

O'Rourke came upon the river with a sense of instant recognition and breathless awe. Its banks were lined with filthy dark buildings. Yet it was somehow majestic and noble in its reach and curved sweep through the city. It brought to him suddenly all the remembered history of dark and tortuous times —the remembrance of the river's thread through the nation's history.

It possessed for him no resemblance whatever to the great rivers of his homeland—the mighty, slow, silt-laden rivers that veined the vast and lonely land of Canada—the great rivers, coiling naked across the plains, slow and heavy with the sense of dark and haunting sorrow as summer grew, or frozen, blue-iced and windswept and utterly lost in the wastes of winter.

He stayed there on the Embankment a long time, gazing upon the ancient river. The evening light faded. New Waterloo Bridge, its fresh concrete startlingly light in the dusk, seemed to bound across the river in a series of short jumps, each jump an arch of perfection. Beyond the bridge, the city crept back into a dark pall, half smoke and half night. Behind St Paul's a high balloon caught a dying ray of light, and for a moment shone like a new moon. As darkness came, a dull faint hum of traffic, of shuffling feet, of million-footed life, escaped through the streets to the river, to the old, weary, ancient and sorrowful river of dark time.

On the way back up town he turned into a corner pub. It was noisy, smoky and stank of stale beer. He did not particularly want to go back to Barbara's place, though he had not dismissed her charms and her hunger from his mind. But with darkness, the city's streets became alive and mysterious with a thousand feminine promises. He heard a woman's laughter, a soft, sensual cry, and he had seen a couple making love in a half-dark doorway and the sight of the woman's arm clinging to the back of her man, and her body arched backwards, awoke in him the old man-animal lust.

He drank six beers and smiled ruefully as he left the place and started back for Barbara's flat.

'I wonder if I'm as young as I ought to be,' he thought.

'A few years ago I would have been after the skirt hardest to catch, and now I'm content to stick to what I've already discovered.'

He knew Barbara's door would be unlocked. He knew she would be waiting, though he had left her with no promise.

He let himself into the dark living room. She called as he closed the door.

"Who's there? Who is it?"

"Who did you expect?" he asked.

"Bob!" She came from the bedroom and stood in the door. Her green dressing gown was wrapped tightly around her.

He dropped his cap on a chair.

"You expected me back?"

She lowered her eyes and half turned to the bedroom. "I . . . I hoped."

"I'm probably asking for trouble," he said. "I don't know if you are married. I don't know if somebody will break in any time and claim I'm out of order. What the hell do I know about you?"

She looked at him and her eyes goaded him. "Do you care? I shouldn't think so. . . ."

At that he seized her and kissed her fiercely. He carried her to the bed and laid her down. As he took off his boots he asked her abruptly, "Are you married?"

She turned her head away.

"I was."

"Divorced?"

"No." She kept her head turned to the wall.

He dropped his boot on the floor and kicked it away. "Tell me."

"He's dead." She said it so quietly that he hardly heard. "He was shot down at Dunkirk. I didn't see him for a month and I think he was too tired to fly in the end. They were up all the time then. . . . They were so few. . . ."

"Were you married long, Barbara?"

"Three months." She sighed, and he felt her body tremble. "We were together only twice and then he didn't come back."

She reached out and grasped his hand. "Don't feel sorry for us, Bob. Don't, please."

They lay together and each fed the hunger of their souls and remained empty. Toward dawn the sirens sounded through the dark and cold streets. They drew closer together and finally slept in the deep and heavy-bed warmth of their locked bodies.

He awoke in the morning and found her gone. He rolled over and slept until noon.

In this way he spent four days in London. On the after-noon of the fifth day he left the flat and took a train from Waterloo back to his unit. He did not leave Barbara a note, nor did he write. Time passed quickly, somehow, and when he thought of writing her, weeks later, he decided it was too late. Someone else undoubtedly had taken his place. Life makes its own laws and finds its own justification.

# 8

O'ROURKE returned from leave and for a few days resumed his former duties. But now he had no interest in what he did. The locality palled on him: he thirsted for a change. Had he taken the trouble to define his new restlessness he would probably have said that he wanted to be in his "own outfit." For, certainly, so long as he was a reinforcement, he belonged to no unit and might be drafted to any within the existing divisions. He was no different from any other soldier in that he wanted to belong to an "outfit," to be part of a unit organization and to be able to share in the exploits of that unit, whatever they might be, past, present and future.

Fulfilment of his wish came soon. He was notified for draft to an Infantry Brigade Company one evening and the next morning at dawn, with a dozen others, he paraded for kit inspection. After breakfast they were loaded aboard a lorry and proceeded "to the field."

## 2

The estate of Brown Hill Manor lay atop a broad rise that overlooked a spacious valley. Beyond the valley over a low line of hills, lay the English Channel, some fifteen miles distant. It was a magnificent view. The valley itself was cultivated from Brown Hill down to the line of a tiny stream that meandered through a grove of ancient trees. Beyond the stream the land was grass grown and emerald in the sun, with waves of burnt brown bracken through it.

The company occupied the manor house, a fine seventeenth-century building with an enormous fire-place in every room. There was very little design to the building: it wandered willy-nilly with undefined limits. The roof was broken by in-numerable tiny gables: half a dozen staircases leading to the most unexpected places gave the house a sense of mystery. But, although it had endured the wear of time, it had never been built to house a company, and had begun to crumble in a hundred little ways under the cyclonic energies of the soldiers —the racing up and down stairways, the shuffle and shake of stamping boots. Floor boards had come loose, stair boards had been torn to shreds, fire-place tiles were cracked, plaster had fallen, and the whole building seemed to groan in protest and despair.

The farmyard and outbuildings were still in the hands of the farmer, who lived in a small cottage some distance away. This individual took a very poor view of the army. He went about each day with a long sour look and had only a grunt for answer to any greeting given him. His farm labourers were of the same mood, but they exerted the privilege of underlings by not giving any sign of recognition whatever. The farmer had reasonable grounds for his dislike of the army. Lorries churned up the dust of his barnyard and scattered his precious chickens: he complained that this discouraged them from laying entirely. This was accepted with regret by the company commander. For a time neither the officers' mess nor the sergeants' mess served fresh eggs, although the lorries continued to come and go through the barnyard as before, and after a while the matter was forgotten.

The soldiers fed the pigs the swill from the platoon kitchens and in return stole what they could. A pullet, an egg now and then, a handful of carrots or a capful of strawberries were tempting delicacies that varied the daily rations.

Nothing disturbed the sleepy monotony of the estate. Days telescoped into one another without event. The hay stood high in the pastures and a slight golden flush crept over the grain fields; roses bloomed beside the kitchen wall; black ducks dusted themselves in the noon sun. In the evening rabbits ventured out of the hedges, and the sergeants amused themselves at pistol practice.

The days were long. Light came upon the land at 4.30 in the morning and stayed until midnight. Overhead, day and night, the planes roared—the Hun coming in over the coast and gaining altitude for a run inland after strafing a coastal town, or the R.A.F. going out over the Channel. The roar of the planes was like a constant thunder, but the soldiers paid no attention to it, and the farm animals and the fowl seemed never to notice. The farmyard remained the same tranquil rustic spot that it had been for centuries. The clatter and bang from the nearby workshop, and the rumble and whine of the lorries coming and going made no difference to the place. One felt that when the war was over and the soldiers had gone, the farmer had only to pick up the litter they had left behind, the empty fuel cans, the bits of scrap metal and the weathered paper blown into hedges, and then the farm would sink back into its ancient withdrawn quietude.

A few hundred yards from the manor house and its adjoining barnyard, a dozen Nissen huts had been erected under a group of enormous elms. These were the quarters for the men. The company headquarters was in the manor house on the ground floor. Upstairs on the first floor the headquarters platoon was billeted, and in the attic the sergeants had their quarters. A six-room, two-storey wing of the house, facing south, housed the officers. The wing was fairly modern, having been added perhaps a century after to the original dwelling.

A winding, half-hidden road led through the farm to the house and ended before the great south doors in an abrupt circle, in the centre of which some long-forgotten lord of the manor had erected a sandstone memorial to a likewise forgotten dream. The sandstone had weathered with the ages : whatever inscription had been wrought thereon had worn to dust. Birds found it a handy perch from which to survey the valley. At high noon its shadow lay across the roadway and pointed to a meaningless family crest carved over the doorway of the house.

There was less activity than one might have expected around a company location. Dispatch riders came and went all day, but so routine were their duties that they entered and left the area with a strange casualness. Occasionally a staff car or a utility car drove in and officers disappeared into the house, while the drivers sauntered over to yarn with a fatigue man or a batman working in the scullery yard behind the house. The platoons were self-contained with their own H.Q. within their areas. Only the officers and senior N.C.O.s kept contact with Company H.Q.

And yet, despite the appearance of outward calm and tranquillity that pervaded the scene, the company was always in a state of flux. Within the company lines there were a hundred daily chores to be performed—the mounting of guards, the regulation of sanitary details, kitchen fatigues, hut orderlies, runners, water-duties men. Daily maintenance of the unit vehicles had to be carried out. The syllabus of training went on day in and day out, six days a week : it was realistic and intensive. In addition to these affairs there were the demands of supplies—rations, petrol and lubricants, and ammunition, to be hauled for the brigade.

For a week after his arrival O'Rourke did little more than observe and adjust himself to the daily routine. The first two days he felt utterly lost and bewildered. Everything and every man was strange to him, and no one was particularly friendly. Gradually his bewilderment vanished and he sank his identity into the platoon to which he had been posted. He came to feel that it was the best platoon in the company; the men were tougher, harder; they worked hard and played hard· and when they laughed it came sudden and wild; they liked their N.C.O.s and their officers; their equipment on parade was better than that of the other platoons. O'Rourke counted himself lucky, and came to feel pride in the platoon.

At the end of his first week with the company he was given a section of his own. His predecessor had run into the hind end of a lorry while riding his motor-cycle back into camp one night. The driver of a ration lorry had found him beside the road the next morning with a fractured skull, both legs broken and some minor cuts and bruises. They took him to the nearest casualty clearing station. Though he was still alive, no one in the company was inclined to bet on his future.

3

O'Rourke took his section on parade for the first time with heavy misgivings. He knew that he and not the men of his section was under close scrutiny by all the company. Whatever happened on that first parade of his would set the seal upon him in the eyes of the officers and the other N.C.O.s. He did not care so much what the officers thought of him, for he reasoned that he was only a corporal and away beneath the direct hand of retribution. It was what the N.C.O.s and the men might think that concerned him most. They would classify him as "good" or "lousy" on his first appearance. If they decided he was "lousy" it would take a lot of living down.

The morning parades were held in a large clearing encircled by giant oaks. The ground was level, but pitted in spots. He went out the evening before and surveyed the ground. Sitting beneath an oak tree he smoked a cigarette and planned how he would bring his section up. Then, as a precaution, since he did not know the order in which the sections might be marched on to the parade, he rehearsed his role for every possible eventuality. Having satisfied himself that he knew the ground well enough, he went back to his hut and wrote a letter to his wife.

Writing did not come easily to him, and it was Tattoo before he had finished it. In it he described the events of his life during the past two weeks, since his last letter, and though he did not know it, he gave her a thumb nail sketch of the company location and his role in it. It was to be the most descriptive letter she had received from him and the only one in which she caught the setting of his distant and strange life. Thereafter, that momentary sight and sense of his life was to fade from her, never again to be rekindled by anything known and tangible which she could grasp.

The parade in the morning went off without a hitch. O'Rourke's section made a good showing, though he himself noted a dozen flaws in it. Still, nothing was said, and that was the important thing. He felt that he had made a good showing, certainly not an unfavourable one.

After the parade he marched his section back to the platoon area. There he stood them at ease and spoke to them. In a few words he told them what he expected of them. His demands were simple and clear. A few of the men heard him in surly silence and tough sneers. For their benefit he concluded:

"Don't get the idea that because I'm new I'm soft. I'll take your best work and no guff with it. If any of you have different ideas, I'll be glad to straighten you out—but it will be in my own way."

He broke them off. As he moved away he saw, out of the corner of his eye, two of the toughest talking in whispers.

"Something will brew up before long," he observed. "They wouldn't be worth a hoot in hell if they didn't try something."

The platoon officer called him in. He had a lecture on discipline and man-management to deliver to him. He was a small man with a crisp red moustache that twitched as he spoke. O'Rourke, towering over him at the desk, measured him. He didn't think much of him: he decided that in a jam he wouldn't be any help to anyone. To all the officer's comments he interposed a punctual and well placed, "Yes, sir."

At lunch, across the mess table, the platoon officer remarked to the C.O.:

"I think O'Rourke, the new corporal, will work out very well."

The C.O. stared for a moment at a spoonful of watery

soup. "What do you make of him?" he asked. "What will he be like?"

Without hesitation the subaltern replied: "In a tight place I think he would be marvellous."

"Ah! Good!" was the C.O.'s reply, and he returned to his soup.

4

O'Rourke expected trouble, and it was not long in coming. He reasoned that someone in the section was bound to resent a newcomer being brought in as N.C.O. instead of one of the section being created a corporal for the job. Furthermore, they were certain to test him out, to see how far they could bend him.

On the third morning after he had taken over the job he found two of the men missing at Roll Call—Murray and Otter. They were the two from whom he had expected trouble. He broke the section off to its duties with a sour look. He kept the absence of the two to himself and did not report it. At dinner parade they showed up. He let them finish their meal, then called them out, one at a time.

The orchard was a quiet corner of the garden. It was out of bounds to the men and enclosed by a high brick wall to which cherry and peach trees were impaled. He took Murray in there and stood him against the wall.

"We're going to settle this between ourselves, Murray," he said. "I like doing things this way—it's quieter."

Murray stood ready for a fight.

"You aren't going to do anything, big boy," he taunted. "You just talk." He jabbed a finger into O'Rourke's chest. "Be careful, or I'll tie your ears around your bottom."

O'Rourke rocked on his heels and feinted. Murray struck out and went wild, and as he tried to recover his balance O'Rourke landed an uppercut that sent him sprawling and clutching at the wall. He sank to the ground slowly and sat rubbing his chin, but he made no effort to get up.

O'Rourke went back to where he had left Otter. He found him behind a lorry. There was no one around.

"Well, Otter," he remarked, slowly. "Do you feel like going A.W.L. again?"

The other looked at him with hard pig's eyes.

"Well, do you?"

Otter made no reply. He waited for the next move. O'Rourke reached out slowly and seized him by the throat. The movement was so casual and slow that it was the last thing Otter expected. Before he could put up a defence O'Rourke had clouted him twice so sharply that his head struck the back of the lorry and he crumpled to the ground and fell on his side. O'Rourke decided he was not badly hurt, and after leaning him in a sitting position against a wheel, left him there in the sun.

No one saw these incidents, and yet, in some mysterious way, it got about. It travelled from the section through the platoon, and in a few hours had reached the H.Q. staff. There the clerks whispered about it and the sergeant-major overheard. This individual, five foot six of brisk efficiency, was a soldier of the older school. He merely smiled and bit his moustache, and at the first opportunity passed it on to the subaltern. The officer in turn saved it up a few days until the C.O. was in a jovial mood, and then, one evening at dinner, passed it over the table as a particularly choice and unusual piece of Company gossip. It raised a chuckle from the Old Man.

"You've got quite a corporal, Simpson," he said, turning to O'Rourke's platoon officer.

Simpson glowed and wagged his head. He felt he had scored a hit. Had he not, after all, discovered this fighting corporal? Well—if not discovered, at least he had been the first to bring notice of him to the Old Man. He, Simpson, was certainly a judge of men; there was no mistake about that.

Of all this O'Rourke was completely unaware, or if he knew of it he gave no sign. But he had no further trouble with the men. They developed an almost immediate and healthy respect for him—healthy because there was in it no vestige of fear, but only admiration. He had two hooks on his arm, but he didn't need them to handle men. Still he HAD two hooks, and the *Manual of Military Law* to back him up. The combination admitted of no argument as to who was boss of the section.

In other ways, too, they developed an admiration for him. On his motor bike, when his section was out on convoy, he was a riding fool. He was neither reckless nor cautious, but he was everywhere along the line of vehicles, always on the spot when there was trouble. He seemed to care nothing for the weather—rain or shine, dark or moonlight, he rode like a demon, sitting forward in his saddle with his long arms bent at the elbows and his hands lightly upon the handle bars. His section kept better interval in a convoy than any of the others, because he MADE them. Their mounted drill became precision itself. In harbour he taught them camouflage that was actually effective, though he had never been taught it himself. He saw that they got their leave when it came due, and when the platoon officer evaded a decision and sought to put leaves off, he bullied him into granting it. He never overstepped the bounds of his rank, but he stood astride it and could not be brushed aside.

He had his faults. They were daily self-evident. He was peaceful by nature, but dangerously easy to rouse. In a flash, out of nowhere, or for the most irrational and unexpected reason he would flare up. It was said of him that he would rather fight than eat, and this may have been true. He never knew it himself. Even when roused he was aware of an immense and powerful calm deep within himself; what happened to the outer man seemed always to surprise him. He never really lost his temper at anyone—people merely annoyed him at times and he showed it easily. Perhaps he never really knew himself. He had a curious and intense flare for everything he did. It was more than infectious vitality with which he tackled everything—a vitality so intense and determined that none who knew him ever escaped being caught up in it and thrust along.

He was one of those strange and intriguing humans who, in moments of history, have risen out of a dark abyss and unknown past to become breathless legendary figures imprinted upon a recorded page of earth's agony or man's glorious dream. He did not know this. He did not know himself. He was compacted of all the people he had ever seen and admired. He preserved within himself the fabulous adventures of all the adventurers he had ever encountered, and had sought, in his brief lifetime, to parallel them all. Therein lay the source of his immense vitality and interest, for in everything he did he found a strange new world of discovery, of opportunity.

He had been a vagabond, a hobo, upon the fabulous continent. Had he lived in another age he might have been a pirate or a buccaneer or rebel leader, or frontiersman. He had them all within him. He had all their strange inward strength and overpowering restlessness, all their glorious dreams, and all their mortal faults. And with it all he was still one of the earth's little men.

5

The summer ripened like a woman touched with love. Brown Hill became a great park. The hedges filled out, and the trees that hid the brook in the bottom pasture lost their incredible flush of green and deepened. A host of birds fluttered through the noonday heat. The field crops were like strips of soft gold carpet laid on the hills. The air was steeped in a soft voluptuousness, blood-warm and wine-rich.

The men soldiered as well as ever, but their eyes wandered into the fields and the cool shady lanes. In the evenings they watched the village girls out walking. The swing of their hips and the fullness of their breasts showing beneath the cotton summer dresses had a new and deeper meaning. In the late twilight couples walked in the lanes arm in arm, or lay whispering in the fields.

Restlessness rustled through the camp as summer advanced, but there were few defaulters. Each in his own way sought diversion. The girls of the countryside were not unwilling to make friends. And there were the village pubs—cool, pulsing places of refuge on the warm nights, places filled with the smell of beer and tobacco smoke and bodies, where one could raise one's voice and become, for a little while, mildly ribald over a joke or a lewd situation expertly retold. And then there were the long walks from the pub back to camp under the darkening sky, with wild songs of remembrance; and then, passing the camp guard with good-natured drunken curses and abuse, to find one's bed in the unlit hut and slip quickly off into deep, sound sleep, remembering nothing, knowing nothing, but the warm blood-beat and contentment of the body, and the quick, clear, sudden unwinding of the mind.

There were dances in the village halls, with an overflow of girls, pretty, plain and homely, to satisfy every man and every man to his taste—so many unclaimed girls that, as a lance-jack in "C" Platoon expressed it one morning while shaving: "Jees—you've got to beat 'em off with a respirator."

"I had one last night," Mitchell reminisced. "I offered to take her for a walk down the road between dances—innocent-like, you know.

" 'I'd love to,' she says, wiggling her bottom nicely, and me not knowing why.

" 'Well, let's hoof it, then,' I says, and takes her by the arm and allows myself to be dragged out of the joint.

"Well, we walks down the road a piece, and bye-'n-bye we comes to a fine garden—all roses and blue flowers. And I thinks to myself: No guy ever snitched this babe a flower, probably, let alone bought her one. So I steals a blue flower and hands it to her, nicely, y'see."

Here he leaned against the wash bench and laughed till he shook.

"Gadalmighty!" he roared, slapping his knee, "You should've seen her. She takes the flower and holds it in front of her for a while and keeps looking at it. When we got to a lane she stops all of a sudden and looks at me and says: 'Do you like me that much? . . . Because if you do, I . . . I like you.' And then, believe it or not, she starts to cry."

"You sure have a helluva time in an innocent sort of a way," remarked Staynes, a mechanic who had a bad stomach and a perpetual grouch.

"Oh, I get around," laughed Mitchell.

6

O'Rourke wrote to his wife every week. When he had time he wrote twice a week. He gave her all the news of his company and of the army that he dared, and he concluded every letter, as an afterthought, with the simple statement: "P.S.—Am well." He was well. There was nothing the matter with him, and he could think of nothing else to say on the subject.

Gerda, too, wrote him regularly, but her letters came to him in bundles of five or six, sometimes a dozen at a time. She gave him a daily record of life on the farm, including even the smallest details. Nothing that she did, no one she met, old friends of his or newcomers to the region, were omitted. Her letters brought to him the form and substance and atmosphere of the life he had known, the life to which, in quiet moments, his mind returned. He would catch upon the images and personalities Gerda painted in her letters, and he would sink into the past and give himself up to an orgy of remembrances, bitter-sweet and haunted with the sense of departed time.

When he recalled the past, the memory of Gerda's loveliness came back to him with an overwhelming wave of warm desire. He would close his eyes and see her beauty as he had known it—all his and his alone. And then a great restlessness, immediate and unfathomable, would rise in him. He could not resist it, could not reason it away. He would hastily put away her letters and stride quickly from the camp out upon the road. At such times he would walk for hours, seeing nothing of the country through which he passed, walking hurriedly with bowed head along the lanes, driven by a nameless and over-powering restlessness. He was homesick and lonely—lonely as the prairie wind on a winter's night—and he did not know it.

It was on one such evening that he met the sheep girl.

She was sitting on a stile talking to her dog. Although his footsteps must have sounded clearly, she did not appear to notice him as he came up. She held the dog's head in one hand while with the other she caressed the back of its ear, slowly. O'Rourke stood for some time watching her. She was not pretty; if anything she was attractively homely. Her face and arms were freckled, and her nose, blunt and slightly flattened, accen-tuated her unusually full lips. Her chin and throat were well moulded. She gave an impression of agility and strength, and something of whimsical wildness.

When, finally, she did notice O'Rourke standing beside her, she pushed the dog away and stood up.

"She's very old," she said, by way of explanation.

"Have you had her long?" O'Rourke asked.

"Oh, yes. Ever since I was a girl—eight years come winter.'

O'Rourke looked at the sheep in the pasture and then across to a cottage half hidden in the trees.

"Do you live there?" he pointed to the cottage.

She laughed. "Oh, no. The bailiff's man lives there. I just watch the sheep. If I didn't do that I'd have to join up."

"It must be lonely, watching them all day. There can't be anything in the country to bother them, anyway."

"No, nothing ever bothers them. But they are better if they are watched."

O'Rourke noticed that her teeth were very white when she smiled and the tip of her tongue was a deep pink. He was not sure if her eyes were light hazel or green.

"I've got to go home now," she said, suddenly, but she made no move to go. She turned her head away from him and rubbed her back against the fence slowly.

"Do you live nearby?" he asked.

She nodded her head, but did not look at him.

After a few minutes of silence she said, "I've got to go home."

She took a few steps into the pasture. The sheep nearby

stopped grazing and looked at her. She stopped, but did not turn toward him. The breeze billowed her cotton skirt and showed her thighs.

O'Rourke jumped over the fence. "I'll walk with you."

The sheep stepped aside to let them pass. The dog followed at her heels. As they passed through the meadow the sheep fell in behind them. Now and then the dog would stop and look back and the sheep would stop, too. When the dog went on again the sheep followed.

O'Rourke took the girl's hand. It was warm and felt familiar. She walked closer to him.

"Do you ever have to be guard?" she asked, suddenly.

He looked at her puzzled. "Be guard?"

"Yes, you know—stand on guard a long time."

"Oh. No. Not now I don't. Why do you ask that?"

"I just wanted to know. I've always thought that must be the loneliest job in the world. If you could look at a field or a cloud or a tree or something—why, then it wouldn't be hard. But just to stand all day . . ."

He laughed and put his arm about her waist.

"You're funny. I like you," he said, and his eyes sought response in hers.

"Funny?" she asked. "I think a lot all day. I haven't anything else to do. Thinking is fun."

They came to the edge of the pasture. A small gate led into a wood. At the gate she stopped.

"I just live a little way now. I can go alone."

She held the gate open after her and made no move to go on her way.

Slowly, sure of himself, knowing she would not resist, he took her in his arms and pressed his lips to hers fiercely. Her arms grasped him and she gave herself up to his kiss. When he looked into her eyes again he was certain of his conquest.

He led her into the woods and there, beneath an ancient elm, had his way with her. The dog, sitting on its haunches a few feet away, looked at them and then turned away and yawned and lay down. The lambs in the pasture cried to one another. Wind stirred in the trees. A full pale moon rose in the twilight sky, and after it, a tiny star set its course across the night.

# 9

THAT summer the Canadians spent on schemes and exercises. Reinforcements poured over from Canada. They came as complete units, even as whole brigades; and they came in drafts as reinforcements without a unit identity. They took up positions in the south of England, occupying large estates and country houses, farms and even whole sections of villages. Their equipment either came over with them or followed shortly after. Within a few weeks of their arrival, each unit was ready for action. In this way, imperceptible from a distance, another division joined the originals. Infinitesimal in strength as they were in comparison with the strength of vast armies, they nevertheless helped to tip the delicate balance of the scales against the Huns' lingering and indecisive intention of invading the island fortress.

By the fall of that year there was no longer any logical possibility of the Germans attacking across the Channel. They had waited too long : the scales had been tipped against them. It was to be recorded, in the impartial view of later years, that Hitler's indecision about attacking across the Channel in the months that followed Dunkirk was the greatest military misjudgment ever made. Had he attacked during that period, Britain would have been his—his, though every street and every lane, every ditch and every bridge, would have been fiercely contested.

By the autumn of 1941 it was plain that his chances of invasion were gone. It may have been this final fact that made the little beer-hall strategist turn his armies to the east and attack Russia. He had to do something. His victorious armies could not be held inactive for long : they could not rest on their victories while the Allies grew in strength. He ordered an all-out attack on Russia, and made his second and fatal misjudgment. He was never to conquer Russia; he was never to set foot in Moscow : that dream became as remote as his dreams of entry into London. His armies found an adversary waiting and prepared. After the initial shock and momentum of the mighty panzer attack had subsided, the Russian lines held; they stretched and bent, but they could not be pierced. When winter came to the steppes, the Russians struck. In the spring the land was sodden with the blood of a million Germans. Though the German armies reeled eastward, again and again, victories turned into defeats: the cost of a village, a railway line, a pocket of earth mounted astronomically. And, finally, the vision of victory faded completely: the vaunted armies of the Reich fell back in retreat along the whole thirteen hundred mile front. In retreat they were no different from any other retreating army that had been before them. Their invincibility, once feared, had become equipped with rear-vision.

All this began in the summer of 1941—in those long days of summer when, microscopically, nothing seemed to happen—at least to the Canadians stationed and waiting in England.

2

Britain, always a little late, finally fell into full-time war stride. The workers had been in stride from the beginning. Administration trip-stepped along beside labour until it eventually caught on. Socially, the country resembled an all-breed dog show on a wet afternoon: the mongrels and little fellows waddled along and did their best, while the long-nosed thoroughbreds stepped gingerly and very high and made a charity effort. The little man of Britain worked his best and endured the worst, quite cheerfully. When asked to double production he somehow managed—a little more effort, a few hours longer each day: he did not know how he did it, and it never occurred to him to wonder if he could.

The upper middle class and the aristocracy did their bit, too. Their bit was considerably more than their contribution in peacetime. But it was quite a different effort from that of the workers. They gave up their large homes because the Government requisitioned them; they gave up their beautiful gardens and the undisturbed calm of pre-war days. They gave up sugar and sausage and kidney breakfasts and champagne and motorcars. They became subject to draft laws and industrial effort in the same measure as the little man. But Britain remained Britain throughout, with its marked and adhered-to classes. The haves worked with the have-nots, but made it clearly understood that it was not on a basis of fraternity, and certainly only for the duration. Those who believed that the war would accomplish what centuries had not, and that there would be a tendency toward levelling-off of class distinctions, saw their hopes die when they examined beneath the surface of the common struggle. Only on top there was a levelling: underneath, differences were maintained as they had always been, and by the same methods of accrued social benefits.

3

The Canadian Army, or those formations and ancillary troops, totalling in all four divisions, that were overseas at that time, occupied practically all of southern England. In all this area there were only a few British units. The Canadian strength was in depth, from the Channel coast north to a line approximately from London to Southampton. Along the coast the divisions alternately stood guard. Each division, when relieved, took up positions in old estates, in country homes and villages as far inland as twenty miles.

The beaches were mined: barbed wire covered the mines and blocked all approaches, coils and coils of it, rusting in the sun. Upon the height of land overlooking the beaches stood the artillery shore batteries, heavy and light artillery, ack-ack. The roads behind the beaches were straddled with concrete road blocks; concrete and steel tank traps ran from the beaches up across the land, across roads and ditches, through fields and villages, not in straight lines, but in wavering contours that followed the land. Every approach to the hinterland of the island was blocked. Barbed wire straddled fields, lay stretched, concertina-fashion upon hedges and fences.

There were areas of defence forbidden to the public. There were places where children could not play and places where lovers could not walk. There were farms requisitioned for tank manœuvre grounds, and forests filled with ammunition and petrol dumps. There were ammunition dumps along the roadsides and in old gravel pits and stone quarries.

But this was not all.

Old vehicles had been dragged into open fields, poles had been driven into pastures, and where no poles were available old culvert pipes had been stood upright and filled with concrete, and across straight stretches of road, overhead trip wires had been stretched—all this to smash up any enemy aircraft attempting to land.

Everything was denied the enemy. There were whole units trained in demolition of bridges, roads and buildings. Every unit was called upon to defend its area; and, more than that, every area was plotted and defensive action charted and and kept up to date.

Airfields dotted the country. One rarely saw them, but this was due, not so much to skilful camouflage, as to the fact that the patchwork landscape of England was in itself a natural camouflage.

Planes roared overhead all day and night. They never seemed to rest, racing across the skies like strange dark birds which could not ground, but had to go on diving, soaring, with breathless and incredible beauty, until they were spent.

So they seemed to the watching multitudes upon the earth. They went roaring up to meet raiders, battled them outnumbered, yet out-manœuvred them, out-shot them and turned them back. After every encounter they swept back to their bases with gaps in their formations, numbers missing. Still, the next day, their losses reinforced, they would be up again, racing to the challenge, sweeping breathlessly across the treetops, then climbing, climbing, climbing, and finally, in the ice-blue heavens, the watchers below could follow the dog-fights by the vapour trails sketched in the sky.

Such brave men! So few, then.

Over Britain they fought, and over the Channel and the French ports, and even deep into the heart of occupied France. With each passing month their strength grew; they lengthened their offensive sweeps.

The soldiers' admiration for the fliers was boundless. Chained to the toilsome earth they could only watch, openmouthed and mute with admiration, the boundless and ferocious courage of their winged brethren. Had the airmen been Afghans or men from Mars the admiration would have been no less intense. To the British it was thrilling to think that they were Britons. To the Canadians it was a proud possessive fact that Canada flew with the Britons and Australians and South Africans and New Zealanders. It was not possible to say who were the best flyers, though countless arguments endeavoured to decide. No one, however, ever denied that the Canadians ranked with the best.

Yet all this was but a small part of what might have been termed "the Military Occupation of Britain."

There was another side to this strange condition of life—a facet of everyday life that was never seen.

Every lathe, every village smithy, every workshop, every factory produced something for war. A plumber's shop produced a certain specified piece of copper tubing for aircraft, or a fitting for a ship. An automobile workshop turned out a part for military lorries. A pre-war fencing company produced portable landing fields from materials supplied by a company which had once made safety pins. The factory which had made fish nets was turned to the manufacturing of camouflage nets. The carpet company produced burlap sandbags.

An engine block was produced in one town, bolts and nuts in another, pistons in another, bearings in another, cylinder heads in another and gaskets somewhere else. In the night, lorries transported these parts to still another town, where, in a central assembly plant, a finished engine was produced. As the lorries hauling the component parts converged upon the assembly plant, other lorries left the plant with fully assembled engines for some distant destination where they would be installed into the fighting unit.

So it was.

The roads of Britain roared with civilian transport lorries, all carrying some cargo of war, some small part of a mighty weapon. A thousand heavy trucks roared along the Great North Road and Watling Street every night. In the roadside transport cafés the drivers would stop for tea and rest, and in the grimy, smoke-filled rooms would exchange gossip about wives, women and towns. They never talked about their loads. They wheeled their vehicles through the nights, through air raids and depressing newspaper headlines. They were not heroes; they were simply doing their jobs, as the men and women at the lathes, the blast furnaces and the factory benches were doing theirs.

All day and far into the night the military convoys roared through the close-cluttered villages of the countryside. Gone was the quiet tranquillity of rural life. The army camped in barnyards, in the fields and in the villages. Units settled into billets as though for a long stay, then suddenly, hurriedly, broke camp and moved on, and were replaced by others. Villagers and townsfolk never came to know them: their movements were utterly bewildering, unaccountable. They left as they had come, hurriedly, with incredible efficiency, and in the morning there was nothing left to show that they had ever stopped there at all.

And all the while, day and night, the planes roared in the

skies and the sirens wailed. In the early morning, in the crisp sunny air, they thundered overhead and played circuses in the heavens, tracing strange magical trails across the blue : in the afternoon it was the same, and it seemed the dogfights, then, were even fiercer. Night was the time of dread—a long, blacked-out space of terror and waiting wedged between the days. In the day, when the sirens wailed, raiders came and the terror from the skies was not so bad : one could at least SEE. But at night the interval between the siren's wail and the "Raiders Passed" compressed all the blind fear and foreboding into hours in which neither hope nor faith afforded a shield. At night one stood at one's post or crawled into the earth, and waited, waited, waited, while the world rocked and flamed and centuries were shattered into rubble.

There was scarcely a village that did not bear the scars of war. When the rubble had been cleared away and the street craters filled in, the villages looked much as they had before, but with gaping holes, sudden and ugly, like missing teeth, in the neat lines of the streets. The people took the rubble and the brick and built static water reservoirs, and waited for the next raid. In time, weeds and even flowers grew amid the ruins, and people forgot who had once lived there. And strangers from far dominions came who gaped and passed on and never knew the beauty and peace that had once flourished there.

The amazing thing to be recorded was not that Britain survived at all (for there was a time when the possibility of survival itself was taken from the people, and placed into the hands of destiny), but that, during those fatal months, the heart and soul of the British people remained unchanged. It was an extraordinary thing, this. Something should have changed in the national character, the national consciousness. The face of Britain altered; the ways of life altered; yet the heart of the people did not change. Deep, deep within him, the little man and the big man of Britain remained the same as they had always been. In this way, as they had stood before, in other wars, they faced the country's most critical hour.

4

The monotony of the daily life bore down upon the young Canadians. From dawn to sundown they were kept continuously training, with weapons, drill and transport. The battle exercises which took place from time to time through the year brought them fresh interest, but immediately they returned from the exercises they slipped again into the heavy listless boredom of training.

What the men wanted was action. Instead they got more training. A thousand useless devices were invented to keep them occupied, until they almost forgot how to relax, how to laugh. Only at night, when they invaded the pubs and dance halls, did they forget the gloom of the days, and then they threw reserve and discipline to the winds.

In the days just before each pay-day the world took on an even gloomier aspect. In the camps it was impossible to find two silver coins to rub together, much less to spend on beer and girls. When pay-day came again the men brightened, the pubs were crowded, and after pub-closing, the dark streets echoed with their wild western songs. English folk could not understand them. They called them "wild" and sometimes they smiled tolerantly, sometimes frowned. The truth was that the men had reached their peak of training. They were spoiling for a fight. Any amusement, and the wilder the better, found easy interest among them.

After each battle exercise O'Rourke found himself restless and caged. He went to the pubs with the others, got drunk and sang and on occasions brawled in the dark streets with strangers. But these things did little to satisfy him. He needed more than that—what, he could not tell.

In the evenings, when he did not go to the pubs with the others, he would strike off across the fields to meet the sheep girl. Sometimes he would find her by the edge of the woods, or along the road leading to her home, and always she would be the same—whimsical, fiery, impulsive and wildly passionate. And yet she gave him nothing of herself. Each time he left her he would ask himself: Why? Why? Why? Not remorse, but a disgust that the physical hunger of man should need so little to satisfy it, filled him with momentary horror. It was like rape. It was like going to a brothel. It was simple copulation.

He knew that he was not the only one to whom she gave her favours. Whom else, he did not know, but he suspected, cynically, that she was for the taking of any passer-by. There was an artillery unit stationed within a mile of her cottage. Often, walking back to his billet, he wondered how many of them knew her, and was surprised that the thought made no impression upon him.

One evening in September he took a different route to meet her, cutting across the country, through a stubble field and through the woods. In this way he approached the sheep pasture from a different direction than usual, coming out of the woods near a new hay rick which had only been partly thatched.

As he approached the rick he heard muffled voices, and laughter, and a woman's wild cry. Astonished, he stopped and listened. The laughter and the woman's cry died, but the sound of muffled voices and the thrashing movements in the hay came to him where he stood at the edge of the woods. Cautiously he approached, stopping now and then to listen. His eyes burned in his head and a tiny muscle on his jaw twitched. He heard someone call in a sharp voice:

"Quickly! Get it over with!"

Another voice, like a low growl, spoke.

Through these voices ran a low, murmured moan. It was not the sound of terror or pain. There was something lascivious and wild in it—something animal.

He quickened his steps and turned the corner of the hay-rick and stood stock still, galvanized at what he saw.

Four men were standing in a group pushing at each other and snickering. On the ground at their feet lay the sheep girl, her head on one side, eyes wide open and staring, and her lips parted as though to sound an exclamation. Her skirt was pulled off her and lay beside her and her blouse was open, showing her firm red-bruised breasts. Her legs were parted shamelessly. Her hands clutched into the straw on which she lay. As O'Rourke watched, one of the men fumbled with his trousers and bent over her.

Blindly, O'Rourke turned and fled, and as he ran he heard the loud laughter of the men behind him.

The incident made a deep impression upon him. A week after this he had occasion to act as guard escort to a corporal who was going up for court-martial on a charge of rape. He did not know the corporal, who was from another formation, but in the lorry on the way to the court, he listened to the fellow's story. The corporal, it appeared, had kept company with a girl for weeks and she had resisted all his advances. He admitted he had tried to take her several times, but, as he put it to O'Rourke, "she said she wasn't like that." And one night he had gone to meet her and had caught her with an old man. He said nothing, but went away quietly. The next night he took her forcibly.

The corporal ended his story.

"My wife—what will she think when she hears this about me?" he cried, biting his lip.

Neither of the guards answered. O'Rourke sat silent,

thinking of the fellow's wife. The other guard remarked stupidly:

"There's only two kinds of women, the good ones and the bitches. We marry the good ones and whore with the bitches."

O'Rourke, thinking of the sheep girl, silently pondered this truth.

### 5

The last battle exercise in which O'Rourke's company took part that year began the last week of September. A few days before they embarked upon it a rumour circulated that this scheme was to be the last before the units went into action. It was the same rumour that had preceded all the other battle exercises, yet this time it was given more credence. If the Canadian troops were to go into action that year it would have to be before the winter weather set in. Hope, therefore, ran high—the last hope of the year.

The day before the scheme began, O'Rourke's company moved south and westward across England to take up its position behind the line of attack. They moved in column, the major leading in his car, with two advance D.R.s out ahead. The roads were lined with military traffic. Convoy after convoy—artillery, infantry, engineers, signals, ordnance, army service, medical—moved south and west into position. Traffic control on cross roads kept the converging convoys moving in order.

The day was hot and breathless: the heat on the roads was stifling. The drivers sweated and cursed the snail's pace they had to keep, and the constant gear changing. The troops, crowded in the back of the lorries under the tarpaulins, groused, sang, smoked and spun yarns.

At noon the company halted on the side of the road for lunch. The men filed past the cook's lorry with their mess tins. One sweating cook's helper dropped a spoonful of bully-beef mixed with potato into one mess tin, while his mate plunked a spoonful of sweetened, watery boiled rice into the other tin and added a couple of hard-tack biscuits. The men dipped their enamel mugs into the tea as they passed. The rice pudding had a few raisins in it. Some got one or two raisins, others had only the rice. The raisins looked like dead insects.

"Look at that—they didn't even pick out the flies," someone remarked in a loud voice, and the whole line burst into laughter.

"They're not flies," said the shoemaker, putting his fingers into the other fellow's rice and squashing the raisin. "No, sirree! That's a black Chinese Palapatoot."

This brought more laughter. The shoemaker wiped his fingers across his bottom and leaned back on his heels. The cook frowned, but said nothing. He was rather a sensitive, temperamental individual, having been a pastry cook in a big hotel before the war.

They ate standing beside the vehicles with their mess tins resting on the mudguards or on the bumpers, or squatted in the ditch under the hawthorn hedge. The D.R.s ate sitting in the saddles of their motor bikes. The officers talked for a time in a little group some distance from the column. The batmen-drivers brought the officers' food in the mess tins to the Jeeps and set the meal on the flat engine covers. Then they went back to the cook's lorry for their own.

The men eyed the officers and wondered what they were scheming. Something unpleasant. . . . But the major seemed in a good mood; he smiled at one of his subalterns and waved his arms conversationally. The D.R.s, who were wise to the moods of the officers when the company was on the move, winked at each other—a silent understanding that nothing very important was in store for them in the afternoon. They knew the major. When he had any plan he chewed gum and smoked cigarettes continuously.

O'Rourke had very little to do while his section ran in convoy with the company. He rode his bike along beside the lorries, sometimes falling in front of the lead lorry of his section, sometimes dropping behind to ride beside the corporal of the following section. The two often thought of leaving the column and riding off somewhere for a pint of beer, but the country bristled with M.P.s.

A halt was made before each even hour. The men climbed out of the vehicles and made water beside the road or against the hedges. They smoked and cursed the slowness of the move and then, when the whistles blew down the column, they mounted again and moved off.

The cook was in a towering rage. His petrol burner continually broke down. He was trying to make a bread pudding for the evening meal: the lorry lurched and sent his pots and pans crashing, and one particularly hard bump had caused his box of precious supplies to tumble over, spilling everything. The burner would not work long enough to boil a Dixie of water, and his utensils from the noon meal clattered, unwashed, about his feet.

"Sonovabitch! Sonovabitch!" he continually shouted to the driver, who, in his cab, could not hear him above the whir of the engine, but drove blissfully along thinking of the charms of his blonde girl friend in far away Regina and the passionate letters she wrote him.

That night the company bivouacked in woods on the edge of a village. The trees provided good cover for the vehicles from the air, but the ground was soft and marshy, and several vehicles bogged down. The men sweated and pushed and eventually got them out of the mud, and, as usual, cursed the "higher authority" who had consigned the company to such an area. They had a late supper, leaning against the trees while they ate. The tea was cold, but by that time they were too tired to grumble

Latrine pits were dug, and because it was an "exercise" and critical colonels and lesser fry might drive in to observe and report, they dug weapon slits in the mud. The platoons posted their sentries and set up their light machine-gun and anti-tank defences. The lorry drivers hauled petrol cans and refuelled their vehicles. In the back of a lorry the adjutant and his corporal worked by the guarded light of a gas lamp, setting up a war board on which they drew the position of the company and flanking companies, in preparation for the "Fire" order the next morning, which would signal the beginning of the battle scheme. The major went off in his car to liaise with Formation H.Q. Most of the men spread their blankets in the lorries and lay down to sleep.

Thomas, the youngest of the D.R.s expounded tactical theories to Therio from "B" platoon who was just starting a two-hour stretch of sentry-go. Therio was not interested in tactical theories, but the lumpy meal he had hastily swallowed settled heavily in his stomach and made him unaccountably sleepy, and he was glad of Thomas's voluble company to keep him awake. He knew the sergeant-major would make a round of the sentries before he turned in. If he could stay awake until the sergeant-major had gone, then he might steal forty winks while the camp slept. It was, after all, only a scheme.

By midnight the last movement in the camp had died. Even the adjutant had snuffed out the light in the orderly-room lorry and gone to bed. The sky was an enormous inverted bowl, black-lacquered and studded with a thousand frozen stars, incredibly bright. The world was still and brooding, save for the far-off hum of an occasional motor cycle speeding across the country. An hour after midnight distant sirens wailed like a faint animal cry, and hidden searchlights threw sudden brilliant tapers into the sky. The drone of planes flying high and far to the east sang through the night, followed by intermittent gun blasts, so distant that they sounded like the dull rumble of a vehicle over a plank bridge.

The senior captain and the adjutant slept on their camp beds beside one of the H.Q. lorries. The captain smoked several cigarettes in the dark before he fell asleep. The sentry, roving back and forth along the lines, watched the glow of the cigarettes. When, finally, he saw the last cigarette drop from a sleeping hand, he moved noiselessly over and stamped it out under his heel. He stood over the captain for some time, gazing at the dim outline of his face in the dark. In sleep the face did not look like the captain's at all: it was soft, relaxed and almost boyish. It was not like the hard, tightened face that had looked at him once and sentenced him to twenty-eight days for being A.W.L. The sentry turned and tiptoed away into the deeper shadows. In the pitch darkness under a lorry he stretched out for a nap. Someone, sleeping in the lorry above him, snored loudly, and he listened, smiled and fell sound asleep.

At dawn the battle began along the imaginary line separating the two make-believe enemy forces. It forced no change in O'Rourke's company location that day, but as the day progressed news came back to the rear about the progress of the scheme and the movements of front-line infantry and tank units. Late in the afternoon O'Rourke saw a bridge company moving up toward the front and knew that some advance had been made or was soon expected.

The function of O'Rourke's company was to supply ammunition, petrol and supplies to an infantry brigade. It was, therefore, tied to the movements of that brigade, although it operated from rear to front and was located several miles behind the brigade lines. All day it remained in its location. The petrol and supply platoons had their stores on wheels and would issue during the night. The ammunition platoon, to which O'Rourke belonged, had no ammunition, since the battle exercise was only make-believe. It had been decided, however, that the ammunition platoon transport would operate as an extra supply platoon and thereby participate in the scheme in a more or less realistic function.

Throughout the day the men lolled about, sleeping, gossiping or doing odd jobs to their kit. The day was brilliant with sunshine and warmth. In the fields nearby some farm labourers ploughed the stubble under, and the sound of their voices calling to the horses sang in the golden heat.

O'Rourke set his section to work mending their camouflage nets on the vehicles. It was a lazy sort of job for them, but one that needed doing. The platoon officer and the sergeant had gone off together after breakfast. He had seen them talking together by the cook's lorry, and guessed they had something planned in the village. The sergeant pandered to the lieutenant, who in turn thought the sergeant was the best in the company. The sergeant-major, on the other hand, had a very poor opinion of the sergeant, and only the lieutenant's protection saved him from being reduced.

Mullens, the corporal from another section, came over to chat with O'Rourke. They sat under a tree near the vehicles. Mullens brought out a package of Canadian cigarettes and offered one to O'Rourke.

"Jees! You know, I haven't had any cigs from home in two months," O'Rourke said, offering his match to Mullens.

"It goes like that sometimes."

"Sure! Sure! But the last ones I had were sent in May. The wife told me so. What happened to the ones she's sent since then?"

"Some bastard got them, you can be sure."

Mullens was not sympathetic. Whenever anything went wrong he attributed it to "some bastards" and let it go at that. O'Rourke noticed that most of his men had drifted away, one at a time. Only three of them remained repairing the nets.

"Hell," he thought, "it's a good day to bum. Let them go."

"Whatcha think of this scheme?" Mullens asked. "Me . . . I think it's nuts."

"I don't savvy it at all," O'Rourke admitted. "How anybody figures it's good training to sit on your tail while the brass hats think out a phoney war is beyond me. But there you are."

"C'est la guerre," Mullens remarked in a philosophic tone, with a flick of his cigarette ash.

O'Rourke looked at him.

"What the hell does that mean? Are you a French-Canadian?"

"No. It means . . ." Mullens spread his hands and pretended to translate, "it means 'It's the war'."

"Where did you pick that up?"

Mullens put his hand down his trousers and lazily scratched himself.

"I got it from my girl friend. She's French—in the A.T.S. She's a great girl." He went on scratching himself.

"She's got a will of her own, I'll admit. But she always gives in and says 'C'est la guerre.' So long as I keep her supplied with candy I'm the greatest fellow on earth. And that's easy, 'cause I get lots."

"Naafi stuff?" O'Rourke asked, without interest.

"Hell, no. My girl friend and my ma send me loads of it all the time. It's got a good trade value."

He stood up and stretched himself. Then he looked down at O'Rourke, who lay sprawled against a tree with his eyes closed. As though he had never seen him before, Mullens studied the other secretly—the full nose, the broad forehead, the tight, close ears, the hard, perfect chin, the mouth which seemed to hold a continual expression of merriment or perhaps derision.

"He's a handsome bugger," Mullens reflected to himself. "He's hard as nails, too. But there's something eating him, and he doesn't know what."

With a shrug and a hitch to his trousers he strode away.

When his footsteps had died, O'Rourke opened his eyes and watched the farmers ploughing in the field beyond the hedge. Near the ground the hedge was thin and he could watch the ploughs moving along, one behind the other. The earth curled out from the plough-shares and rippled, bright wet in the sun. He could see the horses' legs and the legs of the farmers moving slowly, rhythmically, but he could not see their bodies for the hedge. The agitating scent of autumn came to him, the intangible scent of musky straw and hot earth and sweet dried grass. He rubbed his arm across his face as though to brush aside a fine clinging spider web.

He closed his eyes and thought of Gerda. He saw himself with her, walking across the stubble of their fields at home after the thrashing. They had done that once. It seemed long ago. By the brook they had stopped and gazed at their reflections in the pool. The grass there was thick-green and sweet. He had drawn her down upon the grass and caressed her, and suddenly she had slipped out of the dress and lay naked and lovely as a peeled birch.

High summer and the heavy heat upon the land. . . . Time of ripeness . . . time of love and the hot blood beating. . . . The grain cut and stored, the prairie land golden, reaped and spent. . . . The high soft thrum of silence.

Afterwards, Gerda had lain beside him with her face pressed beneath his arm. How warm she was in the sun. How sweet the grass where they had crushed it.

"Perhaps we made a child, Bob," she said, simply, sighing with contentment.

"Do you want a child, Gerda?"

"Yes, yes. Your child, darling . . . more than anything in the world."

Two years . . . there had been no child. He understood now why she wanted one, something of him . . . something of her . . . an image, the fruit of their love. If he died she would have nothing but memories, but at least he knew they were good memories.

He fumbled in his pocket-book and brought out one of her letters. It was the sweetest letter she had sent him. Faded, dirtied with handling and a hundred re-readings, he unfolded it and read:

"I had an order for fifty pounds of green beans yesterday and some rabbits, so that is why I didn't write as I intended. I'm sorry I missed a day. Maurice and Sylvia are coming over for supper to-night. How I wish you could come, too. What fun we'd have around the big table . . . but if you were here I'd send them both away, as then I'd want only you. But soon, Bob!

"I picked white daisies and set them in the blue Moorcroft to-day, near your picture on the mandarin chest.

"The days are hot now, and the evenings long and warm. Last night there was a great golden moon shining down when I went out to close the barn. It was so bright that my shadow moved ahead of me across the yard. I thought of you, darling. It is the time of year you liked best—the harvest time.

"It's a wonderful country, this land of ours, Bob. It's rich and fine and good. It's a whole lot more, too, but I'm not good at saying those things. But it is yours, Bob. Don't ever forget it. Come back to it. Come back to me. I will wait, always."

The letter trembled in his hand. As though she were beside him he heard her cry across the gulf of time and distance, and a terrible longing for her lay like a stone within him.

How long will it be before we are together again? he asked himself. A year? Years and years, perhaps.

And time, heavy with the weight of his longing, pressed down upon him.

That night there was considerable activity along the front. The company was ordered forward: the enemy forces along the make-believe battle front had apparently been pushed back. The platoon commanders met with the company commander, and immediately thereafter returned to their platoon lines and began preparations for the move.

For two days the brigade moved forward, and O'Rourke's company, a few miles behind. followed. The make-believe enemy rolled back, and their weakness was exploited to the full. No-one rested. No-one dug in. Finally, early in the morning of the third day, the advance slowed. Whole units halted and could not go on. In the forward lines the infantry dug in, the tank regiments withdrew to harbours, and anti-tank units prepared to meet a counter-offensive. Along the whole front, imaginary though the battle was, the lull in activity came like a sudden calm in the midst of a gale.

O'Rourke's company halted in a little village. Ahead of them the road was blocked by an artillery regiment going forward slowly. The company halted beside the village green and the cooks began to prepare breakfast. In the stillness of the morning the blast-roar of the petrol cookers sounded unusually loud. Dead with fatigue, the men sat in the vehicle cabs and fell asleep. Some crawled out of the vehicles and lay in the dew-soaked grass, and, oblivious of the damp and chill slept like drunken men.

The platoon lieutenants stretched out beside a Jeep, not far from the cooks. They rolled themselves in their greatcoats and smoked.

Lieutenant Sampson, a fat, red-faced little officer, whose face bore a striking resemblance to a new-born child, stretched himself slowly, cracked the knuckles of his fingers, yawned and declared :

"Another day would finish me. I've too much weight on me to keep going forever. You two scarecrows can stand much more."

"I suppose that means you want us to whip your platoon into shape for the next move while you sleep. Is that it?"

"If you go sick now, I'll clout you one."

They smiled good-naturedly at each other.

"I wonder how many more of these schemes we'll have to do before we see the real thing? God, but they're dull."

"There won't be many during the winter. In the spring they'll begin again."

"You think we'll be here in the spring?"

"Where else?"

"We might get into action before then."

"Do you see any hope of that?"

"No-one can tell."

The others shrugged. They held no such hope.

After a brief silence, during which each officer smoked thoughtfully, Lieutenant Sampson said :

"I wonder how long the war will last. I'm tired of it already."

Wharton, a thin, six-footer with a beaked nose, snorted disgustedly.

"You should be tired of it! Why, damn it all man, the ink is hardly dry on your attestation papers. You've only been in the army nine months."

"I suppose you're a veteran."

"Hardly. But I didn't wait for a commission before I joined up. I jumped in the day war was declared—and as a private."

"Now, lads, no quarrelling," the third lieutenant pleaded. "Not everyone could get into uniform the day war was declared. If they could, the war might be over now."

Wharton was still belligerent.

"But a helluva lot of fellows could have been in," he said with heated emphasis.

"Yes. Still . . . there's no point in making an issue of that now. It's small change. By the time we're out of service we'll be old men."

"That's a happy thought . . . and I with a young wife at home."

"She'll keep."

"Yes, I know that. But some won't. It's a terrible thought for any man who isn't sure."

Lieutenant Sampson rose and ground his cigarette out under his heel.

"I've got work to do," he said, stiffly, and strode off to his platoon.

The two lieutenants watched him go, and then looked at each other.

"It's like that with some," Wharton remarked.

The other did not answer.

"Yes," Wharton said, thoughtfully. He shivered suddenly. A tiny fang of uneasiness and doubt licked at his mind.

# 10

UNDER an azure sky the town lay like a dark round clotting upon the golden prairie. A narrow river, muddy-brown in the sunlight, circled the northern limits of the town and veered away in a sharp bend to the north and flowed on through rolling scrub land, finally disappearing from view in a dense pine forest.

One wide street, broad and paved, cut the town in two. On the west side of this main street, behind the row of stores and business buildings, stood the railway yards. The tracks gleamed silver in the afternoon sun. The station house and platform, weather-bleached and dust covered, huddled close in the oblique shadow of a towering grain elevator. Farther down the tracks four other grain elevators, rising like giant watch towers, dominated the town and the surrounding countryside.

Main Street was almost empty. In front of the drug store a farmer's wheat wagon with a team of grey horses waited. The wagon was empty, but the floor of the wooden box was smooth and gleaming from the grain it had carried to the elevators. Two small children played on the pavement in front of the bank building. From his first-floor window above the bank the dentist Hamilton picked his teeth and watched the children. Further down the street a gasoline tank truck cut a corner and disappeared, leaving a cloud of grey dust across the road. The screen door of the butcher's shop slammed, and a fat woman in a black coat came out and walked slowly, heavily, down to the druggist's and entered. The two waiting horses lifted their heads momentarily and turned their ears towards her as she passed.

The second year of the war had left no marked change in the town. There were fewer young men to be seen on the streets. Labour was scarce, though if one paid high enough wages the land could be worked. There was talk of rationing foodstuffs and fuels. There was even talk of mobilization of manpower. A lot of families in the area had sons in the army or air force, and even a few in the navy. Most of the boys in the services were still in Canada. It was something to have one's son or husband "Overseas."

True, there were unmistakable signs of neglect here and there, where farms had been deprived of male hands. The Reddick farm, just outside the town limits, bore eloquent signs of abandonment. Jim Reddick had joined a First Division tank regiment and was overseas. His wife could not keep the place going herself and had rented it and moved to the city. The tenant, too, had joined up and was in a training centre. The gate of the farm sagged on its hinges. Burdock and mustard weed grew in the barnyard. Boys had broken the windows of the house and carried off the front door. Obscene pictures had been scratched on the parlour walls. On stormy nights the wind cried through the house and frightened children hurrying homeward along the road. But asters grew in the beds below the front windows—bleeding red and dusty purple asters dancing in the sun.

2

Gerda O'Rourke closed the gate of the farm and stood a moment, looking down the dusty road toward the town. The five grain elevators, two miles away, appeared to lean against each other, and cast a solid block of shadow across the buildings of Main Street.

Along the edge of the road, goldenrod grew amid the high, dry grass, and in the dust of the cart ruts little tufts of wild cotton hovered, fluttering in the faint breeze. The wild rose along the fences no longer bloomed, and the leaves were tipped with red and brown and gold. In the fields, the stubble was bleached, yellow, the earth dry and powdered.

Far across the fields she saw that the Martins had started ploughing already. Down the centre of their north quarter the plough had cut a wide straight band of dark rich earth that seemed to sever the field in two.

"It's all very well, that, if you have menfolk at home," she thought, as she walked along. "We would have our plough-ing well started now, too, if Bob were home."

"It's strange to be buying a Christmas present in September," she mused. "It takes so long for parcels to get there."

A toad jumped across the road and came to rest in a

cart rut. It looked like a dusty stone lying there. Gerda stopped to watch it. Then she broke a stem of goldenrod and flicked the dust with it beside the toad. It jumped twice and cleared the road, disappearing into the grass.

In town she went first to the news stand. Bob was very fond of detective thrillers, and she bought three of the magazines with the most lurid covers.

"I suppose I should read them," she thought. "He would like me to." She paid for them and put them under her arm. On the newspaper rack the new editions of the city papers were spread. She glanced at the headlines. Strange, the different ways the papers said the same thing.

"Germans Drive on Black Sea."

"Zero Hour Nears for Hitler Drive into Black Sea."

"Four Russian Armies Trapped."

The newsman, busy counting papers on the counter, looked at her out of the corner of his eye. When he had finished counting the pile of papers he said, with finality:

"The news is not good."

Gerda looked at him. "No," she agreed. "I don't understand it. We never seem to make any headway."

The newsagent tapped his fingers on the glass counter and his watery red eyes flamed with sudden hot anger.

"I tell you, Mrs O'Rourke," he shouted, "there's too much of politics in this war. You don't know what's going on."

"We will win in the end," she said, brightly.

The newsagent nodded his bald pate.

"That we will. But it will be a long time." With that he turned his back and began to straighten his tins of tobacco.

For a moment a dark cloud swept across Gerda's mind . . . a long war. . . . But Bob had said it might be a year or a little more. Surely it could not go on for years . . . not to see him for years and years. . . .

A cold dread filled her, momentarily. Then she shook her head and left the shop. Bob had said it would not be long, and she believed that. She would go on believing it. Impossible to think anything else! This town, the fields, the sunshine on the distant land all belonged to him. He had to come back to it before anything changed, before it had grown dim in his memory.

Nevertheless the war news was disturbing. He had been gone almost a year, and yet victory seemed as far off as before. Surely the Allies would invade Europe soon. Then there would be a decisive battle and it would all be over, and all the men could come home.

By the time she arrived at the drug store, all the life had left her; she felt unaccountably listless and disinterested. With a pang of remorse she remembered with what enthusiasm she had dressed and started for town to shop for Bob's Christmas present. Now, somehow, the weight of sorrowful and empty time pressed heavily upon her.

Gerda had decided upon a leather toilet set for Bob. They had seen one in a window once, and she knew he had wanted it. The druggist had only three in stock. He brought them out and laid them on the counter, making room for them by moving several jars of face cream and a case of razor blades.

She immediately rejected one of the sets. It was of cheap leatherette covering and lined with green linen. One of the other sets was of a dark brown grained leather, the third was a light tan. She put the two sets together, wondering which one Bob would like best. She tried to imagine him standing beside her, tall and lithe and impatient as he always was when she shopped, and she thought he would pick the light tan. It was of fine leather lined with oiled silk and contained two brushes, a toothbrush holder, soap container, a razor holder, steel mirror, scissors and nail file, shaving brush and shaving stick.

He would like it, surely. She could not imagine him using the scissors or the nail file, for he always bit his nails short. Nevertheless, all the other things were useful.

The druggist packed the set in a strong cardboard box, wrapped it carefully and tied it with bright green string. On the way out of the shop she passed the rack of Christmas cards and stopped to look. She chose a humorous one to put into the parcel.

There was no-one on the street when she came out. Strange, she thought, how quiet the town is now. Before the war it was filled with noise and hustle and a lot of people drove through on their way north. Now it is like a deserted place.

She turned her steps toward the river, hardly realizing that she did so. She left the street and took a mud path across a field. At the end of the field the path led into deep woods that covered the river bank. The woods were wrapped in silence. Dead leaves lay thick upon the path, and as her feet turned them over they gave off a damp, pungent odour. Long slanting rays of sunlight came through the trees and laid bars of riotous colour upon the tangled undergrowth. A faint sudden breeze stirred the poplars, and brought down a tremulous shower of gold.

She sank down on a log and gave herself up to the haunting poignant memories which the place evoked. In these woods, she and Bob had walked just a year ago. The sweet and lovely memory of that time came back to her as though it had been but the day before. Breathless, she listened, and was carried away on the memory of that moment that had been.

Strangely, magically, she felt the touch of his hand, smooth and strong, in hers. She sank into the drift of gathered leaves and lay outstretched, pressing her body into the soft rustling bed. Her breasts ached, and a deep gnawing hunger crept into her. She closed her eyes and the flood-gate of loneliness and yearning opened. The parcel lay beside her, half-buried in the leaves, the green string startlingly bright.

How long she lay there, dulled by hungry yearning, lost in memories of ecstatic joy and soaring happiness, she did not know. The sun had set and left floes of rose and washed yellow upon the sky. Through the woods a chill breeze whispered the approach of night. She rose and brushed the clinging leaves from her coat and turned homeward.

The street lamps were lit: dusk descended upon the huddled town. She met no-one she knew on the street. On the corner in front of the drug store a group of soldiers from the army camp north of the river lounged sprawling against the shop front. They whistled as she passed and she quickened her step.

When she reached her gate it was quite dark and a fine sliver of moon lay low over the brooding land.

Her father-in-law was in the barnyard. His lantern laid a circle of warm yellow light upon the ground at his feet.

"That you, Gerda girl?" he called to her as she climbed the steps to the kitchen door.

"Yes, dad," she replied.

"Amy has gone to her church meeting," he said. "You'll find your supper warm in the oven."

She went in through the kitchen, warm and smelling of fresh milk, and climbed the stairs to her room. She laid her parcel on a chair and struck a match and held it to the wick of the table lamp. Sudden light sprang up in the room, and with a sense of tender and intimate recognition she swept her eyes about the familiar, beloved objects.

In this room she always felt close to Bob. Something of his spirit dwelt there—something of his warmth and intense vitality, and of his immediate presence. It was as if he had just left the room. And always at night, with the blinds drawn and the door closed, she felt his nearness and was happy.

She took off her coat and hung it in the cupboard. Then she set his Christmas present on the table under the lamp and stood for some time gazing at it, trying to project herself upon the unknown and unfathomable journey the parcel would take. There was so little of that far "Overseas" life of his that she knew, so little for her mind to grasp with any sense of reality. A few picture images that he had tried to describe in letters, that was all she had.

"Some day he will come back to me," she said aloud. "Some day, in this room, he will tell me all his life there and then I shall share it."

The thought released a flood of tenderness and love so passionate and intense that she felt she could reach out across the vast distance and embrace him. Every fibre of her being yearned for him; and her body throbbed and ached with a hollow hunger.

With a sudden small cry she buried her face in her hands and wept great silent tears.

# 11

In the last week in November the company abandoned its summer location and moved to within a mile of the Channel coast, where it took up a position in a fourteen-room manor house, with an enormous stable yard and several outbuildings. All this accommodation was not enough to house the entire company, and two of the platoons were put under canvas until Nissen huts could be erected.

It was a bleak existence for those under canvas. At night the cold Channel winds swept over the fields and shook the tents. The men shivered all night and in the morning found their clothes cold and heavy with moisture, and cursed their comrades who slept indoors in the warmth. They had to march to the manor house to wash, to eat and to go to the latrines. The sun rarely shone; the days were a dreary expanse of fog or rain or wind under a leaden sky. The area around the tents was trodden into ankle-deep mud.

The men were set to the task of hauling gravel from a nearby pit to fill up the mud holes. Lorry loads were dumped and spread between the tents, and the gravel settled and disappeared and the mud was as slimy as before. Only after weeks of work did they succeed in making pathways that could be used. They dug slit trenches for protection against aircraft, and as fast as they dug them, they filled with water. Finally they had to abandon the trenches, and dug new ones on higher ground several hundred yards from the camp site—too far away to reach safety when an aircraft warning came.

The vehicles were parked on the hard-surfaced lane that led to the manor house, under a line of consumptive elms. At night the guards patrolled the vehicle lines in the rain and driving wind, and when they met on patrol they squatted beneath a vehicle and smoked and cursed the army, England, and the fate which had caused them to be born into such a world. Their one moment of pleasure came when they were relieved, and, trudging heavily through the mud, they entered the sudden light and heady warmth of the kitchen and had their tea and biscuits. Then they were loath to go to bed, and lingered by the stoves, swapping yarns while they dried themselves, until the orderly sergeant came through and sent them packing.

The men grumbled among themselves and fell silent when their officers passed. They found ample food for discontent—the quarters, the mud, the cold rains, the endless training, the air raids night and day, the food and, above all, the lack of mail. The mail from home, at this time, was particularly bad: for more than seven weeks no letters or parcels came from Canada. Men worried about their families, imagining all manner of evils at home. Whenever they met in groups they began to grumble and curse.

With the turn of December the rains abated and the weather grew colder. In the mornings the land would be covered with a delicate, shimmering frost that disappeared magically as the sun rose. By four o'clock in the afternoon it was again cold, and the countryside seemed to draw back into the mists. By supper time it was dark and the world became confined, hostile and blind.

Air raids were daily occurrences. The Luftwaffe came over across the Channel and were met by the fighters. In the pale heavens vapour trails traced the dogfights, and sudden black plumes of smoke descending to the earth marked the aerial casualties. The ferocity of these dogfights was extraordinary. In a short time the men came to distinguish the Allied fighters from the various machines of the Luftwaffe, and would stop their work to watch and cheer.

One morning a group of men from "C" platoon were cleaning up the vehicle lines when the alert sounded. The sirens had scarcely stopped when they heard the high faint gathering roar of the Huns coming in over the Channel. They stopped their work and stood searching the sky. Three waves of bombers traced faint dark pinpoints across the sky over the Channel, ominous specks that became winged roaring monsters. As they came in over the coastline, flying at a great height, the anti-aircraft batteries opened up. Sudden puffs of smoke appeared around the planes as the shells burst. The thunder and bark of the guns was terrifying, growing in frenzied, frantic crescendo as the gun crews fed the guns at maximum speed. Still the planes flew in, through the barrage, keeping their formations tight. For an instant the first flight seemed to waver in the face of a terrific wall of shrapnel. The puff of a bursting shell appeared suddenly around the tail of one of the leading bombers. Seconds after it had burst the bomber fell back, as though a giant unseen hand had laid hold of it, then it burst apart in a black cloud and the pieces spiralled earthward, one fragment burning a long-tailed plume across the sky as it fell.

From inland came the Spitfires, climbing to do battle. They passed over the camp, over the group of men standing in the roadway, and their passing was so swift, so deafening, like birds of unbelievable flight, that the men ducked instinctively. In a split second they were overhead and gone, climbing with incredible speed, with a sense of rocketed destruction. Behind them they left a sharp scream of air that died away to a hollow moan. The ack-ack guns fell silent. Guns blazing, the Spitfires closed with the bombers. The aerial circus was on! Over and through and around the raiders the Spitfires flew, banking, diving, rolling. Faintly, far away, the watching men heard the split-second bursts of gunfire, saw first one bomber go down, then another, then a Spitfire spiralling dizzily toward oblivion, then a bomber frozen momentarily in a sheet of yellow flame.

From the north-east rose another squadron of Spitfires. They kept out of range of the bombers' guns, gaining altitude and rising so high that they were lost to sight of the watching men. Then, suddenly, they appeared, diving down out of the sun, each fixed upon a single bomber, hurtling out of the sightless immensity like rockets, their guns blazing as they closed. Three of them were stopped short in their flight, hovered an instant, then fell, burning, leaving a three-plumed design of incredible beauty in the sky. Their comrades dived on the bombers, then banked swiftly, sharply, and climbed back into the sun.

The bomber formation broke. Four of them came down in flames; three crashed in the remote distance, one disappeared over the Channel. The remainder banked and peeled off and turned back for the coastline, jettisoning their bombs on the first objects they could hurriedly aim for. The Spitfires followed them, diving on them like swallows after a raven.

Two of the bombers flew close together northward along the line of the coast before turning out to sea. They passed almost directly over the men watching in the roadway. One after the other they jettisoned their bomb loads. For a moment the bombs seemed to ride along beneath the planes, then they dropped leisurely in two close clusters, one beneath the other. For several seconds the men watched, fascinated, realizing no danger.

Suddenly one of the men screamed:

"Mother of Christ! They're for us!"

There was a rush for cover. One soldier slipped in the mud of the roadside and fell headlong into the ditch; another fell on him; both lay there huddling together. The others ducked behind the trunks of trees, behind the banked-up ditch mud, or fell flat in the mud.

The bombs studded a road crossing half a mile away and along the roadside for several hundred yards south of the crossing. Even at that distance the explosions were deafening.

One by one the men raised their heads, then rose and gathered in the road again.

"Well! Well! The show's over boys," a chap named Stockwell remarked, breezily.

"Some show," added another.

"Bastards," shouted the fellow who had fallen into the ditch and was covered with wet clay from head to foot.

Everyone laughed at him. He cleared the mud from his eyes, then blew his nose fiercely between his fingers.

"Laugh, you hyenas," he cried, dancing with rage, while the mud fell from him. "Laugh! Go on! Laugh your empty heads off." Then, viciously, he picked on a thin runt of a boy and thrust a knotty finger into his face. The boy backed away and gulped, swallowing his adam's apple like a rubber ball descending an ostrich's throat.

"You think I'm funny, do you?" the muddy one demanded of the runt. "Now you listen to me, you pup. I'll bet your drawers need changing right now. . . . That's how brave you were. . . . I'll just bet that's so. Let's have a look at him, boys."

Wide-eyed with terror, the lad sprang from the encircling group, dodged behind a lorry, dived through a hedge and ran like a frightened deer across the field toward his quarters.

The men stood in the roadway laughing. The soldier who had fallen into the ditch strutted around cockily, flicking the mud from himself.

At that moment the duty sergeant appeared in the roadway. He stopped and looked at the men and his hair bristled. Ordinarily, a sergeant stirred no terror but only a healthy respect in the men. Sergeant McRury was not like that. He looked: his head and shoulders hunched as though ready to do battle; then with a bellow that knocked every sparrow off the fence for half a mile he sent the men scattering like chaff in a tornado. After they had disappeared he stood in the roadway, chuckling to himself.

"Now, if I just stroll around the back of the barn I'll bet I'll find them all there telling each other what a dirty dog I am."

Taking a reef in his trousers he set off slowly down the vehicle line, cut across the field and sauntered around the corner of the barn.

"Sure enough," he said to himself and stepped out into clear view of the men who were standing in a tight group beside the manure pile, heatedly expressing their similar opinions about sergeants in general and "the bull" in particular.

One man caught sight of him and nudged the others. One by one they slunk away to their work.

Smiling ruefully, Sergeant McRury strode off to the cook-house to bull-doze the cook into making him a cup of tea.

2

December promised snow. One could almost catch its tantalizing freshness in the air. Out over the grey restless Channel seas snow fell frequently, or what appeared to the men to be snow. Beyond the dark, grey cloud that hovered over the water every day, lay the coast of France, only a few miles away. It was close enough for the shore batteries at Dover to whistle mighty shells across, and, when they fired, their rumble was quite distinct, and the whole coastline trembled. Across that narrow stretch of grey turbulent winter sea stood the enemy. So near, and yet so far. Not miles of Channel sea separated them from the enemy, but months of preparation, training and dreary waiting. Each day the men cast their eyes upon the far water and each said to himself, "Some day." As the winter advanced, that word, in itself a promise, came to replace hope and the eagerness for battle.

Civilian engineers erected Nissen huts just before Christmas on concrete floors poured on the meadow in front of the manor house. Water was piped and washing stands built between the huts. Beside a group of saplings the latrines were erected, of corrugated-iron sheeting found in a salvage yard. The men moved from the tents to the huts, the tents disappeared, and only round trodden patches of dead grass showed where they had stood. For two days the men washed and shaved in cold water. They groused and kicked about this, utterly forgetting their recent discomfort in the cold, damp tents.

At the washing trough in the morning they were snarling among themselves about it.

"A week of this and my face will feel as smooth as a pig's rump," one man remarked.

The soldier standing behind him sharing his bit of cracked mirror swore : "Damn it man, stand still, or I'll slit my throat."

"Good! That will be one less to hear from."

"All the same, fellows, it's time we did something about this."

"Try the Ritz. You'll get your boots shined there, too."

"Where's Finkle?" someone called from the end of the line.

"Where's Finkle?" same the chorus.

Private Finkle at that moment emerged from his hut carrying his shaving kit and towel in one hand, and an assortment of stuff in the other. Obviously he heard the clamour of his name being called, but he pretended not to hear. Casually he laid his shaving kit on the washing bench, took a tin basin and rinsed it under the tap, then half-filled it with water. Then he produced a tin of canned heat, which he had mysteriously stolen from some Compo pack rations. Lighting the can, he set the basin on top and stood with his hands in his pockets waiting for the water to heat. Out of the corner of his eye he saw the line-up of men staring enviously and admiring at the fine flame licking the bottom of his wash basin. Nonchalantly he whistled a tune and rocked on his heels.

At last he asked, in a bored tone : "You chumps were asking for me?"

"Sure, Finkle. We were talking about you."

Finkle cast a bloodshot eye toward the top of the nearest tree and stroked his beard gently, then scratched his neck.

"Yes?" he said.

"We were wondering if you could do something about getting us hot water out here. This is pretty grim."

"How would I be able to fix hot water?" Wide-eyed innocence and modesty attended the question.

"Ah, Finkle. We know you can fix anything."

"Not me."

Delicately he dipped a finger into his basin, and then flicked the water from his finger into the eye of a fitter who was shaving opposite him.

"Why, you . . .!" the fitter roared, and was cut short with a kick in the shins from a lance corporal.

"Now, listen, Finkle. You can fix up hot water easily. We all know that. How about it?"

Finkle lifted his basin off the can and snuffed the flame.

Then he rolled up the sleeves of his underwear. Black rings of dirt showed around his wrists.

"Inasmuch as my talents are practically inexhaustible, I suppose I could," he remarked. "For a price."

"What is it?"

"Well, there's my time. And my ability, to say nothing of the work in it."

"How much?"

"Ten bob."

"It's a deal."

"In advance."

"All right, Finkle. A shilling apiece, boys. We'll balance it out later. Pass it up. Shylock wants his flesh."

Finkle pocketed the money without comment.

"When do we get the hot water?"

"Why, to-night, I suppose," was the casual answer.

Finkle was the mechanical genius of the company, and he knew it. There was nothing he could not repair or make. He drove a lorry and stoutly declined all the attractive offers made him by the workshop officer.

"If I go to work in the workshops I'll have to do everything for love. This way I make more," was his answer to all entreaties.

And he was right. He charged for everything, from fixing a watch to making a pair of sock stretchers for the major. His platoon officer maintained that Finkle and the company barber made more than the major.

Finkle belonged to O'Rourke's section, although this was only temporarily. Actually he was moved continually throughout the company, being bribed from one section to another. After breakfast he took O'Rourke into his confidence and, with some cajolling, he got permission to take a 15-cwt. lorry away for the morning.

At noon he returned with a load of assorted junk scrounged from salvage dumps—an empty, rusty 40-gallon petrol drum, some rusty lengths of pipe, taps, valves, an old oil pan from a car engine, some scraps of metal, and an armful of bricks. When lunch was finished he set to work. For an hour the site of the hot-water installation looked like a miniature junk yard, but eventually the pieces of scrap took shape. When the men came in before supper from the vehicle lines they gathered around the boiler to admire. They turned the taps and felt the hot water, and one by one they shook their heads.

Finkle had done it again!

It was all quite simple. Digging a foot into the earth he

had laid the old oil pan; over this, resting on the bricks, he laid the rusty petrol drum on its side, and sealed the bricks with wet clay. From the water tap in the barnyard he piped the water into the bung at one end of the petrol drum. Then he disconnected the cold water supply leading to the row of taps at the washing troughs and ran a pipe from the bung on the top side of the drum to the row of taps. Into the old oil pan beneath the drum he poured a mixture of used motor oil and petrol, and lit it. The intense fire heated the cold water that flowed into the drum from the bottom and hot water flowed out the top pipe to the taps on the washing trough. Lastly, he rigged up a gravity feed reservoir of old oil to keep the fire going.

"You see," he commented with just pride, when he was finished, "you take some old junk, and you add your brains, and you have hot water! Simple!"

3

The village was not far from the company camp. It stood on the northern slope of a gradual hill and looked down over a broad, sweeping valley, patchworked with tiny hedged farms. On the south side of the hill was a deep forest. Through this forest wandered a lane that led to the unit's lines. On the brow of the hill, facing each other across a road, stood two tiny churches.

It was Christmas Eve. There was a dance in the church hall. The girls of the village were already there, waiting for the soldiers to arrive. Old women bustled about the hall with refreshments they had brought. From the centre of the ceiling a great Christmas bell hung suspended by paper ribbons. The three piece orchestra tuned their instruments. The flat, broken music of their tuning carried out on the still night air and mingled with the thin, delicate sound of the bell from the Catholic church.

As the soldiers came along the path through the forest they heard the church bell, muffled and delicate in the distance, like music from an old-fashioned music-box. Overhead, through the naked, silent trees, some stars twinkled in the north. The air was crisp and exhilarating, and the men walked briskly in little groups, talking and laughing.

And then, suddenly, in a shimmer of magic silver out of the night, snow began to fall. A faint whisper crept through the forest and a soft confining weight seemed to press down upon the earth. The men stopped still and, unbelieving, looked up into the fine swirling mantle. Across the mind of every man swept the ecstatic memory of the snowlands of his beloved Canada. With a wild quickening blood-beat they shouted for joy.

"Yi-pee! Yi-pee!"

"Snow! Snow! Look! Feel it!"

They danced in the roadway; they turned their faces to the sky to catch the soft melting crystals on their faces; they even stuck out their tongues and tasted it. Mad, like drunken men, they continued on their way, reeling, singing, shouting, and their uproar rolled through the night. Villagers standing at the crossroads heard them and watched them approach, and, frightened, drew back from them.

"Canadians!" a woman snorted, and turned her child away from them. But the child, wild-eyed with curiosity, peeked around at the men.

In the dance hall the girls and old women heard their shouting and singing as they approached.

"The Canadians are coming!" someone shrieked.

"They're drunk. Hear them!"

Titters and faint shrieks mingled in the suddenly tense air of the hall. Everyone stood with caught breath waiting for the "drunken Canadians" to appear.

The men burst into the hall in a wild clamour. They stormed the timid orchestra. One soldier dragged the pianist from his instrument, stool and all, and standing over the keyboard, thumped out the opening bars of a wild reel. Another took the violin from the bald man's hand with a "Thank you, daddy," and began to fiddle the reel. The soldiers on the floor found breathless but willing girls, and in a moment the hall rocked to the wild, happy surge of the old-time reel.

The night was half gone before the people realized that the Canadians were not drunk at all, but simply full of wild soaring spirit. Impossible for the English, with their utter lack of emotionalism, to understand the wildness of the soldiers. Had anyone explained to them that there were on earth people to whom the miracle of falling snow brought a wild, unutterable happiness, they would have shaken their heads in complete mystification.

Time and again throughout the night when the men went out into the darkness and stood in the falling snow, breathing the fresh crispness, feeling the blood quicken in their veins, and, drunk with a nameless ecstasy, thought of their homeland. A thousand voices seemed to whisper out of the snow, hushed, tense, beckoning voices: "Canada! Canada! Canada!" The snow swirled in the darkness, and the voices died away: the snow stilled and hovered like a cloud and the voices caressed the air.

And out of those moments when each man stood alone in the snow, out of the mantle of blessed night, came the thrum and beat of the life murmur of that mighty, magic country that was to each man "Home." It came like a faint echo out of time, as of something once heard and long forgotten. Across the mind it stabbed its instant recognition. Primitive, wild and savage as as a symphony of wind in wilderness, the faint echo soared into deep and powerful music. It sang the heavy homesickness of each man. It lulled through his haunted time-dark forests, it moaned and sighed and whispered through the night streets of his village; lonely, wild and savage it swept across his snow-covered plains: it caught the murmur of his great and eternal rivers that flowed a thousand miles: upon the wild northern cataract it roared and swirled and died in liquid rainbow notes; in rhythmic tidal beat it laved the ocean shores of the far earth span; in hot secret, sensuous beats it expressed the thousand inland summer pools, wove rich and powerfully through the half-wild aroma of hayfields and dry prairie lands, through the rippling ecstatic fragrance of new spring growth, in the forests, in the plains and through the deep hidden valleys of the far western mountains. Wild and powerful, soft and sensuous, soaring and savage, it sang the song of loneliness, of homesickness, the song of man's love for his wilderness, his wilderness of hope, of beauty, savagery and hunger, of riches and toil and miracle.

In the hall the music throbbed; the men paired with the girls, each to his taste, and they let restraint go with the night. Couples disappeared into the darkness and returned and danced. The food was served, plain food made fancy by the old women. And the dance continued. At midnight everyone gathered in a great circle and sang "Auld Lang Syne." When "God Save the King" had been played, the dance broke up. The young people left the old to clear up, and hurried away. Along the roads and lanes that night, by fence gates and hedges, many a couple whispered love and made vows that were forgotten at dawn.

O'Rourke had danced with a pretty freckled-faced girl all night. In her eyes he could read his favour, in her body that moved so lightly with his own, he sensed a warm desire, a willingness. As he danced with her he knew he had but to take her in his arms and she would be his. Once, in the dark entrance by the door where they had gone to smoke cigarettes, he took her in his arms and pressed his lips to hers. With one hand he caressed her, touching her breast beneath her blouse, and ran his hand down over her firm thighs and felt her quiver. Yet no desire rose in him. He felt nothing for her, neither need nor lust nor tenderness. Behind her, over her shoulder as he caressed her, he saw the face of his wife, vague and ethereal in the darkness. It was as though Gerda were watching him, with a faint mocking smile. He did not take his hand from the girl, yet he knew she sensed a sudden change in him and he felt her stiffen and move back from him. With a slight shrug of hopelessness she turned from him and went back into the hall. Though they danced together the rest of the night they did so without any warmth or friendliness, and when the last note of "God Save the King" had died among the shuffle of feet, he bade her good night stiffly and left, his cheeks and neck burning with a sense of unaccountable shame.

Snow still fell as he walked back over the hill to camp. Behind him he heard the clamour of voices outside the hall, the shrill laughter of the girls. Near the top of the hill where the forest began, he stopped and looked back toward the tiny clustered village. A mantle of snow lay upon the rooftops and the church spire and topped the dark stone wall of the graveyard. Where people had walked at the crossroads there was a strange maze of trails across the virgin whiteness.

Through the dark naked trees he saw, faint and high, ten thousand stars twinkling through the falling snow, and suddenly he felt cold tears in his eyes. He recalled the winter night of his marriage, the sleigh ride with Gerda from the village to his father's house. He remembered the warmth of her under the fur robe, the pressure of her knee against his, and the crisp animal smell of the fur, the smell of the trotting hoar-frosted horses, and the jingle of the two tiny bells on their harness.

He remembered the day they had parted, the first day of winter, and the falling snow that had obliterated the sight of the crowded station platform at Yellow Prairie as the train roared out across the land. He saw it now, vague and nebulous, like a scene out of early childhood, and though he knew the village and every building in it, he could no longer construct its picture in his mind.

There was something terrifying for him in this. He stopped still and stared at the ground as though to fix and steady himself upon the whirling planet. Was all the past to dim and be forgotten like this? Was it all to be like a dream out of which, waking, he would find himself a stranger in an unknown place? Would he, in time, forget what his wife looked like, the sound of her voice, the touch of her hand? Was nothing real and enduring on earth?

He closed his eyes and pressed his palm against his forehead. With deliberate and intense will, he recalled the image of his wife's face; across his mind's film it appeared dim and soft, and even while he clung to it with all the intensity of his mind it vanished abruptly, and in its place he saw some chance scene from childhood that came like a mockery.

Slowly he walked between the naked trees through the falling snow toward the camp. His body ached with a numb, mysterious hunger and his mind lay crushed and dazed by an intense and bitter loneliness such as he had never known.

As he emerged from the snowy woods, Bubbles, the fox-terrier mascot of the company, crept out of the darkness and silently sniffed at his heels. The camp was deserted; no voices sounded from the quarters.

He took off his wedge cap and hung it on a nail over his bed. For some time he sat on his mattress looking at the floor. When he looked up at last he was gazing into the dark, expressionless, unfathomable eyes of McKinley, the negro, who was sitting on his bed half naked with his legs crossed.

They looked at one another for several minutes in silence. Finally McKinley asked: "You have a good time to-night, corporal?" His voice was very respectful, but it carried a faint suggestion of mockery.

"No, not very," O'Rourke answered. "Did you?"

"Me? I nevah went out. Not me, mistah?"

"Why not? There was a dance."

The negro leaned forward a little toward O'Rourke, and his voice sounded as though he were talking to himself in a whisper.

"I'se a black man. White girls don't want a black man—leastways, not often."

"Do you ever get lonely, Mac?"

"Lonely? Gawd! I'se black—I'se ALWAYS lonely. There ain't nothin' else in me."

"But the boys all like you. Don't you feel that?"

The negro sighed, and leaned back on his arms. The ceiling light shone across his chest.

"I like the boys. They's a good bunch. If I was in the American Army they'd put me with niggers. They'd never stand fo' me with whites. No, siree! But, brudder, yo' don't know what loneliness is. Not ever."

"Where's your family, Mac?"

"I ain't got no family. I'se just me."

He looked at his toes thoughtfully for a while, then he remarked, with a broad, sudden grin, "We's got pork for dinner to-morrow. I heard the cook say so. I like pork."

"As good as turkey?"

The grin vanished. "Maybe no. . . . I dunno. But there's folks on earth ain't even got pork for this Christmas—ain't even got NOTHIN'."

After another pause he went on, "I'se lonely—sure. Cause I'se black, and black men ain't ever been happy. But I'se lucky, just the same, mistah. I'se from a country that don't mind me being a nigger, an' workin' and livin' like I want to, and fightin' for things same as white folks. Seems to me it's the only country that let's a nigger be. Some places, they call it democracy, but it ain't the same. In Canada they don't call it nothin'."

He stretched and lay down, with his face turned to the ceiling, his black eyes staring sightless into the electric light bulb.

O'Rourke unlaced his boots slowly, put them together at the foot of his bed. As he undressed he fell to thinking of the first Christmas he and Gerda had together. He crawled between his blankets in his underwear, and turned toward the wall and gave himself up to the orgy of happy remembrances. He did not know when he fell asleep, but he seemed to drift all night through a dream of living beauty. When he awakened in the morning to the white earth he could not remember the dream, but he felt happy and excited.

Bubbles, the fox-terrier, came and sat by his heels and looked across the white fields with him. Together they set off for a walk, making fresh tracks across the soft virgin snow.

# 12

I

A LIGHT spring wind billowed across the land. Everything seemed to waken and stir again.

It brought to the camp at Broom Hill Farm a new promise, a re-birth of hopes. Every man, from the cook's helper to the sergeant-major, was of the belief that an Allied invasion of the Continent was imminent, and with that belief, the men indulged in the luxury of day-dreams, utterly fantastic and beyond the realm of reason.

It was said that Germany would collapse the moment the Allies landed on the European continent. It was said that the German people were ready to overthrow the Hitler régime at any moment, and were but waiting the signal from the Allies. Many said Germany had no oil left, no steel, no aircraft, no rubber, no food. The more conservative were ready to agree that Germany, indeed, must be in a very bad way—that she would not long continue the war. All that remained before victory was the actual invasion of the Continent. Upon that signal the crushed, beaten peoples of occupied Europe would spring to the fight for their liberation, and a great series of bloody pogroms would purge Europe of the Nazi war dogs.

How all these events were to take place, none could tell. A dream, a hope, needs no justification in the heart of man; it is its own justification.

While it was true that Russia held the German military might pinned to the earth, there was at that time no indication of the turn events were to take in the following months along the Eastern front. In the Mediterranean the Axis forces grasped victory after victory from the Allies: Cairo and the Suez stood in peril. In the Pacific the Japanese were everywhere in the ascendancy; Australia prepared to resist invasion that seemed not only imminent but completely certain. Within the European continent the peoples of the occupied countries could hold no hope of immediate liberation; the Nazi grip tightened;

mass murder, butchery and torture, quenched any outward flutter of hope. In Britain itself, the citadel of strength in the west, there waited the balance of the British armies, re-grouped and re-equipped after Dunkirk. American forces, although growing constantly more numerous, were as yet but the vanguard of immense forces that were to cross the Atlantic in the late months of 1942 and throughout the following year. Canadian forces had grown from the original expeditionary force of one division in 1939, to four divisions and ancillary troops. More were still to cross the Atlantic. Such, then, was the view of the global war in the spring of 1942. There was, in reality, little basis for hope of an Allied invasion of Europe that spring. Yet hope lived and grew more fervent as the weeks passed. The men responded to training with unusual fervour—training which they had already undergone a dozen times before. They itched for a fight and were happy to prepare.

2

The one noteworthy event (and one that was fraught with excitement and nervous tension) that occurred in O'Rourke's unit that spring, was the litter of nondescript mongrel pups which "Bubbles," the fox-terrier mascot of the company delivered in the last week of February.

Technically, Bubbles belonged to the company as a whole, though her popularity rose and waned from time to time. She was claimed successively as the property of each platoon. When the platoons were busy hauling ammunition and petrol, or on special tasks, the men ignored her and she was left with the company headquarters. When they were idle and hanging about the camp they all claimed her, petted her and she would wander from the lines of one platoon to another, spending a night in each, curled up in the blankets of some snoring soldier's bed nearest the fire.

Immediately before the arrival of the pups she was treated with special care and tenderness. The canned milk in the army rations was not, generally, regarded as suitable for her, and fresh cow's milk was bought from a farmer. A soldier who professed to have been a dog breeder in civilian life maintained that it was wrong to feed her Naafi cake, which she was inordinately fond of. It soon became almost a crime to be caught feeding Bubbles anything that had not been generally agreed upon as suitable for her condition. The men never refrained from taking her with them when they went to the tiny pub near the crossroads, for she loved beer in a saucer and would sit by the door and howl when it was not forthcoming.

Despite all this tender care, Bubbles produced five pups of such indefinable antecedents and variety that, clustered groping around her on a blanket in the corner of the quartermaster's stores, they looked less like dogs than five distinct species of rare animals. In each one, however, there did exist a trace of Bubbles herself. The tail of one was fox-terrier, albeit it had not yet been bobbed. The snout of another was terrier; the feet of another were dainty and short haired. Each had some trace of its mother, however vague and suggestive. But Bubbles was infinitely happy over the groping, staggering, blind litter and seemed proud of the attention they drew from the men.

It was, indeed, an event. Before their birth wagers were made on how many pups might arrive. But since such bets were limited to the maximum procreative capacities of dogs, a sweepstake of much wider scope was started. Guesses as to the time of delivery of the first pup were bought at sixpence a ticket. This had infinite possibilities, but those who knew when Bubbles had been bred and had any knowledge of dog life, had a better chance in betting on the time of arrival than those whose ignorance of the subject eventually cost them sixpence without the consolation of being even near winners. A machinist in the workshop finally won, his guess being just ten minutes early of the arrival of the first pup.

When the pups had been weaned, there took place what might be termed a re-allocation of the dog establishment within the company. The first born, who showed unmistakable signs of a tendency toward a water spaniel, was given to the workshop. He was named "Crank"—shortened from crankshaft. The second born, a dainty bitch of Cairn blood, was called "Oh! Oh!" and went to headquarters. She did not live long, however, for she ran beneath the wheel of a lorry one dark night. The third born, named "Bull," after the sergeant-major, was given to one of the platoons. "Whistler," who promised to be an Irish terrier, went to the ammunition platoon. "Bishop," who had a very solemn face and two black-ringed eyes, and who had a retriever's body and a spaniel's legs with a terrier's nose, showed a distinct preference to be left with his mother, and so he remained unclaimed, wandering through the company's lines at will.

# 13

MAJOR BREST, the commanding officer, decided to hold a parade.

He had spent a wild and dissipating week-end at Torquay with an infantry company commander—a graduate of the Royal Military College—whom he had not seen for two years. Over several bottles of Scotch whisky the two men had rekindled an old friendship which war had cut adrift.

Major Brest found several changes in his friend—changes which, he had to admit, were, if somewhat eccentric, certainly becoming to the man as a soldier. In place of the rather mild and retiring fellow he had known, he beheld a dapper strutting infantry officer who exuded efficiency and "command." He carried a cane which he swung with an air of great assurance and determination, in the manner of English officers, and wore a short, cropped, bristling moustache which gave his rather florid face a look of ferocity. This was all the more accentuated by bushy eyebrows, which he now brushed vigorously upward. He spoke slowly, with frequent pauses and throaty rumblings, in order to hide his weak voice, and while speaking he raised his right eyebrow affectedly.

The conversation, while it included dubious women, liquor and greyhounds, constantly reverted to army affairs, and both unburdened themselves of their military problems, their political doubts, and their intrigues. There was one point upon which they were in complete agreement; they believed that the morale of the army was sinking at an alarming rate. Major Brest was of the opinion that action alone could give the men new life and new hope. His friend insisted that the root of the evil could be attributed to poor discipline and too much fraternity between officers and men. Stricter discipline was the answer! And this could only be accomplished by a return to parade square methods of exacting obedience and respect. There was no more ideal place than the parade square for re-establishing the proper gulf between those who commanded and those who were meant to obey. The solution, he proclaimed, was not action, but more training, more parades, more discipline.

Major Brest was deeply impressed. His conscience pricked

him when he thought of the few parades he had held. Secretly he hated them, and he was honest enough with himself to feel that he could not demand from others something which he himself disliked so intensely. Yet it was, obviously, a duty. Or so it seemed to him at Torquay. He returned to his unit with a determination to hold a parade and inspection immediately, and to carry one out every week. The knowledge that it was a duty, and that in carrying it out he was beating down his own weakness, glowed within him.

Immediately on his return he called the sergeant-major and ordered him to prepare a parade of the entire company. The sergeant-major twitched his moustache as the only outward sign of his surprise. He could not recall a time when he had seen "the old man" in so decisive a mood. Swiftly he examined the events of the past few weeks for some clue that would explain this strange and sudden turn. He found nothing that might have disturbed the quiet, easy-going course of events, and he came to the conclusion that the major had received a "shake" from Formation H.Q.

Having dismissed the sergeant-major to work out the necessary details for the parade, the major slumped into his chair and began biting his nails absently. The room suddenly palled on him. He saw himself confined and prisoned by the everlasting red tape of army affairs, the endless papers, the dull routine of administration. All at once the room, filled with warm sunshine and throbbing summer heat, stifled him. The basket of routine papers on his desk seemed very dreary. The brown copy of *Manual of Military Law* lying across his blotter had bleached to the colour of cheap cowhide. With a fierce sweep of his hand he sent it hurtling from the desk. It struck the wall and landed on the tin security box with a clatter. He scowled at it, and then, with a vicious jab of his forefinger on the button, rang for the adjutant.

Somewhat startled, the adjutant appeared in the door.

"Yes, sir?"

"Send a message to all platoon commanders that there will be a parade on Saturday morning at 0830 hours. Go over the details of it with the sergeant-major."

He looked up into the watery blue eyes of the lieutenant, and then for a moment studied the large mole on his soft chin.

'He's like a woman,' he thought. 'There is something feminine about the fellow.'

"Well!" he said, finally, with a snort of exasperation.

"Yes, sir," replied the adjutant, and, grinning sheepishly, he closed the door.

After he had gone the major rose from his desk and began to pace the floor. Now and then he stopped to gaze out of the window to the downward slope of the land toward the sea. The fields were a tawny gold rippling in the summer heat. Through the open window drifted the scent of new-mown hay and the smell of straw dust. Three planes flew out toward the Channel. He heard the far-off throb of their engines, and for a moment saw their bird-like shadows sweeping darkly across a stubble field.

Turning from the window his eye caught sight of a swirling dust cloud rising over a far valley road. He gazed at it for a while, and then, puzzled, he took his binoculars from the desk drawer. On a rise of ground a tank emerged from the dust cloud. Immediately behind it followed another. He could see only the turrets and the upper part of the hulls.

His second in command, Captain Brodin, entered the office. With a nod the major turned back to the window and again examined the tanks. Then he handed the binoculars to the captain.

"Take a look at those Rams wheeling along the valley road. I don't know who they can be, I'm sure. They seem to be in a rush, though."

The captain sighted the tanks. The gold signet ring on his finger glittered in the sun as he adjusted the focus to his eyes.

"I don't think they are Rams. They look like Lees to me," he said, after a pause.

Impatiently the major snatched the binoculars from him and took another look, but the tanks had disappeeared in a fold of the land. Only a long cloud of dust rose above the road.

"They were Rams," he said shortly. "The Lee has a totally different turret from the Ram. There is no mistaking them."

He turned abruptly to his desk.

"I thought you had made a considerable study of tank recognition at one time," he added, caustically.

"Sufficient to identify all the Allied tanks and a few of Jerry's."

The two men glared at each other. With difficulty the captain controlled himself.

Though usually the best of friends the two men had recently found cause to quarrel over trivial differences. The rift had begun over a matter of discipline, when the major had dismissed a charge against a man whom Captain Brodin had placed under arrest for a minor offence. Brodin had taken this as a personal affront, and began harbouring the belief that the C.O. would not support his officers' disciplinary measures. He did not voice his opinion to the major, but brooded over it secretly.

On this small ember of resentment he heaped coals. The major had lost all interest in training. All proposals which he, Brodin, put forward were rejected or shelved. Moreover, the major had begun to deal personally with a great many matters which, formerly, he had delegated to the captain.

Captain Brodin had never developed a philosophy which might have enabled him to extract from his years of service what few comforts and enjoyments army life could have offered him. But he was at heart a careerist. He saw the war as an opportunity for personal advancement, and he pushed himself forward with an almost unprincipled zest. He was undoubtedly efficient, though heartless. In short, he was one of those peculiar individuals who read into army orders all the justification they require for the full liberty of deeply rooted anti-social tendencies. He insisted upon the strictest obedience to all army orders, and permitted no deviation nor interpretation which was not allowed in cold print. The men feared him, and his fellow officers despised him for his inhumanity.

In the numerous small quarrels and differences between himself and the commanding officer he began to detect a threat to his advancement. He stood high on the seniority list of captains, and would, shortly, receive his majority and the command of a company, if his record remained unblemished. On the other hand, he had no political or social influence to enable him to pass through a period of adversity.

He thought the matter over for some days, and came to a decision. The quarrels were gradually assuming a more belligerent nature, and it was only a matter of time before an open rift would occur. He had two courses open to him. He could retreat from every situation which threatened a quarrel with the C.O., and diplomatically appease him. Or (and this was more to his nature) he could bide his time until some situation arose which he might exploit to his own advantage and gain prestige in higher quarters. He decided upon the latter course.

He had not long to wait.

# 14

I

THE high summer heat beat down upon the earth. Life seemed to murmur indolently with a voluptuous sigh. Far up in the azure sky the planes hummed faintly, and sometimes a plane flew low over the camp at tree-top height, passing like a monstrous savage bird, leaving behind its rocket-like roar to soften and fade in the woods. But for the most part, life about the camp dragged out in a tedious, stupefying round of chores and regimental duties, without interest or event. The men were gripped in a heavy apathy. They spent most of their time talking in listless tones.

The weekly parades were elaborated to occupy a full morning. The sergeant-major had the men re-dig all the weapon and air-raid trenches about the area, and even had them reinforced. All the vehicles were painted. The cook house was whitewashed. The fire buckets were scoured, and the trunks of the trees along the driveway were whitewashed. Yet, with all this, the men were idle, listless and not one of the officers had the courage or the energy to propose more training. Everyone waited—for what they did not know—while the summer wore on.

The major decided to begin each day with a period of physical training. Reveille was sounded at 05.30. Ten minutes after the bugle everyone was out on parade. Then the whole company, by platoons, was led at a trot down the tree-lined drive to the highway for a two-mile run. Afterwards, there was opportunity for desultory conversation, for there was three-quarters of an hour before the breakfast gong.

"Some life, my boys!"

"They do this sort of thing in prisons."

"I dunno. I was never in one."

The old man runs like a mare in foal."

"I'm going sick to-morrow. Just see if I don't."

"I'll bet my wife is lying in bed this minute wondering

what I'm doing. 'I hope he's happy,' she'll be saying to herself."

"I can smell bacon and eggs for breakfast."

"You're dreaming. You shouldn't run on an empty stomach. It gives you a light head."

"Did you see the 2 i/c? He looks like the coach for a varsity track team."

"He's so mean he'd put a man on charge for just thinking. Why—he's decided to have the latrine buckets painted white with black handles. He'll have us relieving ourselves by numbers next thing—you know, sit, one, two, three. Stand, one, two, three! Button up, one, two, three!"

"All right! Fold your blankets on someone else's bed. Mine's all made up."

2

One morning in September, while his comrades were at breakfast, a private in "A" platoon sat on the end of his bed, placed the muzzle of his rifle to his body, and, with a stick, pressed the trigger. The bullet tore a long, black hole in his upper abdomen.

The sound of the shot brought men running from the mess hut. They found him crawling on all fours into the bracken beside the hut, a trail of bright, smudged blood following him. When they reached him he stopped crawling, and, still on all fours, turned his head and laid it on the earth, with his eyes staring upwards, frozen in their sockets. Blood bubbled on his lips.

"I did it! I did it . . . I . . ." He sighed and sank down into the bracken.

They carried him to the side of the road. Someone ran to start a lorry, but he was already dead.

This incident caused great excitement in the camp for a day or two. Everyone put forth a guess as to the reason for the suicide, but when it was discovered that no-one really knew the man, the general belief was that a hopeless love triangle had driven the fellow to his death.

No-one knew the man. That was the surprising and grim fact which emerged out of the Court of Enquiry. Everyone knew him by name, some knew the district from which he came, and that he was married. And yet, search their minds as they did, not one of his comrades could call him "friend," not one could recall any time when he had spoken of his wife, or any personal matter. They knew him : they had taken him for granted. It was not until he had left them that they realized that they knew nothing whatever about him. He was a stranger to those with whom he had lived and worked. Day by day, for a thousand days, they had rubbed shoulders with him, talked and laughed, groused and sweated with him; and yet he was a stranger.

And this realization was in itself the beginning of a sort of immortality. It was as if, by his sudden and brutal death, he had left a message for his comrades, a message contained in the heart of every man. For every man is to his comrade a stranger, and every man dwells in his own wilderness. And when he dies, he dies alone, and the faint glimmer of light which he shed goes out.

Within a few days the dead man's name was almost legendary. When it was spoken it was in a hushed tone. He was attributed with feats of skill and courage which, in reality, had been every-day events in his mediocre existence. Because they knew so little about him, they endowed him with qualities he had never possessed. In time, events came to be dated by his death. When reminiscing upon a matter it was said that, "such and such happened before Snowden killed himself," or "that was after Snowden died."

No-one thought of the man's wife—no-one, that is, except the officer who was president of the court which inquired into his death. To this officer fell the task of gathering all the dead man's possessions for disposal. His army kit was returned to the army for re-issue. His personal effects were to go to his wife, his next of kin.

The President of the Court sat at his desk with the dead man's effects before him. The naked electric light shone on his bald head and his bushy eyebrows cast shadows over his eyes. A half-smoked cigarette burned in the ashtray. In the corner of the office lay a heap of worn and soiled army clothing—a rifle, web equipment, mess tins, tin helmet and respirator. On the desk, scattered upon the pink blotter, lay a number of letters and scraps of paper.

Slowly, with a feeling of distaste, the officer began to sort the letters. He put them all together, and then sorted them into two piles, one pile containing letters from Canada, the other letters from within England. He began reading the letters from Canada. They were all from the man's wife. They were letters of love, of devotion and tender solicitude, and though frequently she expressed the wish that he would write more often, there was no note of complaint or admonition.

"A fine woman," the captain said aloud to the empty room, and put the letters together in a neat pile.

He began reading the second group of letters. They were all from the same woman, and, as he read on, covering a period of almost a year, he followed the development of a passionate and wild love affair from a casual meeting to its sudden and tragic end. It was a task he had no relish for, and as he drew each letter out of its soiled envelope and unfolded it upon his desk, he had to overcome a repugnance that was almost nauseating to him. He felt like a Peeping Tom. Before him lay bared a woman's heart, expressed in such terms of shameless intimacy and endearment that only a woman touched with love could utter to her lover.

When he had read them all he pushed them aside and sat looking at his fingernails. Finally, drearily, he turned to the few remaining objects. There was a wisp of woman's hair—red curly hair. Could it be his wife's, he wondered. To which group of effects did it belong—the wife's, or the other woman's? Slowly, hesitantly, he placed it with the letters from the other woman. After all, he thought, I am not sure. He looked through the scraps of paper—addresses, scrawled notes of no significance. He tore them into fine shreds and made a pile of them on his blotter. There was the fellow's signet ring. It was, he decided, safe to assume that it had not been given by the other woman, and he put it with the wife's letters.

Into a large envelope he placed all the things which he decided the man's wife should have, including her letters. Methodically he arranged them in the envelope, sealed it and marked it. Then he took out his cigarette lighter and lit it, holding one of the other letters to the flame. When it had caught and blazed he put it into the fireplace grate and touched another letter to it. One by one he burnt the letters and the lock of hair. As he stood watching the last letter darken and crackle on the hearth, the door opened and the hawk-like face of Lieutenant Vantry, a platoon officer, appeared inquiringly.

"Come in." The captain's voice was listless.

"Not a happy tone, that," the lieutenant replied as he entered. "Working you too hard these days?"

"I've just completed an unpleasant task."

"Oh! The Snowden affair?"

"Yes. There is the last of it." The captain indicated the crisp, black burnings in the grate, from which a fine wisp of smoke fluttered.

The other looked at him questioningly.

"I've just burnt the other woman's letters. No good can be served by letting the wife know the story. Let her believe—she obviously did believe in the fellow all the time. And now—now she has only memories."

"And the other woman?" the lieutenant asked cynically.

The captain swept his hand toward the fireplace. "Now she doesn't exist, does she? She will probably write, inquiring. But who will answer? The army is so impersonal, isn't it? There is only you and I, and in a few months' time, in a few weeks' time, we'll have forgotten all about it." He raised his eyes and there was a faint glint of animosity in them. "Won't we?" he asked.

"Quite," the lieutenant replied, and then, after a moment's hesitation, he said, "I hope someone remembers to do the same for me some day, if it's ever necessary. I hope to God someone does"

They looked at each other for a minute and then, suddenly, they shook hands in silent pact.

"Come! A drink is in order."

They turned out the light and closed the door and went along the corridor to the mess. Behind them, in the dark room, a faint burnt odour mingled with the night air.

3

One day there was liver for dinner. This was an event, not because the men were particularly fond of liver, but because the appearance of it on the mess menu denoted the arrival of mail from home. The relationship between liver and mail was prevalent throughout the army. Men of the first division had begun it. To them the appearance of liver was a certain omen that a mail convoy had reached Britain safely. In time it became an accepted fact. There may indeed have been a basis of truth in the belief, for it is quite likely that mail for troops overseas was dispatched from Canada on fast boats which were also, because of their speed, loaded with perishable meats and other supplies.

This day the cook appeared outside the cookhouse door with his giant spoon in his hand. He stood for some minutes beside the bent iron dinner gong, with his hands on his hips and his head thrown back, eyes blazing into the sun. His posture was that of an official who is about to announce great tidings to a multitude.

At last, with a great flourish, he brought his battered spoon down on the iron gong and began to hammer out a tinkling dinner call that brought the men running at the double, mess tins clattering. As they came, the cook put his spoon beneath his left arm, in the manner of a sergeant-major instructor handling his stick on parade, and, cupping his hands to his lips, shouted:

"And it's LIVER!"

Hearing this, the men passed the word back to those following, who in turn shouted it back. But by this time it was no longer the cry, "And it's liver," but instead, "the mail's in."

True to custom there was a mail parade among the platoons that evening after supper. Some got a letter, some half a dozen, some a handful. Some were suddenly radiantly happy; others were afraid to open their letters. And there were those who, when all the names had been called, knew there was nothing for them and turned away with a dry lump in their throats.

In a remote spot in the pasture beneath a great elm tree, O'Rourke sat and read his letters from Gerda. Twilight! And the soft murmur of life abating, the sweet smell of the grass and the faint odour of burning wood. He opened the first letter and began to read. Images sprang to his mind—images of his home, of the fields, of the trodden roadways, of the beauty of his wife. He heard the sound of her voice, heard her laughter, saw her beauty in a hundred forms of intimacy and embrace which he had known and forgotten and remembered again. Out of her letters these things emerged, close and captured, and yet elusive. He tried to draw them to him and set their image upon his mind forever, but they endured a moment and were gone and others floated across his vision and disappeared. All that remained with him was a strange and haunting remembrance of Gerda's loveliness.

"I know now, Bob," she wrote in one of her letters, "that I will not see you home this year. I know that now. I have hoped for months that you might come back—that something would make it possible for me to see you again if only for a little while. But now I know that it cannot be this year. The war is far from over. It has hardly begun and I must realize that now.

"Then next year? Surely it must be next year, Bob! It must be! We must believe that. I shall go on believing that until next year has gone. And the next year after if that is necessary.

I'll go on believing and waiting for ever for you. But oh, not with patience! No woman ever lived who loved a man and had patience for a war. War is man's business. If this were a woman's world there would be no war.

"I will always wait for you, Bob, no matter how long it is. You are all my life."

He lay beneath the tree with the opened letters in his hand while the sky gradually darkened and the light died from the earth. A great flight of bombers roared high overhead going out toward the Channel, but he did not lift his eyes to follow their sound. After they had passed, he rose and walked across the pasture to the camp through the heavy and palpable darkness.

# 15

I

ON a warm sunny February morning Captain Brodin left the company area to attend a meeting at Formation Headquarters. He had begun the day in a particularly evil mood for, when he was dressing, he noticed a crust of mud around the sole of one of his boots. He had kept his batman-driver standing at attention in the centre of the room for ten minutes while he delivered an acid-tongued lecture on the boy's duties and the penalties that would accure if he did not "pull up his breeches." Thereupon he had flung the offending boots across the floor to the batman and had angrily gone down to breakfast wearing his oxfords.

At table he found the toast cold and the tea insipidly weak. Commenting upon this in injured tones to the major, he received only a grunt in reply. His further attempts at conversation were met with silence. The major was engrossed in his morning paper and seemed not to notice him. The other officers at the table exchanged knowing glances. After a quick gulp of tea, Brodin pushed his chair back noisily, threw his napkin upon the table, and left the room in a black rage.

And so, huddling his head into the collar of his greatcoat, he climbed into his jeep beside his driver and started for the meeting. He had planned on borrowing the major's staff car for the trip, but after the events at breakfast he decided against broaching the subject and ordered his driver to get the jeep ready for the trip.

Passing down the driveway from the manor house to the road barricade marking the company entrance, he stared at the pasture and at the dark, squat Nissen huts of the platoons, with bloodshot eyes that still smarted from his anger. At the barricade his driver stopped, waiting for the guard to open the barbed-wire swing gate. After a minute of waiting the driver honked his horn. Still no guard appeared. The driver looked at the captain as though to say: 'I am only a small man. Such mysteries are for you to unravel.'

Captain Brodin puffed out his cheeks, snorted and looked around for the guard. Presently, almost at a loss to know what to do, he snapped at the driver:

"Well! Don't sit there like a fool! Open the gate."

Obediently the driver got down and opened the gate, drove the jeep through, and closed it again behind them. Then, with a last look at the empty sentry box beside the gate and a shrug of his shoulders, he got back behind the wheel and set the little car careening down the road through the flashes of brilliant sunshine that cut between the roadside trees. Now and then he glanced slyly at the captain out of the corner of his eye, and the frozen angry face he beheld made him turn his eyes quickly back to the road. When they had gone a mile, the captain stirred in his seat.

"Turn about! I want to see if that sentry has returned to his post yet."

The driver swung his jeep around, and as he started back he crossed his fingers.

"Poor Jetson," he said to himself, "he'll catch hell now. I'm glad I'm not in his shoes. Or maybe it's not Jetson—maybe it's Crawford. Anyway—somebody is going to get skinned for this. God! I'm glad it isn't me!"

So happy did he feel over this thought that he began whistling softly through his teeth.

When they returned to the sentry post the guard was still absent. Captain Brodin glanced at his watch, and then methodically made a note of the time in his message book.

It occurred to him, in a moment of swift reflection, that the guard might have gone to relieve himself, in obedience to a natural urge that was, conceivably, stronger than any army order. Yet he did not entertain this possibility for long. His temper, already frayed, and his ego injured by the events of the morning, he seized upon this incident of the absentee guard. The guard, whoever he was, was absent from his post, an outrageous and inexcusable crime. Suddenly he saw it as his duty to charge the man for it, and to obtain the severest penalty for it in order to stamp out any possibility of a recurrence within the unit.

In a somewhat happier mood, grasping at this incident as a sop to his vanity, he proceeded on his way, determined to bring the offender to charge in the afternoon. He looked at the green, hedged pastures that swept past them, at the tiny withdrawn cottages that seemed to peek out of dark, naked bushes beyond the fields. The grass seemed greener, richer and in the balmy air there was a faint suggestion of spring—something wistful, tender and exciting. The captain smiled benevolently upon his driver, who, distrustfully, pretended not to see it. The boy had served the captain long enough to regard with deepest suspicion any display of humanity and goodwill from him. Usually it was the prelude to more work, or an unpleasant task.

The captain began to feel a sense of well-being with the world. Spring, he decided, was almost in, and with spring and good weather and the revival of hopes that it always brought, he would be able to go ahead with a new training scheme he had been fathering all winter. He decided to introduce this subject at the meeting, if the opportunity presented itself. It would place him in a good light. At the least it would serve to show that he was alert and looking ahead.

The events of the morning came back to him. and he experienced a stifling oppression when he saw the incident at the breakfast table in retrospect. He almost sensed the sneering smiles of the lieutenants at the major's silent rebuke to him. He would have to score one on the major, somehow, or be the laughing stock of the company. The situation had become intolerable.

All through the meeting, listening to the drone of voices discussing army matters and new policies, Captain Brodin's mind was engaged in the development of a crafty plan. He heard what was being said around the meeting table, and in a curiously abstract way he digested and criticized it. All the while his eyes roved over the panelled walls of the old room and gazed through the french windows to the square of sunlight upon the vivid green lawn. He offered no comment himself when it came his turn to speak. He merely nodded his head and smiled ingratiatingly.

As the meeting broke up and the officers filed out to their waiting cars, a burly lieutenant remarked to another in a loud voice :

"Did you ever see Brodin miss a chance to talk before? I couldn't believe it.

"We usually have to listen to more boom from him than there is in a training memorandum. All he has done, or is going to do.... Frankly, I'm suspicious of his silence to-day.

"The poor fellow is merely trying to get ahead. We have to suffer him, I suppose."

2

That afternoon, back in his office at Company H.Q., Captain Brodin sent for the sergeant-major.

"For some time," he said in a brusque tone, "I have been very dissatisfied with the slovenly and haphazard manner in which the unit guards have conducted their duties." He paused and let his words sink in, watching the sergeant-major's eyes for some indication of his temper. But the other, standing severely to attention, gave no indication that he had even heard. He stared back at the captain with a respectful but faintly amused smile in his eyes.

Captain Brodin continued :

"This morning at 0925 hours I found no guard on duty at our 'out' gate. I checked again ten minutes later and the man was still not at his post.

"I needn't remind you of the seriousness of this, sergeant-major. You know it as well as I. I am determined to make an example of this case—to stamp out, here and now, this laxity, this . . . this disgraceful lack of discipline !"

The sergeant-major shifted his eyes from Captain Brodin's face to his hand that had thumped the desk and now lay spread-fingered and white-knuckled across the blotter like a claw.

"I have not been informed of anything of this sort before, sir," he said.

"Informed?" Brodin blew the word at him out of a crimson face. "Then, sergeant-major, it is high time you made a deeper acquaintance with the state of discipline of this company."

"The commanding officer has made no complaint, sir."

Inwardly Brodin recoiled from this piece of insolence. Had it come from any other N.C.O. in the company he would have stormed him down, charged him and had his skin and his rank before the sun had set. But the sergeant-major was of a different breed. Military law protected him from the wrath of junior officers, and assured his rank of an integrity that made him virtual lord of all his N.C.O.s. Not even his commanding officer could reprimand him. It required none less than a Briga-dier to do that. And while any guilt of insolence laid him sub-ject to the same military laws which governed everyone else, he knew, and Captain Brodin knew, that any statement of truth such as he had just made was not insolence at all, though it was, definitely, in the captain's mind, an insult. No statement could have been more calculated to put the captain back in his position as the second-in-command of the company, and at the same time to imply that the matter of discipline should be referred to the higher authority of the major. It left Brodin with the necessity of defining his position in relation to the case.

"I am laying the charge against the man who was supposed to be on guard duty this morning, sergeant-major. Is that clearly understood? I want the man's name, the name of the guard corporal and a full report of the matter. I want this from you to-day.

"That is all, sergeant-major."

Sergeant-major Betts saluted. It was not what he termed his "whiz-bang" salute, which he reserved for officers he admired. It was, however, a salute smart enough to be beyond criticism. He simply drew his arm up, paused and dropped it again with the faintest suggestion of boredom.

When the sergeant-major had gone, Brodin sat at his desk, clasping and unclasping his fingers in uncontrollable rage.

"I'll make this a court-martial case. I'll push it right through. There is the guard and the guard corporal, whoever he is. And there is the sergeant-major. I'll take some of the snot out of him in short order. Technically he is responsible for the guards. If I handle the evidence right it ought to be easy to implicate him. I'll make an issue of this."

Hollow silence, and a barren coldness filled the room, in spite of the sunshine. A lorry growled in the workshop yard; someone shouted and was answered by a coarse laugh.

He, Brodin, would have to give evidence in the case before the court. Well, he would be happy to oblige. Simple evidence, it would be. Nothing derogatory to the company, mind. But he could insinuate that this particular case was but an example of the discipline of the company. That ought to be enough, entered as evidence in the court-martial and eventually read and studied by the formation commander, to set critical eyes upon the company commander. It might put a whole series of critical examinations in motion—examinations that would be embarrassing to the C.O.

He felt it would work. Moreover, he felt perfectly safe.

3

The sergeant-major checked his duty roster of guard corporals. He found Corporal O'Rourke doing duty. Frowning, he closed the book, and locked it away. Then he stood by the window biting his moustache. A small, long-legged bird fluttered in the gravel outside.

"The truth is, I suppose, that I'm tired of the army," he said aloud. "I'm tired of the waiting, and the training, of holding the men together."

He shrugged his shoulders. "There must be two types of soldiers. People like Brodin are in this war for what they can get out of it. And then there is my sort. . . . We simply want to get the job done and get back to our families and our homes. I suppose Brodin's kind make the best soldiers in the long run. They've a personal interest in it. But when my kind lose sight of all the pep talk about fighting for democracy, and saving the world, and making the world a better place to live in—well, then, we've nothing. Absolutely nothing, but waiting. What's democracy? It's the right of people like Brodin to live and disturb people like me. Making the world a better place to live in? For whom? For all of us, of course, including the scoundrels and the Wops, and the Germans and the Japs."

He picked up his web belt and snapped it on.

"I suppose I'm losing my perspective," he said with a wry smile, "and I'm blessed if I know whether it's a good thing or not."

On his way to see O'Rourke he walked by the barnyard. It was a little out of his path, and though he had marked it "out of bounds" to the men, he liked to go past it and dally there, looking at the fowls and the animals. Secretly, he had a fervent wish to set up in farming after the war. Everything about the barnyard interested him.

He stopped to look at the hens scratching and powdering themselves in the dust. There were brown hens, black, white and a few speckled black-and-white ones. He knew nothing about chickens, and wondered which kind laid the best eggs. He decided he would ask O'Rourke. The lad was from the farm and would know.

He found O'Rourke beside his hut, cleaning his motor cycle. A can of dirty washing petrol was beside the machine.

"Afternoon, O'Rourke."

"It's a great day, sergeant-major. Too nice a day to be wasted in the army."

"Tell me, O'Rourke. You're a farmer. What kind of hens are the best for laying—the black-and-white ones?"

"I always figured Leghorns were about the best. Depends on the climate a lot, though."

"I've wondered. I'm going to keep some hens after the war."

O'Rourke went on cleaning his machine. He hummed absently to himself.

After a silence the sergeant-major asked, "You posted the guards this morning, didn't you?"

"Sure thing, sir. I put them out at eight o'clock to relieve the night guards. Why?"

"Well, it seems that Captain Brodin went out the gate about 0930 this morning and the guard had bitched off. There was no-one on the main out-gate at all. Who did you post there?"

"I put Private Crawford out there, from eight till ten. I suppose Brodin's raising hell?"

"That is putting it mildly. But the point, I'm afraid, is that you're Joe."

O'Rourke stopped his work and looked at the sergeant-major. When the sergeant-major spoke like that it meant something. He was a good fellow, as a rule. Friendly, in a regimental sort of way. When he tipped a fellow off he declared himself on that fellow's side. And THAT was always a help to weather trouble.

"I don't see how I'm Joe just because Crawford buggered off from his post this morning. I put him there. I can't sit and hold his hand all the time, or play rummy with him so he won't get lonely and go looking for company. I've enough to do playing nursemaid to my section."

"That's true enough corporal. But you see you're responsible for the guards to-day. That makes you Joe, doesn't it? The guard will be crimed, sure. But it will involve you, too. Don't you see? Captain Brodin's really hot about this. Now, just take my advice and be careful you remember that you did all the things you were supposed to do to-day in connection with the guards. Brodin's after blood, for some reason. Just see that it isn't yours he gets."

"Right, and thanks for the tip, sergeant-major."

"By the way, did you read the orders to the guards when you posted them this morning?"

"No. We never do."

"You're supposed to, you know."

"Yes, sir. But it's never done—not by anyone. The guards all know their duties."

"All the same, it's a point, and it's not a good one, either."

The sergeant-major retraced his steps towards headquarters. He did not go by way of the barnyard. He walked along briskly, looking every inch like a man who is just going up for promotion. But he was worried. The fact that O'Rourke hadn't read the standing orders to the guards that morning was, he felt, a grave omission. Certainly it was one that Captain Brodin would not miss when he came to sift the facts of the case. It put the case in a far more serious light, as far as he, the sergeant-major, was concerned. The guard could claim that he wasn't aware of his duties because they hadn't been read to him. And it was up to the guard corporal to read them. Finally, it was the sergeant-major's responsibility to see that they WERE read to all the guards.

It was exactly the sort of case that Captain Brodin would love. Fishing for a case against a private, he would be able to bag a corporal and a sergeant-major at the same time. Not bad, that.

The sergeant-major smiled into the sun. But there was not the slightest vestige of amusement in his eyes.

At his desk he drew out a clean piece of paper, sharpened his pencil. Slowly, in a rather cramped hand, he marked the date on the upper right-hand corner. Pencil poised over the paper, he sat for some time unmoved, wondering where to begin his report.

"What the hell can I say?" he asked aloud.

He laid the pencil down and methodically began to search his mind for the various points of the case which had come to light, ticking them off on his fingers one by one. . . . Item 1—O'Rourke is Guard Corporal of the day. . . . Item 2—O'Rourke posted Private Crawford, G. F., on sentry duty. . . . Item 3—therefore Private Crawford, G. F., is the man guilty of the offence. . . . Item 4—Corporal O'Rourke failed to read the Standing Orders for guards to Private Crawford when he posted him on duty. No, on second thought, that last point had better not be mentioned. Let it come out later if it had to, but for now it was too meaty a point to give Brodin. It was just what he wanted.

Suddenly, viciously, the sergeant-major crumpled the paper up and hurled it across the room.

"I'll give the bloody sod the facts and no more," he said,

and pushing back his chair noisily he went off down the corridor to Captain Brodin's office.

## 4

At dinner that evening neither the major nor Captain Brodin spoke. For the major's part he was preoccupied with a report on his company from H.Q. command which he had that afternoon received. It was not an unfavourable report. Neither was it complimentary to him. It listed too many petty faults in the internal organization of the company, faults which suggested a slip-shod control of discipline. On the whole, the major was not greatly worried about the report, for petty faults could be found in any company. Yet it was annoying, coming as it did at a time when he, the major, stood high on the seniority list for promotion.

Captain Brodin knew nothing of this. Throughout the meal he reviewed the case of the absentee guard and inwardly resolved to push the case as far as possible.

When the major left the table and went back to his office, the captain waited a few minutes, chatting with one of the lieutenants, and then followed the major.

Across the desk, upon which the naked light shone with hard, cold brilliancy, the two men faced each other. Each regarded the other with faintly concealed hostility.

"May I have a word with you, Major?"

"Certainly." The major fingered some papers on his desk and waited.

"It's about Private Crawford, sir. I found him absent from his guard post this morning."

"Crawford? Crawford? Who is he? I don't seem to recall the name."

"He's in Corporal O'Rourke's section."

"Ah! Oh, yes! I recall him. Smart young lad. Well set up. Mm . . . and what's this he's been up to? Eh?"

"This morning he left his guard post without being properly relieved."

The major bowed his head to hide a frown of annoyance. He stared at the papers on his desk with a morose, angry look. His lips trembled as he replied:

"What has this got to do with me, Captain Brodin? I shall deal with the charge when it comes before me. In the meantime, I trust that you are capable of supervising the details. It is, after all, a minor offence, is it not?"

"The man deserted his post, sir."

"Is that your charge against him?"

"Yes, sir."

"Have you seen Crawford's crime sheet? Is it bad?"

Brodin hesitated.

"Well, no, it isn't. There are no entries on his sheet. But this is an extremely serious offence, sir."

"It is serious, Captain, if you choose to regard it as such. I, myself, am inclined to take a more compromising view of it. This is the man's first offence. Surely there are some circumstances which, if not excusing him, at least lessen the severity of this, his first crime. Have you investigated it fully? Have you talked with the man?"

"I have investigated it fully, sir. I saw no reason to interview the man. I am a witness that he deserted his post."

The major gave a sigh of exasperation.

"You are a hard man, Brodin. Couldn't you charge the man with absence without leave, which is a minor offence, comparatively. Couldn't you be satisfied with that, since he has no other crime?"

"I fail to see, sir, why I should change the charge merely because the man has had no previous crime. It would in no way lessen the seriousness of this crime. Unless you direct it, sir, I will let the charge stand as desertion."

"We shall see, Captain. We shall see. That will be all for the present."

Alone, the major sank into his chair and lit a cigarette. Toying with his cigarette lighter, he thought:

'I must be careful. If I insist that he change his charge to one of absence without leave it is quite likely that he will take the matter to higher authority for a ruling. He would be quite within his rights to do so, and of course the Judge Advocate General's branch would support him in his charge, as being correct, for they don't know all the circumstances. It would put me in a dim light, really, if it went that high. Damn it all, it would be quite a triumph for Brodin and that is what he is after. It isn't Private Crawford he's out to get. It's me! There's no mistaking that.'

He puffed on his cigarette for a time, lost in deep thought. Presently, in a soft whisper to himself, he said, reflectively:

"Brodin is a bit too cocky altogether. I'll send his name in as a candidate for the senior officer's course. It's hardly likely he'll pass it. He hasn't the education, for one thing, and he can't make friends. Even if he passes, it will not be with distinguished marks. There is a good chance he'll fail it, and his chances for promotion will be gone. In any event I'll get rid of him for a month.

"But this case—I must break it down in some way. It's ridiculous to charge a man so seriously. Somewhere there must be an extenuating circumstance on which I can justifiably reduce the charge to A.W.O.L. or throw it out entirely. . . . Somewhere. . . . "I'll question the sergeant-major."

Rising from his desk he rang for the night orderly.

"Is the sergeant-major about the house?"

"Yes, sir. He's in his office."

"Tell him I wish to see him."

The sergeant-major, somewhat surprised, clicked his heels upon entering the major's office and stood severely to attention.

"You wish to see me, sir?"

"Oh, yes." The major assumed a confidential, friendly tone. "Stand at ease, Sergeant-major."

He coughed, moved the papers off his blotter, and looked nervously at the electric light.

"It's about this Private Crawford, who, according to Captain Brodin, deserted his guard post this morning. I wanted to speak to you about it. Have you any facts about this case that . . . er . . . that would interest me? That is, before the case comes up before me formally to-morrow. As the case stands now the man is charged with deserting his post. A very grave charge, as you know."

"I daresay Captain Brodin has given you all of the facts that I know, sir. There aren't many to the case. Apparently the man was posted on guard and left his post shortly afterward. I don't know his reasons, sir, but I believe he will produce a good one when the case comes before you. After all, sir, Crawford's record is clean, and it isn't like him to simply leave his post. Besides, he didn't really desert. He was seen in the company lines about the same time that Captain Brodin noticed him absent from the guard post. That's hardly desertion, sir."

The major sucked the end of his fountain pen, reflectively.

"Quite correct, Sergeant-major," he agreed. "It isn't quite desertion. It really amounts to this: the lad absented himself from his place of duty without permission. Doesn't it, now?"

The sergeant-major nodded in vigorous agreement.

"Exactly, sir. That is exactly how I see it, myself." He

coughed nervously. "If I may say so, sir, it seems to me that Captain Brodin is being a bit severe in this matter."

"Perhaps, Sergeant-major. Perhaps. But you must bear in mind that each of us performs his duty as he sees it.

"Is there, perhaps, some side of this case that you know of, and didn't impart to Captain Brodin? Something, let us say, that would allow me a more lenient view. Think, please."

"Well, sir, when it comes to that, there is no case against Crawford at all. Not if he takes a court-martial and gets a smart officer for his defence. You see, sir, the man was posted on guard, but no-one read the standing orders for guards to him. It's a technicality, I know, sir; nevertheless, he can cry innocent because he didn't know how long he was supposed to remain on duty, or what he was to do."

Major Brest tried to hide his pleasure at this disclosure. It was, he felt jubilantly, too good to be true. Now he could sweep the case away completely and take Brodin down a step. Cautiously he inquired:

"Are you sure of this, Sergeant-major? Quite sure?"

"Certainly, sir. Quite sure. I myself questioned the guard corporal about it, and he admitted that he had not read the Standing Orders to the guards."

"Did you tell this to Captain Brodin?"

"No, sir. He didn't ask me."

"And who was guard corporal this morning."

"Corporal O'Rourke, sir."

"I see. I see. You must in future make absolutely certain that Standing Orders are read to all guards by the guard corporals of the day. It is your responsibility, you know."

"Yes, sir."

"Have the charge against Private Crawford changed to A.W.O.L. Give him an opportunity of bringing in any witness in his defence that he may have. I will hold Orderly Room tomorrow morning. Also, parade Corporal O'Rourke before me, immediately after I have disposed of Crawford's case."

"Very good, sir."

5

The next afternoon O'Rourke sat on the edge of his bed with his kit and belongings piled untidily on the floor at his feet. He picked up a kitbag, then dropped it suddenly.

He looked down the length of the hut and then lifted the kitbag again, wearily. He stuffed a cardigan into it and jabbed it down viciously with his fist.

"The bastards! The dirty bastards!"

The door opened and Corporal Mullens stood leaning against the wall.

"Hello, Bob. Moving?"

"I'm moving."

"I heard you were up before the old man this morning. I came across to see if I could help."

"What have you heard?"

"Nothing. What's the story?"

"It's grim, Mullens. The major asked me to revert at my own request."

"He what!"

"You heard the first time."

"But, good God, man, what for?"

"For not reading the Guards' Standing Orders."

"But, damn it, Bob, an admonition would have done just as well, if he wanted to pull that chestnut out of the fire. We've all been guilty of that. Say! You're sure you didn't blow up and say something to him you shouldn't have?"

"I never had a chance. It was all cut and dried before I went in. Revert, or I'll have you paraded to higher authority. Just like that. So I signed the little piece of paper.

"Afterwards he seemed quite nice about things—said he'd see I got my rank back if I kept my nose clean for a couple of months. You know the baloney."

"There's something wrong about this. Something very fishy. It isn't like the old man, at all."

"I can't make it out either. I guess I'm just Joe."

"I'll speak to the sergeant-major about it."

"No, don't. I had a word with him afterwards—asked him the real reason."

"Did he tell you?"

"No. All he said was that 'when little people like us get involved in big people's affairs, it's the little fellows who always get hurt!' It doesn't give me any good reason to stop thinking what I am thinking right now. I've been a corporal a long, long time. That ought to mean something in this bloody army. But I guess it doesn't.

"So now I've got to move. They posted me to another platoon—said it would be better to make a fresh start with fellows I didn't know."

"Christ, man! They know damn well your own boys will

go to bat for you. Sure as shootin'. That's why they move you to another platoon. Out of sight, out of danger."

"I'm going over to 'C' platoon. Maybe it's just as well. The only tough thing about it is how I'm going to tell the wife. She'll take it badly. She'll feel badly about the army, you see. And she'll worry about me. I don't care for myself."

"Sure, I know, Bob, I know. Maybe I could write her a note explaining it. Coming from one of your buddies, she'd maybe see it wasn't your fault."

"Thanks, Mullens. That's a mighty nice offer. But no, I'll write her. She'll know it isn't my fault, even if I didn't write at all, and she only heard it by local rumour. That's one thing about her—she believes, and nothing will ever change that. She's a great girl. I just don't want her to worry about me."

"Okay, Bob. You know your missus. Come on down to the 'Ploughshare' to-night and we'll get stinko. Right?"

"Thanks, I feel just like it."

"Here, I'll give you a hand to get settled in your new home. Has it a nice view with hot and cold water? I've heard the service is lousy over there."

"You aren't funny, Mullens."

"No."

"But you're a good head."

"The boys will miss you."

O'Rourke did not answer. The two of them struggled across the field to "C" Platoon lines with O'Rourke's kit and belongings on their backs. Mullens carried the heavier load.

"You'll be back with good old 'B' Platoon, Bob. Just you see if you ain't. Won't be long, either."

"Maybe you're right, Mullens. But if I ever get those two hooks back on my arm, I'll be a wiser and tougher corporal than I ever was."

"Could be. But I'd be surprised if it was so. You see, the trouble with fellows like us—we believe everybody's just as honest and as good natured as ourselves. We forget there is always some dirty guy waiting to stick his knife into us. We're too bloody good-natured, and what happens? We get it in the back first time we close our eyes. You see, they make us something but they don't make us important enough to count for anything. They put us up and knock us down as often as they feel like it. And we do all the work! Now take a sergeant! He's cock o' the walk. Takes a lot to break him."

"Yes, I know. I've thought of all that, too."

"Well, I was just talking. I guess I talk too much."

"You're a good Joe, Mullens."

# 16

MAY. Nineteen forty-four. The South of England.

Along the invasion coast the days were hot and cloud-less, the nights cold and frosty, with cutting winds that swept in from the Channel. A new moon rose with the month. Night after night, as it swept across its bed of stars, it illuminated a coastline which gave no clue to the vast movement and prepara-tion of the mightiest military operation in all history. To all appearances the south coast line of England in the moonlight differed not in the slightest way from what it had shown in the five years of war.

The Hun suspected great concentrations of landing barges, naval craft and armoured might. Reconnaissances re-vealed empty harbours, clean, surf-swept beaches, empty fields and moorlands. He bombed with what few aircraft he could afford—bombed at random where he believed, strategically, military concentrations existed. The bombs landed on homes, churches and in open fields. It was the feeblest effort the German had ever made.

By day the roads of the south coast teemed with military traffic. Yet this vast movement never congested, never seemed to hurry. From points all over the South of England the convoys moved towards the invasion coast.

Out of old estates and farms inland moved the myriad units that made up the assault divisions. Along the roads lead-ing to the south coast the convoys rolled, by day and night. Into the woods and towns, under the trees of old lanes, under camouflaged nets, along hedges, in disused lime quarries, in the shade of houses, even into rock caves, they disappeared, and the earth gobbled them up and gave no clue. For once the quaint charm of England's shaded lanes and tiny woods had a practical purpose. For once the labyrinth of winding roads served a purpose other than to confound the traveller.

Gazing at a small-scale map of southern England, one

would have said that it was impossible to conceal a million men in such a small area, not only that—to hide their activities and movements by road. Yet such was true. Bournemouth and the Poole harbour areas contained enormous concentrations of amphibious equipment and crews. Southampton and Portsmouth areas contained several divisions of assault troops and great naval forces. Worthing, Brighton, Eastbourne, Bexhill, St. Leonard's, Hastings, Rye, Folkestone, Dover—all were invasion ports and concentration areas. Farther to the north, along the East Anglian coastline, American forces were forming up. To the west other vast American forces were concentrating.

By night, over the English countryside, the pulse of activity throbbed at the same high steady tempo. Through the sleeping villages the convoys rolled southward, Infantry, Artillery, Armoured Corps, Tactical Air Force, Signals, Engineers. Tanks roared through the streets, tore up kerbing stones, scraped the sides of buildings and rushed on across the countryside. Tank transporters, carrying tanks and armoured bulldozers and even railroad engines, belched black diesel smoke into the narrow villages, rumbled and rattled on their way, leaving a heavy roar like the passage of a great flight of bombers behind them. All night long there was the whine of gears, the roar of exhausts, the sharp stabbing cataract of sound rising and falling and rising again across the land. And yet, with the coming of dawn, at any given spot in the country, there was no sign of the forces which had made havoc of the night. Nothing was altered; everything was the same. No troops, no vehicles, were to be seen. The earth had swallowed them up, had thrust protective arms of green verdure around them, had folded the contours of hills about them, had taken them unto itself, as the snipe blends into its nesting ground.

Trained, poised, without nervousness or fear, a million men stood ready to launch the greatest attack in history.

2

In the early part of May, O'Rourke's company moved into the Portsmouth area with the brigade which it served, a part of the Third Canadian Division. They bivouacked in the Fareham area, five miles to the north of Portsmouth, on the western slope of the Ports Down—that magnificent height of land which commands Portsmouth and all its sea approaches.

Their area was a wood of ancient elms and scrub. Nearby, a meandering brook fingered its way through banks of gnarled roots to its mother stream, the Wallington River. An old, rotted cart gate, opening on to the main road that skirted the forest, became the main entrance to the encampment. The morning after the unit arrived this gateway was widened to allow the largest vehicle to enter. The vehicles simply crashed their way through it. The oaken gate itself completely disappeared as firewood for the camp fires. Only the gate posts remained, and these were set further apart, whitewashed, and adorned with "In" and unit signs. The farmer to whom the property belonged complained of the damage to his gate. The guard listened to his complaints with indifferent silence. When the farmer said all he had to say about his gate the guard turned his head slowly and deliberately spat half-way across the road, then, eyeing the farmer for a full minute, asked, "What gate?"

The undergrowth scrub disappeared. Tents and tarpaulins nestled under the giant trees. Washing stands were built and water was piped. Workshop fitters became plumbers. Petrol tins were made into wash basins, even into improvised ovens, the tins stacked and sealed with clay, like bricks. Although ten thousands troops were "on the scrounge" in the same area, the men found old boards, signs, pieces of metal and slabs of stone to use for improvised tables. Telephone wires became clothes lines, stretched between the branches of trees. Old motor oil mixed with water served for flash fires to heat water. Along the edges of the unit lines, slit trenches were built for protection in the event of bombing. In some parts of the camp the only possible way to identify the slit trenches from the ablution pits was by remembering that the slit trenches were zigzagged. Jokingly the men reminded each other that in the event of a night raid it would matter very little which one dropped into. In a few days' time the ablution pits were glorified by the addition of a peeled crouching pole, supported precariously on two crossed poles at either end. As time advanced and the camp took on a semi-permanent appearance, burlap netting was strung around the ablution areas—a refinement which was utterly wasted on the men.

From the roadway the encampment presented a strange appearance. There was something reminiscent of a gipsy encampment about it. The bushes were adorned with drying clothes of every conceivable shape and kind. Long winter underwear that would never be snow-white again consorted in the breeze with ragged shirts and oil-stained overalls. Summer underwear in all stages of repair made crazy tumbling patterns upon the clumps of trodden grass between the trees. Here, too, appeared precious bits of colour that were never to be seen on a regimental parade—red bandana handkerchiefs, bright socks, gay sweaters and sports wear. These, the bright colourful tatters that were the soldiers' most prized possessions, had survived innumerable kit inspections and unit house cleanings. Though the equipment of every man had been reduced to an absolute minimum that could be packed into a large and small pack, these bright tatters endured. Nameless were the dodges and means employed to hide them on each inspection. Other things more vital to comfort had been sacrificed to make room for them. They were cherished because man loves colourful and useless things—a love which he defends by attaching to them a sentimental value.

Washday (and every day was that) was an excuse to loaf in the sunlight beyond the trees, where, over a petrol tin full of clothes and muddy water over an open fire, the men yarned and bragged, or talked of home and the girls they had left behind. It had all been said before, a hundred times, yet it was ever new. Each fond recollection of the beloved homeland, every association of time and place within the memory, expressed a hope, a fervent longing. It was good to think of home, good to laugh at things suddenly remembered anew, good to share the love of things common to all.

To-morrow was another day. To-morrow there was a battle to wage—perhaps the fiercest, bloodiest battle of history. But the mind does not dwell upon to-morrow's peril : it drinks the nectar of memoried joys and thirsts for the past, the unforgotten, unrelinquished past.

At night there were exercises for the entire company. By moonlight they drove their vehicles down to the tidal shore and practised loading them on the invasion barges. Many of these exercises were on a grand scale, with entire divisions involved. Control of movement on the night roads, the timing and co-ordination of all the various units converging on the port area from their unit locations, was practised. Faults were discovered. Orders were altered, and again the practices were held, time after time, until the smallest detail was perfect. Tanks roared from their harbour areas down to the beach, loaded on the barges, and stood ready. Convoys of armoured cars, troop carrying lorries, petrol, ammunition and supply lorries, artillery, from the heavies to the anti-tank. There were great long convoys of tanks, ducks and bridging equipment, and there were convoys of M.10's—self-propelled anti-tank guns mounted on tank chassis. There were underwater recovery tanks, with a compartment for a driver and another for a diver and co-diver—equipment that could be submerged to recover tanks which had been lost from landing barges close in shore. There were special signal equipment, special engineer equipment. There were mine-clearing tanks that pushed great nets of chains before them to clear pathways through minefields— Sherman tanks with great sprocket-operated chain booms in front of them. There was medical equipment and administrative vehicles and tank transporters laden with every conceivable type of load, from tanks to engineer bulldozers for clearing and remaking roads, to great staff cars of the army chiefs. Every inch of space on every vehicle was utilized.

Such was the detail, infinite and microscopic in the planning.

In the first few exercises of embarkation that took place in the early part of May, one outstanding fault developed—a fault which threatened to destroy the precise timing of the operations. It was found that all equipment could be moved from the nearby harbour areas to the barges on the time scales laid down for all the various units, with the exception of some heavy engineer equipment, such as mighty armoured bulldozers, excavators, shovels and the like. These were too slow and unwieldy to move along the dark roads and at the same time keep up with the mass movement toward the port. And yet it was imperative that this equipment be loaded on to barges in the order of its priority on debarkation. Finally, to solve the problem, the Command called in a platoon of Canadian tank transporters. These giants, capable of lifting a forty-ton load, had carried every type of equipment from tanks to railroad engines. Now they were set to the problem of loading the special engineer's equipment and delivering it to the barge slipways according to the precise time-tables laid down. They did it, and the problem was solved.

Other problems arose. Officers and men were at first slow to grasp the necessity of adhering to the time-tables. A blunt warning drove home the essential truth that the success of the operation depended very much upon individual adherence to issued orders.

And so, all through the month, night after night, the exercises went on. Whole divisions were practised : smaller units held rehearsals, then merged with larger formations for combined operations. Every officer, every N.C.O., every D.R.

had to know the roads and turns by memory. During the day the dispatch riders went over the routes again and again, until they could guide their convoys along them blindfolded.

With all this there was the inevitable prelude to invasion —air-raids from the Hun, who raided not so much with a purpose to destroy (although that, too, was their task) as to reconnoitre. The Hun did little damage: it was the sound and fury of our own anti-aircraft bombardment that turned the night into a white wilderness of terror.

Along the south-eastern coastline a great force was assembling and preparing for an amphibious assault. Rumour in high quarters had it (and it was only a rumour that whispered in the train of the ranking officers) that this force was to attack Norway. But since all the areas in which invasion forces were concentrated were closed to public traffic completely, and the only movement allowed to civilians was granted on special permits which were so difficult to obtain that people were discouraged to apply for them—because of such restrictions, information about the operations within these areas never leaked out. Citizens all over England knew that preparations were going forward at full speed. They were told this in the Press. They were also told only what the Ministry of Information deemed it necessary for them to know in order to partially appease the insatiable human curiosity. "Security" of information had never been better within England. It is possible that the Hun knew more of the Allied preparations in any given area than the residents of that area. But the Hun, fortunately, was in a position where he could do nothing about it. The master card was withheld from him: he did not know WHEN the Allies would strike. He only knew, or shrewdly guessed, that they were ready.

During May, O'Rourke's unit, operating with the Infantry Brigade to which they belonged, took part in twenty-three practice moves from their location to the sea, on to their barges, and returned to their unit lines. For twenty-three successive nights they stood at the ready, not knowing whether they would be called into the schemes, whether (if they did) it would be for "keeps" or whether it was to be merely a "Stand to" alarm. For two weeks the weather changed from the warm, sensuous heat of the typical English May to bouts of squally winds, cold nights and lashing rain. On these nights they worked their convoys down to the sea coast and loaded into the barges in total darkness. Sometimes for an hour or more they would huddle, shivering, in the lee of their vehicles, bracing themselves against the lash and throw of the barges in the surf. They looked out on the darkness of thrashing seas and stinging spray, toward the unseen, unknown and ominous coast of France. There the enemy waited.

O'Rourke, standing in the waist of his barge beside his vehicle with his Sten gun in his hands and his loaded magazine at his waist, looked out to sea and wondered what the long, cold interval before dawn would bring him. Beyond the noise of the surf, beyond the faint opaque void upon the sea he was to meet the supreme adventure of his life. Would it be this night? Or to-morrow night? When would the grim macabre rehearsal end and the signal for the attack come? He tried to construct a picture of what the landing would be like—a picture which never completed itself but recurred again and again as a series of brilliant flashes in a terrific din, of shell bursts and water spouts, of tracer shells starlighting the enemy shore in flights of wondrous slow beauty that impelled one to pause in the shoreward race for cover and look heavenward. This was all that he could envisage, and part of it was evoked from memories of "battle courses," part from pure imagination.

The month of May waned. The days were interminable; the nights, in spite of exercises and training practices, were strangely unreal and empty. The men were kept continuously at games and training to prevent them from softening up. The weak ones had been weeded out; there remained only the strong who could take physical punishment without showing fatigue— men who could dash a hundred yards at top speed laden with full equipment and still have their wind when they finished, who could hurdle an eight-foot ditch with an easy leap, or climb precipitous ropes, men who could endure any weather and any strain which a battle might impose.

As the month drew to a close the night exercises and embarking practices ceased. The planning staffs had tested the operations. Everything was in readiness. Almost twenty divisions were locked away from the rest of the world. They neither saw nor spoke to men of neighbouring units. Over the embarkation areas a veil of secrecy and silence fell. Half a million men lived in a world apart. Half a million men looked into the unknown.

3

A chilly wind blew under the trees and shook the tent flap noisily.

O'Rourke, squatting on a jerry can, turned his head at the sound, then cocked his eye at the sky.

"We're in for a blow," he remarked to his companion seated on another jerry can across from him.

The two were on night kitchen fatigue. A bucket of peeled potatoes, faintly white in the muddy water, stood between them.

"S'pose so," was the laconic reply. "Let it blow. Maybe we'll get good weather tomorrow."

O'Rourke cut an eye out of a potato with surgical deftness, and surveyed the neat result for a moment. Then with disgust he let it drop into the bucket with a splash.

"No. We won't get good weather to-morrow. Haven't you noticed? When the sun sets clear it will be clear the next day. I remember my dad pointing that out to me when I was knee high to a grasshopper. And it's a fact. Any farmer knows that."

"Well, I'm no farmer. I'm just a bloody wet nurse to a bagfull of potatoes. Do you know why I always get stuck on kitchen fatigue? They say I can't do anything else. I'm sick of it. For two pins I'd go A.W.L."

"Look, Webster. You're a right guy. Don't let 'em kid you. You aren't on fatigue because you can't do anything else. It's because you've got that goddam silly, insolent way of looking at an N.C.O. when he tells you to do something. When it comes to making up a roster for fatigue duty—well, your name just heads the list—all the way down. Me—I just got stuck for not shaving yesterday. I was feeling browned off. At that I'm lucky. If I'd come up before the old man—you know, conduct to the prejudice of order and military discipline—well, I'd probably have been soaked three days' pay."

"Hell! How can I help looking the way I do? I've got a hairlip. When I smile I look like death warmed over. But if that's an offence in this army, then it's time I was going home."

"Can it, chum. You're just feeling fed up."

"You can say that again. Say, when do you think this show is going to start?"

"I don't know. But they can't keep us on ice like this for ever. It's got to break soon."

"You think the weather has something to do with it?"

"It isn't doing us any good."

"I get seasick awfully easily. Why, I got sick if I went fishing. Got a weak stomach, I guess."

"They give you pills for that on the barges."

"Before I get sick or after."

"I dunno. But it's a point."

"Well, come to think of it, I guess I won't take any of those pills. I'll just get seasick and stay that way. Then when I get to the other side I'll be so sick I won't give a damn what happens to me."

Webster cut a potato in half and threw it at the kitchen cat that was lying asleep beside the warm earthen wall of the outdoor oven. The cat leapt into the air and disappeared into the bushes."

"I'm going to go over and see Mullens for a while," O'Rourke said, jabbing his knife into a potato and rising. "If anybody comes snooping around, you know what to tell them."

"I might shock 'em," Webster commented.

Humming to himself, O'Rourke skirted the trees of the kitchen area and struck across the open ground between the headquarters and his old platoon that was half-hidden in the trees beyond the field of hard clay. When he reached the woods he picked up a well-trodden path that cut through an overgrown hawthorn hedge, across a plank bridge spanning a dark brook, and thence along the lower edge of the woods to the entrance to the platoon bivouac.

As he came to the stream he saw the company commander and Lieutenant Vantry sitting on the bridge with their feet hanging over the water. They were deep in conversation and did not notice O'Rourke. He stopped, hesitant to cross behind them. They sat across most of the tiny bridge and there was only room to shuffle past them. O'Rourke had not seen the major since the day he had reverted in rank, and though there was no longer any bitterness in his soul he felt an instinctive wariness to put himself in his notice again. He was already in the "dog house" for not shaving. Perhaps the major had been told. . . . It was too late now to turn back. Screwing up his courage he stepped out on to the bridge.

The two officers looked up at O'Rourke with surprise. For a moment an expression of annoyance showed on the major's face, as though he had caught an eavesdropper. Then, recognizing O'Rourke, he smiled warmly.

"Can you get past?" he asked.

"Yes, sir. Thank you."

As O'Rourke shuffled past the major reached out a hand to steady him from falling. The hand touched O'Rourke's trousers and he felt the slight tug. So unexpected was this gesture that he stopped for a moment, unable to move, and looked down into the major's eyes. He saw nothing but friendliness there—friendliness and something more that he could not define. For a moment he thought that the major would rise and shake his hand out of some mysterious impulse. Murmuring another "Thank you, sir," he passed on.

He had only gone a few yards when he heard the major call his name. It was not a command, but a friendly call. He retraced his steps.

"How are you getting along, O'Rourke? I've often wondered. I don't get around to the platoons as much as I'd like to now."

"I'm just fine, sir."

"Everything well at home, I hope?"

"Yes, sir. The wife is well."

"I daresay you'd like to be back now? You come from the West, don't you?"

"We'd all like to be home, sir, whether it's east or west. It's Canada, and that's all that matters."

"Well spoken, O'Rourke. We all have a hunger for home. But first we have a job to do." The major spoke consolingly, as though to himself.

O'Rourke made no reply. The two officers looked at each other. After a silence Major Brest said, with a warm, engaging smile :

"Lieutenant Vantry is understrength one corporal in his platoon. Corporal Kindrat has been struck off strength to the hospital. The vacancy is yours, O'Rourke, if you want it."

O'Rourke feigned surprise to cover some quick, cold calculating. Why jump at the chance? Obviously it was his if he wanted it. But did he really want it? His integrity demanded some appeasement for what was still to him the mysterious and unwarranted storm of ill fortune which had cast him from good graces and cost him his former rank. He knew that he wanted his rank back only for Gerda's sake. She had said little about the matter in her letters, yet it was obvious that she had been hurt for his sake.

Interpreting O'Rourke's silence as doubt of sincerity, Major Brest added :

"Lieutenant Vantry has asked for you, O'Rourke."

"Thank you, sir. But I don't know. I'm happy as a private. It doesn't matter what I am, so long as I can do a job. That's the way I see it now, sir."

"That's hardly an answer, is it?"

O'Rourke did not conceal a faint shrug. More eloquently than words it said: I am only a private soldier. An opinion can't cost me anything: I have nothing to lose.

Major Brest looked at O'Rourke. The silence became uncomfortable. He felt O'Rourke's eyes boring into his mind, probing there among the lurking shadows of his conscience, as though trying to draw from him the admission of the wrong he had once done him. There was almost mockery in the other's gaze: O'Rourke saw too much. No wonder he gave an evasive answer. He wanted him, Major Brest, to admit the injustice, to offer up some token of apology.

Yes, the fellow was too damned clever. He was touching a sore spot. Since the time he had reverted O'Rourke to private his conscience had troubled him. Often he did not know what it was that haunted him with vague remorse. His quarrel with Captain Brodin had been patched up, and the captain had been transferred to another division. They had parted almost as friends. Yet the ghost of their quarrel had remained. And that ghost was O'Rourke. There were whole weeks when the major could forget that it was O'Rourke who had paid the price for the compromise that had settled the quarrel. It was only when he heard the name of the ex-corporal, or saw his name on a nominal roll, that his conscience disturbed him. Then he was reminded that he had never really settled with Brodin at all, had never really set him in his place. All that he had done was to effect a compromise, and that, at the cost of a man's rank—a rank which, he conceived, had been as precious to O'Rourke as his own was to himself.

O'Rourke did not answer. When the major lowered his eyes and looked into the stream, O'Rourke brought his heels together and stood for a moment at attention. Then, turning quickly, he went on his way along the bank of the stream.

When he was out of earshot, Lieutenant Vantry spoke.

"I want that fellow for my corporal more than ever now."

"And you shall have him, Vantry. As soon as we cross the Channel you will have your corporal."

"He may refuse," the lieutenant mused, gazing after O'Rourke's retreating figure.

"No. You are wrong, Lieutenant. He won't ask for it, but he won't refuse it, either. He simply wants ME to give it to him. You see, he and I share a little secret."

## 4

The platoon sergeant called out the names quickly, in an irritable, clipped tone. The foreign-sounding names he did not even take the trouble to pronounce correctly, though he knew better. As he called each name the man stepped forward and took his mail, and then broke off to find a quiet, secluded spot to read it.

It was an hour before supper. A dull, throbbing heat pressed down upon the earth. The trees were strangely still : not a leaf moved. It had rained the night before and now the bright, intense heat smothered the woods with a smell of over-ripeness and rank vegetable growth.

O'Rourke heard his name called, and stepped forward. A minute later he was walking slowly toward a shaded, grassy spot near the kitchen tent, and he could not remember taking the letters which he held in his hand.

This was very strange, and he stopped suddenly and looked at the letters clutched in his hand. He raised them to his eyes, and scrutinized the handwriting of each. Yet he could not identify them. They were as familiar to him as his own name, each written in the same small meticulous script, but he could not find the name of the person who had written them. The writing was familiar and yet it was terrifyingly strange.

He dropped his hand to his side and walked on, with his head bowed over his chest. When he came to the grassy spot he lowered himself very slowly, feeling suddenly tired. There was a sour, dry taste in his mouth and he licked his lips. He laid the letters out on the grass in front of him—there were four altogether. He made them into a square pattern that looked very white against the green grass. He folded his legs under him, Indian-fashion, and picked up one of the letters. With his teeth he nipped off one corner of the envelope, then inserted a finger and opened it with a jagged tear. Then, as he had always done (and the real reason why he chose to be alone) he put the envelope, cupped open, to his nostrils and sniffed. A faint perfume tickled his senses. It was almost imperceptible, but it was there. It was Gerda's perfume—not the perfume she used behind her ears; not the perfume he had watched her daub ever so lightly with the bottle stopper to the side-swelling of her breasts at night before she put on her nightdress. This, in her letters, was mysterious. One by one he opened the letters and held them to his nostrils. Then he put them on the grass again, re-forming a white square with them.

There is something wrong, he told himself. I've never felt like this. I don't even want to read them.

And then he thought of the mad, deep, secret joy he had always known on mail days . . . the waiting for his name to be called, the happiness of holding her letters in his hand, and the stealthy, animal-like searching for a secluded place to read them, to be alone with Gerda for an hour, to dream mad, wild dreams and tear from her words, her phrases, the living form and substance of her life, enshrining it in his heart and in his mind, so that he might resurrect it again and again in the days to come.

He felt nothing now, and he searched his mind for the reason. He had given something up, changed something between Gerda and himself. Or something had been taken away from them—some precious thing that had held her close to him during the years of their separation.

He did not want to read the letters. There was nothing in them that he wanted or needed from her. That was the truth and it fevered in his mind. What he needed from her, and needed with a hunger which consumed him, she could not write into her letters. There were no words for it. There was no language on earth that could express it. All at once he felt a great sorrow for her. There was nothing she would not give him of herself. But she was so far away and he could not tell her what he hungered for. There were no words for it.

After a long time he began to read the letters, reading line after line of her small neat handwriting slowly, trying to give the words that came up to him from the white pages the substance of the time and place in which Gerda had written them. Across his mind, evoked by Gerda's mention of places and people and even by minute things such as buildings and woods and flowers which had been familiar to him since his childhood, there swept the vision of the prairie spring. He could almost feel the soft wind on his face, the fragrance of bursting, murmurous life. His pulse quickened with the blood beat of awakened life, and an overwhelming desire to stretch out his arms and enfold the vast, rich, mighty land of his home, to draw into his tortured, hungry soul the wonder, power and beauty that he had known.

When he had finished the letters he put them in his pocket and lit a cigarette, and sat thinking of Gerda and the things that her letters had contained. He could look back upon his life and see the thousand scenes and events with perfect clarity, and yet he could not see Gerda. It was strange that he could see the faces of people who had never meant anything to his life, and yet he could not see hers. He belonged to her and yet she was hardly real. He knew more about her than he knew of any other living person, but when all was said that could be said, when memory gave up all its store of treasure, what did he really know of her? What did one ever know of anyone, or of one's self? Very little. One learned another's habits, gave hunger for love and shared the mould of common clay. One loved and was loved in return. You could carry that within you to the end of time and your life was sweeter and richer with it. But it did not kill the hunger and the loneliness within you.

He found himself wondering, without any emotion whatever, if he would ever see Gerda again. It was a matter of luck and belief. He believed in his own safety for Gerda's sake. Life would be very long and empty for her if he did not come back.

Far off he heard the clang of the triangle gong summoning the men to supper. He rose and stretched himself. He was not hungry, but he would eat. That, too, was a habit.

# 17

I

On the night of the fifth of June the invasion forces set sail for the coast of Normandy.

For days everything had been in readiness, but the weather, unusual for the month of June, had played strange caprices with the plans of the military leaders. Strong winds lashed the Channel seas and made the crossing a hazardous prospect for the light, shallow draught invasion craft. The skies were overcast and at times the sea was shrouded in mist, which made impossible a complete umbrella of support to the ground forces such as had been planned.

Originally planned for the fourth of June, the fourth anniversary of Dunkirk, D-Day was postponed for forty-eight hours. The weather improved slightly, but the moments of sudden calm and clear visibility were broken by buffeting winds and fast-driven clouds. Everything depended upon the weather. The assault upon the enemy beaches had to be made at low tide. A delay of several days would alter the entire plan; might, in truth, alter the whole course of the war.

The weather continued to improve slightly. There were longer periods of calm and sunshine, of clear skies and summer warmth. Weather experts were divided in their predictions : it might grow worse, or it might improve, or it might remain variable and wholly unpredictable.

Finally, on the night of June the 5th, in Supreme Allied Headquarters, one man made the decision—the decision upon which the fate of millions rested. Within an hour the greatest armada ever assembled on one spot of the earth's surface, set sail. Cradled by the battle fleets of three nations, protected overhead by tens of thousands of aircraft, the invasion armada sailed out into the darkness, into the hands of an unknown fate.

British and American airborne divisions landed at dawn and moved to take bridges and strategic positions. Shortly thereafter, the invasion barges touched down on the sandy beaches along the great arc of the bay of the Seine, from the mouth of the River Orne in the east to the Grande Rade in the west. In the first wave the 6th Airborne Division of the British came down along the east side of the Caen Canal, between Caen and the sea. The 3rd Canadian Division landed at Courseulles and Bernieres. A few miles to the west the 50th British Infantry came ashore, and began the thrust toward Bayeaux. Still further west the 1st and 29th U.S. Infantry supported their 82nd and 101st Airborne Divisions, which had landed at dawn.

Of the 3rd Canadian Division two infantry brigades landed in the first wave. One brigade of Westerners landed at Courseulles-sur-Mer. The other, an Eastern Brigade, touched down on a fine stretch of landing beach between Bernieres and St Aubin.

Prelude to the landings was a mighty naval bombardment by destroyers, cruisers, monitors and battleships, steaming slowly offshore as a seaward screen to the landing craft. Under this mighty barrage of screaming shells and thundering explosions the infantry streamed from the yawning doors of the barges across the sandy beaches toward the land. Engineer sappers cleared mines and forged pathways across the sands over which the infantry advanced in long, scattered lines, zig-zagging as they went, half crouched, at times flat to fire at a sniper, or a mortar crew on the higher ground along the beach road, then making another dash of a few yards, and falling again to blaze away at the Hun.

Cleverly entrenched, German snipers took their toll of the advancing infantry and mortar fire cut the moving columns to pieces. But barge after barge disgorged its load of men, and in time the beach swarmed with the Canadians. Machine-gun fire from pill boxes swept the length of the beach, and men fell all about, but still the advance continued, yard by yard, foot by foot. The Canadian mortar sections set up on the open beach and begun to return the Huns' fire, blasting their mortar crews off the higher ground, knocking out pill boxes and clearing the hidden ground for their comrades.

The naval bombardment from off-shore ships had lifted and moved inland, laying an ever-advancing wall of shell bursts over the towns of Courseulles and Bernieres and beyond them along the roads. The invaders broke through the beach obstacles, cut through the barbed wire and stormed the strong points at close range.

At Courseulles, the Western Brigade had as their first objective the strong coastal defences on either side of the inlet at the mouth of the River Seulles, which gave entry to the heart of the town itself. Here the Hun put up a withering mortar and artillery fire, devastatingly accurate. Inch by inch the Canadians advanced through the beach obstacles, barbed wire and mines, and fought their way into the concrete emplacements and trench systems. The enemy fought tenaciously to the very end, giving no quarter and asking none. Tanks came ashore in support of the infantry and raced through mine-cleared lanes for the town itself. Infantry and armour over-ran the beach defences, silenced the guns and swarmed into the town, through the stone streets which rocked in the din of the battle. With machine guns, rifles and grenades the infantry cleared the streets in a slow advance toward the market-place, backed up by the roaring, rumbling tanks, whose guns smashed the German artillery to shrapnel, dissolved fortified road blocks to dust. Smoke clouded, shattered, littered with German dead, the town was finally occupied, and with it fell the prize of an elaborate German headquarters. Behind it, amid the wreckage and litter of the battered beach, the brigade left hundreds of its dead and wounded to the care of the landing craft crews.

Outside the town, one company broke off and captured Graye-sur-Mer, a short distance to the west. Others, racing forward on foot, took the villages of Banville and Ste Croix to the south-west. Linking up their main forces again, they struck at Riviers, where the Mue river from the south joins the Seulles river on its way to the sea. Fighting their way through this village the brigade struck due south down the western side of the wooded Mue river valley. Now, nearly five miles inland, they were forced to slow their pace. Winding indolently through wooded banks the tiny stream winked bright metallic flashes of light at the hostile new-comers. The valley shimmered its mantle of greenery and seemed possessed of an ageless, forgotten beauty. The narrow road that wound along the course of the river, at times through an overhanging tracery of boughs and deep, soft coolness, emerging suddenly into the bright daylight to skirt the side of farmyards, only to disappear again into the woods, seemed to lead to nowhere in particular. Overhead the Air Force roared with a continuous deep, throaty rumble, and, far off yet thunderously near, the mighty roar of the naval guns shook the earth. Somewhere ahead of the advancing column the shells were bursting and the thunder rolled across the land and up the winding valley.

Meanwhile the Eastern brigade, landing at Bernieres and St Aubin, a mile or so to the east of Courseulles, met tremendous resistance on the beach and in pill boxes and large emplacements along the shore line. Even as they left their barges and plunged into the surf, machine-gun fire raked them and artillery blasted at the barges. The dead floated upon the water, bobbing up and down on the surf. The men plunged ashore through the surf, grasped at the floating dead and wounded nearest to them, without taking their eyes off the shoreline, or deviating from their path, and dragged them to the sand. It was strange to see the men fall all along the beach and in the water —strange and terrifying to have your comrade next to you suddenly drop, and feel an instant sense of deliverance, and then an overwhelming frenzy of rage.

The first staggering lines of men to leave the barges were mowed down. Only a few reached the sand and sprawled behind the beach defences and the barbed wire, not hidden nor covered at all, but lying spreadeagle out on the sand behind the tangle of darkened, rusty defences, blazing away at the enemy, whenever they could see him. And the second wave came on and were mowed down, and still some lived and reached the sand and dug in with their elbows and toes and opened fire, while the machine-guns raked them and reached over them to the water's edge, and artillery shells tore up the sand and the men and even the defences themselves. It was not an assault, for those first men—not in the real sense. It was a fight against a hellish terror to reach the sand, and then it was a fight simply to lie there and hold on to a bit of sand while all the world rocked and belched and thundered and everything all about them flew into a thousand dark, stinging little pieces.

The water was dark with floating bodies that were like pieces of bobbing cork in the surf. And the beach, along the tide water lines, was littered with dead and wounded, and the wounded were as motionless as the dead. Behind the barges, out to sea, the thunder of the naval bombardment was like a long hard, splitting thunder-roll that came over the beach again and again and had no ending. There were moments of strange, startling quiet in the rattle of the enemy machine-guns, and even the artillery fire seemed to rise and fall away and then come again. But these moments of tense, unreal calm along the beach were so brief as to be almost little more than the way a continuous sound rises and falls when it is caught by the wind. In those moments the men did not breathe, but lay waiting, for the shell burst that would be the end, for the hot, instant, tearing shock of a bullet. Blood seeped into the tide-washed sands; blood floated momentarily on the sea, bright ruby red on the green surf lulls, to disappear in an instant in the fury and lash of the water upon the shore.

But men did live in that hell, and they reached the dry

sands. If courage was the price of freedom, the men of D-Day bought it for the world, for all time.

Slowly, infinitely, dashing zig-zag across the sands, through the tangle of the defences, through the hidden mines, through the barbed wire, through the hail of bullets and blasting shells, they stormed the pill boxes and the big concrete emplacements and over-ran them. With the support of their tanks they stormed Bernieres and took it, by grim hand-to-hand street fighting. A large part of St Aubin had to be by-passed, for the street fighting there was so fierce that it threatened to hold up the advance inland. The centre of the town was left to be cleaned out by British Commandos who had landed, and the brigade swept inland. Across the open farm fields they struck at Tailleville, a hamlet sitting astride an east-west road, due south of their landing point. The fields were alive with German positions, and for each one a bloody battle in miniature raged; across the rolling farmlands a dozen battles raged at once. In one position they came upon more than a dozen 77-millimetre guns in deep concrete pits with an elaborate trench system connecting the guns. The fields were mined, and the network of tiny lanes was blocked with anti-tank guns. Every mile or two there were German strong points that had to be cleared from the path of the advance. Men and tanks littered the fields and roads and a pall of smoke hung over the land.

But the brigade, once in the open, advanced with gathering speed. There were many small groups of enemy left behind in the heat of battle, and these lay in hiding for days, sniping at the beachhead reinforcements that later passed through, until they were cleared out.

Swinging south-west from Tailleville, they charged at Beny-sur-Mer, a town four miles from the coast which commanded the road to Caen. Here in the woods and orchards surrounding the town the infantry fought hand-to-hand with the Germans. Snipers, hidden in trees and behind stone fences, took their toll and mortar shells fell like hail. Slowly, foot by foot, the Canadians took the woods and the town itself, and stood astride the road to Caen.

The third brigade of the division, a Central Canadian formation, landed at midday at Bernieres. Fresh, and itching for a fight, with the infantry riding on the tanks, on bicycles, on Bren carriers and every piece of mechanical equipment, the brigade raced inland to take up the battle. At Beny-sur-Mer they swept through the lines of the Eastern brigade and drove southward along the Caen road through the village of Basly, and down the eastern side of the Mue river valley. Here, in this rich farmland country, the enemy had established cleverly hidden defences and forward artillery observation posts. Resistance grew stronger with every mile the brigade advanced. Artillery and mortar fire at times threatened to paralyse the columns, and snipers took a heavy toll. Finally, late in the day, in the area of Villons-les-Buissons, enemy tanks and infantry charged out to do battle. The battle for Caen was on, a battle which was to rage with increasing ferocity for weeks.

Meanwhile, along the western side of the Mue valley, the Western brigade was pushing southward. From the wooded slopes on either side of the valley the Germans dropped mortar shells upon the columns working up the river road, and snipers, firing from the valley caves, from trees, from stone fences, from farm buildings and churches, thinned the long single lines of marching infantry and picked off the transport drivers at will.

One after another the tiny, clotted, river villages fell to the Canadians. In the rear, the men had time to snatch moments of rest, though the nerve-racking sniper fire made them take cover. Overhead there was a continual whistle of shells thrown over by the ships that stood offshore in the Channel, and the thunder of the bursting shells in the enemy's lines ahead filled the valley and made the earth tremble. In the spearhead of the advance there was no rest. Every farm building, every stone fence, every thicket and tree had to be explored. The scouts, working well ahead of the columns, reported anti-tank guns around the bends of the road, sighted toward the advancing tanks, or in ditches and woods commanding the road.

From one position after another the enemy was blasted, and steadily, slowly, like a great irresistible wave the brigade pushed southward down the valley. They cut the Caen–Bayeux road and took up positions on high ground across it. There, for days to come, they held on, beating back every savage attack which the enemy threw against them.

2

When the invasion craft, carrying O'Rourke's company, touched down on the French coast and the great yawning doors opened one after another to expel the loads of men and equipment, the beach had been won. An unbelievable confusion of litter charred, twisted and sand blasted, lay all about. Along the water's edge some boats were still burning, others were swamped, while others were strange, unidentifiable masses of twisted, surf-washed scrap. Among the ruined ships bodies floated. O'Rourke, looking over the side, saw one body float past his ship as it came in. It was floating chest upward. The face was greenish-white and horribly swollen. It bobbed up and down slowly, as though it were very tired, and gradually it was drawn out to sea by the wake of the ship.

Dozens of craft were already unloading along the beach, and streams of vehicles and equipment of every kind poured out of the dark caverns of the ships, down the ramps into the water and up across the beach, converging into one dense, throbbing column moving along the beach road. Many vehicles had stalled in the water, between the ships and the first sands. Others, disabled, were scattered along the sands. Armoured bulldozers were forging road paths across the sands, building up tidal embankments, and pushing the litter of blasted beach defences out of the way. Along the sands, too, mine-clearing tanks worked at clearing new pathways for the unloading equipment, their great spinning chains flailing the sands unmercifully. Now and then they struck off a mine and a cloud of sand enveloped the tank and the whole beach trembled. The tanks worked on slowly, as though nothing unusual had happened.

Far down the beach, in front of a concrete beach wall, half a dozen landing barges were loading wounded. The wounded lay in long rows under the beach wall. Medical orderlies put them on stretchers and carried them across the sands, weaving in and out of the litter and around the dead, and then through knee-deep water to the barges. The orderlies brought back empty stretchers for more wounded. They worked as though they were in a separate world, seen only through heavy glass from the other end of the beach. They seemed utterly indifferent to what was going on a few hundred yards from them. Their job was to dress the wounded and put them on the barges for evacuations to Blighty. They did not seem to even hear the thunderous naval barrage from the great fleet in the Channel, the thunder that crashed the sky and had no ending but rolled on and on forever overhead.

The vehicles of the company had to wade through a few feet of water. Some stalled and were left to the water until the barges were empty, then they were towed out by armoured recovery tanks. Along the beach road and in the area directly behind the beach, in the sand dunes, the platoons formed up. One platoon carried supplies, another carried ammunition, another petrol, and then there was the workshop platoon and the company headquarters, consisting of administrative vehicles.

A wave of excitement swept through the company, down through the lines of vehicles. The men laughed and shouted to one another and made jokes about the sanity of army commanders who had prophesied a swim to shore, and all manner of gruesome possibilities. Here they were ashore in France and no-one had got wet, no-one had been fired on, and no-one cared a damn whether he ever saw England again or not. Not at that moment anyway.

Between them and the hinterland lay a fringe of consumptive-looking trees, which, here and there, had been blasted and stripped bare by gun fire. Behind the trees, on a gradual upsweep of grain fields, two peasants worked beside a dirt road. Only their heads and shoulders could be seen above the standing grain. What they worked at was a mystery, and their appearance there on what had been a battlefield only a few hours before, seemed so strange that they might have suddenly appeared out of the earth. Shell holes broke the smoothness of the grain waving in light and shadow over the land.

Over the crest of the grain fields, beyond the fringe of trees, lay the real France. Somewhere up ahead the brigade was fighting. The company would make contact with it during the night. Already the liaison officer had gone forward in his jeep, disappearing in a swirling cloud of dust. The men were in high spirits.

All along the beach there was feverish activity. Ack-ack batteries were moving into position; artillery was coming off the sands and moving forward: engineer beach parties with bulldozers and shovels were setting to work levelling off pathways through the sands to the roads. Already the vast minute organization of a vast army entering upon an operation was setting to work to keep the lines of communication from tangling, and to feed the forward areas.

One by one the platoons moved inland, along a dusty road which tanks had already churned up, through a dreary grey stone village, and out into the country. The village was almost deserted. A small, dirty boy, in a torn calico dress and wooden shoes, sucked a finger as he watched the convoy whirl past from the safey of a doorway. No glass remained in the windows of the houses, and many of the buildings had neat round shell holes clean through them. The church spire, which must have contained a sniper, was cut half-way by a shell. A large crucifix standing in front of the church was untouched.

Now and then along the road they came upon dead. Some

were Germans and some were Canadians. You could tell from the type of helmet or the respirator that lay with them. There was no other way of identifying them, their faces were black and shapeless, or they had no faces at all, and their bodies were twisted and stiff, as though encased in dirty cement casts.

There were dead horses and cattle in the fields, too, lying shapeless and dark around the shell craters. The smell over the land was nauseating—that sickly-sweet putrefying stink of the battlefield. Across the fields, through the standing grain, were thin waving pathways trodden by the infantry as they had advanced, alert to the slightest movement of the hidden enemy. Sometimes these pathways cut clear across the fields and disappeared. Or, again, they ended abruptly in the fields, and there the dead lay too, where they had fallen, killed outright, or from long-bleeding wounds. Tanks, too, had swept across the fields and their tracks made strange flowing patterns through the grain that, from a distant height, looked like dark-lined shadows in the gold. Here and there across the countryside lay a blasted, burned-out tank, looking like a dark, grim spectre with its cannon pointing out into nowhere.

They halted outside a small village, in a lane of tall trees. Over the village, from the other side, a great pall of black smoke rose into the sky.

Each man cooked his own meal in his mess tins, with his Sten gun lying on the ground beside him as he squatted. A peasant girl came along the road leading a donkey that pulled a small water cart. She was fat and dirty, but her face shone with a bright innocent smile. The men teased her, and flirted, some in English, to which she shook her head, and others in French, to which she replied in a fast patter and with a coquettish shrug of her shoulders. Once she stopped and replied to a French-Canadian and her donkey wagged first one ear and then the other, inquisitively.

One by one the men crawled under their vehicles or into the ditch to sleep. Near the head of the column two sergeants smoked, and argued about the possibility of a piece of work one, or both were supposed to do.

"Go to hell, you two, and let a fellow sleep," someone yelled from beneath a lorry.

The sergeants glared down the column, but the voice was suddenly quiet.

"Yeah," another added. "Take your damned two-bit worry and drown it. Let's go to sleep."

"Shut up!"

From afar came the dull, continuous thud of artillery.

Sometimes it seemed quite close, and then it fell away into the distance. When it came close it was suddenly terrifying, and many a man shivered and pretended to himself that he was cold. And some thought of the infantry along the front line ahead, who crept between the fire of the guns and lived only from minute to minute.

"Listen to those guns. God! Those poor bastards up front are getting hell!"

And a wiseacre replied:

"Who knows? They might be George's guns, and then it's all right. So why worry?"

A burly driver, shirtless and grisled, with a chest like an ape, kicked out at the speaker with the heel of his boot.

"That for you, you bastard, and if you want to make any more bright wisecracks, stand up, and I'll tie your ears under your trousers."

Silence then. They slept fitfully. The artillery pounded away all night, and tank reinforcements swept across the country, roaring through the darkness. Shortly after midnight the German planes came over, and the mobile ack-ack gunners threw everything into the sky but the guns themselves.

In the early morning the company unloaded its ammunition and petrol and supplies of "compo" rations in a large wheatfield beside the road. They did not know if the field was mined or not. Nor did they care. Their orders had come through by then, and everyone was impatient for the work ahead. They stacked their loads and returned to the beach for more supplies. By the time they had returned, loaded again, to the wheatfield, the stacks of ammunition and supplies had dwindled. Front line transport had already drawn the requirements for the day's fighting, and had returned to the fighting lines.

Thereafter, for many weeks, through a long whirl of rushing days and nights that were filled with toil and sweat and terror, first and second line transport strove to keep the fighting men supplied with the three essentials—ammunition, petrol and food supplies. No-one cared a damn if his trousers were torn, or burnt, or if he had a tunic or not. Nothing mattered, so long as there was ammunition to fill the guns, and petrol to push the columns forward, and food to fill the stomach. Mail from home was a luxury—the rarest delight of all. It came forward with the supplies. With these bare necessities the men fought, and held to their lines.

Each night the men in the line dug themselves their foxholes. Rarely did they sleep in the same spot. Times there were when they slept in the holes the Boche had dug for himself the night before; and, again, the Boche slept in theirs. The line wavered back and forward, whipping into a straight line like a stretched band reverberating back and forth and finally becoming a hard, taut line. Human life was the line, and it was human will and guts that beat the line straight and held it there until the next assault set it again into frenzied animation.

# 18

LATE in June, O'Rourke was made corporal of a section. He had expected it, for rumour had whispered it through the platoons. It was, therefore, no surprise when he was formally paraded and given back his old rank.

After his parade, he took the afternoon off and sat by the side of his foxhole and wrote Gerda a long letter. It seemed to him long weeks since he had written to her, and it was with a twinge of conscience that he realized how anxious those weeks had been for her. He tried to make up for it in his letter.

DEAREST GERDA,

I am squatting beside my foxhole trying to write you this letter with the paper on a ration case. It's a bright sunny day, for a change, and it feels good to be alive. In the mud and rain you don't think life's worth a damn, but when the sun shines it is all right.

We all sleep in foxholes at night—or all day for us, because we work at night, mostly. The rain seeps down into them, no matter what you do to keep it out, and it's good to get a warm day like this to dry things out. Still, it's better to be wet and alive than wet and dead.

The food is all right. It's all canned stuff, but it keeps us going, and in case we run out of our own cigarettes there's an issue with the rations to help out. I'd like you to send me some tinned stuff—like meat balls and steak and onions, if you can get them, and some Postum, because you can make that with just hot water, and often times you have to get moving before the water boils, and Postum is easy to make. Oh, yes, and some chewing gum. If you can put yourself in the parcel, come along, and I'll dig the foxhole big enough for the both of us.

Well, Gerda, there isn't much to tell you. I'm feeling fine, and nothing has happened to me yet. The boys are held along this line and it seems they'll never be able to get farther, but I guess they will some time.

The country around here is very much like home, Gerda.

The land is rich, too. The buildings are all heavy grey stone and not like ours, but the land is like home, and now the grain is ripening. I think of our place a lot, Gerda, and wish I were back. Another year, I think, and we'll all be come home—all that are left, that is. There's a good many buried in these fields hereabouts that won't see home again, and when I see their little crosses it makes me think of their families who won't see them again.

Your letters are coming fine, darling, and I read them over and over. At night when I am on the road in the dark I think of the things you say in your letters, and then I don't worry about what's ahead. In a few more months I'll be home with you. It won't be long now. You have all my love, for always.

BOB

After he had finished the letter he laid it on the grass in front of him. He took off his shirt and stretched out in the sun, lying on his stomach. The air was heavy with the smell of clover and ripe grain. There was another smell, too, faintly nauseating, rather like the odour of mouldy, damp rubbish.

'I wonder what Gerda is doing now,' he thought, fingering the letter. 'Very likely she is just getting up, or having breakfast.'

He let his mind wander back through time. Breakfast with Gerda had always been a sort of adventure. It began a new day, and every day with her had been different—like turning the pages of a picture book.

He remembered how she always kissed him before she poured his coffee, bending down to him, with a hand on the back of his head, and her lips slowly pressing against his. And sometimes she said, softly, "Thank you, Bob, for the lovely night." Sometimes, though, she only looked at him, and her eyes were misty and soft. As distinctly as though she stood beside him again, he could feel the touch of her hand upon his head.

He rolled over on his back and groaned. Thoughts were all a man had, really, and they tormented him almost to madness. In thoughts you could have all that you had ever known —all but the physical body and substance of the past. You could recall everything of the past, but you could not catch and hold it. Love was like that. You could dream and think of your wife, and it brought you happiness. You could remember how it was, loving her, possessing her, but you could not FEEL it. You could not reach out and touch her, hold her again in your grasp. Memory was of the same stuff as dreams.

Somewhere down along the Bayeux road some field guns started firing. At first there were only two shots, then, a moment later, half a dozen opened up in quick succession. A full minute of silence then everything along the front started firing. It was not thunder they made, but a vast jumble of staccato noises. It seemed to sweep along the line, and the conglomerate of roaring sound rose and fell and came again and again.

O'Rourke looked along the vehicle lines of his company. No one had moved at the sound. Everywhere everything was the same. Some men lay in the sun, sprawled naked, others sat in tight circles in the shade of vehicles gambling and cursing. One man was shaving, another was gazing at a photograph, another was writing. Over beside a clump of bushes two men were in the latrines and three more hung around waiting beside the waist-high canvas screen. Nothing had changed. Everyone behaved as though the artillery barrage was no business of his.

"If anybody had told me a month ago we'd sit around and pay no attention to a barrage like this, I'd have called him a liar," O'Rourke reflected. "Like as not this won't even wake the Old Man out of his siesta, though it might crack his bottle of Scotch."

Indeed, no-one cared about the artillery barrage, though the logical reaction to it would be a counter-barrage on the Canadian positions from the German lines. It wasn't like the Hun to sit and take it for long and not give it back with interest. Some people said the Hun didn't have the artillery he should have, but even if that were true, he still had a lot of mortars, and when he was out of mortar range he just sent his mortar crews forward with covering infantry and grenadiers, and they held the ground while the mortar men peppered the Canadian lines so accurately that at times they laid down a square pattern, or a circle just to show they could do it. They were so accurate they could have written their names in mortar bursts along our lines, and even dotted their i's. In fact, some said that the Hun could spell out some very obscene words with mortar craters if you wanted to stick around and read them.

O'Rourke set to work washing his hair, using a cutaway biscuit tin for a basin. When he came to rinse his hair he filled an ammunition case with water and poured it over his head. It was then that he remembered how Gerda had always rinsed his hair, pouring the water over his head slowly. Sometimes she laid a hand fondly on his back as she held the jug over him, and sometimes, too, she let some of the water run down his back in a playful mood that sent him chasing her about the room. When he caught her they had a tussle that always ended in love-making.

He shook the water from his dark hair, and began to dry it.

"Almost everything I do makes me remember something about her," he said to himself, aloud. With a sudden, overwhelming wave of tenderness for her he took her photo out of his inner pocket and gazed at it while the water dripped from his head.

# 19

---

I

THE first light of day was creeping across the drenched earth. It brought cold comfort. Ceaseless lashing rain drove across the fields. The ditches overflowed and flooded the roads. Where shell craters cut the roads great pools of water lay, hiding the deep holes and the rutted fillings. Tethered cattle in the fields stood cold and forlorn against the grey that crept stealthily in under the dark night sky.

The world was strangely still. The guns that had blazed all night along the front were quiet now. No traffic moved on the roads. There was only the wind-driven rain that lashed the earth and made the trees moan and cry in torment.

Along the battlefront no sound broke the ceaseless cry and moan of the driven rain. It was as though the night-long downpour had washed from every soul the will and desire to fight. It was like a world from which all life had fled.

Into this desolate scene rode a dispatch rider. The lonely guard by the orchard gate heard the machine long before the tiny disc of its riding light broke out of the semi-darkness and came slowly across the open stretch of road toward the platoon location.

The guard remained close in under the darkness of the hedge by the orchard gate. He lifted his Sten gun slowly and set it at the cock, and his numbed fingers moved down to the trigger guard. He watched the motor cycle approach along the road. With a faint smile he saw it slow down to a crawl when it hit each shell crater, saw the sudden slow splash of the water around the machine, heard it sputter and then go on again. He knew where each crater lay in the road. Had there been anyone with him on guard, he would willingly have bet on a chance that the approaching D.R. would take a spill before he could reach the orchard, for the craters were filled with water and could not be seen. But the D.R. negotiated each crater expertly: he was no greenhorn. Long before he had reached the orchard entrance the guard had decided the D.R. was someone who knew the road, and knew it well. Either that or he was wearing horseshoes.

As the D.R. turned in toward the orchard he was challenged by a command to halt, shouted loudly enough to be heard by the guard corporal, if that individual in a nearby tent were awake. The D.R. took his time to obey the order. He brought his machine to a halt exactly at the entrance, and sat astride his machine with a bored expression on his streaming face. The usual formalities of guards amused him. There was never anything original in their challenges. Now the guard of an infantry unit was different. He really meant it, and a stranger halted on the spot.

The guard moved out of hiding by the hedge. When he saw the unit sign on the motor cycle he put his Sten gun on the "safe."

"What's your name?" he asked in a surly tone.

"Lemke is my name, as you bloody well know, and I'm D.R. from company H.Q. You know that, too. What you don't know is that I've got a message for the O.C. of your platoon, and it's urgent. So if you hold me up with it any longer you'll still be doing guard duty when we reach Berlin."

"Cut the lip, fellow. I'm doing my job. Stay here while I get the corporal."

The D.R. lit a smoke and listened while the guard woke the corporal. He heard the muffled curses from the tent, and laughed to himself.

The guard returned to the gate. He was in a more amiable mood. He recognized in the D.R. a kindred soul, drenched to the skin as he was himself, miserable and tired, while others slept dry and warm. He felt in secret conspiracy with the other in getting the corporal out of his warm blankets.

"He'll be out in a minute. I can't take the message myself," he remarked apologetically.

The D.R. smiled tolerantly, but made no reply.

"Think we'll ever get any summer?" the guard asked, conversationally.

"We're getting it. Hitler had his number one magician fix this up specially for us. Personally, I like it."

"The rain must have soaked into your brain."

"No. It's better than the dust, when you're riding one of these things. Try it, some time."

The guard corporal came trudging up through the mud, a gas cape thrown over his shoulders.

"Message from H.Q. for the platoon O.C.," said the D.R.

The corporal snorted.

"Why the hell couldn't they hold on to it till after breakfast? This is no time to be waking people up."

"I don't know, Corporal. But I'll give the major your question if you like. Do you want me to give him your compliments with it?"

"I'll give you a cuff on the ear. Hand over the message."

"Here it is, and here's my book. Just sign for it there and enter the time. It's now 4.30 or thereabouts. Let's see. . . . Yep, 4.35."

He turned his bike around.

"Don't get your feet wet, boys," he called over his shoulder as he drove away. He accelerated deliberately, and his rear wheel threw a stream of mud over the corporal.

"Why you——!"

But the D.R. was already a dim figure receding down the road, lightly, almost gaily, flipping his bike back and forth across the roadway, dodging the puddles and shell-holes.

"I'll have to wake the boss up, I guess," grumbled the corporal. He peered at the message, already rain-soaked. "It doesn't see to be very urgent."

"You can't tell, Corporal. Might be. They say there's a war on hereabouts."

With that laconic remark the guard began to pace back and forth across the orchard gate, in an exaggerated guardsman fashion, but whistling softly between his teeth the tune of "The Old Grey Mare."

Scowling darkly and wiping the rain off the end of his nose with the back of his hand, the corporal plodded down the lane to the lieutenant's tent. The tent was dark and smelled strongly of damp clothes and petrol fumes. He tapped the sleeping form on the back. Getting no response, he shook the Safari bed violently. The lieutenant jumped and sat up, startled, rubbing his eyes.

"It's the guard corporal, sir."

"Corporal, never wake a man like that. Do it gradually. It's really a fine art. I recommend you to make a study of it in your spare time. Are you a married man?"

"No, sir. Why?"

"Then, Corporal, you won't know what I mean."

"No, sir. There's a message, sir."

The lieutenant scratched himself sleepily.

"Do we have to move our location?"

"No, sir. It's a detail for a section to go out."

"That's disappointing. I've always believed that messages

that came in the dead of night were for location moves. This upsets my theory. Strike a light and I'll have a look at it. There's a good lad."

The corporal held his flashlight over the officer's tousled head. The officer read the message, and sat thinking for several minutes in silence. The corporal's hand grew tired of holding the light and he fidgeted.

"You can put out the light, Corporal. Wake Sergeant Ganter and send him to me."

When the corporal had gone the lieutenant lit a cigarette and lay in the darkness listening to the rain lashing on the canvas. He rubbed his stomach under the blankets and thought of Sunday mornings at home when he used to lie in bed in the warmth and read the papers before getting up. He did not think of his wife when he thought of the comforts of home. She was neither passionate nor vivacious, and reminded him always of the atmosphere of a hospital. She looked after him, had a flare for music and was a good cook, but she occupied no place in his dreams.

"I'll send O'Rourke on this detail," he said to himself, suddenly, as though the sensual act of rubbing his stomach had produced the solution to a question.

He heard someone cough, heard the sucking sound of boots in the mud, then the tent flap parted."

"You wanted me, sir?"

"Yes, Sergeant, come in. I'm just getting up."

"We'll have to tow most of the vehicles out of the mud today," the sergeant remarked, as though he was concerned with much greater issues than the lieutenant's effort to get out of bed.

"We ought to move location, sir," he continued. "We ought to get out of this mud before the vehicles sink out of sight."

"We ought to, Sergeant," the officer replied, wearily. "We ought to, indeed. But where could we go? One field is as muddy as the next. However, that's unimportant just now. We have to send a detail of one section out on attachment to a tank outfit. It may only be for a couple of days, but possibly longer."

He handed the sergeant the message.

"It's all there. Corporal O'Rourke will take the detail. Tell him to report to the Regimental H.Q. at the map reference given there. See that he has the necessary map, too. They will give him all details there. The vehicles must be at the R.H.Q. by 0800 hours, so you will have to nip to it to get the men fed and on the road. When you have done that report to me, will you?"

"Right, sir. I'll get them away as soon as possible. Will they take rations with them?"

"Give them a day's rations. No, on second thought, the tank unit will undoubtedly provide rations, so don't bother. It will give our cooks a bit extra to work with, won't it?"

"That's right, sir," was the ready answer. There was a sly note in it.

After the sergeant had gone the officer sank back in his blankets, lit another cigarette and consciously drew back across his mind the reveries which had been interrupted. For a moment the war faded and he was home again. So mellow were his thoughts that he felt the stirrings of a genuine deep affection for his wife, and laughed quietly to himself at this discovery, thinking of her starched, crisp, perfumeless person. War and time, he decided, had changed him.

2

The rain had lightened by the time O'Rourke got his section out of the orchard and headed down the pock-marked road. They travelled slowly; there was no traffic on the road, for it was the dawn lull.

His route took him down the Caen road through Pierrepont, Camilly and Cairon, then south along the west bank of the Mue river to where the R.H.Q. was located.

R.H.Q. was busy that morning. A new assault was being prepared and everyone was engaged on working out the tasks for the various squadrons. As O'Rourke's section was to supply two of the squadrons, he had to wait for his orders until the plans were prepared.

While they waited the men lit oil fires and boiled water for shaving. One man who had missed breakfast made tea for all. Everyone contributed something from their hoard of stolen supplies, and soon a meal was in preparation.

"What's this detail all about?" a man named Seltzer asked, as they sat around the fire.

"Hauling ammo and supplies for tanks, that's all I know about it," O'Rourke replied, sipping a mug of tea and munching a piece of hard tack.

"A lot of night work, I suppose," the lance-corporal commented.

"That won't be any different, then."

"The point I don't like about it," observed O'Rourke, "is that we'll have to off-load to the tanks out in the open. They'll give us some co-ordinate to pin-point on the map, and we'll have to be there and no guessing about it. We'll have to be right every time. Tanks can't stand in one spot for long, at least not in this open country."

"Who is this cocker now?" asked someone.

Everyone turned to watch a tank corps man plodding across to the vehicles.

"You corporal of these vehicles?" asked the man, when he came up to the fire.

"That's me," replied O'Rourke.

"Here's your dope, then." And he handed O'Rourke his orders.

"The major says you're to get cracking right away."

"We'll finish our tea first," replied O'Rourke.

"You don't know the major?"

"No, never met him."

"Then, brother, take a tip. Get cracking, or you'll meet him, but not the way you'd like to."

"Okay, fellow. Thanks."

"Come on, boys, get ready while I unravel the mysteries of this order, then we'll get under way."

The orders listed the co-ordinate where the section was to load, the types of ammunition to be loaded, the amount of compo pack supplies and the co-ordinate to which they had to be delivered to the squadrons, as well as the time of delivery. This last was repeated and stressed as urgent.

They set out across the rolling plain. By mid-morning the rain had stopped and a feeble sun shone out from between great rolling clouds. Between the swift, racing clouds, a brilliant azure sky promised good weather. So swiftly did the clouds collide and break and race across the sun that the alternating light and shadow made strange, sudden shapes over the plain.

By noon the clouds had gone, the sky was a washed blue from which the sun beat down unmercifully upon the weaving, snake-like streams of movement upon the roads. Along the roadsides the mud of the night had already dried and clouds of dust swirled up from the wheels. Far across the Normandy plain, too, gigantic dust clouds marked the runways of the invasion airports where fighter planes were already taking off, every fighter, with a bomb under each wing, like a strange dark bird hugging eggs to its breast. The planes rose and banked and circled above the roads, then turned inland to their targets. Above them the air circus flew in neat formations. These, the rocket-firing planes, flew in queues, waiting for orders from the ground forces. As soon as they received a target they peeled off and went diving earthward at tremendous speed.

On the Tailleville–Delivrande road, O'Rourke picked up the tank ammunition and petrol and further down the same road, in a very muddy field, he loaded the cases of supplies. It was already past noon and he decided to move along his route for a few miles and find a place where he could take the section off the road for the midday meal.

He found a pasture field with a crossing over a deep ditch. The field had harboured tanks at one time and the earth was laced with their tread marks. This was what he had hoped for. Where tanks had been there would be no mines. He pulled the vehicles into the field and scattered them about, not so much as a precaution against an air attack, as for appearances' sake, should a brass hat drive past.

The men made a fire, burning oil in a tin, using sod in the bottom of the tin to produce a slow-burning fire. They brewed tea in a cutaway biscuit tin. At the supply point where they had loaded the compo rations for the tank squadrons they had filched two extra cases. These would last them for two days: there was no need to starve with so many supply points in the country and so many vegetables growing in the fields. They made a hearty meal of canned stew and new potatoes. When they had finished some cleaned the fire-blacking off their mess tins with sand, other left them dirty, stowing them away behind their seats in the lorries.

O'Rourke, sitting sprawled against his blanket roll some distance from the fire, watched them with a smile of amusement. He felt he knew them all so well. The fellows who were dirty about little things like mess tins and shaving were the ones who had to be watched. They were the ones who neglected their vehicles. There were only three of them, really—Aylmer, Josephs and Curtin. Of the three, Josephs was the worst. He was an Indian, a Cree from northern Manitoba. He had a short, ape-like body, with rounded shoulders and a bull neck. His face, seldom washed, looked like a mask of some ugly, inscrutable god. His only expression was a broad smile that revealed a mouthful of dirty teeth. This smile would appear quite suddenly and for no apparent reason. Often, in his darkest moods, he smiled like this.

Aylmer and Curtin had been "dead-end kids" at one time.

Though the army had taught them discipline and something of cleanliness, still the result was little more than a dubious compromise between the old way of life and the army's way.

All three of them were tough. Aylmer and Curtin had served more time in detention than most of the men had church service. It didn't bother them. It was all part of army life. They may, in the dim past, have broken their mother's hearts, but it was certain no one would ever break theirs.

Lying back on his bed roll O'Rourke soaked in the sun. There was no reason to hurry about the detail. So long as the section was at the delivery point by 2300 hours that night, all would be well. It was, he reflected, better to take the section into the rendezvous point before dark in order to get the lie of the land. But this depended upon where the front was and what was doing there. Mulling it over in his mind, he decided to halt the section on the road near the delivery point and go ahead to recce the location. That way there would be no hitch to it.

He dozed off to sleep, only to be awakened a few minutes later by Curtin, who was bending over him, shaking him by the leg.

"What do you want?" he growled.

"Don't get sore. I just want to know if we're going to be here long enough to do some washing."

O'Rourke rubbed his eyes and then turned over.

"Have you got enough water to do washing?" he asked, indifferently.

"No, but I can get some."

"You'll get a swift kick in the tailbone if you wake me up again."

"Ah, go fry an egg."

O'Rourke sat up.

"What did you say?"

"Nothing, boss. Nothing at all. You're too touchy."

Late in the afternoon when O'Rourke awoke he could find few of the men around the lorries. He went in search of them and found them splashing naked in a great stone trough in the centre of a farmyard nearby. Three peasants stood near the house watching them, grinning from ear to ear. Between the peasants and the trough some geese stood nervously, arching their necks and hissing in alarm.

Bob O'Rourke left them and went back to his motor bike. The heat was stifling and he opened his shirt. He wanted to take it off, but some officer on the road was bound to see him. He started his machine and set off down the road, to recce the rendezvous point.

There was a lot of divisional transport moving down the road toward the front, and the dust was as thick as fog. It got in his eyes, and in his nostrils, and filled his throat. There was no way to escape it. The traffic moved at a snail's pace. It was as though every one on the road that afternoon was drowsy and heat-sick. And yet, when he lifted his eyes and turned his head to one side, he could see the far country as though through a dirty window of a train coach, and the land looked bright and golden, and the green of the trees and pastures was a deep, soft, cool green.

Traffic crowded him over. He was in the ditch as much as he was on the road. Oncoming traffic came up on him out of the dust, and he had to pull over. The jeeps were the worst: they swept past contemptuously, and, because they had speed and could take the bumps and holes they cared for nothing else on the road. They could dodge anything, squeeze through any hole in the traffic, and get into the clear. O'Rourke cursed them aloud. It was a well-known fact that many of the jeeps on the roads carried junior officers from the base lines out on sight-seeing trips of the front. They went up until they heard the artillery, and then they turned around and went back to base with tall stories of adventure. He had no love for them. He had respect only for vehicles that bore one of the divisional signs.

As he neared the front the traffic thinned. For a distance every field along the road held a unit of some kind—signals or engineers, bridging, artillery heavies, service corps, sometimes a medical post, sometimes only a lone ack-ack gun out in the field, surrounded by its earthwork, the gun gleaming dully in the sun. Then, abruptly, the fields were empty: the grain was untrodden and except for the broad, crazy pattern of tank tracks across the land there was no sign that an army had rolled across to the front. Near the front itself there was equipment again, but it was cleverly camouflaged against trees and hedges and farm buildings. There was nothing in the open on which the enemy could range his guns.

O'Rourke rattled along. He passed a military policeman covered with dust in a little village. Beyond the policeman the last building in the village had a gaping shellhole in its wall, through which protruded an anti-tank gun. The crew were brewing tea on a smoky fire. Coming to an orchard beyond the village, he stopped and looked at his map, then turned off on to a dirt road that skirted the orchard and climbed the rolling, open country behind it. Ahead, not more than a mile, lay the woods where he was to rendezvous with the tanks that night.

The road ran directly through the woods, dipped sharply

into a ravine and climbed away into open country again. German infantry had used the woods. There were several neat slit trenches, dead boughs of trees with the leaves withered and crisp that had been used for camouflage, and tatters of enemy equipment lying around—steel helmets, respirators, belt ammunition, clips of wooden bullets and wisps of paper and photographs blown about by the wind. Even had there been no equipment lying about he could have recognized it as a one-time German position, for, unlike any other soldier, the German always left a litter of personal letters, printed forms and photographs lying around a place that he had hurriedly vacated. Several tall trees were burnt and splintered and there were three large craters in the midst of the diggings.

It was not a good place for vehicles and he decided to skirt the outer edge of the woods, around the fields. On the eastern side he found a good spot where he could pull the lorries partly in under the trees. For the rest, the camouflage nets would hide them in the daylight.

He knew little about tanks. He could not venture a guess where the tanks would come from that were to take his loads that night, or whether they would enter the woods or remain in the open. It was quite probable that they would harbour elsewhere, and send a guide to bring the lorries to them for off-loading.

The men were sleeping by their vehicles when he got back to the section. He woke them and they started out on the road. The sun had set when they reached the woods. They parked the lorries in under the trees, then went out to explore for convenient foxholes to dive into when the night barrage opened up, as it did without fail every night as soon as the last light had gone.

Slowly night came upon the earth, and with it a brilliant moon rose across the sky. Far off, etched against the silver sky, a line of tall poplars bent toward the moon. From a half-hidden hamlet lying in a fold of the earth moonlight sparkled on the slate of the church steeple.

The men sat in a group looking out across the land. Far off they could see the dark density of the city of Caen lying low in the rolling land. It presented no shape or form, but only a dark clotting upon the earth.

"It's a beautiful night," a man said, softly, speaking the thought to himself. No one answered. For the moment the earth was at peace.

Then suddenly the field guns along the Canadian line opened up and burning flashes licked at the invisible enemy.

At first the interval between each gun was almost equal, and then, as the barrage carried down the line, the thunder rose to a fury.

The lance-corporal crawled over to O'Rourke.

"Are you sure this is where we are supposed to be, Bob?" he shouted. "It's likely there are some twenty-five pounders behind us just about ready to open. This is going to be a hot spot."

"This is where we are supposed to be and where we'll stay. So sit down and relax. Look at me! I'm almost shaking apart."

They both laughed, and then the men laughed, though they did not know what the joke was.

"Those shells are greased with sweat," someone remarked, in a deep voice.

"I wouldn't be a bloody gunner for a brigadier's pay." This from Aylmer, who lay on his stomach near O'Rourke's feet.

"You wouldn't be, because it takes brains and you've got callouses where your brains are supposed to be."

"Look! There's Jerry opening up."

Far across the plain spurts of orange-red flame broke out. They travelled back and forward over the land. Then, coming with a long, slow, whining crescendo the shells began to burst in the fields. They watched, fascinated, until a shell whistled low overhead and exploded behind the woods. Almost in a body the section dived for cover in the foxholes among the trees.

Curtin, O'Rourke and the lance-corporal rolled into the same hole, with the lance-corporal at the bottom. They extricated themselves and looked around. Heads were popping up out of nearby holes. Josephs stuck his head up over the edge of his hole, grinning from ear to ear. The moonlight made his teeth seem very clean for the first time, thought O'Rourke.

"This isn't a healthy place to be, Corporal," someone called.

"I can think of better."

"You don't suppose Jerry knows we're here, do you?"

"Naw! The brigade forgot to send him our location. The administration in this army is dogawful."

"Well, I don't want to give the Graves Commission any trouble. But so help me, if one of those ammunition lorries goes up they'll never find me."

"Has anyone a water bottle on them?" a voice asked from a nearby hole.

"Imagine a man wanting to drink water at a time like this," said Curtin in a low voice.

"Suppose we can smoke?" asked the lance-corporal, who was sitting on his haunches at the bottom of the hole.

"Sure, pass them round."

They knelt together and lit their cigarettes. The hole was crowded, but it felt good to be together. Now and then a shell burst in the open field nearby, and the earth shook.

"I'm getting mud down my neck," complained the lance-jack.

"It's better than shrapnel."

"If you moved your fanny out of my face I'd have more room."

"You're lucky it isn't my fist."

"God! Listen to those guns. Did you ever hear anything like it?"

"I'm glad the ones I can hear are working for George."

"Well, can you hear this one?"

A screaming shell landed in the trees. Mud and splinters of wood rained down on them. The sides of the foxholes caved in, half-burying them. They shook themselves and looked up. Where the shell had landed a cloud of black smoke seemed to bounce on the earth. Around the smoke there was only one tree standing. It had no branches and stood like the spar of a sunken ship, stripped white and shining in the moonlight.

Curtin had lost his glibness.

"How much longer do we have to wait for the tanks, Corporal?" he asked.

O'Rourke looked at his watch closely.

"Just about an hour to go if they are on time."

"Don't you think we'd better move the lorries, Bob?" the lance-corporal asked. He looked up at O'Rourke with a white, strained face.

"I thought of that, but where could we move them that would be better than this? We can't stand them in open country. Besides, we'd only have to come back when the tanks came. "No. We'll just have to stick it out. The boys along the line over there are getting the same thing."

"O.K. You're the boss. Who's got a cigarette?"

"That's funny. What happened to the cigs we were smoking."

"Here's a package," moaned the lance-corporal. "Just leave one for me. I need something in my mouth to keep my teeth from rattling."

"Don't those plates of yours fit yet, Sam?" asked Curtin, as he bent and scratched a match across the seat of his trousers. "You were going to have them fixed way back in England."

"Go to hell."

After a time the enemy barrage grew lighter. Only an intermittent shell came over, but the Canadian guns kept up their murderous fire. The tempo seemed to increase until it was almost a frenzy of crashing thunder.

O'Rourke lifted himself out of the foxhole and made his way over to the vehicles. He stood by the edge of the trees looking out across the moon-bathed land.

Across the fields to the south he saw a tank appear over a slight height of land, then it disappeared again to come up on a contour rise near an orchard half a mile from him. There it stopped. Other tanks followed it. From where he watched, each tank seemed curiously like a great dark insect.

He got on his bike and started across the fields, travelling at a snail's pace, dodging the shell craters. Over a rise of ground he picked up a rutted cart road. Between the ruts it was smooth and he hummed along. When he was abreast of the first tank he swerved off the road and cut across a pasture field. He swung around behind the lead tank and came to a stop. Sitting on the turret of the tank was a man in coveralls, with a pair of field-glasses hanging around his neck. He looked down at O'Rourke and smiled, and then slowly, nimbly, slid to the ground.

"I was just wondering when you'd come out of that bush," he said. "Figured if I waited long enough you'd come out."

"Yours are the tanks I'm looking for, I guess," observed O'Rourke.

"If you've got supplies and ammo, we're the ones. I'm OC of this outfit. Pleased to meet you, Corporal."

"That bush over there is the co-ordinate your R.H.Q. gave me," said O'Rourke defensively.

"That's right. But I couldn't come across to meet you. You see, that field you just drove over is mined."

"Well, it's been a nice quiet night," observed O'Rourke, ruefully.

They both laughed and then the officer brought out a package of smokes.

"Have one?"

"Thanks, sir. I'll get along and find a way to bring the lorries over to you. I guess you're in a hurry to get the stuff?"

"Well, more or less. We're going to bed down here for the night and the sooner we get some sleep the better. If you take that dirt road there and stick to it, it ought to be fairly safe for your vehicles. But don't take to the fields . . . we want those supplies tonight."

Following the farm road brought him to an east-west tank track and he turned westward to the point where he had parked the section. The tank track was deep with fine powdered dust, and his machine stalled in it. He pushed and lifted it on to the side and rode along the verge. After the officer's warning about mines he expected to hit one every minute, and by the time he reached the woods he was sweating.

The men were out by the vehicles, waiting for him. They had watched him approach.

"I'm going to ride the edge of the tank track, but you fellows stick to the track, and then to the road when we turn. You'll have to go in four-wheel drive along the track. The dust is knee-deep."

He led them along the track, and then over the farm road between the fields. Instead of turning off across the fields to the tanks he took them down to the corner of the orchard and turned them there, in line with the tanks. Then he rode over to the officer, who was sitting with his crew around a petrol heater on which they were making tea.

"Where do you want us to unload, sir?"

"Right along beside the tanks. The boys will give you a hand as soon as they've had a bite to eat. It won't take long to off-load and then you can pull out. To-morrow morning you report to R.H.Q. Unless they give you a change meet us at this map reference same time tomorrow night."

He tore a page out of his message book and handed it to O'Rourke.

"It's an orchard just south of Villons. We'll come along the road on the west side of the orchard. You can check that later on your map. Right?"

"Right, sir."

"Good lad. We'll win this war yet, if we get enough sleep. Good night."

"Good night, sir."

He went back to the lorries and waited. The moon was low in the sky now, and the earth was darker. A cold ground mist crept across the fields in slow, wavering floes. It seemed to catch and snarl on the heaped, littered earth around the shell craters. The artillery barrage continued, but it was less intense.

A Tank Corps sergeant came across to where he stood leaning against a lorry.

"We'll get you unloaded now, and then you can get going. It sounds noisy around here, but it's not a bad spot to spend the night if you want to. Trouble is, you'd have to get out before daylight. Jerry wakes up awfully early these mornings."

"Thanks, sarg, I think I'll get on my way as soon as we've unloaded. Jerry seems to have stopped shelling."

"Don't kid yourself! He's let up on his artillery. But, boy! He'll be pasting hell out of our positions with mortar further up the lines. We're a bit out of the Canadian sector here—just a flank, really. He hates the Canadian guts, and his mortar fire is killing. You've got to give him credit for that. Those guns of ours across there are lobbing over smoke shells now, hoping to blind Jerry's mortar men. Don't suppose it will do any good, though. Well—let's get cracking. I want to get some sleep to-night."

The moon had set by the time they had unloaded. In pitch darkness O'Rourke led the section out of the tank harbour, across the farm road and onto the tank track again. They turned westward and crawled through the dust at a snail's pace, past the clump of trees where they had lain during the bombardment.

Looking back now and then, O'Rourke could sometimes see the dark form of the lead lorry behind him as he rode the edge of the dust track, but he relied on the sound of the racing gears and the rattle of the lorries over the bumps, to tell him that they were following. It was a nice close sound—the whine of those gears. He could see nothing ahead of him and the darkness bound him round in a tight, tense circle of danger. Yet so long as he could hear the lorries whining in the dust, hear the tail board chains clanging, he was not alone, and there were no dangers that they would not all share alike.

After what seemed an eternity, he picked up a crossing. Without hesitating, he blinked his tail light in warning, then turned to the right. It was only a dirt track, badly rutted but it brought them out onto a metalled road. Here he turned right again, and after a while he began to feel the familiarity of the road. He passed the dark shadow of a shattered cottage, rounded a slow bend that he knew well. He was going in the right direction.

They slept under the lorries in an open field. Within a few minutes Josephs was snoring loudly. Curtin struck his head on a hot exhaust pipe, and in a stream of rich profanity cursed the manufacturer of the vehicle and all his relations unto the tenth generation. Someone laughed—a tired, quickly stifled laugh. Then there was quiet around the lorries. From far off came the dull rumble of artillery fire. Dawn drew a faint smudge of grey across the horizon. The stars blinked out, one by one.

3

In the morning O'Rourke sent the section back to the dumps to load, then set out for the R.H.Q. at Lasson.

Keeping off the main roads that were thick with slow-moving traffic, he cut across country, going entirely by sense of direction. He admitted to himself that it might be longer across-country: still he had the trails to himself, and the only dust was what his machine threw up behind him.

He felt happy. From time to time he sang at the top of his lungs—old cowboy songs he had sung when he worked in the fields at home. He even broke into a love song which Gerda would ask him to sing when she knew he was very happy.

The fields were beautiful. Although the heat of the day was full upon the earth, there was something sweet and cool in the smell of the ripe grain standing so golden in the sun. It was a pity, he thought, that the farmers had not taken down the bleak wooden poles which the Germans had erected to thwart invasion by air. They studded the land and were un-believably ugly. Probably, he reflected, the farmers left them there because they were mined.

He came to a stretch of country that was completely pock-marked with shell-craters, and the earth was brick-red in the sun. It was a scene of utter desolation. Not a square yard of earth had been missed. The craters were huge. He had never seen any so wide or deep. They had been made by enormous air bombs, or by a bombardment from one of the great battleships that had supported the landings on D-day. Weeds had begun to grow on the crater rims—tender green and startling against the rich Normandy earth. Down in the hollows between the craters grain grew, heavy-ripe with bright red poppies to keep them company. And, half-covered in earth, rusted and gaunt, lay the litter of enemy artillery, lying as it had fallen when the great shell bursts had smashed it to shrap-nel—here and there a broken wheel, a gun barrel, a gunner's seat, a riddled shield plate.

O'Rourke, curious, steered his bike up on the rim of one of the craters and looked down. The shell had made a perfect cup in the earth. At the very bottom the mud was of a burnt grey colour, something like wet wood ash. Tatters of German uniforms stuck in the mud on the sides, and on the rim opposite him a hand stuck out, blue-grey, enormously swollen, almost unrecognizable. The stench from the hole was sickening.

'And yet,' he thought, as he turned away, 'a poppy will grow . . .'

He crossed a main paved road, cutting in between a convoy of field artillery, and took another dirt track. He came upon an old farmer and his wife harvesting a field of rye. The old man cut with a scythe while the woman followed him, tying the grain into stooks with braided grainstalks. Once the man stopped, and drank from an earthenware jug. While he drank the woman rested, standing in the cut grain with her legs apart, her hands on her hips.

O'Rourke stopped his machine on the pretext of repairing something, and watched them. It was nice to see the way the grain fell across the blade of the scythe, to see the stubble suddenly revealed against the wall of standing rye. It was nice, too, to watch this old couple, in the twilight of life, working together. Terror and death had passed them : it was already just over the horizon on the new battlefield. But war promised a long winter of hunger and want, and so they worked.

When, finally, he rode down the wooded road into the village at R.H.Q. it was noon. The men were lining up at the field kitchen for their meal, clanging their mess tins with exaggerated impatience, and making dirty comments about the cook and the "service". He picked up his orders, neatly typewritten and stuffed them into his pocket without reading them. Unstrapping his saddle-bags he pulled out his mess tins and mug and fell into the line.

4

That night the Normandy plain was aflame from end to end. It began even before the sun had set. Usually there was an hour of peace and quiet in the orchards where men lay and rested, and across the fields the cool of evening was like a soft caress. Usually, too, it was the time when the dust in the roads seemed to settle for a little while, when the hideous desolation of ruined buildings was graced with long, deep shadows—the hour when men drew away from their comrades and sat in ditches, or lay sprawled in the fields thinking of home, of the treasures that the past gave up, of boyhood days, of wild youthful love, of pretty girls and the gang down on the corner of Main Street in the old home town.

But there was no moment of reverie this night. Late in

the afternoon aircraft reconnaissance reported that the Germans were forming up for an attack in the vicinity of Carpiquet south of the Caen–Bayeux road. The answer came within a very short time. From the beachhead landing strips rocket-firing Typhoons and fighter-bombers rose into the air and went racing across the front lines to the attack. Simultaneously the artillery opened up all along the line in a drum-beat barrage that shook the earth. Under the creeping barrage the tanks moved forward. Behind them went the infantry. Tanks and infantrymen moved cautiously. The task for the aircraft was to wreak havoc in the enemy's forming-up area, to nip the attack before it could be launched. The task for the tanks was to meet the enemy armour and hold it on enemy ground, should the air force be unable to prevent an attack from being launched. The infantry was to hold the ground taken, to meet what lay between the tanks, and, more important still, to hold advanced positions through the night against anything that might come across the plain.

The air force did indeed wreak havoc among the German tanks and self-propelled guns in the forming-up area, and drove the infantry to cover. But the enemy was no fool. From west of his forming-up area he launched an armoured attack of terrific fury, designed to drive a wedge between the Canadian and British flanks. Then, although somewhat battered and dis-organized, he attacked from Carpiquet with everything he could muster.

So it was that the intended main attack from Carpiquet became the minor one, and, in reality, it limped forward, dazed by the salvos of the air force, with feeble momentum and very little organized support. To break through the Canadian lines before dark, to hold the territory until dawn and then to launch another attack had been the intention. But what armour escaped the air force and broke into the open met Canadian armour that opened fire at long range from picked positions. Moreover, the German tanks had to advance into the artillery barrage. Their supporting infantry was forced to cover, pinned down before the creeping curtain of shell-fire.

It was not what the German liked. To be sure he gained some favourable ground, and it was not long before his mortars were in action with their usual deadly effect, but what he gained he gained at a terrific cost, and made no appreciable dif-ference to the Canadian line. As darkness descended his attack was turned. The best that he could hope for that night was to be able to hold his positions against a counter-attack which had already been launched.

A little to the west the armoured wedge attack aimed at

splitting the Canadian and British flanks had even less success. They ran up against a British front which would not move. The British knew what the game was, and they held the German armour in the open while the air force, using the last light of day, swooped to the kill.

Again it was not the sort of situation the Hun wanted. He called his tanks back and turned them up to Carpiquet to support his positions in the north against the Canadian counter-attack. By this time the last daylight had gone from the sky. The air force swept homeward over the blazing front to their dusty beachhead airfields, and the roar of their flight was like a wild high song of glee.

It was just after dark when Bob O'Rourke brought his section down the Cruelly–Caen road toward the front. They had started out from the supply dumps along the main north-south road from the beach area, but at Basly they were stopped and diverted south-west. O'Rourke had argued, cursed and threatened, but the provost in Basly was adamant.

Next, they were held up by an artillery unit moving forward. Through smothering dust and darkness, they crawled forward.

Wedged in behind the artillery convoy O'Rourke turned his mind to the problem which the diversion from Basley had led him into. He knew he could go only a mile or two before he struck the front line. Indeed, as he emerged from a village on to higher ground the land ahead was ablaze with fire. The front seemed only yards away. Somehow he had to turn left and cut across country behind the front line to reach his rendezvous. He tried to remember the map of the area, but his mind refused to focus upon it.

"Hell," he said to himself aloud. "I'll take a chance and trust to luck."

Ahead, a short distance, he remembered where a dirt road cut in from the left between two blitzed buildings. He had passed it several times and wondered where it led. He decided to take it.

"I just hope, baby," he said, patting the tank of his machine, "that we won't run into a convoy up there. If I get through this night I'll be a hero or a private to-morrow, for sure."

He led the section up the road. It turned left and then dipped down below a contour. He could feel the thick dust drag at the wheels of his machine. For half a mile the road snaked and followed a line of trees on the left. Above the trees the sky was bright with moonlight, but along the road, the shadows were deep.

The road narrowed between hedges and stone walls, then broke out again into open country. He came to a crossroads and halted. He took off his helmet and spat the dust out of his mouth. Behind him he could hear the whine of the lorries pulling up to a halt. Overhead, across the hill-top, a stream of orange tracer shells flew westward, then a starshell burst, giving off a ghostly light.

O'Rourke lit a cigarette. A lorry door banged. The lance-corporal walked up beside the vehicles. He looked very small, and seemed to stumble.

"Are you all right? You walk like a drunk?"

"I got it in the leg, back there. It was a sniper. I saw the flash of the shot from the side of the hill."

"Sit down. We'll have a look."

The men crowded around. O'Rourke cut the man's trousers. There was a gaping, torn wound, but the bullet had not reached the bone.

"You're lucky, I'd say."

"Damned lucky. Put a first-field dressing on it. It won't need a tourniquet. Then get me a drink of water and I'll be all right."

"How'd it happen, chum?"

"Like I said. I saw the rifle flash on the side of the hill back there. If the truck hadn't been bouncing on the road I'd probably have had it through the head. It was meant for the driver, no doubt about it."

"Well, let's get out of here. Put him in the back of the second lorry. It hasn't a full load, and someone had better ride in the back with him. All right, let's go. This isn't a funeral."

They crawled up over the hill to the plain. Now they could see the whole front lit up—Very lights, tracer shells, artillery flashes and, far off, the throbbing orange hue that marked the German lines.

They passed a burning farmhouse. A white, shaggy dog sat on the side of the road looking at the flames. He turned his head and looked mournfully at O'Rourke as he passed. Across the plain in wide-open country that looked down upon the battlefield they passed an ack-ack gun-site. A stream of tracers flew over the crew, but they did not move. Their dark forms stood at the gun like shadows.

They came, eventually, to a village and slowed down to a crawl. The houses stood crowded against each side of the street. Some were intact, some had shutters hanging loose on the walls, others had gaping holes, half-filled with rubble where shells had torn through the village. The narrow street was filled with choking, musty-smelling dust. There was a strong smell of the dead, too, a smell that did not fill the street but lay only near the dark places where the dead were, in the houses and in the rubble. A green light blinked and waved across the road. O'Rourke stopped the convoy.

"What the bloody hell do you think this is—a parking lot?" came a booming voice out of the dark. Then a provost came into sight.

"Green's green and red's red," the white-gaitered provost began.

"Yeh, but I just want to ask a question. You don't mind?"

"Well, why the hell don't you ask it and get going. I'm supposed to keep the traffic moving. There's an artillery move through here to-night."

"Sure, sure," soothed O'Rourke. "I'm looking for an orchard where I'm supposed to meet some tanks."

"Won't any orchard do? I haven't time to show you our large selection. Just take my word for it that all the orchards hereabouts are very cherce."

O'Rourke lit a cigarette and offered one to the provost.

"Well, it's this way," O'Rourke said. "This has got to be a very special orchard, you see. It's got to have a southern exposure and be on the edge of the town. And it's got to have a dirt road running alongside of it, due south. Otherwise I'm not too particular. If it isn't fenced—well, there's a war on. You know how it is. And if the gate sags a bit I won't kick, so long as the neighbours are nice clean people and don't throw their tin cans over the hedge."

The provost stood, legs apart, rolling his cigarette between his fingers.

"You know," he said, finally, "you're in luck. I know the very place and it came vacant only last night. About this time it was, too. They pulled out in an awful hurry and whipped past me here, going hell-bent for election. Someone yelled that Jerry had taken over the orchard and was coming through. But I stood here until my fanny dropped and no Germans came along.

"Funny way for people to behave, wasn't it? I hope you'll like the place and not go moving out without giving notice."

"What I want now is the direction to this super-duper parking lot you've been bragging about. Come on, give!"

"Well, you keep going until you come to a fork. Take the right and keep going till you come to the end of the hedge. It isn't really a hedge, but a bunch of bushes on the side. Anyway, pretend it is a hedge, and when you come to it—there's your orchard, buddy."

"Thanks. So long, chum."

"Don't forget to duck."

They turned up the right fork. A few hundred yards along the road they were hailed and stopped.

"Where are you going?" came a shout from the dark.

"I'm pulling into an orchard just ahead."

"Take it easy, then. There's infantry in rest along here."

As they continued on their way, O'Rourke could see the dark forms of infantrymen lying against the embankment of the road.

They were in the orchard, too, lying everywhere. Some rose from the path of the vehicles as they drove in under the apple trees. The cracking of the branches against the lorry tops and the hail of falling apples wakened the encampment. By the time O'Rourke had scattered the vehicles around the orchard, each lorry had gathered a circle of curious infantrymen around it. Then, their curiosity suddenly satisfied, the figures melted away into the darkness.

The high fringe of scrub that enclosed the orchard from the open plain shut off the blazing battle front. It felt secure there.

O'Rourke slept, and did not know it. Hours later he awoke with a start. Tank engines were roaring nearby. The infantrymen had vanished. The sky throbbed, flame-red over the battlefield. He went through the hedge and out across the field toward the tanks. A figure loomed suddenly before him. He stopped and dropped his hand to his holster. Out of the night came a sharp challenge, in English. He answered it, feeling absolutely certain that the other had already covered him with a weapon. Even after he was commanded to approach, he did so warily, and not until they were a few paces apart did he recognize the dark figure as a tank corps man in his black overalls.

# 20

I

Six or seven kilometres from Caen, on a rise of land dominating the river Orne and the city itself, three little villages formed a triangle—Buron, Gruchie and Authie. Their apex pointed northward toward the sea.

It was here, on the night and morning of June 7th and 8th, that the Canadian assault battalions caught the full savage force of the first German counter-attack upon the Normandy plain. Suffering heavy casualties, the Canadians fell back to their support lines. There they dug in grimly and held their positions against the almost continuous hammer blows of the Germans. They dug in and held, until the counter-attack had spent itself. Then they brought in their dead from the field—all that they could reach, and buried them, then set about strengthening their positions.

They held there for thirty days, within sight of the three little towns. In time they gave the place the name of "Hell's Corner," and even back on the beaches, among men who had never been there, the name inspired a reverence and awe for those who lived in that savage inferno.

For thirty days they waited, giving no ground. Not a day passed when they weren't shelled. Their foxholes became as familiar to them as the houses on their home-town streets, and when a bomb knocked out a foxhole they viewed it as a Londoner viewed the bomb devastation in the middle of his street. Through rain and mud and blistering sun they held on and could not be broken. Their strength dwindled and was reinforced. Night after night their patrols went out into No-Man's-Land under the artillery fire. Often the patrols had to lie doggo while a German patrol passed, and sometimes the patrols fought it out to the grim end. In time they came to know more about the Germans who faced them than they knew about their own comrades on their flanks.

But there was no fraternizing with the enemy, in spite of

the bulletin board which one wiseacre erected by his foxhole, which proclaimed the daily market-price which the Germans were prepared to pay for commodities such as bully-beef, cigarettes and wool socks. On this list, three Iron Crosses were worth a tin of sardines, and a trenchful of Jerries was worth one grenade. No, there was no fraternizing, for the Canadians in Hell's Corner faced the 12th S.S. Panzers—the most fanatical of all Hitler's hoodlums.

The plain before the three villages was dotted with the burnt-out wrecks of tanks—Shermans mostly, but there were Tigers and Panthers there, too. The three villages gradually crumbled. Tons of artillery shells crashed into them and through them. They were no longer villages, but only heaps of broken masonry and dust. Here and there a wall stood to mark where a house had once been, and even these had neat shellholes through them. The orchard trees were blackened, splintered ghosts that brooded over the desolation and the dead lying in the ruins.

Then, exactly one month from the morning when they had rolled up against the terrific onslaught of the fast German counter-attack, the Canadians rose from their positions and attacked across the fields. Their long wait was over: now their revenge came for that month of hell and fury.

It was the hardest fought battle since D-Day. The attack opened with a terrific artillery bombardment from the Canadian twenty-five pounders and mediums. The infantry went in under it, fanning out across the fields. The Germans opened up with a heavy mortar barrage which met and overlapped the Canadian barrage. The Canadians went in without protection, standing up. The Germans kept in their weapon pits and allowed their positions to be infiltrated. Then they opened up with their small arms, firing through the curtain of their own mortar barrage into the backs of the Canadians.

It was small arms and grenade fighting all the way. Every trench, every foxhole, had to be cleared, one by one. It was man against man, hand to hand, in the fields and amid the ruined houses, under the overlapping artillery barrages. The Panzers knew how to fight and how to die a fanatical death. Their positions were strong.

One by one the trenches and foxholes fell, filled with German dead. Across the fields the Canadians advanced. By noon they owned the three villages and opened up the country to the south as far as Franqueville. What was left of the 12th S.S. Panzers were prisoners and there were not many. The rest lay on the battlefield.

The Canucks owned Hell's Corner for good, thou
it had cost none could then say. They did not stop to co
dead. The next morning they pushed on across the plai
heart of Caen.


2


A few days previous to this action men of an eastern
Canadian regiment on the immediate right flank of Hell's Corner
had staged an attack of their own. Their neighbours on either
flank knew little about it for some time. The commands knew,
and word of it filtered to the rear and then came forward again,
spreading from foxhole to foxhole, from one gun position to
another. It was spoken of as "an advance of a mile or two,"
and "tough going," but for the time being it meant very little
to the individual soldier sitting in his weapon-slip looking out
across the front. Somebody had done something, and in a stale-
mated period of war that was good news, but not such good
news that it would make anyone uncork the last bottle of
looted, frenzy-fixin' Calvados.

In reality, this attack was of considerable importance
when, in a few days, it became linked to the grand offensive
for the city of Caen. For the attack was against the village and
airfield of Carpiquet. When it fell it unlocked the enemy's defence ring around the city—that ring of steel which had come
to be regarded as almost impenetrable. Caen was the enemy's
right flank : it was also the Allied left. If the enemy could gain
control of the plain north of Caen, by turning the Allied flank,
he could command the beaches. Disaster to the entire campaign
would be the result. Caen had to be taken.

Carpiquet was the first wedge that the Allies drove into
that ring. The village, three miles due west from Caen, was the
centre of a great German airfield. True, the airfield had been
almost completely destroyed long ago both by aircraft and
artillery. But the Germans had built the remains into a solid
defensive position. Day after day, night after night, the Allies
had poured a withering barrage of artillery into it. Patrols
probed it nightly. Tanks and self-propelled guns covered it from
close range. The village held, even when there was no village
left, but only a ghostly mass of ruins rising from the plain. The
fight for Carpiquet had been long and grim. The Germans held
out in their concrete encasements that had walls of reinforced

concrete six feet thick and steel armour plating that could withstand any reasonable seige. Behind them they had reinforcements, and supplies that poured in over the network of roads leading to Caen.

The Canadians advanced like an inexorable tide. They had tanks, tank busters, flame throwing tanks, sappers and heavy assault equipment to back them up. It was more than an attack: it was an all-out assault upon a defensive position so strongly fortified that it had stood continuous artillery bombardment for weeks. The infantry cleared the open country, mopped up the trenches and machine-gun nests. The flame throwers scorched the enemy out of his concrete emplacements and the infantry mopped up. Sappers cleared pathways for the tanks, laid charges that literally blew pillboxes into the air, demolished whole buildings upon the nests of snipers in hiding. Tank fought tank to the death. They cut the enemy lines to pieces.

The Germans counter-attacked with strong armour. The attack was beaten off, and blazing Panthers littered the land— funeral pyres for their crews. Yard by yard, foxhole to trench to concrete pillbox, the infantry advanced. The enemy put up a terrific artillery and mortar fire that carpeted the battlefield. Casualties soared, the ranks thinned. But the attack swept on.

They took Carpiquet and consolidated on the south side of the village, across the east-west road through it. They held there for five days in that small bulge in the battlefront which they had created, until the attack from Hell's Corner began, and closed their exposed flank to the east.

Those five days and nights seemed an eternity. Every position they dug into was shelled and mortared by the enemy, who still held firmly on the great airport beyond the village within hailing distance.

Carpiquet was to be remembered as one of the hardest, bloodiest battles of the war. It was also something more. It was the first wedge driven into the Nazis' strongest front in Normandy. The small bulge which the eastern Canadians had made in the battle line was like a finger protruding from a clenched hand—a finger pointing the way out of France.

Five days later the Canadians broke out of Hell's Corner and swept down across the plain into Caen, the city of the dead.

# 21

I

DAWN broke across the fields like a curtain lifting slowly across a vast stage. Night mists still clung to the ground. The trees rose above the mist and appeared to float in the sky.

O'Rourke awoke, stretched and scratched himself indolently under the blanket; then he began to dress. His clothes were dry, for he had folded them in a piece of tarpaulin. His blanket, though, was heavy and wet with dew. He decided to have his breakfast, then ride over to the tank R.H.Q. for further orders, leaving the men to sleep on. There was no need to move the section until late morning.

He found an empty biscuit tin and threw a handful of earth into it, then poured in a couple of inches of oil. With a piece of toilet paper he lit the oil, then set a tin of water on top of the fire. While he waited for the water to warm he laid out his shaving kit and his mess tins. Digging into the saddlebags on his bike he found a small tin of tea, a handful of broken biscuits and a tin of bacon. When the water began to steam he took it off, then filled a mess tin with fresh water from the can on a lorry. Into the other mess tin he put the tinned bacon. Setting them on the fire he began to shave himself, wedging his splinter of mirror in the bow of a nearby tree. By the time he had shaved and washed breakfast was ready. He added the compo tea to the boiling water and took it off the fire. Sitting cross-legged like an Indian he ate.

The air is so clean in the early morning, he thought: It was like this at home, too—cool and sweet at dawn, and then warming gradually in the sunlight so that, if you walked across the fields at daybreak as he had so often done at home, you could feel the change of air upon your body. At first you shivered, your body covered with hard goose-pimples, then gradually your body warmed, felt smooth and sinewy, and you wanted to run—run wildly, madly over the earth. Mornings like that brought heavy, languid heat at midday when the crickets sang in the still grain, and far off, far, far away upon the horizon the golds and blues and browns melted into a dancing ever-changing mirage.

Mirages were strange things. He remembered the first one that he had ever seen, when he was just a kid. It was a lake he had seen—a vast, shimmering lake far out upon the prairie to the north. He could even see the waves flashing silver in the sunlight. Suddenly he had turned and raced for home to tell his father that he had seen the lake, running so hard that his mouth burned dry and a sharp pain shot through his chest. His father had laughed and gone on with his work, but his mother had said, "Yes, son," and given him a piece of berry pie. Afterwards, for a long time, he felt the lake had been real because his mother had not laughed.

He shook himself. It was not good to remember things too much. All the good things were in the past. The future, the distant future beyond the war—that was a promise. But one could not be certain of it. It lay somewhere in the opened book, the pages were being flicked over slowly by the wind of fate, one by one. If the wind ceased. . . . Then the story would end there, abruptly.

At the tank headquarters there was a great bustle among the lorries and tents. Clerks and officers wove in and out, each intent on some mysterious task of his own. O'Rourke asked for his orders and was bluntly told to wait. He hung about the office lorry for a time, then strolled over to his bike and lay down. It was amusing, for a while, to watch the staff going and coming, talking and gesticulating. They were like so many ants swarming around an obstruction to their anthill. He dozed off.

He was awakened from his nap by a clerk who stood over him with a piece of paper in his hand. O'Rourke saw his boots first as he opened his eyes. The boots were laced very loosely, and somehow he knew it was a clerk.

"Here are your orders," the man said in an annoyed tone. "As you'll see they're cut and dried—you return to your unit."

"That's cosy. When?"

"Read it yourself. It's enough that I have to run around looking for you, without spelling it out."

O'Rourke tore the message from his hand, and with a hefty shove sent the clerk spinning.

"That for your lip, you dog-eared brat."

Two officers and a sergeant stood nearby, talking, and pretending not to have seen.

In a way O'Rourke was sorry that he had to go back to his unit. The little that he had seen of the tank corps men had impressed him, and in his own way he had developed a profound respect for them. He had not had time to learn their ways. The operation of tanks in battle and the organization behind them remained a mystery to him. There had been, moreover, a far greater freedom for the section than they would have had with their own unit. They had been completely independent, and he, as their leader, had held the sole responsibility. Still, it was good to be going back to their own comrades.

They found everything as they had left it. There was the immediate atmosphere of feverish activity, the unending movement of vehicles coming and going, the banging and clattering, the shouting and the cursing. There was Smokey, the platoon cook, leaning against a tree, squinting at the sun and chewing tobacco, pretending not to notice the new arrivals, looking deliberately away with an extravagant air of boredom. There was Sergeant Swarchuck shouting at a fatigue man who staggered with a load of two swill buckets. There was the lieutenant standing in front of the orderly-room tent, looking very dusty and very irritable as he watched O'Rourke's section drive down through the orchard location. And there was the smell of dust, of ripeness and that indefinable smell the army carries with it. There was, too, the air of transient being, as if everything were about to move on an instant's notice. It was precisely the same in the next orchard, the next company, in every orchard and every farmyard in Normandy. But one's own unit was "home," the hub of everything in one's immediate world.

O'Rourke parked his vehicles among the trees and went over to tell the cook that he would have "extras" to feed for lunch. But that worthy individual was in a singularly cantankerous mood.

"The meal's all ready, and you're too late," he announced. "Besides, you've been on your own now for days and seem to have gotten by. So just keep on. You're doing fine."

O'Rourke tried to humour him.

"Smokey," he said, "you oughtn't to take that attitude. We're all in this war together, you know."

" 'Taint my fault. A fellow's got to put up with the good and bad in this world, I says."

"What's for lunch?"

"For them that's having it, it's stew."

"No apple turnovers, Smokey?"

Smokey was visibly touched. He moved from one foot to the other, then resumed his original leaning position against the tree. He was very proud of his turnovers.

"How the hell can I make pastry if I ain't got no drippings to make it outa?" he growled.

"That's too bad. If the boys don't get a bit of your pastry a couple of times a week they get disgruntled. Why, that's the one thing we were looking forward to all the time we were out on this detail with the tanks."

"Mighty nice of you to say that, Bob, even if it ain't true. Say—tell me. How do those tank fellas eat? It must be a helluva job for a cook, following those Leapin' Lenas around. A fella couldn't lay on a meal schedule no matter how he tried."

"Well, it's this way, Smokey. They're on their own—no cook, no water trailer, no nothing." Then slyly, "Just like we were. . . ."

Smokey spat out his tobacco.

"God's truth! That's an awful way to treat men—no cook, no meals, nothin'! Men can't stand their own cookin' for long —they breaks down. 'Course," he mused, "I guess them fellas in the tanks don't feel it so much as you and me might, 'cause if you ride around in one of them things for a while you wouldn't have no stomach to bother you any way."

He gazed up at the green, spotted apples on the tree for a while, thinking hard.

"Them poor devils," he said after a time, sympathetically. "Them poor devils. What they wouldn't give for an apple turnover now and then. It's a bloody shame—no cook, havin' to shift for themselves all the time. 'Tain't natural. You can't run an army that way. No, siree!"

"You're dead right, Smokey. Dead right. Well, I've got to pick up the mail now. I'll tell the boys to just fall in line for lunch as usual, eh?"

"That's right, Bob. And if I get a wiggle on I might just have time to turn out a bit of pastry to tickle them. Something special. I just remembered there's a tin of drippings from that pig the lads killed last week. Tough old sow, she was, too. So long, Bob."

Cooks, Bob O'Rourke, reflected sagely, as he went for the mail, were always temperamental. If you flattered them they did better. If you didn't, they wilted. They were like women.

There was a great bundle of mail for the section. The men came running when they saw it. They spread the letters out on the grass, sorted it in piles for each man, then each went off to a quiet place to read, as men always did when they had mail from home.

O'Rourke had eight letters and a bundle of newspapers from home. Five of the letters were from Gerda, two from his parents, and one from his old school teacher. He lay in the shade of a lorry and opened Gerda's letters first, feverishly, avidly. The present faded away and he was back in Canada, living amid the every-day events she described, seeing the things that had delighted her weeks before. He was at peace, and Gerda was with him. Life was good : it was exciting, fresh with promise and hope.

There was a farm near his father's place which was for sale. Gerda was sure they could buy it with their savings, and with what the Government might provide in gratuities after the war. To her the place symbolized a home of their own, independence and security. She discussed, with an irrepressible naïve enthusiasm, the changes they would make in the house, the colour of the curtains she would make, painting and decorating and heating. Typically feminine, as though the purchase of the place had already been decided between them, she was convinced that green window shutters would give the house just the right effect and that it would be the only place of its kind in the area.

Bob laughed outright at her total disregard for the practicalities of such a purchase. The house was all she thought about—the house and the children she wanted, to make it a home. But he laughed indulgently, for he knew the place and knew the land was good : tired, perhaps, and in need of work, but worth the price asked.

It became for him instantly the place that he, too, wanted more than he had ever wanted anything. It had been all very well to work with his father : it was a good business arrangement, but he wanted his own land, his own stock, his own home. There was a difference between what you might inherit, in time, and what you actually owned.

The letters, too, filled the interval of time. In her last letters spring was just bursting upon the prairies, wild, passionate, intense. And there her letters had left him, to wait until more mail came across the ocean to the beachhead in France. Now it was early June upon the home lands, the grains sown, the livestock fattening on the pastures, the earth drying under the hot sun, the trees spreading their fresh, tender green : and dust on the roadways—dust under the cantering horses' hooves. And over all the blue, limitless, empty sky.

When the next letters would reach him the wild rose would be blooming in the fence thickets, the tiger lily dancing stiffly in the breeze, and in the hayfields the slow, murmurous symphony of insects in the noonday heat.

It was July in Normandy, and Canada was far away. It

was far away and yet it was right in his hand, in the precious letters from Gerda, in the thousand images that crowded his mind. Summer and autumn and winter, and yet another spring would pass before the dream, the hope could come true. There was so much in his heart that he wanted to express, so much that his heavy, empty hands wanted to do.

A loud banging of a tin can resounded through the camp. He swallowed the lump in his throat and went to eat. His eyes burned and he rubbed them, pretending it was the heat.

2

In the night the platoon hauled ammunition from the base depot up to a tree-lined road directly behind the front. It was stacked along the roadside and left for the front-line transport to pick up when it was required.

Traffic on the roads leading forward was unusually heavy —guns, tanks and wheeled vehicles moved up slowly, in total darkness. The dust was an impenetrable fog, filled with the roar of engines and the ominous clanking of tank treads. There were accidents, many of them. Dispatch riders were killed, vehicles crashed into one another. Up forward the Germans shelled the crossroads intermittently, and at times with accuracy. But the vehicle casualties were pushed to the side and traffic moved on, tortuously, slowly, blindly. Everyone sensed that "something was up." With so much equipment pushing forward it had to break out somewhere.

Under these conditions, moving forward with its first load of ammunition the platoon was soon split up. The sections lost contact with each other: vehicles became separated and lost. Thereafter the responsibility of getting the loads to their destination lay with the section corporals. All they could do was to post themselves along the road, at intersections, and check the steady stream of traffic to find their own vehicles. In this way they managed to direct most of them to the road upon which they were to dump the ammunition. It was a narrow side road: the heavy traffic passed it by.

On the first turnaround, from the depot to the dumping area, O'Rourke lost one vehicle. It was not until he had completed the third trip of the night from the base depot that he found it. He did not really find it, for it mysteriously reappeared in the stream of traffic with the rest of the section in a way that never was explained. Afterwards O'Rourke forgot to question the driver.

Often, during that night, he cursed his old lance-corporal and the sniper who had sent him to hospital. He had never felt that the lance-jack was of much use to him, but this night he needed him, and missed him. The other corporals had help to control their sections, but he had to work alone. The matter of creating a new lance-corporal to fill the vacancy had been passed over, forgotten, by the company.

Sergeant Ganter rode down the road on his motor cycle, checking the work of each section. O'Rourke was helping Josephs, the Indian, to unload twenty-five pounder shell and cartridge cases when Ganter came putt-putting along in the dark, and he whistled to him. His sergeant stopped his machine and came over.

"That you, O'Rourke?"

"It's me, all right."

"How's your section making out?"

"Well enough. This is our third turnaround. I was wondering when someone would show up to take a bit of interest in what was going on around here."

"You sound as though you've got a huff on," the sergeant observed, in a tone that was meant to be a reproach. It only angered O'Rourke.

"I'm in no huff. Not me. I'm bloody well mad."

"Do tell."

"It will be a pleasure," O'Rourke replied, leaving his work and moving up close to the sergeant.

"Since you're the sergeant of this half-baked outfit, maybe you can tell me why I can't get a replacement for the lance-corporal I lost. Or did you know I lost one?"

"Why blame me? You'll get one as soon as it can be put through orders. There's lots of good lance-jack material around."

"Listen, Sergeant—I'm not blaming you. I'm ASKING you! And if you can't answer me, you can get the answer from the high-priced help. I just want you to know that I need a lance-jack—badly—in case you didn't know."

"All right, O'Rourke. Keep your shirt on. This war's apt to last a week or so yet. I'll see about it first thing in the morning. It's a promise."

"Good enough, Sergeant. I'll remember that. Come noon to-morrow I expect I'll have a brand new lance-jack just a-wiggling his ears to learn the job, eh?"

The sergeant held out a package of cigarettes.

"Have one?"

"Thanks. A cup of coffee would be better. That bloody ammo is heavier to-night, seems to me."

"Well, one more haul and you're finished for the night. In fact, that will be a bit over the quota, but it won't matter."

"Hell's a-popping around here to-night. Some of Jerry's stuff is coming over awfully low."

"Must be the build-up for a big blow," observed the sergeant.

"We've heard that before," commented O'Rourke.

"Well, we've got to break out of this country soon. We can't hold here forever."

"That's true. There's something in the wind. I feel it. Whenever something is about to happen I feel it inside, and I get jumpy, like a cat on a hot stove. Once it does happen I'm fine."

"It affects everybody differently. Me—when things are just about to boil over—it affects my bladder. 'Course I blame it on the bike-riding, but that's the way it is, just the same. By the way, before I forget, have you anyone in your section who would make a good lance-jack?"

O'Rourke thought for a moment. He had a preference, it was true, but he hesitated about stating it. He knew beforehand what the sergeant's reaction would be.

"Well, truth to tell, Sergeant, I'd like to see young Curtin get the hook." He said it blandly, as though it were a comment on good weather.

"What? That candidate for detention? Why, he's got a crime sheet a mile long. You can't be serious."

"Yep, dead serious. He's all you say, but I'll bet he'll make a good lance-jack. Perhaps if we gave him a hook and some responsibility, it might be just what he needs. Up to now he's had nothing. No-one ever believed he'd do anything but get into trouble. Why, he'll be prouder of that one hook than he ever has been of all the trouble he's caused."

"I don't know, Bob. I can just imagine the reception I'll get when I put his name up to the boss."

"Sure, I know. And you can tell him the same thing I've just told you. If you believe it will work out, and I believe it— why, he's a cinch to get the hook."

"Well, I'll do it and be damned! If anyone else had suggested it, I'd just laugh. But you're right, Bob—about men, anyway."

"Keep ducking 'em—and I'm not kidding. Jerry seems to be getting a little too accurate to-night, with his eighty-eights."

"Well, so long. Tell old Smokey to make extra coffee for breakfast. We'll need it."

O'Rourke stood in the road watching the tail light of the sergeant's motor cycle recede down the road. It shone red and intense, like a burning ember in the darkness.

'I wish to God I were on that bike,' thought O'Rourke. 'I wish to God I were getting out of this area. I've got a feeling Jerry suspects what's going on here. He'll get a range on us before dawn.'

He watched the red light of the bike until he could see it no longer—watched it with a poignant loneliness. Star shells burst overhead, forming meteor-like bursts of exquisite beauty. The roadway, the vehicles and the sweating men stood revealed, shadowless, motionless, with the frozen immobility of sheer fright. Every face was staring at O'Rourke where he stood in the middle of the road, between the tall, grotesque trees. He could see each man's face, and he knew that his own was bathed in the same ghostly light. Every man looked to him, and waited. He cleared his throat and spat the phlegm across the road, then gave a hitch to his trousers and went to help Josephs with his unloading. The men resumed their work : the star shells died out slowly, and there was only the nearby bark and roar of artillery that lulled and rose and lulled again.

O'Rourke did not know it, but as he watched the red tail light of the motor cycle grow dim and finally disappear in the darkness he was witnessing the last ride of Sergeant Ganter upon this earth. A man's fate so often hangs by a thread. Does it not often depend upon the pure accident of place and time, or upon another man's digestion, or whether he has slept well and is in a good mood?

At the beginning of the night's work the platoon commander decided to send his sergeant to the unloading point. He himself would go to the depot. The truth of the matter was that the officer had been forced to hurriedly gulp his supper. It lay on his stomach like a rock and made him irritable. At the ammunition depot he knew of a lieutenant who had a snug billet underground and who would be glad to produce a cup of strong coffee or tea in exchange for conversation about the movement of personalities with whom they were both acquainted.

So it happened that Sergeant Ganter rode forward to meet fate, encountering on the way one or two incidents which became relative to it. If his motor cycle had not broken down, and if the traffic had not been so heavy, he would have arrived much sooner at the unloading point and thus have missed his fate entirely. As it was, between getting his machine started again, and being held up by the snail-pace of the traffic, he lost more than two hours. If, also, he had cut his conversation short with O'Rourke, or had stopped to talk a minute longer, he would have outlived the night, might indeed have survived the entire war. And finally, IF the German gun behind the village of Buron had not hurled its shell into space at the precise moment it did. . . . As it happened, the shell landed on the edge of the road beside Sergeant Ganter as he rode along.

O'Rourke, a moment or two after the red tail-light had disappeared, heard the shell burst down the road. He paid no attention to it: many shells landed in the area that night. No one knew what had become of the sergeant. For days he was "missing," and then came the report of his death—"due to enemy action." It was probable that he lay for days quite un-recognizable in the field into which the shell burst had thrown him and his machine. In that area there were many dead lying about.

The sections finished their work and withdrew. In that pre-dawn hour the mighty night-long bombardment was fading out. All things must end. The army commander had ordered a barrage of several thousand rounds of shells to be dropped on the German lines. The order had been carried out—with a few extra rounds thrown in for good measure.

That was the morning the Canadians broke out of Hell's Corner.

# 22

It was two o'clock in the morning. The sky was deep velvet blue, studded with intense quivering stars, but low down in the south a fierce orange light glowed upon the rim of the earth. It was too far away to hear the thunder of the guns.

O'Rourke looked upward to the stars. The world was quiet, and in the heavens there was peace and infinite wonder. And then he turned his face toward the glowing flash of the guns, and the magic wonder of the night vanished suddenly.

The lorries stood scattered about. Out near the centre of the field the faint glow of a covered fire made a tiny circle in the darkness. The men had built the fire in one of the German excavations for the hull-down position of a Tiger tank. The tank lay on its side, burnt out, a few yards way.

Someone began strumming a banjo, chording at first, then swinging into a song. A voice took up the song, but no-one joined in, and after a time the player began another. This time it was "The Red River Valley," and several voices rose with the plaintive cowboy song. It haunted the darkness like the cry of a lonely animal.

O'Rourke listened to it across the field, with the palpable darkness between him and the singers. It brought to him an overpowering sense of loneliness, and he had the impulse to reach out to grasp something that the darkness and the faint, far-off light seemed to contain for him. The mournful chant spoke to him of the rich and powerful land of home, of the mighty slow-winding rivers of the prairies, of the solitary, lonely man upon the vast curvature of the earth. It spoke of his boyhood, of the magic of the earth's discovery, of warm sun and the rich deep smell of ripeness and seed. It spoke of the quiet spirit of sleep that enfolded Gerda in that familiar distant room, of the voices of the night that encircled the house upon his father's land. of the gate he knew so well, the step, the known door.

The song ended. Then through the night burst another song, throbbing with life and revelry, and a chorus of voices caught it up. It was a new song that the men along the front had made up, sung to the tune of a dance piece:

*Lay that Luger down, kid,*
*Lay that Luger down;*
*Luger-luggin' Ludwig,*
*Lay that Luger down.*

*Lay that Luger down, kid,*
*You haven't got a chance:*
*Luger-luggin' Ludwig,*
*You're all washed up in France.*

The revelry of it was irresistible. O'Rourke forgot his loneliness. He walked quickly toward the light and the voices. As he squatted by the fire and looked at the warm, lit faces of his comrades, he remembered a night of long ago, a night when he had heard the hoboes singing in the jungle around their campfire, and he had gone toward them through the darkness, forgetting his loneliness, forgetting the hunger that had always been with him. And now, remembering that night out of the wandering years, he thought it had been the first time he had ever felt the need of comradeship. He had come down out of the mountains in the dead of night, travelling alone, and there, in the wilderness, beside a slow, gleaming river, he had seen the jungle fire, heard the voices, and knew that he could no longer contain the loneliness within him. He had gone toward the light as a man goes toward a friend.

He sat now before the fire and listened to the songs that poured out, one after another—the soldier songs of interminable verses, and the cowboy songs, the songs of the west. He thought of Gerda and home, and of the years of his youth, the wild, reckless, wandering years. He did not know what hunger had driven him over the mighty continent in those years, nor what he sought. He only knew that his love for Gerda had stilled his restlessness, quenched his hunger, and given him a peace such as he had never known before. Almost. The nameless hunger and the restlessness was with him again wildly rising out of his spirit like the ghost of an evil inheritance.

He rose and stood over the fire. He looked down at the circle of men and saw them as from a great distance. They were his men, his section, and he felt a sudden passionate impulse to grasp them all by the hand, as if, by that gesture, he could express to them the comradeship and love he had for them, for which there were no words.

"It's time to go," he said abruptly, looking at the distant glow in the sky. "Pack it up, boys."

One by one they went off into the darkness across the fields. He heard the lorry doors banging, the engines warming up. For several minutes he gazed into the firelight vacantly and then, shaking himself, he drew a map out of his pocket. Three times, slowly and methodically, he traced his finger over the route they were to take. Then he looked into the sky and went over it in his mind from memory. Satisfied, he lit a cigarette and put the map away, and with his toe kicked earth over the fire. On his motor bike, with his Sten gun slung over his shoulder, he led the section out onto the road into the cold clear night. They turned south toward Caen and the far-off fireglow of the front lines.

It was in the Forêt de Cinglaid that O'Rourke's section had a dawn rendezvous with front-line unit transport which was to take over the loads of ammunition. It was an area entirely new to O'Rourke; he knew it only from the map.

Unknown to him, there had been a change of plans. From behind a tiny hamlet on the southern outskirts of the forest, the Germans had retaken ground which commanded an important crossroads leading southward out of the forest. The company against which the attack was launched drew back, reformed and swung eastward, under cover of a forest road, with the intention of driving below the enemy and outflanking him.

So far as the brigade front was concerned this incident was a minor affair, a slight disturbance on a battle line in constant flux. Still, its effect carried back some distance. Brigade Headquarters, far from being alarmed by the position, calmly notified the forces on either flank of the attacked company (though they already knew the position), and at the same time ordered first-line transport lying in the forest directly behind the endangered front to take up new standings elsewhere.

By the time O'Rourke, in the last hour before dawn, led his section convoy off the Falaise road and climbed into the great dark forest, the position had changed completely. Where he had expected to find armour and transport lying in harbour along the roadside he found only the burnt-out, twisted wreckage of equipment the enemy had lost during the battle for the forest. Instead of encountering traffic coming and going from the front lines, he found the roads deserted. In the distance, beyond the forest, he could hear the rattle of machine-guns and the occasional crack of mortars, but along the roads between the tall dark walls of the mighty trees, there hung an ominous stillness. The first faint light of dawn tipped the tree tops like a breath of mist.

Growing increasingly uneasy at the stillness, the empty roads, the shivering ominous atmosphere of the forest, he slowed the convoy and crawled along warily. Finally, on sudden impulse, he stopped. He felt they were being watched by unseen eyes, yet there was no movement, no sound. For a moment longer he sat in the centre of the road astride his bike, alone ahead of the convoy. A dozen devious plans spun through his mind but he did not give himself time to consider them. He acted instinctively. Leaving his bike, he ran back from lorry to lorry, driver to driver.

"Pull off the road. Get in close to the bush, behind any wreck you can find. Don't bunch up. Keep to the right."

From the centre of the road he watched them until the last was parked. Then he pushed his bike behind a German half-truck that lay on its side.

The men knew something was up. O'Rourke didn't play games. When he gave a long, low whistle they came running. Strangely enough, not a man forgot his Sten gun—the weapon they had so far never used in action.

They squatted around O'Rourke, with broad grins of excitement. They had been half asleep in their cabs. Now they were wide awake.

"I don't like this, boys," he told them. "Something's up, and I don't know what it is. We're on the right road and our rendezvous is ahead, I'm sure of that. We'll lie doggo here for a bit. As soon as it gets light I'll go ahead and find the unit transport."

Josephs, squatting on his heels, looked around the circle slowly, then at O'Rourke.

"Say, Boss," he said, "I ain't seen a single lorry or jeep go by this road since we came on it. It's funny."

"Damned funny, Josephs," agreed Bob. "There ought to be bags of transport moving around here."

"Now listen carefully. Each of you get back and lie low near your lorry. Lie down along the verge where you can see the road both ways, and keep your guns handy. But get this—no-one is to fire a shot until I do, no matter what you see, no matter how good a target it makes. If there are any Jerries around, they might never notice us and go right past, or across the road. If we're seen, there'll be time enough to open up. We're safer to lie doggo. Now scram!"

They lay hidden, and waited. The dawn crept through the trees, spread along the road.

A hundred yards ahead, something moved—something that was grey and part of the dawn. A sapling shivered, and then fluttered still. O'Rourke brought his Sten gun up to his shoulder, but he did not take aim. He fastened his eyes upon the sapling and waited. The sapling moved again and a grey-green figure detached itself from the forest and crouched on the road verge. The figure peered up the road, and then toward O'Rourke. He studied the burnt-out wrecks for some time, and O'Rourke knew that he saw the half-hidden lorries. After what seemed an eternity, the figure turned and in a quick broken run crossed the road and disappeared into the bush.

O'Rourke licked his lips and glanced quickly behind him. Curtin and Josephs had crawled forward to within a few yards of his feet and were grinning at him. They, too, had seen.

He knew that the figure that scurried across the road had not gone far, but lay in the fringe, studying the half-hidden lorries. A patrol, he decided, and turned his eyes along the wall of trees from which the figure had emerged.

"More game will come out soon," he said to himself. "There won't be many, else they'd come crashing out." He felt the cold wetness of the dew seeping through his clothes, and one foot had gone to sleep.

Suddenly he saw five of the enemy on the road verge, hugging close to the bush. In spite of the powerful urge to open fire, he made no movement. At best he could get only one of them, perhaps two: the rest would slip back into the bush and open fire from cover.

When the first had reached the centre of the road, O'Rourke raised his sights and took aim on the half-crouched man. He pressed the trigger. The man whirled, threw his rifle into the air and toppled backward into the bush. His companions wheeled, lifted their rifles, then leaped for the trees on the far side of the road. But in that instant every Sten gun in the section opened up, some firing automatic bursts, others firing rapid single shots. One German went to his knees, still holding his rifle across his chest, and they could see the savage snarl of pain on his face. Another, hit in the back, stood petrified for a moment, and then fell forward on his face. One reached the edge of the forest and stood there, shot through, groping at the bushes, unable to fall. Another jumped to the verge, and with his back against the trees, knelt and coolly began firing. The automatics threw up the dust in front of him, and cut through the trees around him. He got three shots out. One of them screamed past Josephs' ear and hit the side of the burnt-out half-truck. Another buried itself into the earth at O'Rourke's elbow. Curtin, who had been firing single shots, licked his finger deliberately, pressed the automatic button, and with a sigh that had no meaning, emptied his magazine into the kneeling figure.

Hidden in the underbrush, the first German who had crossed the road was sniping intermittently, slowly, but with good aim. His bullets whined close every time. He waited, and fired only when a head appeared. O'Rourke would have given anything for a grenade. He put in a fresh magazine, set his gun to automatic, and settled himself to wait.

Two shots came over; one cut a crease in the road in a line with his shoulder, and he heard it whirr upward and away. He marked the spot it came from, saw a quick movement in the bush, and his finger itched on the trigger. He waited. A full minute passed. Then another shot came, and this time it buried itself into the tyre of a lorry, behind which someone had moved.

Quick as a flash O'Rourke was up and across the road into the bush. He had crawled to a large tree and crouched behind it. There was a chance the German hadn't seen him. If he hadn't, in a little while he would work his way down toward the tree, changing his position each time he fired. O'Rourke smiled to himself and furtively wiped the sweat from his eyes.

He heard another shot, quite close, but saw no movement. He leaned a little out from the tree trunk and peered through the brush. A twig snapped, there was a quick rustle of leaves. Then, suddenly, not fifteen yards from him, he saw the German, half crouching, edging sideways toward him. His rifle was held across his chest, pointing away from the tree, his face was toward the road.

O'Rourke rose. His Sten gun was at his hip. For a moment he stood there in the clear, and the German did not see him. Then, the German turned, his whole body stiffened. He whirled, and brought his rifle up. It was one clear, lithe movement, the whirling body, the lifting arms, the rifle already at his shoulder. O'Rourke pressed the trigger. The burst caught the German in the stomach, almost cutting him in two. His whole body quivered and shook, as though activated by a hidden spring. He fell in a heap, still clutching his rifle.

The whole section was across the road now. They crashed through the bush, crowding around the dead sniper. O'Rourke turned him over with his foot. The face was that of a boy of sixteen. Frothy blood oozed from his half-open lips, set in an enigmatic smile. The eyes were clear bright blue, wide with frozen terror.

"What's he got on him?"

They emptied the pockets of his tunic. No-one would touch the blood-soaked trousers. Some German paper money, some coins, a few French francs, two letters in German, a postcard of a nude, and a small folder containing two portraits of a girl—these, and a membership card of the Hitler Youth, to which was affixed a small photo of the dead boy; that was all that he possessed.

"I'll keep this for a souvenir," said O'Rourke, picking up the Hitler Youth card. "Someday I might get a chance to give it back to his boss."

The others fingered the objects. Curtin took the postcard nude; Seymour, the German money. The rest was left scattered around the body.

They turned their lorries around and O'Rourke led them back the way they had come. He felt nothing, no sense of deliverance or escape. There was only a gnawing ache in his stomach, but it was not a hunger.

Outside the forest he parked the section on the side of the road, and went in search of the unit transport. After cruising through the forest roads for an hour, he came upon the lorries parked in front of a woodman's hut. The men squatted around a fire, cooking their breakfast in mess tins.

"We'd given you up," grinned the corporal in charge, as O'Rourke got off his machine.

"Well, you picked a comfortable spot to do it. Doesn't a map reference mean anything in your outfit? You're about two miles from where you're supposed to be."

"Oh, sure. We were over there, but some Joe came along and told us to move, so we holed up here. Had breakfast?"

"I ain't had anything but trouble," replied O'Rourke, rubbing his saddle sores.

"Hey, fix the corporal up with a bite of food. There's tea in the can, there. Help yourself."

"Where's the ammo?"

"Parked outside the bush."

"We'll come over and get it, soon as we finish chow."

"That's mighty generous of you. Next time let us know where the guns are and we'll deliver right to them. It will be easier."

# 23

I

AFTER his first kill O'Rourke was filled with a strange and tormenting hunger as he had never known before. At times it amounted to a heavy, dreary pain. It grew within him, and he could not cast it from him. He lost weight: his face became haggard and thin, the skin grew taut on his face and gave him an expression of sharp and nervous intensity. He could not sleep. He would lie and gaze up through the dark tracery of the trees at the stars frozen like crystals in the immensity of night, and he would begin to think of the fight, reliving it again.

When he slept his mind unravelled. He saw again the terrified frozen face of the German boy, shaking convulsively as he slumped to the ground: saw him scratch at the earth with the heel of one foot, saw the blood oozing out over his trousers. He remembered, too, the dawn light coming throught the forest, swift and suddenly revealing, and how, when they had turned to drive away, the dead Germans had seemed very dark and strange there in the road.

Of all the nightmares that came back to haunt him, the memory of that dawn battle remained most vivid. In his sleep he would feel again the sense of being encircled: the darkness was filled with a nameless terror. He felt he had to run from it, that he had to scream, and he would wake suddenly and stare up at the sky through the trees, his body shaking like a leaf in the wind, the sweat hot and stinging in his eyes. Who was the German he had killed? Why did it have to be a boy?

And finally he would throw off his blankets and get up and walk about until the nightmare cleared from his mind. He smoked cigarette after cigarette. He wanted to talk to someone —anyone. And then he would suddenly realize that he had nothing to say, that what was in his mind had never been spoken by man.

## 2

Meanwhile, with supreme driving effort, the Allied armies were closing the Falaise gap, sealing off the only escape corridor left to the encircled German divisions. Within that ever-tightening circle all that remained of the German armies in France was milling around in frantic confusion. Torn, battered, bleeding, completely disorganized, they were faced with surrender or annihilation.

From the first light of dawn till nightfall the air forces swept the area, bombing, machine-gunning, shooting up the enemy transport, tanks and guns. The roads within the trap became blocked with wrecked burning equipment. The dead lay everywhere, in fields and orchards and woods, and along the roads, in thousands. They lay among their burnt tanks, among the miles of tangled wreckage of guns, lorries and wagons, among the grotesque swollen carcasses of horses.

From all sides the Allies pushed inward: the noose tightened. Trapped amid their own countless dead, driven to sheer panic by the holocaust of fire and death that swept across the land, the Germans surrendered in droves. Long, dreary lines of prisoners trudged through the dust back toward the prison cages. Gone was their arrogance and pride of might, their flaunting brutality. They were men who had come out of hell. Their spirits crushed and beaten they seemed not to care what fate awaited them.

Many, however, stayed to fight it out, inspired by a fanaticism which only death could end. For them there was only one fate—annihilation. In bands, in small units, they attacked the walls of the ring that pressed in upon them. Sometimes, with the desperate fury of caged, doomed animals, clawing over the masses of their own dead, they managed to force a way through the ring of men and armour. But their escape was shortlived. They still had to cut through a series of lines, and beyond these the long maintenance and communication lines of the Allied armies. Germany was far away; their position was hopeless. They lived, for a day or two, prowling in the fields and woods, driven and hunted, and finally killed.

There were, at this time, when the great trap had closed, many such small bands of desperate, hungry men who crawled from field to field, hedge to hedge, to woods, working their way through the labyrinth of communication roads behind the front. They knew only that they had been trapped, and having broken through the first encircling ring, they hoped to work their way through the rear lines and eventually meet up with a body of their own troops. They did not know that, beyond the Falaise trap, the nearest German position in any strength was a hundred miles away, in the heart of France. Had they known this, it was doubtful if they would have surrendered. They were the fierce, fanatical followers of the mad Fuehrer.

Their tenure of life was short. They were hunted, doomed men, and they lived for the brief period which fate allowed them, with a fanatical desperation and purpose. It was to kill, kill, kill; to kill, not because a man in another uniform was their enemy, but knowing they were doomed, they were determined to take to the grave as many of their fellow creatures as they could. They were trapped and the game was up. They would come out with their hands raised in surrender toward their foe, and then, suddenly, they would throw a grenade and die with their victors. Sometimes it was acid they threw. Sometimes they blew themselves up with their own grenades. In the dark forests, among the strewn dead, they prowled like beasts.

It was into such a region that O'Rourke, after an idle period of almost a week, led his section one hot August evening. They were hauling up ammunition to dump along a roadside. He had no heart for the task. He had, in truth, no heart for anything. For days he had been living in hope of getting mail from Gerda. He needed something from home to still his restlessness, something close and precious which he could think about and live with.

If only he had a letter from her which spoke of the farm they were going to buy. Or if he could be reminded again (insatiable hunger!) of the way the prairie land looked from their bedroom window in the cool, hushed twilight, how it had been to turn from the window, with the beauty and peace and coolness of the land. the fabulous land, throbbing ecstatically in the mind and body, to turn to each other with sudden pulsing desire, so swift, so intense.

If was not Gerda's fault that the mail did not come. For ever faithful, for ever good, she wrote every day, letters which reflected her mood, the mood of the weather, the land, and the events of her day-to-day existence, the eternity of waiting. Somewhere in the vast distance betwen home and the front a train, a ship, a plane was delayed. The mail did not come.

Such a thing may not directly change the destiny of a man's life. But, working its effect within the dark, mysterious tenement of the mind, it produced in O'Rourke a gnawing, insatiable restlessness which no thought, no image, could still. It mounted in him to a climax, clamorous, demanding, soul-destroying. He was possessed by it.

When he brought the section to its unloading point near a small crossroads, he left the men to unload by themselves, and on the pretext of reconnoitring the road ahead, he drove away on his bike. Usually he remained with them while they unloaded, and often helped them to get the job done. But this day he wanted to be alone, even if for half an hour, as never before.

The country, in this area, was thickly wooded, and cut with small farms here and there. In the tiny fields the grain stood high and ripe, ready for cutting. Thin, untamed trees divided the fields. The farmers, driven off by the onslaught of war, had fled; the weeds flourished and tangled in the crops, and amid the lonely, shattered ruins of the houses. In the pastures lay the carcasses of horses and cattle, stiff and swollen. Along the road where it ran through the woods, it was dark and ghostly still : the trees crowded close on either side. Shrapnel, shell and fire had scarred the tree trunks. Here the dead lay in hundreds, in the ditches, beside the trees, or piled in mounds in the road where they had been mown down.

It was a ride that gave O'Rourke nothing—neither joy nor peace. He knew he had gone far enough, and there was no point in riding on. Yet his restlessness urged him onward. There was a bend in the road ahead, marked by a bad crater and burnt bushes. He would see what was around that bend, and then turn back.

So he travelled on, down the long, straight road between the trees, toward the distant bend ahead, swerving now and then to avoid the sprawling dead and the litter. Far ahead he could see the crater, where the road turned. It was a rough, clay-coloured break in the dark surface of the road, and beside it, where the sun shone, the burnt-black bushes.

When he came up to it the crater was wider and rougher than it had appeared from a distance, and he swerved his machine to one side over a narrow strip of unbroken road surface. Clear of the hole, he was on the point of kicking the machine into second gear when he lifted his eyes from the road and saw, not a hundred yards ahead, a bearded German in tattered trousers and field-grey shirt, standing beside a wrecked lorry, lifting his rifle to aim directly at him. So clear was O'Rourke's instant terrifying picture of him that he saw the dirty cord tied around his trousers, the dark hair on his arm revealed by a long tear in the shirt, and the tensed sinews of his neck.

O'Rourke had only one chance, and he took it. He jammed his foot on the brake and swerved the bike toward the scrub growth that lined the ditch. He knew how to fall from a motor bike; he had taken enough spills to do it expertly. The machine plunged into the scrub, the front wheel dived into the ditch. At that instant he let himself go. The impact of the crash sent him flying through space, and he landed in a field of high mustard, rolled twice, and lay still. For a moment he took stock of himself, and then, finding that he was all in one piece, he reached for his Sten gun. It was gone, torn from him in the crash.

He lay for some time and thought of his next move. The German had been in the road; a fringe of scrub stood between them, but it was no protection. Unarmed, his only chance was to get away.

He began to crawl away from the road. He kept stretched to the earth, using the high mustard for cover, crawling on his elbows. He crawled swiftly until he was out of breath, and then lay panting, bathed in sweat. He looked back at his zigzag runnel through the mustard, and over the yellow bloom he saw the top of a great tree.

This was no good, he decided. At this rate it would take him an eternity to cross the field to the far bushes where there must surely be another road. In the bushes he could lie in hiding and wait for passing traffic, or during the night could work his way back to safety. The thing to do was to make a run for it and take his chances—run for a spell and then drop out of sight, and then another sprint.

Slowly he lifted himself in the mustard and peered quickly around the field. The German was nowhere in sight. But, like all hunted men, he had a terror of what was behind him, not of what he could see ahead. With a curiosity stronger than reason, he sprang to his feet, stood for a moment and looked back to where he had left the road. Over the edge of the ditch, directly in the line of his vision, he saw the head of the German, and the long dull glint of the rifle in the sun.

In that split second, from the instant when he saw the head and the rifle of the German sniper protruding above the edge of the ditch, to the moment when he heard the crack of the shot and felt the shattering impact of the bullet, a black cloud of agony engulfed him, obliterating everything with a fiery, choking pain so intense, so consuming, so beyond all conception, that he lost consciousness before his body struck the ground.

Time stopped. He lay in the mustard on his back, legs

wide apart, one knee raised. A gush of bright blood coloured his shirt, spread across his chest and began to creep down his side. Freed, in an instant, from the sudden white-hot choking pain, he lay like a dead man. Deep in the dark depths of his torn body life throbbed faintly, quivered and hung in the balance. The blood oozed from his wound, flowed down between his arm and body and formed a pool under his shoulder.

It was almost twilight when life stirred again in his body. He opened his eyes and looked through a veil, beyond which the mustard blossom waved in the breeze. He could not believe that he was alive in the world he had known. It seemed, to his slim consciousness, that by some strange transformation he had shed the body and soul of that man he had always lived with, had gone from the world in which he had lived, so lonely, so strangely tortured with grief, pain and remorse, bitter triumph and brief ecstatic joy, and had entered a new world, a different life, where there existed only the physical form of his body and in it the body's racking pain. Slowly, through a vast whirling space coloured with blown mustard bloom, he became conscious of more than the burning, dry, intolerable pain. His body felt encased in a hard, dry shell, and a mighty weight seemed to be pressing him down. His first reaction was to struggle. In a moment he gave it up, sank back into himself. Then, gropingly, his hand began to explore his body. He was covered with dry, hard blood—his own blood. He struggled again, this time with consiousness, and succeeded in turning upon his side. Lying in this position, the sense of crushing pressure upon his body vanished : even the pain in his lungs eased a little. He wished he could move his lips; they felt enormously swollen, and yet he could not feel them with his tongue.

Now, fully conscious, he lay on his side and began to think of his position. He was lost in this sea of high mustard. No-one would ever find him here. He had to get into the open, reach a road, where he would be seen. He must hurry, for it was already growing dark.

He dug a heel into the earth and pushed his body. The pain was intolerable, and after a few minutes he had to stop. He lay still and tried to lick his lips and could not. He pressed his hand into his wound to stop the terrible pain. After a few minutes he began again to worm his way head first across the field.

In this way time passed. He felt he had gone a long way, and must surely be near the road at the end of the field. He was sure he had travelled a long way, and was filled with a great exultation. When he stopped and rested, it was this exultation which helped him to bear the terrible racking pain. When he moved again he began to anticipate the end of the field, and he told himself he would strike his head into a hedge or fence, and then he would know he had reached the road.

He could only move a few feet at a time now, and then the pain paralysed his body, the dark veil would fall over his mind. It was the descending darkness of unconsciousness that terrified him, again and again. He knew that if he ever slipped into that darkness he would never return, never escape. It would engulf him, bury him, hold him for ever. He fought against it with desperate frenzy, pushed it back from him, held it off. He did not know where the strength came from that moved his legs, pushed his body over the ground, inches at a time. There was no longer any feeling in his legs, only a heavy dragging weight. He was covered with earth. It matted his hair; it was in his ears and mouth, between his fingers, caked with the blood on his chest and back and stomach, but he did not know it. He felt only the white-hot pain and the threatening terrifying darkness.

At last he could go no further. His legs moved, the heel of his boots dug into the earth, but there was no strength left to push his body forward. Yet for some time he believed he was still crawling, closer and closer to the edge of the field.

He would rest awhile, and then he could reach the road. He had come a long way, a long, long way. The road was further than he had thought. If only the black veil would not threaten him again.

He sank his head back upon the earth and looked into the darkening twilight. A solitary star, gleaming with the blue glint of ice, hung overhead. He smiled to himself : he was no longer afraid of the dark enveloping terror; the star would give him light, keep the darkness away.

And then, suddenly, through the vast hollow night, he heard the long, low, wailing whistle of a distant speeding train. It was far-off, and he could hear the echo of it crying across the lonely land. It died away, and the silence was filled with a nameless dread. Then it came again, closer, nearer, and he could hear the low rumbling thunder of the hurtling train, the racing click of the wheels of the track-spread, the pant and blast of the mighty engine. He saw the long, steady, piercing, blue-white shaft of the headlight, the sudden glare, the flashing flare from the firebox.

The pain vanished from his tormented body, the frenzied fever and the terror left his mind. Filled with a sudden infinite sense of happiness, he smiled, for he knew where he was now.

He was going home. The thundering train was bearing him homeward across the mighty continent that he knew so well.

He saw it all again with an instant recognition of exultancy and surging joy, but with the strange unreality and dream-like vision of a man returning from the dark forest of time. He knew where he was; he knew his beloved land. It was the fabulous land, the vast and lonely land of the north. It seemed stranger than a dream, and more familiar than his own hand.

He saw it all again, instant quick, fixed for one bright intense moment, and then gone, gone forever. It brought to him the tremendous memory of space, of soaring distances, of exultant power and magic; a memory of the great rivers veining the land, of the limitless forests, the mighty mountains. He heard again the magic names—the strange-sounding names of the cities and towns, the rivers and plains, the forbidden places and the undiscovered places, the mountains and the valleys, the lakes and the marshes.

It brought to him the vision of the great trains that hurtled across the continent, pounding and roaring on the rails —the trains that opened city after city, town after town, unlocking the heart and mystery of the vast land. Across the vision of his mind he saw the glow of a city in the velvet night; lived and had his being for a fragment of time upon the hot man-swarming streets, breathed the murmurous destiny of the tenemented life, saw the summer-strolling girls in clinging cotton dresses, heard the drug-store boys cat-calling into the warm night, heard a baby cry, a woman laugh.

The train sped onward into the dawn, across a river that flowed majestically, silently, into the wilderness. A hundred towns and tiny villages swept past his vision. He saw the smoke from breakfast fires rising over the little railroad towns; heard the stomp of a horse's hoof in a livery barn, the sudden cough and roar of a tractor engine starting up; heard the sleepy-soft blanketed murmur of morning love from a cottage window as he passed; smelt the delicious overpowering smell of frying bacon and hotcakes through the screen door of a Chinese café, heard the clink of dishes in the kitchen.

He was going home, and he smiled happily. It was a long way—but his heart sang. This was the last journey, and at the end of it there was home, and Gerda waiting. The restlessness was gone from him now, and the loneliness. The train was heading into the West, and he was going home.

This was the fabulous land. This was the land of rich inheritance, the land so rich, so powerful, that its people could not claim it all. It was the land of immense and lonely skies that bend over man and dwarf him; the land of bitter cold and burning heat, of fierce sun and weathering time, of savage nature and tremendous strength, of wildness and brutality, and of nameless indescribable beauty.

And now the train moved and snaked through country which was poignantly familiar to him: the great slow undulations of the land, rich gold and striped yellow, with here and there a line of startling green, here a known farmhouse, a weathered barn—all so familiar, so precious to the heart. They were cutting and harvesting in the fields. Far off, the men and horses were but tiny suggestive dots of dark upon the land, but close along the right of way they stood strong and real. They waved to him and beckoned, and his heart gladdened at their recognition. The threshing machine threw out a cloud of golden straw dust that laid a shadow upon the earth, and the sacks of rich grain, filled to bursting, stood in rows near the wagons.

The train slowed, quivered and rattled around a long bend, brushed a line of poplar trees that half hid the old wooden school house. And there, suddenly, unbelievably, was his father's house—the open gate, the step, the known door. And there was Gerda, her face lit with a tender radiance, her arms outstretched to hold him.

At that moment life fluttered and died in the body of O'Rourke. He was freed of pain, of hunger, of loneliness—freed of his vassalage to the earth. His eyes closed, his lips sealed in a happy smile.

In the morning, as the sun rose, long columns of transport moved along the road, past the mustard field. The mustard was high, and no-one saw his body lying a few yards from the roadside. The Germans were beaten in France; the convoys raced ahead, throwing up great clouds of dust that rolled across the fields.

Toward evening of the second day an artillery unit, laying up for a rest, moved into the field, cutting tracks through the mustard, trampling it into the ground. They found O'Rourke's body and buried it where it lay. They fashioned a wooden cross and painted it white, and on it they burned his number, his name and initials with a red-hot iron. The next morning, being Sunday, a gunner out for a morning stroll gathered dahlias from a farm garden and laid them on the mound of damp earth beneath the new white cross.

# THE NEW CANADIAN LIBRARY

n  1. OVER PRAIRIE TRAILS / Frederick Philip Grove

n  2. SUCH IS MY BELOVED / Morley Callaghan

n  3. LITERARY LAPSES / Stephen Leacock

n  4. AS FOR ME AND MY HOUSE / Sinclair Ross

n  5. THE TIN FLUTE / Gabrielle Roy

n  6. THE CLOCKMAKER / Thomas Chandler Haliburton

n  7. THE LAST BARRIER AND OTHER STORIES / Charles G. D. Roberts

n  8. BAROMETER RISING / Hugh MacLennan

n  9. AT THE TIDE'S TURN AND OTHER STORIES / Thomas H. Raddall

n 10. ARCADIAN ADVENTURES WITH THE IDLE RICH / Stephen Leacock

n 11. HABITANT POEMS / William Henry Drummond

n 12. THIRTY ACRES / Ringuet

n 13. EARTH AND HIGH HEAVEN / Gwethalyn Graham

n 14. THE MAN FROM GLENGARRY / Ralph Connor

n 15. SUNSHINE SKETCHES OF A LITTLE TOWN / Stephen Leacock

n 16. THE STEPSURE LETTERS / Thomas McCullock

n 17. MORE JOY IN HEAVEN / Morley Callaghan

n 18. WILD GEESE / Martha Ostenso

n 19. THE MASTER OF THE MILL / Frederick Philip Grove

n 20. THE IMPERIALIST / Sara Jeannette Duncan

n 21. DELIGHT / Mazo de la Roche

n 22. THE SECOND SCROLL / A. M. Klein

n 23. THE MOUNTAIN AND THE VALLEY /Ernest Buckler

n 24. THE RICH MAN / Henry Kreisel

n 25. WHERE NESTS THE WATER HEN / Gabrielle Roy

n 26. THE TOWN BELOW / Roger Lemelin

n 27. THE HISTORY OF EMILY MONTAGUE / Frances Brooke

n 28. MY DISCOVERY OF ENGLAND / Stephen Leacock

n 29. SWAMP ANGEL / Ethel Wilson

n 30. EACH MAN'S SON / Hugh MacLennan

n 31. ROUGHING IT IN THE BUSH / Susanna Moodie

n 32. WHITE NARCISSUS / Raymond Knister

n 33. THEY SHALL INHERIT THE EARTH / Morley Callaghan

n 34. TURVEY / Earle Birney

n 35. NONSENSE NOVELS / Stephen Leacock

n 36. GRAIN / R. J. C. Stead

n 37. LAST OF THE CURLEWS / Fred Bodsworth

n 38. THE NYMPH AND THE LAMP / Thomas H. Raddall

n 39. JUDITH HEARNE / Brian Moore

n 40. THE CASHIER / Gabrielle Roy

n 41. UNDER THE RIBS OF DEATH / John Marlyn

n 42. WOODSMEN OF THE WEST / M. Allerdale Grainger

n 43. MOONBEAMS FROM THE LARGER LUNACY / Stephen Leacock

n 44. SARA BINKS / Paul Hiebert

n 45. SON OF A SMALLER HERO / Mordecai Richler

n 46. WINTER STUDIES AND SUMMER RAMBLES / Anna Jameson

n 47. REMEMBER ME / Edward Meade

n 48. FRENZIED FICTION / Stephen Leacock

n 49. FRUITS OF THE EARTH / Frederick Philip Grove

o 1. POETS OF CANADA, VOL. I: POETS OF THE CONFEDERATION / edited by Malcolm Ross

o 2. MASKS OF FICTION : CANADIAN CRITICS ON CANADIAN PROSE / edited by A. J. M. Smith

o 3. MASKS OF POETRY: CANADIAN CRITICS ON CANADIAN VERSE / edited by A. J. M. Smith

o 4. POETS OF CANADA, VOL. III: POETS OF MIDCENTURY / edited by Milton Wilson